STARGATE
SG·1

THE COST OF HONOR

"Damn it!" Watts yelled from the DHD. "This is pointless, sir! It won't stay open!"

Standing up slowly, Major Henry Boyd glanced up at the twisting nightmare in the sky. It looked like some hideous creature come to tear them to pieces. "Keep trying," he told the Captain.

"Sir?" Lieutenant Jessica McLeod ripped her gaze from the sky, voice shaking. "I've been thinking about why the gate won't activate. The gravitational force of the—" She stammered over the word. "Of the black hole would create a massive time distortion effect."

He stalked toward her, frowning. "A what?"

"Time here will be moving much slower than back on Earth, sir. Much slower. The gate was probably open for half an hour at the SGC, but here…just a second."

Boyd felt his heart clench tight. "What are you saying, Lieutenant?"

She looked bleak. "I don't think we're getting out of this one, sir."

Lucy. His daughter was the first thought in his head. Sweet, innocent, adoring Lucy. Her little arms around his neck, her delighted smile when he came home. *Daddy!* He swallowed hard. "I won't accept that, Lieutenant." Lucy, barely old enough to understand. Heather, having to explain why he was never coming home again. "They'll find a way to come get us. They won't leave us here."

An original publication of Fandemonium Ltd, produced under license from MGM Consumer Products.

Fandemonium Books
PO Box 795A
Surbiton
Surrey KT5 8YB
United Kingdom
Visit our website: www.stargatenovels.com

STARGATE
SG·1

METRO-GOLDWYN-MAYER Presents
RICHARD DEAN ANDERSON
in
STARGATE SG-1™
AMANDA TAPPING CHRISTOPHER JUDGE DON S. DAVIS
and MICHAEL SHANKS as Daniel Jackson
Executive Producers ROBERT C. COOPER MICHAEL GREENBURG RICHARD DEAN ANDERSON
Developed for Television by BRAD WRIGHT & JONATHAN GLASSNER

WWW.MGM.COM

ISBN: 978-0-9547343-4-3   Printed in the USA

STARGATE
SG·1™

THE COST OF HONOR

BOOK TWO OF TWO

SALLY MALCOLM

FANDEMONIUM BOOKS

For Tom and the children,
with love.

Many thanks to
Sabine,
for all the red ink.

Kate,
for being so speedy.

The Netnutters,
for hanging out at all hours.

And Jack, Josh and Jamie,
for keeping us chatting.

Author's note:
The events in this book take place during season seven
of STARGATE SG-1.

PROLOGUE

The fire crackled, catapulting sparks into the cloudless desert night. They drifted on invisible wings, like the angels themselves, until their flame was consumed by the icy air and they fell dead to the ground.

Fallen angels.

Just like the One.

Through her mass of dark hair, Alvita Candra studied the *auspicium* where it lay in the cold ruins of Arxantia. It had been silent for fifty years, dark with the corruption of the enemy, but two weeks ago a light had shone in its depths – a hope not seen since her mother was a girl. The light had flared, and then died. Since then, the *auspicium* had remained dark.

"Does it say more?" Atella was impatient, the blood running hot through his young veins. A warrior born.

Closing her eyes, Alvita reached out and placed her hand on the gray dome of the *auspicium*. The familiar swirl of images spun through her mind like the desert wind, kicking up sand into a spiral toward the stars. And through the chaos, through the thousand dead minds, she saw the One.

His eyes were alien, pale like the enemy. But he was no enemy; he had walked with the angels. She could see it in his face, his strange colorless face. "I do not know what he is," she whispered. "He is not Arxanti. But neither is he Kinahhi. He is…different. And yet he has been touched by the angels. He has walked among them."

"You see this?" Atella's harsh voice seemed far away, distant through the clamor. "Are you sure?"

"I see him," she whispered. "But faintly. He has had scant contact with the *sheh'fet*, but it is enough. The *Kaw'ree* fear him. They fear them all, for the *Kaw'ree* have seen the truth – though their black hearts deny it." She shivered, the night air cutting through her thin clothes. Too cold to be out, had the *auspicium* not demanded it. But time was changing – she felt it, felt the wheels spinning backward. "He is of us."

"And does he come?" pressed Atella. Eager, so eager to throw off the chains of generations.

"I cannot see." Atella wanted more than she could give. "He is lost to me now, lost to the *sheh'fet*. He has gone, but he will return. The prophesy cannot be denied. *Salvation will come from beyond the stars, when the angels return.* Can it be otherwise?"

Atella rose to his feet, his boots crunching anxiously in the sand. "But when?"

"I cannot see. I see only the enemy now, shriveling in fear of shadows. They dread his return. They dread us all."

"The One," Atella asked, stopping and crouching at her side. She could feel the heat of his body in the icy night and relished his warmth. "Does he have a name?"

"A name…?" She sent her mind out, recapturing the image. A sharp mind, slicing to the truth like a blade. An unquenchable thirst for justice, too often thwarted. Frustration, outrage and a great anger, tempered by greater compassion. A name… "Yes," she whispered, hearing the alien sound in her mind. "He has a name, a strange name." She twisted her lips in an attempt to form it. "Dan'yel Jak'sun."

Atella sat back on his haunches. "Dan'yel Jak'sun? A strange name indeed." His hand came to rest on her bare arm, strong and warm. "Come, Alvita. You have searched enough. The night is getting cold, and the fire is failing. We must return."

"Yes." But it was hard to leave, to bid farewell to that face. Those eyes. A fallen angel, come to deliver them from the Kinahhi. At last. *At last!*

CHAPTER ONE

General George Hammond was cold. A late-night chill had seeped into the marrow of his bones, fusing with his exhaustion, guilt and long hours of helpless waiting until he felt cold from the inside out. Through the control room window, at the heart of Stargate Command, he stared down at the silent gate as if he could will the vast machine into action. But it remained inert, absorbing his growing sense of frustration and self-recrimination as easily as it handled the awesome power of a wormhole.

Thirty-six hours ago he'd watched his flagship team stride resolutely up the ramp and through the Stargate. At the time he'd known – suspected – that their mission wasn't exactly textbook, but he'd turned a blind eye, as he'd done so often where Colonel Jack O'Neill was concerned. Now, it seemed, his customary faith in his people was going to come back and bite him on his broad Texan backside.

SG-1 were missing. They could be dead. Captured. AWOL. Fact was, he had no idea. Which meant he had no idea how to help them. He cursed silently – as their CO, that was the one thing he should damn well know how to do. He should have demanded the truth up front. Instead, he'd given them plenty of rope and was afraid they'd used it to hang themselves.

Abruptly, a loud metallic clunk echoed through the gateroom. Chevrons locked, and Hammond felt the familiar tingle of static and tension that accompanied any off-world activation. He stood a little straighter, shoulders braced as the event horizon mushroomed and settled into a shimmering pool of light. It never ceased to impress, even at times like this, when his mind was occupied with grimmer thoughts.

"Receiving IDC," Sergeant Harriman reported, scanning the screen before him. Then he looked up, a note of disappointment in his voice. "It's SG-13, sir."

Nodding, the General turned toward the stairs as Colonel Dave Dixon stepped through the gate. The look on the Colonel's face told the whole story. By the time Hammond had reached the gate-room, Dixon's team were bunched disconsolately at the foot of the ramp. "We've got nothing, sir," the Colonel apologized, tugging off his cap and showering the ramp with grit. "Nothin' but sand and ruins. If SG-1 were on '832, any trace of them would have been swept away within hours. The damn wind never stops blowing."

Hammond nodded, the tension in his shoulders twisting into a cramp that gripped the back of his neck like a vise. "Is it possible Colonel O'Neill took his team further away from the gate?"

"It's possible," Dixon shrugged, although his tone belied his words. "But, frankly, sir, I don't know why he would. Like I said, there's nothing there. It's a dustbowl."

Clutching at straws, George. His gut told him Dixon was right – SG-1 weren't on P6M-832. The moon had never been Jack's destination, it was just a staging post on his trip to…where? He should have pressed O'Neill for more information. He should have darn well demanded it.

And now SG-1 were running out of time. Kinsey was breathing down his neck like a rabid dog and Hammond knew the Senator wouldn't back off until he had juicier meat to sink his teeth into. Preferably Jack O'Neill flavor.

Angry at himself, he dismissed SG-13 with a brief nod. "Good work."

But as his men trudged towards the door, Dixon paused. Glancing up at the control room – empty but for Harriman – he lowered his voice. "Sir, if SG-1 are in trouble, my team are willing to do whatever's necessary to bring them home."

"I appreciate that, Colonel," Hammond nodded. As always, the loyalty and bravery of the people under his command touched him deeply. But it never surprised him. "I'll keep you posted."

More quietly still, Dixon added, "We've heard a rumor that Senator Kinsey tried to—"

"Rumors," Hammond interrupted, "are best unrepeated, Colonel." He softened the reprimand with a meager smile. "With any luck, SG-1 will walk through the gate in the next twelve hours with a darn good explanation. If not…"

If not, they were in trouble. Big trouble. And it was his damn fault. O'Neill had been all but relieved of command before this final mission – he had nothing to lose. Hammond should have kept him where he could see him until this whole stupid mess with Crawford and Kinsey had been cleared up. *Bad call, George. Bad call.*

Dixon nodded grimly. "I hope they're okay, sir."

"So do I, Colonel." Hammond looked up at the massive Stargate, its ominous presence offering no comfort. "So do I."

Everything hurt. His right knee was stiff and swollen, despite the Tylenol he'd chewed. Grit had scraped one side of his face raw, and it stung like needles every time he spoke. Not to mention they were into their third day of exhaustion and his eyes were sandy and heavy. All in all, Colonel Jack O'Neill had felt better.

He'd also felt a hell of a lot worse.

Slumped in the co-pilot's seat, feet up on the dash, he stared blindly through the *tel'tak*'s window. Streaks of starlight bled past at incomprehensible speeds as their ship hurtled across the galaxy toward another impossible rescue. Despite his aches and pains, Jack couldn't repress a swell of pride at the thought: his team were the best. No doubt about that.

Speaking of which… Carter had said it would take three days to reach P3W-451, the planet that was shattering beneath the feet of Henry Boyd and SG-10. With her usual optimism, she'd gone on to assure him that the anti-grav device would be up and running by the time they arrived. And if he'd seen a shadow of doubt in her eyes, he'd chosen to ignore it. Over the past few days he'd seen a lot of shadows in her eyes, and felt a few of his own crowding close. He ignored them all; it was the only way to keep going. And that was one thing they damn well had to do.

So he'd sorted through the remnants of their kit in search of food and water and scrounged enough to keep them functioning – if not exactly satisfied – until they arrived on '451. After that… The plan was to fly to the nearest world with a Stargate and hightail it back to the SGC with a happy, healthy and grateful SG-10 in tow.

From that point onward things got a little blurry. But he was pretty sure that it would involve something unpleasant hitting the fan. Jack shied away from the unwelcome thought. Plenty of things to worry about before he had to face Kinsey's politicking;

he might even be dead by then. With any luck.

His companion shifted in the pilot's seat, making a small adjustment to their course. "You appear troubled, O'Neill."

That was the nice thing about Teal'c – he never beat about the bush. He also had the disconcerting habit of knowing exactly what you were thinking. The best response was to play dumb. "I do?"

Teal'c cast him a slow glance from the corner of his eye. "You are concerned that our mission to rescue SG-10 will not succeed?"

Jack yanked his feet from the dash and landed them with a thud on the floor. He sat up straighter and stretched his aching shoulders. "Nah," he yawned. Damn, he was tired. How long had it been since he'd slept for more than a couple of hours? "Carter's on the case, it's a walk in the park."

Teal'c was silent for a moment. "You place a great deal of faith in Major Carter's abilities," he observed. "The task she faces is formidable."

That was true enough, but Jack could read the subtext. Hell, with Teal'c, if you couldn't read the subtext you missed most of the conversation. "It's not like I have much choice right now," he said quietly. "She can handle it." He hoped. But he couldn't shake the image of her sprawled against Baal's gravity wall, nor the brutal revenge she'd tried to exact on a Jaffa barely out of short pants. Teal'c was right; the last couple of days had been tough on Carter. And he'd noticed a brittleness about her that was worrying.

What she really needed was time to regroup and heal, mentally as well as physically. Instead she got short-rations, sparse medical care, and the weight of an all-but-impossible mission resting entirely on her ability to make an alien device work. Not to mention the fact they were in breach of orders and AWOL. A court martial might only be the start of it. God only knew what Teal'c and Daniel might face…

Leaning forward, Jack pushed his hands over his face and screwed his eyes shut. What the *hell* was he doing? *No one gets left behind.* Great motto, but… He sighed heavily. "You ever question yourself, Teal'c?"

"On many occasions, O'Neill."

He nodded through his hands, but didn't raise his head. "You think I'm crazy, dragging you guys out here? Just because..." Hell, Boyd might even be dead by now.

Teal'c's silence filled the room as adequately as words; Jack knew his friend understood guilt. They were two of a kind, brothers-in-arms. "I have sacrificed much," Teal'c said at last, his voice quiet and dignified, "for the sake of principle. If we do not uphold our beliefs, O'Neill, what purpose is there to our fight?"

"Staying alive?" Jack stared down at his scuffed boots. The dust of Baal's palace still clung to them, like memories that could never be scrubbed from his mind. "To live to see another day? Maybe find a little happiness, a little peace."

Another silence followed, and then, "Small men may live such lives, O'Neill. We are not such men."

Jack slumped back in his seat. "We're not?"

"We are not."

No arguing with that. He'd had a hundred opportunities to walk away from the fight, to hand over to someone younger, stronger. Smarter. It would have made a lot of things easier. But he never had. Perhaps he never would. Turning to gaze out the window once more, Jack sighed. "You know, sometimes I think it would be nice to just, I dunno, be a barber in Indiana. You know?" Teal'c's eyebrow rose curiously. "It's just something I think about," Jack muttered. "Not sure why, exactly. But it sounds relaxing, don't you think?"

"I am unfamiliar with Indiana," Teal'c replied, clearly less than impressed. After a moment, he added, "And I have little experience of barbers."

Jack smiled slightly, but Teal'c was right. This was the life he'd chosen and he could no more abandon his principles than he could cut off his right arm. The truth was, Daniel, Teal'c and Carter were no different. It was what made SG-1 so extraordinary – and usually what landed them in oceans of hot water. Like right now.

He glanced at his watch. It was later than he'd realized. "Carter?" he called out. No answer. He stood up, grimacing at the stiffness in his right knee. "I thought I told her to quit an hour ago."

Teal'c turned, his face more serious than usual. "I believe

Major Carter feels she has much to prove."

"What makes you say that?"

"I see doubt in her eyes, O'Neill."

So he hadn't been imagining it.

The golden brand of Apophis glinted dully in the muted light as Teal'c turned back to the controls. "This mission has damaged her faith."

Just do your job! Jack remembered her shocked expression as he'd yelled at her, furious at her deception. Overreaction? Maybe. But she'd made a bad call, for all the wrong reasons, and she knew it.

"I do not believe she will permit herself to fail – whatever the cost."

Slowly, Jack nodded. That was Carter all over; push herself beyond the limit to get the job done. It was both her strength and the fault line in her character: pile on enough pressure and she'd crack. He'd seen it happen on the roof of Baal's palace, when her rage had burned red-hot and violent. He knew what it was like to lose control like that, and he knew she would see it as a huge personal failure.

He clasped Teal'c's shoulder in silent thanks. He should have recognized this for himself. Perhaps, if he'd been less tired, if his own emotions hadn't been so raw, he would have done. But he appreciated the heads-up; that's what teams were for, after all.

"Dig out the rations," he told Teal'c, as he trudged out of the cockpit. "Time we all got some R&R."

The moon cast cold, silver shadows over the snow-clad face of Cheyenne Mountain. It was a comfortless glow in the midwinter night, and deep beneath the rock and stone it seemed to penetrate the restless dreams of George Hammond. He hadn't left the base since SG-1 had disappeared, and now lay on top of the narrow cot in his base quarters, trying to catch enough sleep to keep him functioning. He wasn't having much luck.

"Unscheduled off-world activation!" The sirens blared, loud and dissonant, and Hammond was bolt upright in a heartbeat. A different man might have raced into action, but Hammond knew the value of propriety. It wouldn't do for the base commander to be seen in the control room with his shirt undone and his shoes unlaced. Besides, he trusted his people to handle the situation.

And look where that's gotten you. The quiet voice in the back of his mind was new and unpleasant. He banished it.

With his shirt buttoned and laces tied, he left his quarters and headed smartly for the control room. He could hear the running of booted feet, a couple of barked orders, and knew that the gate security team had deployed. His heart raced a little faster and he picked up the pace, marching up the stairs. "Lieutenant," he demanded, "report."

"Sir." Ashford was on duty. The young woman jumped to attention, nervous fingers fumbling with a stack of papers. "It's the Kinahhi, sir. They're requesting permission to return Ambassador Crawford to Earth – they claim to have dropped all charges against him."

Do they indeed? The Kinahhi were as slippery as snakes, and he didn't trust them an inch. But he could hardly refuse their request. He glanced down at the armed men guarding the gate. They wouldn't be needed – the Kinahhi were more subtle than that – but they'd send the right message. He was not to be trifled with nor mistaken for a fool. "Open the iris," he told Ashford, folding his arms and moving to stand before the window. "And tell the Kinahhi to proceed."

With a metallic swirl, the iris peeled back. A palpable tension rippled through the men waiting in the gate-room as they came to the full alert. All was silent. Then three figures emerged from the Stargate.

Ambassador Bill Crawford was as slick and disdainful as he had ever been. He glanced at the airmen as if they were a bad smell, then up at Hammond. "A warm welcome, as always, General."

Hammond's eyes narrowed. "Major Lee," he said over the PA, "stand down your men and escort our guests to the briefing room." He watched as the soldiers lowered their weapons and the Major spoke to Crawford. Hammond turned his attention to the Ambassador's two companions. One was Commander Kenna, the officer he'd seen at the Kinahhi leader's side during his visit to their world. He was looking around the gate-room with professional interest, his eyes lingering on the soldiers as if assessing their worth – whether as friends or foes Hammond could not be sure. And then Kenna lifted his eyes to the General and gave a brief nod of acknowledgment. Hammond returned the gesture; he saw something in the Commander that he liked, but that he couldn't quite identify. Perhaps it was simply the recognition of a kindred spirit?

The contact was brief, disrupted by the third man, who touched Kenna's shoulder with a long, elegant hand and murmured something in his ear. The Commander nodded, but made no reply. This man was new to Hammond. He was tall and slender, as were all Kinahhi. His skin was copper, his hair falling long down his back. But it was his eyes that caught the General's attention. They were a compelling amber color, like a tiger's, unusual and somehow disconcerting. He radiated mistrust.

As the men were led from the gate-room, Hammond glanced at his watch and realized it was barely 0400 hours. He had no doubt that the Kinahhi had chosen their time of arrival deliberately, but if they thought they could wrong-foot him so easily they were very much mistaken.

"Have coffee brought to the briefing room, Lieutenant," he ordered as he strode out. "And make it strong."

Sam Carter eyed the stodgy, scarcely warm food on her fork without enthusiasm. The pain from the knife wound in her shoulder had shredded her appetite, and MREs were really only half-way palatable when you were starving. Nonetheless, she forced down another mouthful and focused, without much success, on the conversation between her friends.

It was light and inconsequential, and couldn't hold her attention. Her mind was stuffed with schematics, and a technology so far beyond her comprehension that she might as well have been an Abydonian trying to make sense of a computer. And the clock was ticking. Less than twenty-four hours until they reached P3W-451, but if she couldn't get the anti-gravity device to work they might as well fly straight home.

She closed her eyes and leaned her head back against the wall. She could do this. It was what she did. It was her job.

Just do your job!

Wincing, she gritted her teeth and pushed the memory to one side. This was different, this was science. There were no ambiguities in science, no misleading emotions; either it would work or it wouldn't. She would succeed or she would fail. End of story. Literally.

At least she'd been able to initiate the device, but meshing Ancient technology with that of the Goa'uld was proving problematic, especially with the limited equipment she had on board. If she only had—

"Hey." The quiet voice startled her. She opened her eyes and saw that the Colonel had come to sit next to her, arms resting on his knees. He was watching her intently. "You okay?"

"Sure," she lied. "Just tired. And frustrated. If I could just—"

"Ah!" His raised hand stopped her. "Resting," he reminded her. "That's what we're doing, remember? Resting."

She smiled slightly. "Sir, we have less than twenty-four hours until we reach '451. If I don't get the anti-grav device online by then—"

"We'll wait," he interrupted. "We'll wait until you're done."

She nodded toward the ration bar he was slowly eating in lieu of an MRE. "For how long?"

He didn't answer right away, but glanced over at Teal'c. "You can do it, Carter. I know you can."

"If I can't—"

"If you can't, then it's impossible."

Not true. She felt clumsy and unfocused, her usually sharp mind was fogged by pain and dark memories. *Acid beading on the tip of a knife. Her fist connecting with the hard bone of a boy's cheek. Anger so hot it scorched away reason.* Three days ago, she'd thought she knew herself. Now she felt like a stranger in her own skin, and she wasn't convinced she could tie her own shoelaces, let alone pull off this technological miracle.

The Colonel seemed oblivious to her doubts. He patted her arm and wearily pushed himself to his feet. "Get some shut-eye, Carter. It can wait a few hours."

She nodded and tried to look confident. He was depending on her. Henry Boyd and his team were depending on her. No matter what happened, she couldn't let them down.

CHAPTER TWO

By the time General Hammond reached the briefing room, Bill Crawford had entrenched himself at the head of the table – in Hammond's traditional place. Commander Kenna and the other Kinahhi man stood staring silently through the window and down into the gate-room, while Major Lee had positioned himself by the door, hands resting lightly on the P90 slung across his chest, watching their guests intently. Hammond dismissed him with a quiet command, donned his smoothest diplomatic face, and strode into the fray.

"Ambassador Crawford," he said. "I'm glad to see you unharmed." That much was the truth; when he'd left the man at the mercy of the Kinahhi it had felt profoundly wrong. "I trust you were treated well?"

Crawford didn't stand, his tone surly. "Better than at your hands, General."

The comment didn't deserve a reply, so Hammond turned to Commander Kenna. "A pleasure to see you again, Commander," he said. "Welcome to Earth."

Kenna bowed his head slightly. "Thank you, General Hammond. Your facility appears…functional."

As a diplomatic opening, it was worthy of O'Neill. Which somehow only increased Hammond's good opinion of the soldier. "It may be a little rough and ready," he admitted, "but it does the job."

"Of that I have no doubt," the Commander conceded. Then he indicated the man at his side. "General, may I introduce Councilor Shapash Athtar, a member of our Security Council."

Athtar stepped forward, bowing a greeting. "General Hammond," he said, his voice young and lilting, "I come bearing greetings from Councilor Tamar Damaris, and news that is both comforting and troubling."

Hammond's gaze flicked towards Crawford. A smug smile touched the corners of the ambassador's lips; he could barely contain himself. *Trouble*, Hammond thought. *Big trouble*. "Why don't you take a seat, Councilor?" He pulled out a chair at the opposite end of the table from Crawford, and Athtar politely sat down. Seating himself next to the Kinahhi, Hammond faced Crawford along the wide expanse of mahogany. A slight hardening of the ambassador's eyes marked his irritation. Well, if the boy wanted to play musical chairs… Hammond turned to Athtar. "I understand you have evidence exonerating Ambassador Crawford?"

The Councilor nodded. "We do, General. Our *sheh'fet* has determined his innocence. I can assure you beyond a doubt that Ambassador Crawford did not steal the schematics for our gravitational technology."

Narrowing his eyes, Hammond considered his response. "Councilor," he began after a moment, "the plans were discovered hidden in Mr. Crawford's laptop computer. That's pretty strong evidence. You'd stack your mind-reading device against it?"

"The *sheh'fet*," Athtar insisted, "is infallible."

At the other end of the table, Crawford leaned forward. "I already told you, Hammond, I was set up. O'Neill took those plans and must have planted them in my damn laptop. If you weren't so blind, you'd have seen the truth too."

"My people," Hammond snapped, irritated by the accusation, "do not steal alien technology. Colonel O'Neill least of all. Now, I know how much Senator Kinsey would like to get Colonel O'Neill out of the way, but this charade will never—"

Light, icy fingers touched his wrist. "Perhaps this," Athtar said, interrupting the argument, "will help settle the matter?" From beneath his robes he drew a narrow, metal cylinder. "Within are the plans in question. I believe you have technology of your own to determine who has handled them?"

Letting his outrage simmer, Hammond eyed the tube. "We do," he said. Athtar's cold fingers sent a chill crawling across his skin, but he refused to shiver. Glancing up, he saw Kenna watching him, his expression unreadable.

There was no way Jack's fingerprints would be on the plans – the General believed that as a matter of faith. He'd asked him point blank about the accusation, and O'Neill had denied it. In

Hammond's book, Jack's word was golden. He didn't trust these people, and he didn't trust their 'evidence' either. Yet he could hardly refuse to examine it. Reluctantly, he took the cylinder from Athtar's hand, and it felt like a basket of rattlers. "I'll have my people look at it."

Athtar smiled serenely. "Then I leave the matter in your hands, General." He rose gracefully to his feet. "And I trust that when you find the culprits you will contact us to discuss extradition."

Rising too, Hammond matched the man's smile. "*If*," he began, "we find the culprits, we will certainly keep you advised, Councilor." *And they'll be extradited over my dead body.*

Athtar seemed to read the unspoken truth in Hammond's face, because his smile froze and his eyes turned to chips of amber ice. "The treaty is non-negotiable, General. As your superiors are well aware."

"Then I guess we'll have to see about that," Hammond replied, moving aside and gesturing toward the door. "Have a safe trip home, Ambassador." In the corridor beyond he saw Major Lee appear, and with a brief nod Hammond gave the silent order to escort the visitors back to the gate-room.

Taking the dismissal for what it was, Athtar didn't deign to reply. In silence, he flowed past Hammond and through the door. Commander Kenna followed, casting the General a somewhat sympathetic look before he too left. Only Crawford remained, perched on Hammond's chair like the Young Pretender. "You can't protect them this time, George," he said, with a vicious smile. "There's nothing you can do. SG-1 are going down."

Anger burned hard and low in Hammond's gut. "Now, you listen to me, Crawford," he growled. "SG-1 have saved your miserable life more times than you know. Each one of them has given more to this project – to this planet! – than you ever will. So I'm warning you, leave them alone."

"I'm not responsible for this," Crawford insisted, rattled but not contrite. He was as convincing as a snake oil salesman on the witness stand. "O'Neill is guilty. He stole those plans and set me up."

Lies, upon lies. "I know for a fact," Hammond said, very slowly and very quietly, "that Colonel O'Neill is innocent. And even if he weren't, he would never, ever let someone else – even you – take the fall for him. I know this man, Crawford. And I won't let you destroy him. Do you hear me?"

The ambassador shrugged indifferently. "Hope those words tasted good, General." He leaned back in the chair and smoothed his hands along its arms. "Because you're gonna be eating them. Real soon."

Tired of listening to his insulting allegations, Hammond turned his back and stalked from the room. But he could still hear Crawford's thin, nasal voice following him down the hallway. "Cut them loose, George," he crowed. "Or they'll drag you down with them."

Hammond didn't answer.

Daniel Jackson was supposed to be sleeping. The lights in the *tel'tak* were dimmed, and around him he could hear the quiet breathing of his teammates. Teal'c had taken first watch, and his solid presence in the cockpit was reassuring. Nevertheless, sleep refused to come. The floor was hard – cargo ships weren't built for passengers – and the hip he'd bruised during his tumble down the stairs back in Baal's stronghold nagged dully, stopping him from finding even one comfortable position. But it wasn't just bruised bones that kept him awake – after seven years in the field, he was used to that. Tonight, his mind was restless. It was worrying about something he couldn't pinpoint, some unconscious fear that refused to let him rest.

Maybe it was just the general insanity of their situation? Hurtling through space in a stolen Goa'uld ship with no backup, few supplies and a black hole at the end of their journey wasn't exactly conducive to a good night's sleep. His low-level anxiety spiked at the bald description of their situation. Suspecting he was getting close to the root of the problem he decided to pursue it further. Deliberately, he sorted through his thoughts one at a time. Space, stolen ships, black holes…

Black holes.

Wormholes.

Stargates.

A black hole trying to drag Earth through the Stargate. A black hole trying to drag a *sun* through the Stargate!

His heart lurched in sudden realization and he let out an involuntary, "Oh no."

Someone stirred beside him. "Daniel?"

Uh-oh. "Jack?"

"Problem?"

He winced, but there was no point in denying it. "Ah... maybe."

Silence followed. Then, "Gonna share?"

Rubbing his hands over tired eyes, Daniel stared up at the blurred ceiling. "Remember when we were evacuating the Tok'ra from Vorash a couple of years ago?"

Jack grunted. "Not often."

"Apophis showed up with his fleet? Sam blew up Vorash's sun?"

"Daniel." There was an edge to Jack's tone now. "Your point?"

Blowing out a long breath, Daniel frowned. "You know, I'm sure Sam must have considered this. Maybe I should just go ask her what—"

"Daniel!"

"Okay." Sitting up, Daniel tugged his glasses from his pocket and slipped them over eyes gritty with insomnia. He really didn't want to be the one to discover this had all been for nothing. But fate, it seemed, had other ideas. "Remember how we dropped the Tok'ra gate into the sun, while it was connected to '451? The idea being that the gravitational force of the black hole would suck through enough stellar matter to—"

"Crap." Jack was on his feet. "Carter!"

No answer.

"Where is she?" he muttered. "Teal'c, I need some lights in here!"

As the ship brightened, Daniel glanced around and saw that Sam's sleeping bag was empty.

"Oh for crying out—"

"Is there a problem, O'Neill?" Teal'c appeared in the cockpit doorway.

"Oh yeah!" Still in his socks, hair spiked in odd directions, Jack stalked out of the cargo hold. Scrambling out of his own sleeping bag, Daniel hurried after him.

He was one step behind Jack as he barreled into the engine

room. "Carter!" He barked it like an order and Sam started so hard she dropped whatever she'd been holding. It tumbled onto the floor with a metallic clang.

"Sir! I'm glad you're here. Looks like I've—"

"Tell me, Carter," Jack snapped. "What do you think the word 'rest' means? *Exactly*."

A smile quirked the corner of her mouth. Daniel spotted it instantly. It looked like triumph. "Sorry, sir," she said, stooping to pick up the tool she'd dropped. "It's just that the solution came to me while I was sleeping. So I thought I'd—"

"Solution?"

Sam grinned. "I've done it, sir. I've integrated the anti-grav device into the Goa'uld systems. I'll need to test it, but—"

"That's great," Jack mumbled, running a hand through his disheveled hair. The look he shot at Daniel was slightly wild. *Now what?* The timing could have been better.

"Ah, Sam?" Daniel began. "Thing is… I was just wondering, um…"

Her eyes moved to his. She sensed his discomfort, and her triumph fell away. "What is it?"

"Maybe nothing," Daniel assured her, settling his glasses on his nose. "It's just, I was thinking about Vorash."

"Vorash?"

"Vorash," Jack jumped in. "Dropping the Stargate into the sun. Big bang. You remember?"

"Of course. What about it?"

"Well…" Jack cast a helpless glance at Daniel, and plowed on. "As I recall, we sent half a star through the Stargate to '451, where Boyd and his team were waiting…"

"Oh!" Realization dawned with a smile like sunshine. "No, it's okay. The stellar matter won't have exited the gate on '451 yet."

Jack blinked. "What?"

"Given the time distortion, sir, it won't have reached P3W-451 yet." She cocked her head and glanced at Daniel. "You didn't think I'd forgotten about it, did you?"

Daniel was about to issue a blanket denial when Jack said, "I tried to tell him!"

What? He shot his friend a wide look and got an urgent *can-it* gesture in response. Ignoring it, Daniel opened his mouth to protest, but a firm hand landed on his arm.

"You know how he worries," said Jack, ushering Daniel back toward the cargo hold. "So…glad we've sorted that out." And then, over his shoulder, "Good work, Carter. Now, get some rest."

"Yes, sir," came the bemused reply. "Thank you, sir."

Jack grumbled a response, and Daniel just smiled to himself. Nice to see things getting back to normal. In the day and a half since they'd left Baal's palace, he'd sensed a brittleness about the pair of them that had troubled him. They were nurturing inner wounds deeper than the cuts and bruises of battle, and it would take time to heal. Time they didn't have right now.

Back in the cargo hold, Daniel crawled into his sleeping bag, pulled off his glasses and tucked them into a pocket. Beside him, he heard Jack muttering to himself as he tried to get comfortable again. Good luck. But perhaps he could offer Jack a different kind of comfort? "Sam seems better," he murmured quietly, closing his heavy eyes and allowing his mind to drift. "I think she'll be okay."

After a long silence came a careful, "Yeah. I hope so."

"And you?"

"Go to sleep, Daniel."

It was as close to an answer as he was likely to get, but he was satisfied. Jack would be okay – if Baal couldn't break him, nothing could. Closing his eyes, Daniel at last fell into a leaden sleep, oblivious to the hard floor, his bruised hip and the danger they were rapidly approaching.

The almost palatable aroma of instant coffee failed to penetrate Jack O'Neill's fatigue as he nursed his tin mug and yawned. "Okay, Carter," he sighed, "explain it again. This time, take it slow."

Sleep and success had done Carter a world of good. She still looked pale, eyes shadowed, but he sensed optimism beneath the exhaustion. She was half-frowning, half-smiling at him now, uncertain if his request was serious. "Sir, that *was* slow."

He cast her a baleful look. "Slow-*er*."

Gathering her patience, she took a deep breath. "Okay. Imagine this," she indicated a Mainstay bar, "is Vorash's sun. And this"

– half a packet of M&M's –

"is P3W-451, where Major Boyd and his team are trapped."

Jack nodded. "Mainstay. M&M's. Got it."

"Now," Carter began, "because of the time dilation here" – she tapped the M&M's – "the stellar mass has virtually stopped moving. The rest is compacted up behind it, also caught in the event horizon of the black hole."

"And none of it has left the gate yet?" The image of Boyd being incinerated by the tons of burning plasma they'd dumped through the gate in order to save their own asses was not a happy one.

"Probably not."

"*Probably* not?"

"It's a risk, sir," she confessed. "If my calculations are off… It's a risk." She looked away, fiddling anxiously with the packet of M&M's.

"Carter…?"

Her face tightened. "Sir, I didn't mention this because you asked if it was *possible* to save them. Not if it was guaranteed. It is possible. It's also possible that we'll get there and find the entire planet gone, or that we can't penetrate the event horizon, or a hundred other things we haven't predicted. This is just one of the variables, sir. I didn't think you needed to know because—"

"Ah!" He cut her off with a wave of his hand. "You're right, I don't need to know."

She blinked. "Right." Then grimaced and stared down at the M&M's again.

He knew where her mind was, of course. Back on Kinahhi, when he'd torn her a new one for keeping Baal's connection to the planet secret. And now she was second-guessing her decisions; not what he needed in a situation as complex as the one they were facing. She could probably do with one of those little heart-to-hearts Hammond was so good at, but talking had never been Jack's forte. Instead, he nudged her arm, and when she looked up he offered her his coffee. "Here. I'm gonna find the facilities." He stood up, stretched, and sniffed in the general direction of his t-shirt. It was bad. Very bad. "You know," he said, pulling a face. "If we don't find a shower soon, I'm gonna have to open a window."

Carter smiled, and for a moment all the darkness of the past few days faded away. He felt a burst of optimism, shaking him wide awake like good, strong coffee. "We're gonna do this, Carter," he told her firmly. "We're gonna bring Henry Boyd and his team home. We're gonna give a little girl her father back, and that's gonna make all this worthwhile."

She nodded, but her face sobered. "And then what, sir?"

The dice were in the air; he had no idea how they'd fall. Rescuing Boyd would do a lot to redeem his decision to act without orders, but he wasn't sure it would be enough. Not with Kinsey in the picture, baying for blood.

When he didn't answer, Carter looked away. "For what it's worth, sir," she said after a moment, "I think you made the right decision."

"Yeah," he agreed, because he knew she needed to hear it. "So do I." But it wasn't entirely true. He'd crossed a lot of lines to get to this point, and he wasn't sure there was a way home. At least, not for him.

Hammond turned to him, eyes sharp and honest. "Colonel, did Councilor Quadesh give you any stolen technical designs?"

Jack paused, weighing the truth against the lives of SG-10. When he spoke, the lie tasted bitter. "No, sir."

The memory crawled like a snake in the pit of his stomach and promised retribution. There would be a price to pay for his breach of faith, one that might cost more than he could bear to lose.

CHAPTER THREE

There had been many occasions in the past seven years when General George Hammond's world had flipped upside down, inside out, or in any number of other chaotic permutations. He'd seen aliens of all shapes and sizes, traveled to other worlds, and even been privy to the fate of other universes. But nothing that he had seen or done since he had first set foot beneath Cheyenne Mountain had shocked him as much as the slim report that now sat on his desk.

He'd had to read it twice to make sure he'd understood correctly, and even then he'd called Major James Griffith, Air Force Office of Special Investigations, down to the SGC to answer the questions that his report had thrown up. Griffith sat before him now, a bullish man of middle years, with the square-jawed determination of any decent law-enforcement agent. Rank kept him respectful, but Hammond could tell Griffith was unaccustomed to having his conclusions queried. Too bad.

"The evidence is conclusive, sir," the Major assured him gruffly. "Three sets of prints were found on the documents. One we have been unable to identify, the second set belong to Colonel Jack O'Neill and the third to Major Samantha Carter."

Hearing it spoken aloud, Hammond felt a flush of outrage. But he refused to believe it. He'd asked Jack outright if Quadesh had given him the plans, and Jack had denied it categorically. Taking a deep breath, Hammond steepled his hands on the desk and tried a different approach. "Is it possible," he said, "that this evidence could have been forged? I don't need to remind you, Major, that we're dealing with an advanced alien civilization."

Griffith nodded. "Yes, sir. Fingerprints aren't difficult to forge. Which is why we also ran further tests." He paused, then added, "The fingerprints on these documents are what we call latent prints. They're made by the transfer onto the paper of oils and perspiration present on the ridges of the skin." He reached for the file on Hammond's desk and flipped through it to the enlarged photographic evidence. "You can see that the ninhydrin spray reacted with the amino acids present in the fingerprints, turning them this purple color. We managed to extract a DNA sample from these acids, and got a match with Colonel O'Neill. Major Carter's results were less conclusive, but given the circumstantial evidence I stand by the findings of my report, sir. This is not a forgery."

And if it wasn't a forgery, that meant… Hammond swallowed the acid taste of treachery, his fingers clenching into fists. "Could the Kinahhi have somehow forced O'Neill to handle the document? When he was asleep, perhaps?"

Griffith sat back in his chair, arms folded. "I can't speak to that, sir. As you said, we're dealing with an advanced alien civilization. But the pressure and position of the prints are consistent with Colonel O'Neill having handled the documents while they were folded up tightly. The majority of Major Carter's prints are on the actual schematics themselves, indicating that she spent a considerable amount of time examining the plans." He paused, and when Hammond didn't respond, he added, "Colonel O'Neill's prints were also all over Ambassador Crawford's laptop, sir. The evidence is compelling."

The sense of betrayal was staggering. Hammond felt it like a physical blow, stealing his breath away. To cover, he stood and paced to the window. *He'd lied! Jack had lied to him, point blank.* Worse than that, far worse than that, he'd hidden the evidence of his crime in the belongings of an innocent man. The world seemed to sway on its axis for a moment. He'd read O'Neill's file, he knew all the damn distasteful things Jack had been ordered to do in the name of God and country, but this… Jack had exploited Hammond's trust, and by doing so had made him an accomplice.

Investigate Crawford.

The note had been left scrawled on a Post-It inside Hammond's briefcase, and he'd done exactly what it had asked. Because he'd believed in Jack unquestioningly. He'd investigated Crawford, found the fake evidence, and almost condemned an innocent man to rot his life away in an alien jail.

Moving stiffly, keeping his anger in check, he turned back to Griffith. "Thank you for your thoroughness, Major. I'm sorry to have questioned your findings, but I had to make sure."

Griffith rose slowly to his feet, coming to a casual attention. "I understand, sir." He glanced down at the file again. "He was sloppy, though. Didn't even try to hide the evidence."

Perhaps he didn't think he needed to, Hammond thought bitterly. Why bother, when your CO believes everything you say without question? Biting down on his fury, he gave a stiff nod to Griffith. "Will you be handling the case once Colonel O'Neill and Major Carter are placed in custody?" If they ever came back from wherever the hell they'd gone.

"Yes, sir," came the short answer.

"Then my office will be in contact with you in due course."

"Yes, sir. Thank you." Saying nothing else, Griffith left the room and closed the door behind him. Hammond was grateful; he felt drained. How could this have happened? How was it possible that someone he trusted so completely could have betrayed him like this?

That's the wrong question, George. The little voice was quiet, struggling to be heard above the roar of his anger, but it was there nonetheless. *You need to be asking 'why?'*

Why lie to him? Why incriminate Crawford? Was there a reason that could justify O'Neill's behavior? Hammond closed his eyes and let out a long, bitter sigh, hanging onto that question with a tenacity that bordered on desperation. Right then, it was all that remained of a friendship he'd thought indestructible.

They were all crowded into the cockpit, Teal'c at the helm and Sam in the co-pilot's seat. Her eyes were glued to the computer screen, her lips moving in silent mental calculations. Jack shifted at Daniel's side, eyes narrowed as he studied the blurred starfield ahead of them. He was as tense as if they were going into battle – which, in a manner of speaking, they were. Going into battle with the forces of the cosmos. It almost sounded poetic when you put it like that. Perhaps—

"On my mark, Teal'c." Sam's abrupt tone cut through his musings. "Three, two, one. Mark."

The sharp deceleration threw Daniel hard against the back of Sam's chair but his grunt of protest died on his lips when he saw what filled the *tel'tak*'s window. It was awesome, in the truest sense of the word; majestic in its beauty and terrifying in its sheer power. Rainbows of color threaded through shimmering silver streaks that swirled in a frozen pattern against the tapestry of the void, like a tornado captured at the point of creation. It was—

"Big," Jack observed from beside him. Daniel flung him an irritated glance, but only got a shrug in return. "Where's '451?"

"We can't see it, sir," Sam said absently, riveted to the data streaming across her computer. "We're not close enough yet."

"Major Carter," said Teal'c suddenly. "We are already feeling the gravitational pull of the black hole."

Sam replied without looking up. "I know. I deliberately brought us out close enough to feel its effects."

"Carter?" Jack's tone managed to convey both faint alarm and complete trust.

"It's okay, sir. It's nothing that our engines can't handle. But I need to test the gravity shield before we get too close." She glanced over her shoulder with an edgy smile. "Kind of like putting a toe in the shallow end, sir."

Jack's eyebrows twitched. "I hope we're wearing waterwings."

Returning his attention to the black hole, Daniel had a question of his own. "Are we being affected by the time distortion, Sam?"

She held up her hand for quiet. "Just a minute." Then she touched a button on the control panel and the ship shuddered beneath them. And stilled. "Teal'c, bring us to a dead halt."

"Very well."

So slow it was barely noticeable, they stopped. "Now we wait," said Sam, staring out the window toward the frozen maelstrom. Daniel found himself holding his breath, and Jack's nonchalance was too studied to be convincing. After a couple of minutes Sam said, "Teal'c?"

"We remain motionless, Major Carter." Satisfaction was evident in his voice. "The gravitational pull of the black hole is no longer affecting us."

"Way to go, Carter!" Jack slapped her on the back, and Sam grinned in relief. "So," he enthused. "We go in, grab SG-10, and get home in time for breakfast?"

Sam shook her head, her smile slipping. "Not quite that easy, sir. Daniel's right. The time distortion is still a problem."

"I thought that's what Baal's gravity shield was for?"

Baal's gravity shield. Interesting, Daniel noted, that Jack said the name without hesitation. That was new – and healthy.

"The shield is keeping us from being affected by the time distortion at the moment," Sam agreed. "But at some point, we have to get Boyd and his team onto the ship. Once the ring device hits the surface of the planet it'll leave the gravitational bubble and become time-distorted. In effect, it'll stop dead. From our point of view, it could take weeks to retrieve them."

Eyebrows climbing, Jack said, "We have two MREs and a packet of M&M's Carter. We don't have weeks."

"I know, sir. Which is why I think we need to deactivate the gravity shield in order to transport SG-10 aboard."

Teal'c shifted where he sat in the pilot's chair. "Will we not then be subject to the same time distortion?"

"Yeah," Sam nodded. "It'll only seem like minutes to get them on board, but in fact several weeks will have passed back at the SGC."

Jack ran a hand through his hair. "Weeks? George is gonna be pissed."

"Yes, sir."

His eyes fixed on Sam, and something significant passed between them. A question asked, and an answer given. Daniel glanced from one to the other, trying to figure out what was going on. Sam looked unhappy, and Jack's face was as bleak and unbending as stone. "Okay," he barked after a moment, "fasten your seatbelts, kids."

Sam turned nervously back to the computer. "The shield's holding, sir."

Shoulders straight, Jack braced himself against the back of the pilot's chair. His uniform was torn and his face was bruised, but Daniel saw something else in his friend: regret and a deep sense of things passing. Jack looked like a veteran marching in his last parade, and it turned Daniel cold. "Jack…?"

A firm hand on his arm both acknowledged and answered the question. "Punch it, Teal'c," Jack ordered quietly. He was staring out at the black hole as if it held his fate. "Let's go bring our people home."

The Senator's office was quiet, its scent of polished wood and soft leather as arousing as expensive perfume on a young and eager intern. It was the scent of power, and to Bill Crawford nothing was more exciting.

He stood before the desk, watching as Senator Kinsey flipped through the Air Force Office of Special Investigations report. Crawford's eyes were fixed on the Senator's face, watching every nuance of emotion in the wrinkles around his mouth and in the cold glitter of his eyes. Kinsey was pleased. Extremely pleased. Crawford allowed himself a small, contained smile and rocked forward onto his toes in anticipation.

"This is most impressive," Kinsey said eventually, closing the file and looking up. "Even Jack O'Neill won't be able to squirm out of this one. I've got him where I want him, at last."

"Yes, sir," Crawford agreed.

The Senator's face creased into a frown. "That is, if he ever comes back to face the music. Which I doubt – he knows we're onto him. So does George Hammond."

"I was wondering if they were in cahoots, Senator." The memory of Hammond's cool superiority as he'd abandoned Crawford to the Kinahhi was still sour. "He was the one who suggested searching my laptop – where O'Neill had hidden the plans."

"Yes," Kinsey agreed. "Yes, that's right. They must have been in it together." He stood, pacing slowly to the window. "No doubt it was part of their plan to undermine our treaty with the Kinahhi – and my Presidential campaign." He turned and paced back. "Do you have any evidence of Hammond's involvement?"

Crawford didn't. "It may be worth interviewing the General," he suggested. "Without O'Neill there to cover for him, the circumstantial evidence is compelling."

The Senator gripped the back of his chair, dry knuckles turning white. "And if O'Neill comes back, spouting his usual lies? What then? You don't know him like I do, Crawford. He's tricky. They all are. You think you've got 'em!" His fist slammed down hard on the back of the chair, a sudden flash of hatred blazing through his rheumy eyes. "And then they wriggle through your fingers like worms!"

For an instant, he looked crazy. Driven beyond reason by his hatred and ambition, driven toward an early grave. *And there, but for the grace of God…*

The thought startled Crawford.

"What?" Kinsey snapped.

"Nothing, sir." Focus, Crawford reprimanded himself. There was more at stake here than the Senator's obsession; Crawford had his own career to build. Clearing his mind, he said, " I believe SG-1's return is extremely unlikely, sir."

The Senator's grip on the back of his chair relaxed. "Why?"

Because Councilor Damaris told me so… The deal had been to rid Kinsey of SG-1, but they hadn't discussed specifics. If the Kinahhi had methods beyond simply implicating O'Neill in the theft of alien technology, it certainly wasn't something the Senator needed to know. "I believe," Crawford said, "that they're using the stolen technology to try and rescue a team lost within a black hole. The mission is extremely dangerous, and the technology is far from reliable. The odds of SG-1 returning alive are negligible." *So say the Kinahhi.*

The Senator grunted a response, let go of the chair and walked back to the window. A winter moon shone outside, turning his silver hair luminous. A halo on a fallen angel. "So they'll die heroes."

"No, sir," Crawford corrected. "They'll die AWOL. And General Hammond will be left carrying the can."

The sly twitch of the man's mouth was followed by a slow nod. "Yes," he agreed. "Yes, he will." Kinsey stayed by the window, staring out over the icy water of the Potomac. "Time's up, General," he said quietly. "And this time, victory is mine."

And mine, Crawford added, with a smile of his own. But he kept the thought to himself. He was playing a longer game, and playing to win.

CHAPTER FOUR

"This is amazing," Sam breathed, staring out at the massive twist in space-time that was curling the universe all around her. "I mean, think about it... No one in the history of our species has ever witnessed this." It was a phenomenal thought, and did much to push aside the nagging doubts and fears that had haunted her since they'd left the inferno of Baal's stronghold.

"Yeah, it's pretty cool." The Colonel was struggling for indifference, but couldn't hide his own awe. There was a reason he had a telescope on his roof, and it had nothing to do with spying on the neighbors.

Beneath the looming black hole, a small gray planet came into view. From this distance it looked distorted, stretching out into an egg shape as the enormous gravitational forces sucked it towards oblivion. And somewhere down there, frozen in an endless moment of time, were SG-10. She wondered if they could—

The ship juddered, throwing her sideways in her chair. Behind her, Daniel muttered. "Ow!"

"Carter?"

"Not sure, sir." She scanned the data streaming across the screen. It had felt as if their shield had slipped, as if an enormous fist had taken hold of the ship and yanked. "Looks like the power dropped out for a moment."

The Colonel didn't answer, but she heard him shift uneasily where he stood behind Teal'c. "Let's step on it, huh?"

No one else spoke. There was little to say, here in the midst of a cosmic maelstrom that could rip them apart in seconds. Its presence was overpowering and oppressive, as if the gravity well were slowly crushing their minds, if not their ship. They descended in silence until Sam could see red fissures cracking the planet's surface like open wounds. It reminded her of another world she'd seen rip itself apart, turning molten beneath her feet. She shivered, and dismissed the memory.

Teal'c spoke. "I have located the Stargate," he reported. "It appears intact."

"Yes!" O'Neill's voice was determinedly bright, as if he could force back the tension by willpower alone. He almost succeeded.

"Ah…just out of curiosity," Daniel chimed in, "what would happen if, you know, the shield failed?"

"Daniel!" The Colonel warned.

"I'm just curious."

"I believe we would all die a slow and unpleasant death," Teal'c replied shortly. "Let us speculate no further."

Sam glanced at him. Was he afraid? "Actually," she said, watching gray shreds of cloud whip past the window as they dropped into the atmosphere, "multiverse theory speculates that black holes are gateways to new universes. Or, rather, that they create new universes from the matter sucked through from this one. So, theoretically, we could end up seeding a new universe."

"Bits of us," the Colonel corrected. "Bits of us could, Carter."

She glanced over her shoulder and smiled. "Yes, sir. Sub-atomic bits."

"As I said," interrupted Teal'c, "let us speculate no further!"

Sam's smile was cut short by a hand on her arm. "Ah, guys?" It was Daniel. "I think we've found them."

They were beneath the clouds now, skimming across gray sands. Ahead of them she could see the Stargate rising up from the wasteland, steely and dark. Before it, growing closer with each moment, was the team they'd left behind.

"Do they know we're here?" Daniel murmured, his voice thick with compassion.

SG-10 were motionless, like a tableau. Sam could make out one figure crouched before the MALP, another at the DHD and two more staring up at the sky in fear.

"No," Sam replied. "Until we drop the shield, we'll be moving too fast for them to see."

She glanced at the Colonel, waiting for his order, and saw a fierce sense of vindication in his eyes. She shared it – seeing SG-10 right there in front of them, terrified and waiting for death, erased all doubt from her mind. Despite what they'd suffered, despite the dire consequences waiting for them at home, she knew they'd done the right thing.

"Teal'c," O'Neill ordered, "take us into position. Get ready

to transport the two by the gate first, then Watts at the DHD and
Boyd by the MALP. Daniel, with me." He turned, striding toward
the transport rings and—

The ship bucked forward. Someone yelled. Sam was in freefall, forward and upward. Her face smashed against the control
panel, crunching into broken glass, then snapped back against the
chair. Vision dark, mind dizzy, she yelled, "Teal'c!"

"The shield has failed!"

"We're goin' in!" The Colonel shouted, far away. "Daniel!
Hold on to—"

The impact catapulted her into darkness and she was gone.

"Damn it!" Watts yelled from the DHD. "This is pointless, sir!
It won't stay open!"

Standing up slowly, Major Henry Boyd glanced up at the
twisting nightmare in the sky. It looked like some hideous creature come to tear them to pieces. "Keep trying," he told the Captain.

"Sir?" Lieutenant Jessica McLeod ripped her gaze from the
sky, voice shaking. "I've been thinking about why the gate won't
activate. The gravitational force of the—" She stammered over
the word. "Of the black hole would create a massive time distortion effect."

He stalked toward her, frowning. "A what?"

"Time here will be moving much slower than back on Earth,
sir. Much slower. The gate was probably open for half an hour at
the SGC, but here…just a second."

Boyd felt his heart clench tight. "What are you saying, Lieutenant?"

She looked bleak. "I don't think we're getting out of this one,
sir."

Lucy. His daughter was the first thought in his head. Sweet,
innocent, adoring Lucy. Her little arms around his neck, her
delighted smile when he came home. *Daddy!* He swallowed
hard. "I won't accept that, Lieutenant." Lucy, barely old enough
to understand. Heather, having to explain why he was never coming home again. "They'll find a way to come get us. They won't
leave us here."

McLeod nodded, but he saw despair in her eyes. Behind

them the gate started to spin again. How many times now? Ten? Twenty? Grimly, he turned to watch as the final chevron locked into place. *Work. Work, you sonofabitch.* "Get ready to run for it!"

The wormhole spilled out onto the doomed planet, silver-blue with hope and— Then it died. "Dial again!" he ordered.

Captain Watts just stared at him over the heads of McLeod and Reed.

"Do it!" Boyd barked. "We are not gonna die here! You hear me? We're not—"

"Sir!" McLeod screamed the word, her voice drowned out by another, louder scream. An unnatural scream.

Involuntarily Boyd ducked as a small Goa'uld ship came hurtling out of nowhere, lurching wildly as it skimmed above the dunes behind them. "What the hell…?"

"It's gonna crash!" Reed shouted. "Get down!"

Boyd hit the ground as an explosion of dust and dirt funneled up into the sky. Sand pattered down like rain, clogging his eyes and mouth. He spat, and heard Lieutenant Reed coughing at his side.

"What the hell are the Goa'uld doing here?"

"I don't care," Boyd growled, scrambling to his feet. He spat out another mouthful of sand. "They could be our way off this rock." Turning back to the DHD, he yelled, "Watts, keep dialing. McLeod, Reed – with me." He clicked the safety off his MP-5. "And stay sharp."

Consciousness came slowly and painfully. His head was pounding, his left shoulder felt torn and wrenched where he'd been hanging onto the bulkhead, and he was unbelievably tired. Peeling open his eyes, Jack found himself staring at someone else's back. Cautiously, he sat and waited for the world to stop spinning. He glanced down and saw Daniel lying on his side with his left arm… Ouch.

"Daniel?" He gave him a gentle shake.

His friend stirred. "I—Ugh. Oh. *Ow!*"

Jack sucked air between his teeth. "You should have let go," he murmured, pushing himself to his feet, testing his weight on his legs. No damage, beyond the usual. "Don't move," he said.

"I'll be back."

Stepping over Daniel's legs, Jack picked his way into the cockpit. Teal'c was slumped over the controls, blood seeping from beneath his head. Carter was draped like a rag doll, half in and half out of the co-pilot's chair. Her nose was bleeding heavily, face white.

Cursing softly, Jack touched his fingers to her neck and found a pulse. A little slow, but it beat strongly. Thank God. But he dared not move her until he could check for breaks. First things first. He turned to Teal'c; he could hear him breathing and touched his shoulder. "Teal'c. Wake up."

Eyes opened, disoriented for an instant. Then Teal'c sat up, sharp as a knife. "O'Neill."

"How you doing, buddy?"

Teal'c considered the question and reached up to touch the bleeding gash on his forehead. "Well enough, O'Neill."

Jack nodded. "Carter's out. I don't know how bad. Daniel's dislocated his shoulder."

"Our injuries," Teal'c observed, glancing out at the wall of sand covering the nose of the *tel'tak*, "are immaterial. We cannot escape this world."

Oh no, not going down that route. "Come on," Jack objected. "We've been in tighter spots than this."

Teal'c raised an eyebrow.

"Hey!" Jack chided him. "Let's keep a little optimism here." He moved away. "Wake up Carter. We're gonna need her brains."

As Teal'c moved woozily across the cockpit, Jack stepped back into the cargo hold. Daniel had shifted himself into a sitting position, back against the wall. His left arm was clutched against his chest and he was trying to hide his obvious pain. Jack crouched in front of him. "Hurts like hell, huh?"

Daniel nodded. "Ah. Yeah." He glanced around. "Teal'c and Sam?"

"Teal'c's okay. Carter's still out." He paused, considered Daniel's pasty face, then bit the bullet. "If we're gonna get outta here," he said, "we'll need all hands to help fix the ship."

Looking down at his shoulder, Daniel paled. "You mean…?"

"I've done it before," Jack assured him. "Just pop it back in the socket. Won't hurt. Much."

Daniel offered a sickly smile. "Yeah. Okay. Just... Just give me a second."

He watched as Daniel took a couple of deep breaths, bracing himself. "Teal'c?" Jack called.

The Jaffa appeared in the doorway. He'd dug out a medikit and held a dressing pressed over his gashed head.

"How's Carter?"

"Still unconscious, O'Neill. However, I have ascertained that no bones were broken and placed her in the recovery position."

That was good news, at least. But if she didn't wake up soon... Someone had to fix the anti-grav device. He blew out an anxious breath and beckoned Teal'c. "Gonna need your help, T."

Teal'c peered at Daniel. "Do you wish me to restrain him, or reset the shoulder?"

"Restrain?" Daniel echoed faintly.

"You pull," Jack decided. Moving closer, still facing his friend, he said, "Gonna get cozy for a moment." He slipped an arm under the one Daniel nursed close to his chest, and held him tight. "Okay, Teal'c."

Teal'c came to kneel at Daniel's side and carefully took hold of his arm. "This will cause considerable pain Daniel Jackson," he announced. "But it will be of short duration."

Daniel gritted his teeth and screwed his eyes shut. "Just do it."

Meeting Teal'c's eyes, Jack nodded. Carefully, Teal'c began to pull Daniel's arm out straight. Daniel flinched, tried to go with the flow, but Jack held him back. "Easy."

"*It hurts...!*" Daniel hissed.

"I know." Jack grimaced. "Almost done."

With a speed clearly born of much experience, Teal'c pulled the arm out straight. Daniel yelled – loudly, and right in Jack's ear – and then Jack heard the pop as the arm settled back into its socket.

For a moment Daniel slumped against him, eyes still tightly shut and face ashen. Jack gave him a reassuring pat on the back. "You're done," he said quietly. "Teal'c? We got some Tylenol?"

"Indeed." Teal'c rose to his feet and disappeared toward the engine room, where their gear was stored.

Easing Daniel against the wall, Jack sat back on his haunches.

"Hang in there, buddy."

Daniel opened his eyes. "Jack?"

"Yeah?"

"Thanks. I—"

Gunfire exploded into the room. Teal'c fell back through the door, sprawling motionless on the floor. Behind him a voice, harsh with desperation, yelled from the corridor beyond. "No one move!"

Boyd saw the Jaffa creep through the shadows, his fluidity and grace belying his bulk. Identifying him instantly as a threat, the Major opened fire. The Jaffa ducked back through the doorway, but Boyd knew he'd winged him. Reed and McLeod were on his six, and together they stalked along the narrow corridor toward what had to be the cockpit. The ship was small; he'd never seen one before, but there wasn't room for more than a handful of men. "No one move!" he yelled, as they approached the door through which the Jaffa had fallen. There was no time for subtlety. If they were going to get out of here, they had to move fast.

He braced himself for the electronic fizz of staff weapons engaging, but all that came was silence. And then, "Boyd? You sonofabitch, is that you?"

Shock stunned him. McLeod's eyes grew wide as saucers and Reed gaped like a goldfish. No one could mistake that voice. But it was impossible. A trick, perhaps? Not taking a chance, Boyd kept his MP-5 raised as he peeked into the room. The Jaffa lay on the floor, and crouching over him was a very familiar – very angry – figure. "Colonel O'Neill?"

"You shot him!"

It didn't make any sense! "How did you—"

"Doesn't matter," the Colonel barked. "You got a medikit?"

"Yes, sir. Reed, give him yours."

The Jaffa stirred as Reed dropped down at his side. It looked like he was trying to sit up, but O'Neill was holding him flat. "Teal'c, don't move."

Teal'c? Crap! "I didn't see him, sir. I'm sorry, I thought he was—"

"It's okay," O'Neill snapped, eyes fixed on his team mate. In the gloom, Boyd could see the Colonel frowning. "Accidents happen. Even to the best of us."

"He's hit in the arm, sir," Reed reported after a moment. "He'll be okay."

Relieved, but perplexed as hell, Boyd turned back to O'Neill. "Sir, we have to get outta here. There's a black hole ripping the place apart and the gate won't dial, so—"

The Colonel rose to his feet and stepped closer. "I know, Major. We can take you home, but you gotta help us – and we gotta hurry." In the faint emergency lighting, Boyd could see him better. He looked strange. There was something different…

At his side, McLeod gasped softly. "Sir, your hair…"

O'Neill switched his gaze to her, somehow managing to be gruff and sympathetic at the same time. "Yeah, it's been a while, Lieutenant."

Boyd's mouth tightened. "How long?" he cut in.

O'Neill paused briefly but he had never been the sort to sugar-coat his words. "Five years."

"Five *years*?" Oh God. Lucy…

CHAPTER FIVE

Daniel forced himself to his feet, ignoring the sickening pain in his shoulder. It hardly mattered, given the circumstances. If they didn't get out of here soon, they'd be torn to bits along with the planet. And while there was a certain intellectual appeal to having his base elements used to seed a new universe, it wasn't exactly a phenomenon Daniel longed to experience.

As if to underline the point, the ship started to shake. He saw Jack stagger to stay upright, and only a miracle kept Daniel on his feet. The quake only lasted a couple of seconds, but it was enough. The beginning of the end.

"We gotta move," Jack snapped. "Boyd, take your men outside. I need a visual on any external damage. Then get the hell back here as fast as you can."

Boyd, still slack-faced with shock, responded to the order as if it were a lifeline. "Yes, sir. SG-10 – with me." The rest of his team followed, shaken but still functioning. Whatever Daniel might once have thought about the military, seeing them in action was a humbling experience. They'd just lost five years of their lives, they might lose the rest within hours, and yet they kept doing their job.

"Daniel." Jack was helping Teal'c to his feet. "Go wake up Carter. We need her. Now."

Casting a concerned look at Teal'c, whose blood was already seeping through the field-dressing on his arm, Daniel just nodded. Keep doing your job. It was all any of them could do.

He found Sam on the floor of the cockpit, rolled onto her side and pale as death. For a moment he chilled at the sight. Her white skin was stark against the blood that had seeped from her nose, down over her mouth and into her clothing. She'd stopped bleeding now and the blood was clogging darkly on her face. Wincing at the pain in his shoulder, Daniel hunkered down at her side and gently shook her. "Sam? Can you hear me?"

Nothing.

He shook her more firmly. "Come on, Sam. Wake up." Again, nothing. He touched her face, lightly tapping at her cheek. If she didn't wake up… "Sam, come on. We need your help." Slowly, her eyelids started to flutter and her lips moved, sticky with the blood from her nose. "That's it," Daniel encouraged her. "Come on, wake up."

Behind him, he sensed Jack enter the room, radiating tension in waves. Daniel glanced up and saw his friend staring at Sam with an inscrutable intensity. "Carter." It wasn't a bark, but somehow it sounded like an order. "Come on, Major, snap out of it."

Her eyes opened suddenly, wide and confused, and she jerked upright as if from a nightmare. "Easy!" Daniel moved to support her, grimacing as she jostled his injured arm. Supporting her against himself, he helped her sit. "It's okay, take it easy."

"Daniel…?" Sam groaned, putting her hand to her mouth and grimacing when it came away bloody. "What happened?"

"Kind of hoping you could tell us," Jack answered. He'd pulled out his canteen and was using the water to moisten a gauze dressing from a medikit. "We crashed," he added, and carefully began to dab the blood from her nose and mouth. "The gravity shield failed."

Sam's eyes closed. "I'm sorry. I don't understand how that happened…"

"Doesn't matter how," Jack interjected. "We just need you to fix it and get us outta here." His words were abrupt, with no concession to Sam's obviously fragile state. But the gentle way he continued to clean her face belied his brusqueness; it was a tenderness Daniel found difficult to witness.

"How long?" Sam asked at last. "The time distortion effect…"

Jack glanced at his watch. "We've been here twenty minutes. Give or take."

"Twenty minutes?" Her eyes flashed wide. "That's…that's almost three months, sir."

Three months?

Jack absorbed the news calmly. "Then we'd better hurry." He offered her a hand. "Think you can stand?"

Sam nodded, but Daniel saw that the hand she extended was shaking. If Jack noticed, he ignored it as he pulled her back to her feet. She swayed, holding her ground tenaciously, but there was uncertainty in her eyes. Fear and self-doubt. She didn't know if she could fix this, and if Sam couldn't fix it...

Daniel stood up, the motion sending needles of pain shooting from his shoulder up into his neck, and allowed himself a moment of despair. He was battered and bruised, and exhausted at the most profound level. Death lurked above them, mindless and merciless. How the hell could they haul themselves out of this one? It was impossible.

Suddenly he felt a firm touch on his arm. It was Jack. His gaze was as weary as Daniel's, but resolute and unflinching. "Come on, kids," he said quietly. "Let's get to work."

Trussed up in his dress blues, General George Hammond stood alone in the silence of Dr. Jackson's office. It was as Jackson had left it, scattered with books and mementos of a hundred different cultures. Something that looked like a shrunken head was perched on one shelf, a tall ceremonial spear was propped, amid a clutter of books, against another. Nothing had changed in the three months since SG-1 had gone missing, but he felt that this office – which somehow embodied them all – was slowly dying. There was no scent of coffee in the air, no hum of the computer screen, no arguing, no laughing. The spirit of SG-1 was fading, and despite the bitter disappointment that haunted his memories, General Hammond missed it. He missed them.

"Sir?" Lieutenant Ashford was hovering at the door, dancing nervously. "Senator Kinsey has arrived. He's waiting in the briefing room."

Hammond nodded, but didn't turn around. "Tell the Senator I'll be with him shortly."

"Yes, sir." He heard the hesitation in her voice – and was that a note of disapproval hovering in the background? Perhaps. Hammond didn't much care. The inquiry he was about to endure would be better named 'grilling', and he had no doubt that the Senator planned to hang him out to dry. Not that it was entirely undeserved – he should never have allowed SG-1 off-world after Jack had seen Crawford's report – but he'd be damned if he'd rush to his own execution.

Let him have a few more minutes here, with the memories of

his missing friends. Those, at least, Kinsey couldn't steal from him, even if everything else he'd worked for over the past seven years was slipping through his fingers. He sighed and shook his head. This wasn't how it was supposed to end. It was wrong. It was all wrong...

Jumping down from the *tel'tak*, Jack hit the sand with a grunt. A bolt of pain lanced up from his knee and grabbed him viciously around the throat, making him nauseous. Growling a curse, he jammed his cap onto his head and squinted up at the swirling mass that disfigured the skies above them. "Damn..." Jaded as he was, the sight caused him to catch his breath. The black hole glowered like the eye of some malicious god bent on destruction. It was the stuff of nightmares. And he should know.

Snapping his attention away, he yelled, "Boyd?"

"Sir!" The Major's head popped up from the roof of the *tel'tak*. "We've almost completed the visual survey, sir. Some superficial damage to the hull, but nothing structural."

"What about the engines?"

"No damage, sir, from what Reed could tell, and—"

A ripple raced through the ground, rumbling like low thunder. Atop the *tel'tak* Boyd dropped to his belly and held on. Ducking, Jack braced himself with one hand. He hated quakes. When it had stopped he caught Boyd's eye again. "Your guy think she'll fly?"

Boyd nodded. "Yes, sir. She'll fly."

Good. Jack stood, fishing in a pocket for his sunglasses. "Good work, Major. Now get your team inside before—" Someone landed with a thump behind him, spraying sand up into his face. "Hey! Watch it."

"Sorry, sir!" It was Carter, and she wasn't hanging around to chat. She was running even before she threw him the apology, heading over the sand dune toward the Stargate, tool bag clutched in one hand.

Damn it! "Carter?" He started running after her. "What's going on?"

She didn't answer, scrabbling up the dune on hands and feet, then slipping and sliding down the other side. But she was injured, and his legs were longer. He caught up with her as she pelted across the sand towards the Stargate.

"Carter!" he barked.

She slowed, but only because she'd reached her objective, and dropped to her knees in front of the MALP. "I need its wiring, sir." Her nose had started to bleed again, and she wiped the blood away with the back of her hand. "The Ancients' power unit fried the circuitry in the anti-grav device – that's why the shield failed."

Breathing heavily, Jack couldn't stop himself from squinting up at the black hole looming overhead like an anvil waiting to fall. "Fried? Why?"

"Don't know," came the short answer. It stank of self-recrimination. "Maybe I read the specs wrong."

And that was about as likely as snow on Abydos. "Or…?"

She just shook her head. "I don't know." She'd pried off the MALP's cover, and was pulling out wiring like she was gutting a chicken. "This should have a high enough ampage to get us out of the event horizon. But it won't last long. We'll have to move fast."

Jack stared back up at the sky. Was it him, or did the damn thing seem to be getting closer? "How long?"

"I don't know, sir." She sounded genuinely anguished. "I don't even know why it failed. It shouldn't have, if I'd done it right in the first place. The specs were designed to use the Ancients' device. I don't know how I could have screwed up."

Normally such things were off-limits, but given the circumstances he permitted himself a reassuring pat on her back. "Focus, Carter. We'll figure out the rest later."

She nodded, a curt and unconvincing movement. Carter was never easily reassured. "If I didn't—"

"What the…?" Jack jerked back in shock as the Stargate began to spin. Someone was dialing in.

His mind swam with possibilities and hopes, until Carter gasped, "Oh no." She stared at the gate over the top of the MALP, hands clutching an armful of wiring and her eyes like saucers. "Sir, run."

"What?"

Scrambling to her feet, she backed up. "It's us, sir. We're dialing in – from Vorash."

Vorash? The sun… Crap!

"Sir, come on!" Carter was already sprinting back toward the *tel'tak*.

Grabbing hold of his radio, he thundered after her. "Daniel! Teal'c! Fire her up. We're coming in hot! Literally!"

He was outpacing Carter now, the load of wiring in her arms combining with her head injury to slow her down, and he could hear the final chevrons locking. Grabbing one arm, he yanked her onward as they both dived over the top of the dune and half-ran, half-slid down the other side. Behind him, Jack heard the whoosh of the gate engaging. Within seconds, white-hot death would incinerate them like bugs in a barbecue.

Carter was gasping for breath, her bloody nose streaming, but she was still sprinting. In front of them the *tel'tak* whined, sand shivering from its surface as power returned to the engines and it lifted from the ground. Only a couple more meters to go, but Jack's lungs were ready to explode, his heart pounding like a drum in his chest. Carter tripped, but he held her up and kept running. At the door of the ship stood Boyd and Daniel, arms outstretched towards them. Daniel's eyes were round behind his glasses, staring over the top of the dune in shock.

An orange glare sparked in his lenses, a mushroom cloud in miniature. Jack felt a searing heat on his back and then everything turned crimson. Boyd was half-reaching out, his face burnished soot-red and distraught as he stared at something behind them. "Boyd!" Jack yelled, pushing Carter toward him. "Help her!" Boyd grabbed Carter's hand and dragged her frantically up and into the *tel'tak*.

Jack threw himself after her, diving for safety. Smoldering metal hit his chest, knocking the breath from his lungs. He gasped a raw, scorching breath and his fingers scrabbled for purchase, legs swinging in midair. Burning air. Sand, hot as sin, flayed his skin and he was slipping back, falling into searing death…

And then strong hands clasped his wrists and pulled, just as the world exploded into flame around them.

"I've got him!" Daniel yelled. "Go! Teal'c, go!"

Hands flying across the controls, Teal'c was oblivious to the pain and weakness he felt. Weakness was human, humanity meant freedom. Freedom meant strength. He would endure. The ship juddered, lurching from side to side under the intense pressures of the gravity knotted in all directions. Heat seeped through the hull like poison, sending sweat stinging into his wounds. Another pain to ignore as he fought with the controls, pulling the *tel'tak* into a steep ascent.

"Look! What the hell is that?" Lieutenant McLeod was in the co-pilot's seat, staring out of the window at the vista below. The open mouth of the Stargate spat fire in a great flare, like the maw of an enraged dragon. It roared across the sand, turned it into a glassy inferno and blasted away all vestiges of life on the doomed world.

"It is a story of some length," Teal'c told her through gritted teeth, wrestling with the bucking *tel'tak*. Its engines were whining and the ship was shaking as if it would tear itself apart. "I have no time to speak of it now." Even as the words left his lips, the *tel'tak* tipped up on end. Yells and shouts from behind rang in his ears as he struggled to right the ship; the gravity of the black hole was immense. Any attempt to resist would rip them apart. Their only chance was to change course, to fly directly toward the black hole itself until Major Carter could restore the gravity shield. If she could not…

"O'Neill," he shouted, grimly. "You must hurry. We do not have much time."

Daniel pushed himself onto his hands and knees, cursing softly at the pain in his shoulder. At his side, Jack lay on his back, gasping for breath. He looked slightly cooked, but in one piece. Sam was already scrambling to her feet, clutching an armful of cabling. "I'm gonna jury-rig this, sir. We don't have time for anything else."

With a last-ditch burst of energy, Jack rolled himself upright. "Whatever it takes, Carter. Just do it."

"I could do with an extra pair of hands, sir."

Jack glanced over at Boyd. The Major sat, back against the wall, head in hands. The heels of his palms were pressed into his eyes, as if trying to scrub something from his memory. With a frown, Jack said, "Boyd, we need your engineer." He paused, dredging up the name. "Reed?"

Boyd didn't move.

"Major! Come on. Get with it."

"Ah, Jack?"

"What?" Jack snapped angrily.

Daniel's mouth felt full of ashes. "He was behind you, Jack." *Running, screaming, burning.* "Reed didn't make it."

It took half a second for the truth to hit. Daniel saw a flash of raw anguish, and then Jack's eyes went as dark and flat as granite. "Damn."

But Sam's face crumpled in self-recrimination. "No..."

"Carter..." The word held a caution, as well as sympathy.

She visibly pulled herself back from the brink. Not far; just enough to keep going. Stooping to pick up the tool bag, Sam cast a bleak look at the grieving Boyd, but said nothing more. Tight-lipped, she left the room and Daniel heard Jack curse under his breath. "Go with her, Daniel," he said after a moment. "Don't let her dwell."

"It might do her good to—"

"Daniel!" Jack nodded toward Boyd, immobilized by shock and grief. *She doesn't have time for this!* For once Daniel found himself agreeing with his friend's icy pragmatism. If Sam fell apart now, none of them would be going home.

CHAPTER SIX

"**Y**ou do not approve of our technology, General Hammond?"

The voice, soft and lilting, belonged to the Kinahhi Councilor, Shapash Athtar. He stood beside Hammond in the control room, staring down at the busy gate-room while an assortment of crates and boxes were taken from the open wormhole and fastidiously stacked in precise rows along the wall.

"My approval is irrelevant, Councilor." The General had been around enough politicians to know how to dodge that question. "Senator Kinsey has ordered this trial of your technology, and it's my job to make it happen."

His job or his punishment? Kinsey had been spitting bullets when the President refused to relieve Hammond of command after SG-1's disappearance, and the General wondered if the Senator got some kind of perverse pleasure out of forcing him to execute orders which Hammond had so vociferously opposed. Or perhaps Kinsey was simply waiting for him to quit of his own accord? In that case, he'd have a hell of a wait; while SG-1 were still out there, Hammond would never abandon his post. But hope was fading. It had been five months without a word. The odds of them returning alive – of O'Neill restoring Hammond's faith in him – grew slimmer with each day that passed.

"I can assure you," Athtar said, interrupting the General's morose contemplations, "once you see the *sheh'fet* in operation your doubts will be lifted. We can protect your people from harm, just as we protect our own."

Bristling, Hammond squared his shoulders. "I've spent the best part of thirty years protecting my people from harm, Councilor. And I don't need to read their minds to do it."

Athtar inclined his head, bemused. "You would rather live in a world of conflict and aggression? We can offer you peace, General. Surely that is something even a military man covets?"

"Peace at any price?" Hammond restrained an acidic smile. "I believe there are some things more important than peace, Councilor."

The man's amber eyes widened in genuine surprise. "May I ask what you value above peace? I cannot imagine."

"Freedom," Hammond said bluntly. "Freedom of conscience. That's something worth fighting for."

The Kinahhi ambassador stared for a moment, brow furrowing in an uncharacteristic flash of anger. It was unusual in a people who revealed so little, and Hammond paid closer attention; he'd obviously touched a nerve.

"You would grant your enemies freedom to maim and kill your own people, General?" Athtar bit off each word. "I cannot support such 'freedom'. It is the cry of the militant who would sacrifice all for his own gain."

"And peace without freedom is a fantasy," Hammond pressed. "You cannot have one without the other."

Athtar's eyebrows rose. "Peace is freedom, General. Without peace, there·is no freedom."

"And I would say that without freedom there can be no peace – merely a break in hostilities." He paused and deliberately returned his gaze to the gate-room. The last of the crates had been brought through, and a small contingent of long-limbed Kinahhi were clucking over them like mother hens. Behind them the wormhole shut down, the room turning gray and commonplace without its iridescence. It was a testament to the strain of the past few months that Hammond could ever view the gate-room as commonplace. Taking a weary breath, he tried a different tack. "I believe Kinahhi is troubled by terrorists and dissenters, Councilor?"

There was a long pause, and when Hammond glanced back at Athtar the ambassador's lips were compressed into a tight line of thought. "Their attacks serve as timely reminders of the value of peace, General. Lest we grow complacent."

It was a strange answer, Hammond thought.

"Complacent?" A nasal voice whined the word from behind them, accompanied by footsteps clumping up the staircase. "We wouldn't want that, would we General?" It was Crawford, smooth and smug as ever. He smiled a bright smile. "The Senator would like to see you, George. In your office."

Hammond ground his teeth. Kinsey had been ensconced at the SGC for the past two weeks, personally overseeing the final negotiations with the Kinahhi. And, no doubt, digging for a good reason to convince the President to replace Hammond as commander of the base. "Tell the Senator I'll see him when I'm finished here."

"No. He needs to see you right now."

"Then he can come down here and—"

The gate started to spin, startling the visiting Kinahhi. "Sir," Harriman reported. "Unscheduled off-world activation."

Hammond rolled his eyes. *Now what...?*

You screwed up. He's dead. It's your fault. The words circled Sam's head in endless repetition. *You failed. He's dead. Burned alive. Your fault.* Through eyes hot and gritty with exhaustion, Sam focused on the anti-grav device that lay in pieces all around her. She'd gutted it, dispensing with the failsafe backups, dispensing with any redundant circuitry. Make it work, Carter.

Just do your job.

Moving without pause, without mistake, her hands stripped wires, twisting and bending. No time to solder. It looked like an exhibit at a High School science fair. If she was lucky, it would last two minutes. If she wasn't, they'd all be dead. No pressure.

You failed. He's dead. You came here to save him, and now he's dead.

Goddamn it!

"Sam?" It was Daniel, gentle and unobtrusive. She didn't have time for him.

"Not now."

He paused. Then, "Tell me how I can help."

Turn back time? Make it so she didn't screw up, so that Reed wasn't dead because she got the damn ampage wrong? "It's okay, I've nearly got it. Tell Teal'c to stand by."

She couldn't see Daniel; he was standing in the doorway. But she could sense his compassion like the heady scent of a perfumed rose, and it felt like pity – sickly and suffocating. He should save it for Boyd. Or for Reed's family, when they found out he was the only one not coming home – because of her screw-up.

"No one could—" He was cut off by a violent shudder that

rippled through the ship and sent him staggering.

Her pulse accelerated. "We're getting too close to the event horizon. It'll rip the ship apart."

"What should—"

"Daniel!" Her mind narrowed inward, excluding everything but the motion of her hands as she stripped the last wire, made the last insanely dangerous connection. This would work. Or it would blow them to hell, but who cared? They were almost there anyway. *Reed already is. Burning in hell.*

Blood was drying on her hands. Must have come from her nose, she could feel it clogged and crusting on her face. Power cackled through the circuits, making them fizz. The whole rig was as reliable as a leaky boat. But it was all they had, all she could manage before their time ran out. *How many months now? Five? Six?* "Daniel…" The voice sounded alien. Was it hers? "Get out. This could blow."

He didn't move.

"Daniel!" When she looked up, she saw him patiently watching her, as intransigent as the ancient stones he loved so much. His solidarity found a crack in her anger; he wouldn't leave her. There was nowhere to go anyway, but that wasn't the point. He wouldn't leave her.

She didn't deserve his faith, but it was too late to argue. Another violent shudder ripped through the ship. And it didn't stop.

"Carter!" It was the Colonel. She could hear him running back to check her progress. They were out of time. "Carter!"

She clenched her teeth and hit the switch.

Metal screeched, sparks flew, the damn ship was tearing itself apart. "Carter!" Jack half-ran and half-staggered back to the engine room. Life was measured in moments, death reaching eagerly for them all with crushing, skeletal hands. Damn it… "Carter!"

And then the rattling stopped. The impact of the sudden stillness threw him against the wall, cracking his head against the hard metal. "Carter?" A strobe light was flashing dully down the corridor, something was sparking and there was a pungent scent of ozone in the air. Fire? He'd taken two steps when Daniel came barreling around the corner.

"Jack!" They all but collided.

"Whoa! Slow down, Skippy."

"We gotta go!" Daniel panted, dancing around Jack and racing back to the cockpit. "Teal'c!" He yelled. "We've got thirty seconds to get outta here!"

Teal'c didn't need to be told twice. The ship accelerated so sharply Jack lost his footing and smashed against the bulkhead a second time, seeing stars all over again. The metaphorical ones. Stifling a curse, he pulled himself out the door and headed down to investigate the smoke. Smoke was never good.

What he found was Frankenstein's lab. Carter sat amid electrical spaghetti – sparks flying, smoke billowing – and poked and prodded like an insane pasta chef. What the hell was she thinking? "Carter! Get the hell outta there!"

She ignored him, focusing entirely on the device scattered all around her. Something to her right exploded with a sharp bang, shooting sparks and smoke high into the air. The ship lurched but kept going, and Carter began pulling at whatever the hell had blown up, tugging out hot wires with bare fingers and twisting them back together. "Carter!"

I do not believe she will permit herself to fail – whatever the cost.

Picking his way through the tangle of cables, trying not to tread on anything vital, Jack grabbed her arm. "Let's go."

"No!" She pulled free of his grasp. "I can't."

"Carter—"

"It has to work," she growled, fiddling with something else that was spitting and snarling at her. "Otherwise we're all dead."

Something else went up with a bang, clogging the air with a bloom of harsh, acrid smoke. Coughing, Carter tried to carry on. But the smoke was thick and suffocating – Jack could feel it burning his lungs. Light-headed, with blood thundering in his ears, his vision started to gray out. Carter shook her head, heavy and lethargic. Drowning.

Grabbing her arm hard enough to brook no argument, Jack wrenched her out of the knotted mess, staggering against the bulkhead and ignoring her protests. "Sir!" she tried to go back, slipping out of his grip and lurching away. But he was too fast, snatching hold with both hands and slamming her hard against the wall of the corridor. The air was clearer here, and he sucked in a wheezing breath. His throat was raw.

"Stop!" he rasped. "Getting yourself killed in there won't solve a damn thing."

She glared at him. "I—"

"Enough." He shoved her ahead of him down the corridor. "You've done enough. We've just gotta—"

The *tel'tak* jerked to a halt. Engines screamed, rattled and then the ship shot forward with enough force to send them both crashing to the ground. Jack's knee exploded in new pain, and beneath him he heard the breath shoot from Carter's lungs as his weight landed on her back. He hoped she hadn't cracked a rib...

The lights went out. Pitch black. The only sounds in the darkness were the wheeze of Carter's breathing and the fizz of dying electrics. He let his head come to rest on the cold floor and waited for the end.

Game over, kids. Game over.

"Close the iris!" Hammond barked. "Defense team to the gate-room!"

The Kinahhi were milling uncertainly around their equipment, casting nervous glances up at Athtar. He was doing a good job of masking his concern, but Hammond could see it nonetheless. What was he afraid of?

A defense team raced into the gate-room, taking up positions, hampered by the hovering Kinahhi. Grabbing the mic, Hammond barked, "Major Lee, clear the gate-room!"

But the Kinahhi were resistant, reluctant to leave their equipment.

"Councilor," Hammond snapped. "Get your people out of there. We have no idea who – or what – is trying to come through the gate!"

Athtar frowned. "Our equipment is most—"

"Sir!" Harriman's voice was incredulous. "Receiving an IDC."

Mentally, Hammond skimmed through all the teams off-world. SG-13, SG-3, SG-9...

"It's SG-1, sir."

His heart leaped. Not meaning to question his sergeant's word, he leaned over to confirm it for himself. "I'll be damned…" After five months! "Open the—"

"Wait!" The voice was Crawford's, sharp as razor wire. "Don't do it."

Hammond turned, white-faced with rage. "How dare you—"

"How do you know it's them?" Crawford countered. "They've been gone five months. It could be anyone. It could be the Goa'uld."

Curse him for being right. Furious, Hammond spun back to the gate. He felt time ticking by in seconds that lasted an eternity. *Make the decision, George.*

At his side, Athtar slipped away; Hammond was dimly aware of him leaving the control room, like a fading shadow.

Make the decision. Open the iris, and open the planet to attack? Or open the door and bring home SG-1? Keep it shut and protect the planet? Or scatter SG-1 like ashes in the cosmic void?

Make the decision.

It had been five months. Five months! And O'Neill had lied to him, he'd set Crawford up to take the fall and used Hammond to spring the trap. He'd lied. And it had been five months…

"Sir?" It was Harriman, pressing for an answer.

He made his decision.

CHAPTER SEVEN

Daniel hauled himself toward the cockpit, barely keeping his feet under him as the ship rolled and rattled so loud his ears hurt. Blazing agony in his shoulder told him it had dislocated again, and he clutched his arm to his chest.

"Teal'c!" His friend's scalp was beaded with sweat, his jaw clamped as he clung resolutely to the ship's controls. "What's happening?"

Through the window, Daniel saw light. Gray, thin light. Where the hell were they? Back on '451?

"We have emerged from hyperspace above P3X-500," Teal'c said, with disturbing calmness. Somehow, he made himself heard. "But the engines have stalled. We are in an uncontrolled descent."

The ship bucked, and Daniel grabbed for the back of Teal'c's chair to keep himself upright. He cursed silently, shards of fire shooting from his dislocated shoulder deep into his chest. "What about the black hole?" he yelled, throat tearing with the effort of making himself heard. Outside, the gray light was ripping apart like tattered fabric. Daniel caught glimpses of the world below, dry and desolate.

"Major Carter's device allowed me to jump to light speed," Teal'c said, grunting as he wrestled with the controls. "In retrospect, it may not have been wise." His left hand shot out and touched something. Faintly, beneath the ship's death-rattle, Daniel heard the whine of struggling engines. It reminded him of his car.

Below them, the rocky landscape grew relentlessly closer. Mountains gave way to a vast plain. The ship was shaking so hard Daniel could barely see straight, but he thought he could make out the remains of causeways and streets. Some kind of civilization long dead—

"Daniel!" Jack lurched from the back of the cargo hold, Sam in tow. "What the hell's going on?"

"Ah… we're crashing."

"Into *what*?"

"We have escaped the black hole, O'Neill!" Teal'c reported. "But the engines have stalled and I am unable to restart them."

"I'm on it." Sam disappeared back the way they'd come.

Jack cursed, hesitated and went after her. "Carter!"

"Dr. Jackson?" It was Boyd.

"Hang on!" Daniel yelled. "We can't die now, not when we're so close!"

Again he heard the straining engines struggling to work, but the ground kept racing toward them. The sky was opalescent, the alien world desiccated. No life. No trees. Coming closer. Inexorably closer.

"Holy Mary, Mother of God…." Boyd was white-knuckling the back of McLeod's seat. "Pray for us sinners…"

Daniel envied Boyd his faith in the divine; his own rested solely in his friends. "Teal'c?"

"…now, and at the time of our death…"

Blood welled from the gunshot wound in Teal'c's arm, his face gray and his teeth bared in a grimace. Again, the engines whined. Nothing. The Jaffa howled defiance in the teeth of death and—

The engines roared to life.

Teal'c's fingers flashed across the controls, calm and unhesitating. Engines shrieked in protest, wind tore against the windows as the nose of the ship lifted. But they were going too fast, way too fast… A savage roar ripped from Teal'c's throat as he wrenched the ship out of its suicidal dive. Teeth rattling in his head, Daniel watched as the silver blade of the horizon crept up the window. Higher and higher, the ground tilting away beneath them as slowly, inch by inch, the ship leveled.

Teal'c was gasping, shoulders heaving as he gradually eased back on the controls. "Daniel Jackson…" His voice sounded faint. "I believe…we have achieved…" He slumped to one side, eyes rolling back.

"Teal'c!" Daniel pressed his fingers against Teal'c's neck. "Pulse is strong. I think he just passed out."

"Daniel?" Jack appeared in the cockpit, a nasty contusion on his forehead and one hand gripping Sam's arm – holding her upright, by the looks of it. "What happened?"

"He did it," Daniel said, eyes fixed on the wan face of his friend. "He pulled us out of the dive."

Jack cast Carter a pointed look. "Hell of a team, huh?" She just shook her head and Jack frowned, turning back to Teal'c. "He gonna be okay?"

Daniel nodded toward the world that now drifted below them. "Yeah, once we get home. We can land near the Stargate."

Boyd pulled out his medikit and handed Daniel a sterile gauze pad. His hand was shaking, Daniel noticed. "There's a gate down there?"

Taking the dressing with a nod of thanks, Daniel began applying pressure as best he could to Teal'c's bleeding arm. "All part of the plan."

"Believe it or not, Major, we did have one," Jack snorted quietly.

"I believe it, sir."

Daniel attempted a reassuring smile. "Almost home now, Major."

Boyd nodded with the guilty relief of all survivors. "Only been gone a day," he said. "I promised Lucy I'd be home for her birthday. She must be almost nine by now."

There wasn't much Daniel could say to that. Boyd's was an unprecedented loss; years snatched away from him in a matter of hours. A five-year jail sentence served in a day. How the hell could he come to terms with that? "If we could have gotten here sooner," Daniel began. But Boyd cut him off with a shake of his head.

"You came," he said. "That's what counts. I knew General Hammond wouldn't leave us behind, however long it took to get us home. We weren't forgotten."

Daniel smiled his response, not sure how to answer. The truth was they hadn't been forgotten, but they had been left behind. There was a plaque on the USAF Memorial Wall in memory of them, and if Jack hadn't bulldozed his way through the niceties of Kinahhi diplomacy then that plaque would have been all that remained.

Into the poignant silence, Sam spoke. "Major?" she said quietly. "I'm so sorry about Lieutenant Reed."

Boyd shrugged, grieving but under control. "Not your fault,

Captain. I should've ordered him back into the ship sooner, not—
"

"If the device hadn't failed—"

"Hey." Jack interrupted them both. "Enough of the guilt-fest. Truth is, none of us should've gotten outta this alive. The fact that any of us are still here is…well, miraculous."

Daniel cut him a sideways glance. "Miraculous, Jack?"

"It's an expression. Isn't it?"

Oblivious to the exchange, Sam bit her lip and scowled at the floor. She looked haggard beneath her bloody nose and sallow skin; Daniel doubted he looked much better.

"Colonel O'Neill is correct." The soft voice belonged to Teal'c, his eyes still closed and face waxy. "The odds of success were slim. We have achieved the impossible, Major Carter."

Boyd smiled slightly. "Major, huh?"

Sam didn't respond, just shook her head and headed back into the cargo hold. Jack watched her leave for a moment, his expression unreadable, then turned back to Teal'c. "You okay, buddy?"

"I am not," came the frank reply. "However, I will recover."

"That's the spirit." Jack dismissed the gloom with a brisk clap of his hands. "So," he said brightly, "who knows how to land this thing?"

In the end, out of stubborn Jaffa pride, Teal'c himself brought the *tel'tak* in for a smooth landing fifty meters from the Stargate. The planet's sun was warm, its air dry and reeking of sulfur. Jack had no idea why the people of this world had left, but the stench was as good an explanation as any.

"Let's hurry it up," he called to his team as they hobbled from the ship. "Or I'm gonna pass out here!" Carter was silent, and didn't respond to his lame humor. Teal'c looked like a stiff breeze would knock him flat on his back, but he was too damn proud to admit it. And Daniel… Unbelievably, even with his shoulder obviously dislocated again, Daniel was picking his way through the ruins of whatever city this had once been, brow furrowed with interest. Exasperated, Jack raised his hands to his mouth and yelled. "Daniel!"

His friend turned, mouth opening as if to say something fascinating, and then abruptly reconsidered. With a nod, Jack beck-

oned him over. Reluctantly, Daniel came, talking the whole way.
"You know, I think this could have been a Celtic society, because
some of the—"

"Look," Jack said, waving toward Carter and Teal'c, then
Boyd and his traumatized team crowded around the DHD.

Daniel blinked. "What?"

"We're alive."

A curious, unsure smile touched Daniel's lips. "Yes. Yes, we
are."

Jack glanced down at the arm his friend was cradling against
his chest. "You want me to—"

"No." He cleared his throat, squinting out into the distance.
"I…ah, think I'll wait for Dr. Fraiser."

Jack grinned suddenly, hit by a hundred fond memories of this
man. Of this amazing team. But the moment turned sour as he
watched Boyd dial home. He didn't know for sure what awaited
him at the SGC, but he'd crossed a lot of lines this time. Too
many, perhaps. He looked away, down at his scuffed boots. Wispy
flurries of sand were blowing over them, and Jack suddenly wondered if this would be the last alien dirt he'd have to wash from
his feet. Was this dead world the last he'd ever visit?

"Jack?" Daniel's quiet voice touched him. "What's going
on?"

"Nothing." Denial. It worked for so many things, so many
people.

But not Daniel. "Don't do that."

Jack looked up. He could see the wormhole flare out, as wild
and dangerous as always. More so this time, perhaps. "Out of the
frying pan, Daniel."

"What does that mean?"

"You don't know what that means?"

"I know what it means!" Daniel paused, exasperated. "I just
don't know what *you* mean."

Jack said nothing, pulling out his sunglasses and slipping them
over his eyes. He saw Carter and Teal'c moving slowly toward
the open gate, and headed out to overtake. He should be first to
face the music. "Come on," he said to Daniel. "Let's go."

Muttering in frustration, his friend followed. "You know,"
Daniel said as they approached the stone steps leading up to the

gate, "I hope our IDC is still valid after all this time."

It was a good point. Jack paused and straightened his shoulders. "I guess we'll know soon enough."

"Or not," Daniel said with a wince.

There were worse ways to go than being squashed like a bug against the trinium plating of the iris. Jack knew that for a fact. "Last one home buys dinner."

If Daniel answered, his words were lost as Jack stepped into the icy clutches of the wormhole and rode the ferocious roller coaster all the way home. Perhaps for the last time.

"Keep the damn iris closed!" Crawford barked, pushing up into the control room with all the zeal of an angry Chihuahua. "You're making a huge mistake!"

"Maybe I am," Hammond snapped back. "But this is still my command, Ambassador. And it's my mistake to make." He turned to Harriman. "Open the iris."

"No. Don't! You can't—"

"Do it!" Hammond barked, grabbing the mic. "Defense team, stay sharp."

Ten P90s lifted and pointed at the gate as the iris peeled back and the blue shimmer of the Stargate bathed the room. Hammond folded his arms across his chest and waited, his stomach twisting with the mounting tension. For five months he'd been waiting, but these final moments lasted forever.

"Traveler in transit," Harriman reported.

Hammond's jaw tightened, but he didn't reply.

"You could be exposing the base to any number of risks!" Crawford hissed in outrage. "You have no idea what…"

His words faded from Hammond's mind as the General focused everything on the rippling surface of the event horizon. It stirred, a minute indication of activity, and then with an explosion of conflicted emotions Hammond watched as Colonel Jack O'Neill stepped out and onto the ramp. From behind his sunglasses, O'Neill glanced around at the airmen without surprise, hands lifting half-heartedly from his weapon as he strode forward. But when his gaze alighted on the Kinahhi, Hammond saw it pause for a long moment before Jack turned and found Hammond, up in the control room. Deliberately, O'Neill pulled off his sunglasses.

Anger vied with relief in the General's heart. This man had betrayed him, had almost cost him his job and his reputation. Yet there was a mute appeal in the Colonel's eyes that seemed like an apology. And then Jack looked away, wearily turning to watch as Daniel Jackson and Teal'c traipsed through the gate, both walking wounded, and trailed by a downtrodden Major Carter.

Where the devil had they been? To hell and back, by the looks of it. Hammond was already heading down to the gate-room when Harriman's voice stopped him. "Sir…"

The Sergeant was staring in astonishment through the window, and a ripple of disbelief whispered through the control room. A ghost had stepped out of the Stargate. Major Henry Boyd, followed by Lieutenant Jessica McLeod and Captain Roger Watts. Abruptly the wormhole disengaged and seven exhausted people were left standing silent and still on the ramp.

"Impossible," Hammond heard himself whisper.

At his side, Crawford looked like he was chewing nails as he glared at O'Neill. "Son of a—" He spat the words. "Lock him up. Lock them all up." Hammond guessed Crawford's anger was justified; O'Neill had condemned the man to an alien jail for a crime he hadn't committed. But still…SG-10. Jack had surpassed himself; he'd saved three people who'd been dead for five years.

And he lied to you.

The truth refused to be silenced, but for the moment he ignored it. Without comment, he brushed past Crawford and raced down the stairs, along the short patch of corridor and into the gate-room. Major Lee hadn't lowered his guard, and none of the travelers had made a move. Pushing through his men, Hammond came to a halt at the foot of the ramp. For a long moment he just stared at his people. Alive. SG-1 were alive!

"Colonel O'Neill," he said at last. "I…" He was lost for words.

"Been a while, sir," O'Neill replied, squinting around the gate-room. "Sorry about that." Then, with a vague wave toward the team warily following them down the ramp, he added, "We found some old friends."

Hammond's eyes fixed on Boyd. The young man's face was no different from the day he'd stepped through the Stargate five years ago. "So I see, Colonel." Boyd stopped at the end of the ramp, shell-shocked and bewildered. "Welcome home, son."

"Thank you, sir." His gaze ran over the defense team in confusion, and Hammond realized their weapons were still raised.

He turned to Major Lee. "Stand your men down." Then, dredging through his memory – damn, shouldn't he have all the men lost under his command memorized? – he returned his attention to Boyd. "Your fourth, son?"

"Lieutenant Reed, sir. He didn't make it."

"I'm sorry to hear that."

"Thank you, sir."

"I suggest you take your team down to the infirmary," Hammond added, standing back to let SG-10 off the ramp. "We'll begin the debrief tomorrow morning."

"Yes, sir." Boyd waved his team toward the door, but before he followed he said, "General Hammond? I just want to thank you for not giving up on us. Colonel O'Neill said it's been five years." He shook his head as if the truth were impossible to believe. From his point of view, it probably was. "Thanks for coming after us, sir."

Hammond was reluctant to take the misplaced credit, but equally reluctant to say more in front of so many open ears. "Get some rest, son," he said instead. And with a nod of thanks, Boyd led his team out of the gate-room and back into a world that had considered them dead for five long years.

When they were gone, Hammond turned back to face O'Neill. "Why the hell didn't you tell me, Jack?"

"Sir, if I had…" He shrugged, and left it hanging.

You wouldn't have let us go. Maybe. Maybe not. "I assume this is why you stole the plans for the Kinahhi technology?"

O'Neill winced. "Sir, about that—"

"Not now, Colonel." The euphoria of relief was fading, and other darker realizations were crowding in. Senator Kinsey was sitting in Hammond's office, and this mess was not going to disappear.

"I was given—"

"Save it for your legal representative, son." The words came out harsher than he'd intended, and O'Neill recoiled.

"Ah…what?" The question came from Dr. Jackson. "I'm

sorry, I don't know if I—"

"Daniel." The single word from O'Neill cut Jackson off in mid flow, plunging him into a brooding silence. His blue eyes radiated indignation and Hammond was forced to look away.

In the control room above, Bill Crawford was watching them intently. Never had General Hammond felt his duty weigh so heavily. *But he lied to you!* And there was no choice. "Major Lee, please disarm Colonel O'Neill and Major Carter. Escort them to the infirmary and place them under guard." His eyes lifted to Jack's and held his gaze. "I'm placing you both under arrest on charges of theft, deception, and conduct unbecoming to—"

"No!" Daniel's heated outburst chimed in with O'Neill's.

"Carter? Sir—"

Hammond held his hand up to silence them both. "I have no choice, Colonel. You've been AWOL for five months, you stole alien technology. And you lied to me." He encompassed the whole team with a single look. "You betrayed my trust."

A shocked silence followed. O'Neill clamped his jaws shut, at once ashamed and defensive. Daniel just blinked in shock, while Teal'c's face was stony. There was disapproval beneath the surface, mingled with the instinctive understanding of a fellow warrior. Discipline was everything to the military mind.

"He's right." Major Carter sounded drained as she trudged forward a step and handed her weapon to the nearest airman. "We knew this would happen."

"No we didn't!" Daniel objected. He was clutching one arm against his chest in obvious pain, but his eyes were ablaze. "General, we saved the lives of three people. We brought them home. How can you…? This is crazy!"

"Daniel…" O'Neill's voice was resigned, as he unclipped his weapon. "He has no choice."

Pushing himself forward, Daniel was shaking his head. "No, he has a choice. General, you have to—"

"Daniel!" O'Neill whirled on him. But there was only frustration in his voice, not anger. "Not now."

"But—"

"It's not the time," he insisted, voice lowering. He threw a significant look at the Kinahhi, mutely observing from the edge of the room. "And there are more important things."

Daniel's gaze followed O'Neill's, eyes widening in surprise, then closing in something that looked very much like defeat. "This is wrong."

Jack didn't answer, but his focus shifted past Daniel to Teal'c, who stood silently behind them. Something passed between them, some kind of acknowledgement. Teal'c stepped closer and placed a firm hand on Daniel's uninjured shoulder. Wordlessly, he nodded to O'Neill.

Turning, the Colonel cast a sideways glance at Major Carter. Her answering shrug was lifeless, as though all the fight had been beaten out of her, and he looked away unhappily. Then, after a moment's thought, Jack's back stiffened and he met Hammond's gaze with a steady look. "So," he said quietly, "Let's get this over with."

CHAPTER EIGHT

Councilor Tamar Damaris sat alone in her office high above the quiet streets of the Kinahhi capital and gazed at the report that lay on her desk. As usual, the Colonial outposts were demanding more money and more men. Did they think the funds were bottomless? Did they expect another tax increase to fund their inefficiency? Her fingers tapped irritably against the irides-cent surface of her desk, and she looked up at the man who had presented the report. "Commander Kenna, you must know that these requests are unfeasible."

The Commander's weathered face hardened. "It is not more than we require, Councilor, to maintain the Cordon."

He was ugly, Damaris thought. His face was creased by sun-shine, coarsened by the wind. "The Cordon has endured for fifty years, Commander."

"It has," he agreed, jaw jutting slightly in a gesture that seemed to imply defiance. "However—"

"There is no more money," she informed him, closing the report with a soft snap. "There are no more men."

"Councilor, you must understand that the Mahr'bal population is rising and without—"

She stood, her chair scraping softly as she rose. Kenna halted and swallowed his words. "Are you questioning me, Com-mander?" She allowed a note of menace to creep into her voice.

"No, Councilor."

"Good." Picking up the report, she moved to the window. Out-side, all was quiet. Peaceful. She tapped the report thoughtfully against the window frame. "Perhaps," she mused, "it is time for a cull."

There was a long pause. Very long. But Damaris did not move, she merely waited for the man to answer. At length, in a voice more austere than usual, Kenna said, "Such a thing has not been contemplated since before the Cordon, Councilor."

"No, indeed it has not." She turned to face him again. His

expression was neutral, but his hands were balled into fists where they hung by his side. "But if the population is ungovernable…"

"We will find a way, Councilor," he told her sharply. "With the resources available."

Damaris smiled. "Very good, Commander. Then I shall——" A soft rap on the door interrupted her. Most irritating. "Come."

One of her aids entered, hands folded apologetically. "Councilor," he began with a slight bow, "Ambassador Crawford has arrived from the Tauri. He says he bears news of some urgency."

Damaris cast a glance at the Commander; he had traveled to Earth – what a ugly name for a world – and might be able to shed some light on the Ambassador's 'news'. She doubted it would be of much interest; the internecine politics of this crude people bored her. But it would behoove her to learn all she could; the price of ignorance was always high. "Let him enter," she answered, resuming her seat at her desk.

Commander Kenna made to leave, but she stopped him with a gesture. "Remain." Compliantly, he retreated to the far wall. But she noted that he watched the little Tauri official strut into her office with eyes as sharp as a bird's.

"Councilor," the Ambassador began, easy and impolite. "I see you are well."

"I am," she replied. "However, I am surprised to see you here. What news do you bear that could not wait until Councilor Athtar returned?"

Crawford glanced at the Commander, clearly wondering if he could trust the man. Damaris ignored his silent question, and after a moment he hesitantly said, "It's to do with SG-1."

"I see." Perhaps this would be of interest after all. "Please explain."

With another wary glance at Kenna, Crawford rocked forward onto his toes. His eyes, dark like dirt, narrowed with a strange, aggressive triumph. "They're back."

"Back?"

"Yup. So much for their return being 'extremely unlikely'." His arms folded across his chest. "And they brought SG-10 with them. They're goddamn heroes."

This was unforeseen. "They escaped from the black hole? Impossible."

"Apparently not!" He was pacing now. "I trusted you, Damaris. You said you'd get them out of the way. It was part of the deal!"

"Calm yourself," Damaris snapped. "This is unexpected, but not catastrophic." She paused, collecting her thoughts. "Have they been apprehended for the theft of our technology?"

"O'Neill and Carter have. But not with any enthusiasm, I can tell you." He stepped up to her desk, fingers impudently resting upon it as he leaned forward. "They have friends, Damaris. Powerful friends. And if they find out about your deal with the Senator you can kiss your plans goodbye, because they'll—"

"Our agreement," Damaris insisted, "will remain secret." Slowly, she rose to her feet and moved around the desk, thoughtfully. "In fact, this may work to our advantage." O'Neill's mind was strong; his aura on the *sheh'fet* had intrigued her. Resourceful, deceptive and ruthless. Yet loyal, intense and principled. A dangerous combination. And a powerful one… "When you return to your world, Ambassador, inform General Hammond that the Kinahhi Security Council intends to invoke the extradition clause of our treaty with the Tauri."

Crawford stopped dead. His dark eyes glittered with untrammeled glee. "You mean…?"

Damaris permitted herself a thin smile. "I would know more of Colonel O'Neill and Major Carter. Their minds will prove most…enlightening." Her smile faded. "And you can rest assured, Ambassador, that they will never again give you or your master reason for concern."

Crawford bristled. Did he not like the term 'master'? She spoke only the truth.

"You know Hammond will fight this, don't you?"

"He may try." She was indifferent to his concern. "But he is bound by the laws of his land."

"But he—"

"Commander Kenna?" The soldier stepped forward, face schooled. "Did you not meet General Hammond?"

"I did," Kenna replied. His cool gaze gave away little; so different from the lurid emotions on display in the Tauri's undisciplined face. "He appears to be a man of honor." He paused, and then more quietly added, "As does Colonel O'Neill."

Damaris stared at him. "Commander?"

He lowered his gaze, adopting the proper deference. "Merely my observation, Councilor."

Indeed. She studied him for a long moment before saying, "Escort Ambassador Crawford to the Stargate, Commander." He moved instantly to obey. Crawford looked like he might have more to say, but few argued with Commander Kenna. He had almost ushered the disgruntled man from her office before Damaris said, "Upon your return, Commander, ensure that you pass through the *sheh'fet*."

Kenna stopped, only for a fraction of a moment, but the hesitation was clear. "As you command, Councilor." Without lifting his eyes to hers, he closed the door and left her in peace.

But not in tranquility. Kenna's muted defiance aside, the return of SG-1 was troubling. How was it possible that they had evaded the snare? With an irritated sigh, she smoothed down her robes and returned to her contemplation of the city that stretched out before her, beautiful in its passive serenity.

Stretched out on the narrow cot in one of the SGC's premier holding cells, Jack O'Neill listened to distant footsteps penetrating the base's ceaseless electrical hum. He counted the steps as they approached, then passed, his door, and wondered if Carter was listening too. She was over the hall. He'd glimpsed her through the door's narrow window a couple of hours after he'd been locked up. Like him, she'd been patched up in the infirmary, but she'd still looked wan. Nothing like the Carter he knew. He just hoped Doc Fraiser had taken a good look at her – and not just at the physical injuries. Carter had been holding on by her fingernails ever since they'd left Baal's palace; he was afraid Reed's death had loosened even that tenuous grip.

Closing his eyes, he pushed aside his anxiety and tried to focus on the positive. Boyd was home, his family was whole again. That was something worth celebrating, right? And yet... There were Kinahhi crawling all over the SGC, Carter was locked up and driving herself crazy with guilt, and he had no idea what would happen to Teal'c and Daniel. But he seriously doubted that being allowed to continue their fight against the Goa'uld would feature very large in their futures. It was a high price for the lives of three people, and he couldn't help wondering if he'd been foolish to risk so much just to ease his pangs of conscience. *No one gets left behind.* It was beginning to sound like a cliché.

The metallic slide of the lock opening drew him back into the moment, and he swung his legs off the bed. When the door opened and he saw who stood outside, Jack rose to his feet and came to attention. This damaged bond of trust was another casualty of his personal quest for redemption.

General Hammond dismissed the guard who'd let him in, waiting for the door to shut before he spoke. "At ease, son." His voice was flat.

Cautiously Jack relaxed his stance, but he was far from easy. He owed the General an apology, not to mention an explanation. Hammond knew it too; he was watching Jack, eyes astute but distant. Something had changed between them, something profound. And, Jack realized, something that meant a hell of a lot to him. "Sir," he began, but Hammond cut him off.

"I don't know what to say to you, Jack. I don't know where to begin."

"If I'd told you, and you'd approved the mission, knowing that the plans were stolen—" He shook his head. "Sir, I didn't want to involve you in this."

"But you did!" Hammond's anger flared. "Aside from the fact that I considered you – all of you – to be personal friends, I—"

"*Considered*?" Past tense.

Hammond ignored the interruption. "You told me to investigate Ambassador Crawford. You made me complicit in framing an innocent man for a crime you committed."

The truth of that hit like cold water. "I didn't—"

"Didn't what?" Hammond demanded. "Didn't plant the plans in his laptop?" Damn it, but there was a hint of hope in the man's voice. Even now, Jack realized, the General wanted to believe the best of him. Too bad.

"No, I did that, sir. But I didn't mean for you to—" He shook his head. "I screwed up. I'm sorry, I never meant for you to be involved."

Hammond's fury hadn't abated. If anything, it had gotten stronger. "Just tell me why, Jack. Why condemn another man to jail for your crime?"

Kill or be killed. That was the short answer; one he'd learned the hard way during a decade in Special Operations. Sometimes you just had to get things done – it was the law of the jungle. And if Hammond didn't realize that then he was a fool. And George Hammond was no fool. "Crawford's a threat," Jack said at last. "I knew it the first moment I saw him. He's Kinsey's lapdog, sir. He was just looking for an excuse to bring us all down."

"An excuse you gave him."

"He'd already written his report."

Hammond took a step closer. "Revenge, Jack?"

Perhaps. He wasn't above vengeance, or any of the other baser emotions. "You said it yourself, sir. This Big Brother stuff Kinsey's after is dangerous. And there isn't a damn thing you can do about it." Taking a deep breath, Jack lowered his voice. "I did something about it. I threw a wrench in the works. Turns out, I needed a bigger wrench."

"He's an *innocent* man," Hammond said, very quietly. "Framing innocent men is not what we do, Colonel. Not ever. Leave that to the NID."

"This is different—"

"He damn near spent the rest of his life locked up in a Kinahhi jail, Colonel!"

The curveball knocked him sideways. "What?"

"You didn't know?" Hammond snorted an angry laugh. "Our treaty with the Kinahhi has an extradition clause, Colonel. If their technology hadn't proven his innocence, Crawford would still be there."

Shit. A vivid memory erupted; strong, strangling fingers around his neck on the floating city of Tsapan. Quadesh had said it was used as some kind of prison, and as much as he loathed Bill Crawford... "I had no idea, sir. I didn't think we did extradition treaties with alien worlds."

"Apparently you thought wrong, Colonel," Hammond snapped, chewing on words he was trying to keep from spilling out. He failed, exasperation and disbelief pouring out in an avalanche of resentment. "I defended you, Jack. When Ambassador Crawford accused you, I said it was impossible. I told him that we didn't operate that way."

"Sir—"

"I trusted you!"

The disappointment in the General's face cut deep, but he had no answer to the accusation. It was impossible to explain his rock-solid certainty that Crawford needed to be taken out; from the first moment he'd seen the man, he'd felt the insidious threat, like the eyes of a predator boring into the back of his head. But he had no evidence, nothing but the gut instinct that had kept him alive for the past couple of decades. To a man like Hammond, that wasn't nearly enough. And good job too, in the grander scheme of things. So Jack didn't bother to explain, just dropped his gaze to the floor and offered the only thing left. "I'm sorry, sir. It was a bad call."

Hammond was silent. In the quiet of the cell, Jack could hear the General's slow breathing and it sounded like reproof. "You're in trouble here, son," Hammond sighed eventually. "I don't think I can help you."

"I don't expect you to help me, sir." Nothing was said for a moment, but when Jack lifted his gaze their eyes locked. He swallowed hard and said, "Carter, however…"

"Jack…"

"She had nothing to do with Crawford! She doesn't even know about it. None of them do." He took a step forward, lowering his voice and edging close to things he normally ran from. "Sir, she only did it because I asked."

Hammond blew out a short, angry breath. "I'm not sure that helps her case, son. Or yours."

"She was following orders."

"Illegal orders, Colonel. That's no defense."

Damn it. Jack dropped onto the thin mattress of the cot, head in hands. "What about Daniel and Teal'c?"

Hammond's feet scuffed against the floor as he moved toward the door. "I don't know yet." He paused. "A lot's changed since you've been gone, Jack. I'm afraid it's out of my hands."

Looking up sharply, Jack caught the note of foreboding in the man's voice. "Sir?"

Hammond stood by the door, grim-faced. The usual glint in his eyes was missing and he looked his age. Jack suspected the same could be said of himself. "You know what they say, Colonel. The Captain goes down with his ship."

Jack sat a little straighter, a gunshot of adrenaline tightening muscles and accelerating his heartbeat. Fight or flight. He could do neither, and the tension was a killer. "Are we sinking, sir?"

Hammond said nothing, but his expressive face failed to hide his disquiet as he rapped loudly on the door. It was opened immediately by the airman on guard, but Hammond hesitated before he left. Then his shoulders lifted and fell in a resigned sigh and he turned back to face Jack. "I'll do what I can for your team, son."

Jack rose slowly to his feet. "Thank you, sir."

Hammond's scant nod was a brief acknowledgement, nothing more, and with it he was gone. The door closed, but Jack remained standing, staring silently at the wall. Something was wrong. Badly wrong. He could sense it deep down, like the oppressive sweep of a death glider coming in for the kill.

And he had the sudden, horrible sensation that he was responsible.

CHAPTER NINE

Daniel Jackson was ablaze with the kind of fury that had earned him a reputation back during his first years at the SGC. He could feel it coiling inside, like an overwound spring threatening to fly loose at any moment. As he stalked through the gray corridors of the SGC he'd never felt so trapped by the military institution in which he worked. The weight of the mountain above pressed down on him, compressing his outrage into diamond-hard slivers of rage. He refused to allow this injustice to happen. It was a travesty.

Hurrying around a corner, he almost collided with a young airman. Daniel's strapped shoulder was still painful, and he dodged out of the way without missing a step, muttering a curse under his breath. He barely heard the murmured apology. His mind was still back in General Hammond's office, trying to grapple with the fact that the man seemed unable and – far worse – unwilling to help Jack. Hammond had looked haggard, his round face sagging and his eyes clouded with disappointment. *Colonel O'Neill broke the law, Dr. Jackson. And he lied to cover it up. Even if I wanted to, there's nothing I can do to keep justice from being done.*

Justice! They'd saved three people's lives, brought them back from the dead. And now the establishment bureaucrats were going to hang Jack out to dry.

Grinding his anger between his teeth, Daniel slowed as he approached his destination and rapped twice on the door.

"Enter."

He stormed into Teal'c's quarters, then stopped abruptly. It was dark, lit only by the candles his friend bought in bulk from Wal-Mart. Blinking against the gloom, he saw Teal'c sitting as if in *kelno'reem*, although Daniel knew the Jaffa could no longer perform the ritual meditation for real. Perhaps he found the familiar routine relaxing? Daniel envied him. But as he gently closed the door, Teal'c opened his eyes and there was nothing relaxed about the incisive gaze that immediately fixed on Daniel.

"You were unsuccessful in persuading General Hammond to intervene on behalf of Major Carter and Colonel O'Neill."

"Yup." Daniel cast around for a chair and sank down gingerly. "He says his hands are tied."

Teal'c remained cross-legged on the floor, hands resting on his knees. "I had expected more from General Hammond."

"Yeah, me too. It's almost as if…" Daniel shook his head, trying to identify the feeling of dislocation he'd sensed in the General. "I don't know – I just feel like there's something going on that we don't know about."

In a single fluid motion, Teal'c swept to his feet and blew out the nearest candle. "I believe you are right, Daniel Jackson." He moved to the next flame and extinguished it with his fingers. "I believe there is much happening of which we are unaware."

Daniel's mind drifted back to the moment he'd stepped through the gate. He'd instantly spotted the tall men lurking in the shadows, neat rows of alien boxes stacked up behind them. "The Kinahhi for one," he said sourly. "Looks like Kinsey's got his hands on the *sheh'fet* after all."

"Without your presence, Daniel Jackson, who was here to oppose its introduction?"

Daniel sighed. "General Hammond? He was as opposed to it as Jack and me when we discussed it after we got back from Kinahhi. But," he shrugged and shifted in his chair, "he did say it was out of his hands. Kinsey's project."

Teal'c put out a third candle and turned to face him. "You would have protested louder, would you not? As would O'Neill. You would not have been bound by the military structure."

Daniel nodded slowly. "No. No I wouldn't. And Jack… Teal'c, what are you saying?"

An eyebrow rose. "Only that it was fortunate for both Ambassador Crawford and the Kinahhi that SG-1 has been absent for the past five months."

Fortunate…? Realization dawned like a cold, damp morning. "It was a set up." Like a pair of dice landing on sixes, everything fell into place. "Damaris knew we'd oppose the treaty. She let Quadesh give the plans to Jack just to get us out of the way." He slapped his forehead in frustration. "I knew it was too convenient."

Teal'c inclined his head. "You are correct. Councilor Damaris could have had no doubt of our opposition to the treaty."

Daniel frowned, remembering his outburst in the Kinahhi Council Chamber. He couldn't repress the creeping sensation that this was all his fault. Over the past seven years he'd learned to curb his natural openness, but in this case he clearly hadn't curbed it enough. Not that Jack had exactly been diplomatic either. Yet, surely Damaris had understood that Crawford spoke for the government? SG-1 had just been the 'military escort' after all. Unless... "I think it's more than that," he said suddenly, sitting up straight and grimacing at the throb in his shoulder. "Teal'c – the *sheh'fet*. They read our minds. They knew we were going to recommend to Hammond that we abandon the treaty. They knew *exactly* what we were thinking and they manipulated us accordingly."

Teal'c growled softly. "They are indeed a cunning enemy, Daniel Jackson."

"Oh yeah, we've been suckered." Daniel sank back into his chair, pulled his glasses from his face, and pinched the bridge of his nose. "They must have known that simply taking the plans would be enough to undermine SG-1's authority and ability to oppose the treaty. It was a poisoned chalice."

Moving to the door, Teal'c flicked on the overhead lights and dispelled the darkness in his quarters. The remaining candles dimmed to insignificance. "The situation is grave, Daniel Jackson," said Teal'c. "The Kinahhi have successfully emasculated opposition to their foothold in this world."

"Foothold?" Daniel doubted his choice of word was accidental; Teal'c always said precisely what he meant.

"We must assume their intentions are hostile."

The dull pain in Daniel's neck twinged as his muscles tensed, and nudged at a lurking headache. He was exhausted, his previous anger turning despondent. "This treaty is Kinsey's pet project, Teal'c. They're already testing the technology upstairs. And General Hammond..." He paused, remembering his recent encounter, and carefully met his friend's frank stare. "To be honest, I don't even know if he's on our side anymore."

Shock fractured Teal'c's face into momentary alarm, and he sat down abruptly on the edge of his bed. "I cannot believe—"

"I'm not saying he's siding with Kinsey," Daniel explained. "It's just… I think there's something going on between him and Jack. More than Jack just bending a few rules to get the job done."

A slow nod from Teal'c confirmed Daniel's fears. "Then, perhaps, we should first discuss this with O'Neill?"

"Under the nose of the guards in the stockade?"

There was a long pause before Teal'c frowned slightly and said, "Is O'Neill not entitled to private discussions with his legal representatives?"

"Yeah, but we're not—" Teal'c cocked an eyebrow, and Daniel winced. "He's really not gonna like that idea."

"Perhaps not," Teal'c agreed, "however, there are more important matters at stake than O'Neill's pride."

"True. So…" Daniel raised an eyebrow. "Who's going to—"

"I believe you would be best suited to the task, Daniel Jackson."

"You don't even want to draw straws…?"

Teal'c rose, the hint of a smile playing around his mouth. "I do not. Instead, I shall attempt to discover the nature of the experiment the Kinahhi are conducting here." And with a polite bow of the head, he turned and made a swift exit.

Daniel didn't stir. Partly because he hurt too much to move, and partly because he dreaded talking to Jack. He was under no illusion: trying to help Jack O'Neill was tantamount to pulling the thorn from the lion's paw. An apposite analogy, he thought, as he came to his feet and headed for the lion's den.

Sam Carter perched on the edge of a bed in the infirmary, staring at nothing and trying to ignore her guard, who had stationed himself near the door. In case she made a break for it, presumably. He needn't have bothered. Escape was the last thing on her mind. Where would she go, anyway? The SGC was as close to home as it got, and she'd never been the sort of woman to run away from her responsibilities. Truth was, she'd known exactly what she was doing when she'd first taken the Kinahhi plans from the Colonel's hand, and she wasn't about to cry foul now.

"Sam?" Dr. Janet Fraiser's voice was patiently insistent, nudging Sam out of her thoughts.

She mustered a smile for her friend. "Hey, Janet."

"How's the wound doing today?"

"It's better." Which was what Janet wanted to hear; whether it was true, Sam didn't know. Her injury didn't matter, her mind was filled with other memories. The Jaffa – the boy – bloodied by her angry fists. Dead now. All of them dead in the blazing remains of Baal's palace. And Reed, burning too, consumed by the inferno she'd sent through the Stargate. A victim of her failure. If they hadn't crashed on that Godforsaken world, if she hadn't gotten the ampage wrong...

"Sam?" Janet said again, the word accompanied by a soft touch on her hand. "You with us?"

Shaking her head, Sam muttered an apology. "Sorry, miles away."

"Somewhere nice?"

"Not really."

Janet nodded, compassion softening her professional scrutiny. "Colonel O'Neill said you had a tough time," she commented mildly, lifting Sam's shirt to expose the bandaged wound beneath her collarbone. "If you want to talk about it...?"

"The Colonel said that?" For some reason, it surprised her. He had his own problems.

"He's worried about you." Janet removed the dressing carefully. It stung and Sam risked a glance down. The short red rope of a scar was mostly healed, but one end was still weepy with infection. In her mind's eye, she could see the knife falling, feel it cutting through her flesh as if through raw chicken, and abruptly looked away. "It's getting better," Janet assured her. "We'll keep going with the antibiotics for the next few days."

Sam nodded absently. It didn't much matter. Soon she'd be fit enough to transfer to Lackland and await her court martial – she doubted General Hammond would want to keep her under local confinement any longer than necessary. Dad would be mortified; she was probably the first Carter to ever take up residence in a military prison. She knew it should bother her, but all she could think about was that if Reed had made it back to the ship instead of her, then everything would have been a hell of a lot easier. If only... Story of her life.

The gentle tugging of her shirt back into place distracted

her, and she realized that her wound had been freshly dressed. "Thanks," she said, offering another weak smile.

Janet's hand closed over hers. "It's going to be okay," she said quietly. "Sam, we'll sort this out. It won't end here."

The warmth in her friend's voice stirred something deep, penetrating the gray lethargy that seemed to stand between Sam and the rest of the world. Tears lumped in her throat, shaking her voice as she murmured, "It's already over, Janet. There's nothing—"

"Carter?"

She turned at the sound of the voice, and saw Colonel O'Neill standing near the door watching her. "Sir." His escort, Major Lee, lurked uneasily behind him.

O'Neill's gaze flitted between herself and Janet. "How you doing?"

"Fine, sir," Sam lied. "You?"

"Fine." His lie was equally transparent. The bruising on his face might have been fading, but she could see pain in his eyes and doubted it had anything to do with his injuries. "Look," he said, taking a step closer and lowering his voice. Lee didn't move, but his jaw tightened. Probably praying the Colonel wasn't going to cause trouble. "I've talked to Hammond. You just tell them you were following my orders and—"

"Sir?" Lee edged forward. He looked like he wished he was pinned down by a battalion of Jaffa rather than confronting Colonel O'Neill, but he did his job nonetheless. "I'm sorry, sir, but you can't discuss the case with Major Carter."

The Colonel flung him a deadly look. "Excuse me, *Major*? I thought you—"

"Sir," Sam interrupted, "he's right. And I've already told them the truth."

"That is the truth!" the Colonel protested. But she didn't turn around. "Carter!" His voice was cut off by the closing door, and silently Sam followed her guard back toward her cell. What was the point of fighting this? She deserved to be punished. She'd broken the rules, she'd deceived General Hammond. She'd beaten a boy to a pulp and incinerated Lieutenant Reed. Shouldn't she be held to account?

And she was so tired of fighting. So, so tired.

"I'm sorry, sir, you don't have access." The young Sergeant who barred Teal'c's way appeared nervous, his fingers clamped around his weapon as though he would use it as a club. Teal'c ignored his words, looking over the man's head into the empty corridor beyond. Level seventeen was a little used part of the complex, reserved mostly for the storage of equipment. A strange place, he thought, for the trial of the Kinahhi technology.

"Do you know the nature of the experiment being conducted within?" It was a vain hope that the man would answer, but he had to ask nonetheless.

"No, sir. Only Senator Kinsey's staff are permitted inside."

"And the Kinahhi?"

The Sergeant nodded. "Yes, sir. But I—" His attention snapped to something behind Teal'c, and as the Jaffa turned he saw a line of approximately twenty orange-clad men snaking down the corridor. Their jumpsuits, he knew, were those of prisoners and their wary eyes darted from side to side as they walked, in manacles, along the quiet corridor. "Excuse me," the soldier said, stepping around Teal'c and taking an armful of paperwork from the man escorting the prisoners. And then the snake was on the move once more, disappearing through a doorway on the far side of the security checkpoint.

Teal'c made no comment, but looked steadily at the young Sergeant. Under his scrutiny, a faint flush rose to the man's face. "If you're going to ask me why they're here, don't bother, sir," the soldier said. "I have no idea."

"Then these men are not the first to arrive?"

A shake of the head was the only answer forthcoming. "Just doing my job."

Teal'c nodded a silent acknowledgement and turned away. It was clear he would get no answers here, yet he had learned enough for now. The base was still nominally under the command of General Hammond; he would seek the truth there. Despite Daniel Jackson's concerns, Teal'c could not believe that O'Neill's deception had so damaged General Hammond's faith in SG-1 that he would hide the truth if he knew it. However, if O'Neill's actions had weakened the General's authority within the hierarchy of the Air Force, then matters were grave indeed.

When he arrived at General Hammond's office, he found it empty. However, the General himself was visible through the star map, standing alone in the briefing room, staring at the Stargate below. Teal'c stepped through the office, and out into the silent room beyond. After a moment, General Hammond spoke.

"How's your arm doing, son?"

"It is healing well." Teal'c joined him at the window, watching the activity in the gate-room. The Stargate was open, and a small group of Kinahhi were heading up the ramp. Teal'c could not see their faces, although one man appeared familiar. Someone he had encountered during his time on their world, perhaps?

"Councilor Athtar is leaving," General Hammond said. "Apparently he's pleased with the progress of the tests, and wants to report back to the rest of the Kinahhi Security Council."

A convenient opening for the purpose of his visit. "What is the nature of these tests, General Hammond?"

"I wish I knew."

Teal'c lifted an eyebrow in surprise. "You do not know?"

General Hammond compressed his lips into a line of anger. "Even though it's happening on my base, Kinsey has insisted that only his people know what's going on. National security."

"That is most disturbing."

General Hammond nodded. "The truth is, the only reason I'm still in command of the base is because the President stepped in on my behalf. But there's only so far he can go; Kinsey has a lot of friends, and there's an election coming up. The President is walking a fine line."

Tauri politics were a subject of little interest to Teal'c – unless they risked damaging the Stargate program. He waited for General Hammond to meet his gaze. When he did, Teal'c spoke. "You are aware that Tauri prisoners are being brought into the base?"

"I am. And it's happening over my official protest."

"Is there no other way of discovering the nature of this experiment?" Teal'c asked, disturbed by Hammond's apparent passivity. "Can you not refuse cooperation?"

"If I refuse, I'll be out, Teal'c." The General looked away, clearly frustrated. "Kinsey's just looking for a reason. And I've already stuck my neck out one too many times."

Thus the truth of the matter was revealed. The Tauri inability to divorce personal from professional was at once their strength and their weakness. It gave them passion to fight in defense of their kin but on occasion undermined the ground on which they stood. After a moment of silence, Teal'c returned his gaze to the gate-room. The Kinahhi had left, and the wormhole fizzled into nothing. "I do not believe O'Neill intended to deceive you, General Hammond," he said quietly. "Your good opinion is important to him."

Although the General did not respond, Teal'c sensed him shift uncomfortably. The Tauri, he had often observed, were perturbed when confronted by honest expressions of emotion. He continued, daring to say more than protocol usually allowed. The situation was precarious and he deemed the risk necessary. "You should not allow your judgment to be affected by your disappointment in O'Neill." He paused, watching the General's jaw clamp shut. "There is still value in audacity."

"You call it audacity?" General Hammond said at last. "He tried to pin his crime on an innocent man. And he lied to me, point blank. I don't call that audacity, Teal'c. I call it criminal insubordination."

A heavy charge indeed. "To which innocent man do you refer?"

The General glanced at him, his expression unreadable for once. "That's right, Jack said you didn't know." Teal'c made no reply, and Hammond continued. "Colonel O'Neill planted the stolen Kinahhi plans in Ambassador Crawford's possessions. If the Kinahhi hadn't proven his innocence, he would have gone to jail."

In truth, Teal'c had to repress a smile of admiration. O'Neill's actions were sly, yet he could not condemn them. He too had identified Crawford as an enemy, not only to SG-1 but to the Tauri. Governed by ambition, Crawford placed his own desires before anything else – including the freedom of his world. He was a small man, in mind as well as stature, and failed to grasp the global implications of his actions. His limitations were a threat, one O'Neill had attempted to eliminate. "You have trusted O'Neill's instincts for many years, General Hammond," Teal'c reminded him. "Do not doubt them now."

"Trust? He lied to—"

"Ah, there you are." A thin voice that rasped from General Hammond's office; Ambassador Crawford stood watching them, his smile smug and his dark eyes alight with trouble. "Still here, Teal'c? I'd thought you'd be cooling your heels in Area 51 by now."

Not deigning to reply, Teal'c cast a questioning glance at General Hammond, whose head shook slightly in denial. "What do you want, Crawford?"

"A word in your ear, General." The predatory smile broadened. "I can guarantee you'll be interested."

General Hammond's brief nod to Teal'c served as both dismissal and apology. Offering a scant bow before he left, Teal'c kept his voice low. "Consider my words, General Hammond. Eight years of trust should not be so easily overturned. And much is at stake."

The General did not reply but turned to face Crawford with a defiant lift of his chin. Teal'c hoped he had said enough.

"Colonel O'Neill?"

From behind the airman, Daniel could see Jack stretched out on the narrow cot, hands behind his head and ankles crossed. At the sound of his name he opened his eyes and peered at the open door to his cell. "I didn't order room service."

Daniel smiled, and the guard cleared his throat. "No, sir. Your legal representative is here."

Frowning, Jack sat up. "I don't have a—"

"Yes, you do." Pushing past the guard, Daniel stepped into the room.

Jack stared. "You gotta be kidding…"

"Thank you." Daniel shrugged apologetically at the bemused airman. "You can go now. I'll call if I need anything."

Clearly suspecting that he was being taken for a ride, the soldier hesitated but beat a hasty retreat when Jack waved him away with a weary gesture. Daniel couldn't help smiling; even under guard, Jack's commands were impossible to resist. Once the door was closed and silence had settled in the small room, Daniel took a deep breath and began. "So…?"

"I don't need a lawyer, Daniel," Jack said at once, lying back down and closing his eyes. "If I did, I'd hire a real one."

"Good to see you too." He perched on the edge of the small table and studied his friend's tense face. "Are you okay?"

"Peachy."

Whether it was denial, false bravado, or just plain stubbornness, it was typical Jack O'Neill. Irritating as hell. "Jack, we have a problem."

One eye opened. "Ya think?"

"I'm not talking about this," Daniel said, gesturing around the room. "I'm talking about the Kinahhi. They—"

"What do you want me to do, Daniel?" Jack's voice was quiet and heavy; he sounded defeated. "I'm not getting out of here anytime soon. I knew what I was doing when I took the plans from Quadesh."

Daniel nodded, glanced at the door, and in a low voice said, "So did the Kinahhi."

"What the hell does that mean?"

"It was a setup, Jack. I think they let Quadesh give you the plans because they wanted us out of the way. They knew we were trying to scupper the treaty."

Jack didn't move for a long moment, eyes slightly unfocused as he thought it through. Suddenly he sat bolt upright. "Sonofabitch! Crawford."

"Crawford?"

"Quadesh overheard him telling Damaris why we wanted the anti-grav device." Jumping to his feet, Jack paced the short length of the cell and back. "This is all some plot to protect their goddamn treaty?"

Daniel shrugged. "It certainly worked. Kinsey's upstairs testing a prototype as we speak."

"Hell of a lot of trouble to go to," Jack mused quietly. "I can see what Kinsey gets out of it, but what about the Kinahhi? What do they get?"

It was a good question. Daniel had left the negotiations before that subject had been raised; in retrospect he wondered if Crawford would have let him stay that long anyhow. "Teal'c thinks they're using the treaty to get a foothold on Earth."

Jack's grimace was eloquent. "What does Hammond say?"

Another good question, with no easy answer. His hesitation drew a sharp look from Jack. "I don't know," Daniel said at last.

"Hammond seems…"

"Supremely pissed? He is. With me."

"It's not the first time we've broken the rules."

"Yeah, well, he has his reasons." If Daniel hadn't known better, he could have sworn his friend looked contrite. And when Jack spoke again, it was almost confessional. "I hid the plans in Crawford's stuff – I set him up."

"You *what?*" Daniel couldn't keep the shock from his voice. "Why?"

"Because he's a sonofabitch and he's out to get us." He slid a dark look toward Daniel. "Law of the jungle."

"Harsh law."

Jack just shrugged: *what did you expect from a guy like me?*

Better than that. But this was hardly the time to debate relative morality – there were more pressing matters at stake. "So that's why Hammond's so angry?"

"Point is, Hammond doesn't trust me," Jack said, sidestepping the question. "You have to warn him. Tell him what you know."

"And what about you?"

"This doesn't change anything. I'm still guilty."

Daniel shook his head. "But they set you up."

"And I set Crawford up. What's the difference?"

The law of the jungle… "The difference," he said quietly, "is that you hate yourself for it, Jack." His friend flinched, but Daniel pressed on regardless. "The difference is that they read our minds. They knew exactly how to manipulate you to get us out of the way. They exploited you, exploited your need to save Henry Boyd. It's not your fault."

"Then whose the hell is it, Daniel? Yours? Teal'c's? *I* was in command!" With a derisive snort, Jack stalked to the far side of the room. His hands scrunched in his hair for a moment and then fell to his sides, fingers clenching and unclenching as he calmed himself. "Look, Hammond agreed to help you, so just—"

"What about you?"

"Oh, I'm way beyond help."

Daniel couldn't believe what he was hearing. "So that's it?" he said scathingly, frustration edging him into real anger. "You're just gonna give up?"

"I'm locked in a cell, Daniel!" Jack whirled around to face

him, taut as a tripwire. "What the hell do you expect me to do?"

"I don't know! Something. Fight this!"

"Fight *what*?" Jack was incredulous. "Don't you get it? I screwed up. I *deserve* this."

"No you don't!" Daniel's shout rang loud in the suddenly silent room, falling away until all he could hear was his own ragged breathing.

With a resigned shake of his head, Jack turned his back on him. His forehead came to rest against the cold wall, his hands balled into angry fists. After a moment he spoke in a controlled, clipped voice. It reeked of self-recrimination. "Go save the world, Daniel. You don't need me."

Daniel stared in disbelief. "That's where you're wrong."

He got no answer.

CHAPTER TEN

It was late, and Daniel's office was quiet and dark. The desk lamp shone on scattered piles of paper, the static blue glow from the computer screen mixing a cooler light into the soft amber of the lamp. In other circumstances, at other times, it was one of Daniel's favorite places, but tonight everything felt wrong. The air was stale and cold and the constant electrical hum that permeated the SGC felt menacing instead of comforting. Daniel couldn't relax, he couldn't even sit still. Three hours later, and he still couldn't get Jack's words out of his head. *Go save the world, Daniel. You don't need me.*

"This is most disturbing," said Teal'c, halting Daniel's restless pacing.

"Yeah." He dropped heavily into his chair. "It's as if he's given up."

In the muted light, Teal'c's features were lost. "O'Neill values the good opinion of General Hammond. If he believes he has lost General Hammond's trust, he will not forgive himself." Teal'c shifted, still hidden in the shadows. "And perhaps, by embracing his own punishment, he seeks to protect Major Carter and ourselves from similar treatment."

"We all knew what we were doing, Teal'c. It's not his fault."

"Do not underestimate the burden of command, Daniel Jackson." Teal'c paused, moving away from the wall and into the light. It shone bronze on his skin and glinted against the golden brand he wore. "O'Neill holds himself responsible for the consequences of all our actions."

Sinking back in his chair, Daniel absorbed what his friend was suggesting. "I guess he hoped bringing Boyd home would earn the rest of us a Get-Out-of-Jail-Free card."

Teal'c inclined his head. "Had the anti-gravity device not failed on P3W-451 we would only have been missing for a few days. Senator Kinsey would not have been able to conclude the treaty with the Kinahhi, and General Hammond's command decisions would not have been questioned."

"And Bill Crawford wouldn't have been handed over to the Kinahhi." The situation was getting more knotted by the moment, and Daniel was beginning to wonder if it was even possible to untangle the mess. It was no surprise that Hammond was hog-tied. After what Jack had done, Kinsey must have had a field day. The fact that the General was still in command at all could be considered a miracle. He pressed his hands against his eyes. "What the hell was Jack thinking, setting Crawford up like that?"

"That is a question only O'Neill can answer."

Lifting his hands from his face, his vision blurring with the sudden loss of pressure, he glanced curiously at Teal'c. "I'm sensing a 'but'."

"Despite what O'Neill may now believe," he said carefully, "I do not think his instinct was wrong. Crawford represents a threat. O'Neill's attempt to neutralize that threat was judicious."

"If morally questionable. To say the least."

Teal'c raised an eyebrow. "Ambassador Crawford is trading the freedom of the Tauri to further his own quest for power. He behaves like a Goa'uld, and deserves to be treated no better." He moved closer. "I know what it is to be a slave, Daniel Jackson. There are times when morality must defer to the defense of freedom."

Shifting uncomfortably, Daniel put his glasses back on. "Ah... actually, I don't agree. Once you start removing basic human rights in the name of 'freedom', you might as well give up all pretense at living in a free society."

Teal'c stiffened, a subtle gesture of dissent. "And how free will your society be if Ambassador Crawford and the Kinahhi are successful in their plans?"

It was an age-old argument, but one Daniel found impossible to let slide. "Truth is, Teal'c, so far we don't actually know what their plans are."

The eyebrow rose in a sharp line of irritation. "By the time their plans for the Tauri are made apparent, Daniel Jackson, it will be too late to resist."

"And if we go around locking people up for crimes they *might* commit, we may as well hand ourselves over to the Kinahhi right now!" Frustrated, Daniel pushed himself to his feet and stalked to the far side of his office. Teal'c said nothing, and the silence between them grew long. At length, Daniel turned around. Teal'c was still standing by the desk, regarding him carefully. "Look," Daniel sighed, "there's no point in arguing about this. Jack did what he did, and it's landed him in jail. Which means it's up to us to try and stop the Kinahhi."

Teal'c gave a slight bow. "On that we can agree. Perhaps General Hammond will—"

Klaxons blared, disturbing the late-night quiet of Daniel's office. For some reason they sent a chill of apprehension rippling across his skin. "Trouble?"

The Jaffa cocked his head, as if listening to an inner voice, tension bunching in his neck. He felt it too. "Indeed."

Without further discussion, they headed down to the gate-room.

Jack stepped out of his cell and glanced around. "Where are we going?"

There was no answer from the anxious airman who had come to fetch him, but he saw the soldier's glance skitter nervously toward Major Lee, who stood further down the corridor. The Major just shook his head.

Trouble. Jack felt it like a cold, sickly breeze, chilling the back of his neck. The sensation doubled when he realized Carter's door was open and he watched her appear in the doorway looking as confused as he felt.

"What's going on?" she asked. The question was directed at Lee, but her eyes fixed on him.

Jack gave a little shrug. "Lackland?" You knew things were bad when military prison seemed like a good option. "I hear it's nice this time of year."

Carter just nodded tightly and fell in at his side as they headed out of the detention block and toward the elevator. The down elevator. So much for San Antonio. When Lee hit Level 28 Carter murmured, "The gate-room?"

"Briefing room," Jack replied hopefully. It did nothing to brighten her apprehensive expression. "Lee?" he snapped, gratified to see the man jump. "What the hell's going on?"

"I'm sorry, sir," the Major replied without turning around.

"I'm not at liberty to say."

"On whose orders?" There was a long pause. "Major?"

"General Woodburn, sir."

Carter frowned. "Who?"

Still Lee didn't turn around, but Jack could see him tense. "He took command of the SGC a few hours ago, Major."

The hovering sense of unease exploded into full-scale alarm, and Jack found his fingers itching for a weapon. But he kept his voice calm and even. "Where's Hammond?"

"I don't know, sir." Lee sounded strained, back ramrod straight. "I heard he was relieved of command."

Shit. Jack exchanged an urgent look with Carter. Her eyes were wide with shock, but anger sparked more life into them than he'd seen since their return home. He took it as a good sign.

The elevator stopped, and they were led along all-too-familiar corridors. He couldn't shake the feeling he was being led to his own execution. Nevertheless, he followed Major Lee through the blast doors and into the gate-room. They weren't alone. A small team was in position, weapons ready but not raised. At the foot of the gate stood a phalanx of Kinahhi soldiers, their gray uniforms bathed in the blue light of the open wormhole. Before them was a solid man of middle years, steel-gray hair forming a hard line above wild eyebrows. Jack didn't recognize him, but from the uniform he guessed it had to be Woodburn. And next to him stood Crawford, a gleeful smile stretching his lips. "Ah," the Ambassador gloated. "How the mighty are fallen."

Dismissing him, Jack made a swift assessment of the Kinahhi force. A dozen of them, they were watching the SGC personnel with open suspicion, weapons kept neutral but only a heartbeat away from action. The situation was tinder dry. Jack turned to Woodburn, hoping for some kind of clue about what was happening, but he got nothing through the skim of ice covering the man's hard eyes. No friend there. "What's going on?"

"That's, 'sir' to you, Colonel."

Jack returned a flat smile. "Oh, I don't think so."

No response. He'd seen more expressive earthworms. He was about to comment on the fact when a commotion behind them drew his attention. Turning, he saw Daniel and Teal'c race through the door, then slide to a halt and stare around in confusion. "What's going on?"

"Exactly what I said!" Jack turned back to Woodburn. "General…?"

It was Crawford who answered, all but bouncing with malicious delight. "What's going on, Jack, is that you're getting what's coming to you."

"Really?" Jack refused to acknowledge the threat. "Are we talking about a boat?"

Crawford's little black eyes narrowed. "We're talking about justice, Jack." His smile almost cut his face in two. "Kinahhi justice."

Jack's stomach lurched. *Clutching white fingers in the dark, coming out of nowhere…*

"What?" Daniel surged forward. "You can't send them there! They don't even have—"

"Why not, Jackson?" Anger seeped through Crawford's obvious pleasure. "It was good enough for me. Wasn't it, Jack?"

From the corner of his eye, Jack saw Carter's confused look. He ignored her, focusing on Crawford. "I made a mistake." The admission tasted foul, but was necessary. "But it's got nothing to do with Carter, leave her out of it."

Crawford's smile returned and he took a step forward, eyes coming to rest on Carter as though seeing her for the first time. "Leave her out of it? Would that make things easier for you, Jack?"

He said no more. He'd already said too much.

The sonofabitch turned away, addressing one of the Kinahhi soldiers. "As per section three, paragraph four, item one of our treaty, I hereby transfer custody of the offenders to the Kinahhi military." He threw an exultant look at Jack. "Take them away."

No one moved. Major Lee glanced over at General Woodburn. "Sir?" He might as well have said, *Don't make me do this, sir.* Jack felt for him.

Woodburn's jaw jutted out. "Hand them over, Major."

"No!" Daniel rushed forward again, Teal'c at his side. "Where's General Hammond? You can't do this!"

Major Lee bristled and turned toward Daniel with his weapon half-raised. "Dr. Jackson, please…"

Suddenly Teal'c was moving, as fast and graceful as a cat.

He grabbed a sidearm from the nearest airman and leveled it at Crawford. "I cannot allow you to do this."

At once, twelve Kinahhi weapons shot up, matched by a half dozen P90s. No one dared breathe. Jack watched the General's mouth open, an order on his lips. Fire? Stand down? Teal'c's finger tightened on the trigger. Disaster was a breath away.

"Stop!" Jack stepped into Teal'c's line of fire, covering Crawford. "Teal'c…" *Not now. Save it.* The Jaffa met his gaze, steadfast as granite. Letting this happen went against everything Teal'c believed in, Jack knew that. He also knew how he'd feel if the situation were reversed, but he couldn't let his friend gamble everything on a no-win bet. "It's not the time."

"Jack?" Daniel looked appalled, but there was nothing Jack could say, not out loud. *Find Hammond. Come after us. Sort this damn mess out!* He put it all into the long look they shared, until slowly, angrily Daniel nodded. He understood. They both did, and reluctantly Teal'c lowered his weapon.

"Disarm him!" barked Woodburn. Two airmen scurried to obey, pulling Teal'c's arms behind his back. They only succeeded because Teal'c let them, and Jack nodded his approval. Teal'c replied with a slight inclination of his head, but there was a promise in the gesture that Jack recognized. *No one gets left behind.* Then, with a final glance at Daniel, he turned back to face Crawford and the Kinahhi.

An officer stepped forward, middle-aged and weather-beaten. Jack recognized him from their previous visit to Kinahhi, but he couldn't put a name to his face. "Restrain them," the man ordered. Two of his team stepped forward and bound Jack's hands in front of him with some sort of flex-cuff. They did the same to Carter, who was watching them all with guarded trepidation. He shared it and edged closer, letting his elbow nudge hers. *Okay?* She looked over and gave a slight nod in reply to his silent question.

"Move out!" the Kinahhi commander ordered, and Jack found himself urged up the ramp toward the shimmering surface of the wormhole. *Clutching white fingers in the dark, coming out of nowhere…* Fear beat fast in his chest, but he ignored it. Buried it. They'd get out of this. He'd get Carter out of this. His mistake, and he'd be damned if he let her – or anyone else – take the fall for it.

At the last moment he looked back, eyes fixing on Daniel and Teal'c. Their faces were like stone, hard and determined. It gave him hope. But then he caught sight of Crawford, following him up the ramp. *He has a right,* Jack reminded himself. *This is exactly what you did to him, isn't it?* Guilt and resentment mixed queasily in his gut, but the dark part of his soul wished he'd finished the job on the rat-bastard. An M24 sniper rifle would have done the trick, nice and clean.

Crawford spoke. His voice was low, pitched for Jack's ears only. "Ironic," he murmured, as Jack paused before the event horizon. "You weren't supposed to come back at all. And this is so much more entertaining."

Jack stared. "What the hell does that mean?"

Crawford just smiled. "Have fun, Colonel."

A hard shove sent Jack tumbling into the event horizon.

As the wormhole disengaged, Bill Crawford turned and surveyed the silent gate-room. No one was moving. It was like a picture, a tableau of fractured faith. It made him smile. From the first moment he'd stepped into Stargate Command, he'd endured their disdain. He'd been the outsider, the butt of their whispered jokes. Kinsey's lapdog. *Crawfish.* But now the joke was on O'Neill. On them all. Major Lee was unable to meet the eyes of the alien, Teal'c, defiant despite the bonds holding his arms behind his back. General Woodburn shifted awkwardly, new to the base and these men, dimly aware that he'd been drafted into a viper's nest. And finally Jackson, as always wearing his feelings on his sleeve, radiating waves of disappointment and impotent rage. The family was broken, leaderless. And he, Crawford, was responsible for cutting out the knot of misplaced loyalty at the heart of the SGC – the knot Kinsey had always found so impenetrable.

He allowed himself a smile and began to walk down the deceptively steep ramp, his footsteps clanging against the metal grid. In the end it had been too easy. O'Neill was a fool, predictable even without the advantage the *sheh'fet* gave the Kinahhi. They'd offered him exactly what he wanted, and he'd been unable to resist. O'Neill the hero, doing the impossible to bring his people home. Sucker.

Crawford stopped when he reached the end of the ramp. From

here he could look down on them all. "Good work, Major."

Lee said nothing, his jaw moving silently as he kept his eyes fixed on the inert Stargate. Crawford felt a beat of irritation at the man's lack of respect, but tamped it down. He held all the cards, all the power. Lee's defiance was irrelevant. He lifted his eyes to Woodburn. "Senator Kinsey wants to see you in his office for a full report, now that this is over."

The General's eyes narrowed at the implicit order, but he nodded nonetheless. "Major," Woodburn said, "escort Mr. Teal'c to the holding cells and—"

"You gotta be kidding." It was Jackson, latent fury re-ignited. "You can't do that, you—"

Woodburn spoke over him. "And ensure that Dr. Jackson reaches his apartment. His access pass is to be withdrawn before he leaves the base and a man stationed outside his building."

Eyes wide, Jackson pushed forward. One of the airmen half-heartedly reached out to stop him, but he brushed the hand away. "What is this? What the hell's going on?"

"Spring cleaning." The triumphant answer came from the doorway. Daniel spun around, Teal'c turning more slowly and with more dignity.

"Kinsey." Daniel spat the word as the Senator strolled into the room, trailing his usual entourage of assistants and hangers on.

Kinsey smiled nastily. "It's taken me a couple of years, Dr. Jackson," he drawled, "but at last I'm cleaning house. Getting rid of the dead wood clogging up operations, and beginning to make some progress." He waved toward the Stargate. "That thing might start proving useful."

At first, Daniel didn't respond. He stood glaring at the Senator, face flushed and eyes bright. When he spoke, his voice was deadly quiet and precise as a scalpel. "You've sent them to their deaths."

Kinsey shifted uncomfortably. *A sign of weakness*, Crawford thought. *Never show them your doubts*. It was one of the first rules his father had taught him: *never show weakness*. "I'm simply fulfilling the obligations of our treaty, Dr. Jackson. O'Neill and Carter have committed a crime. Even you can't deny that."

Jackson was shaking his head. "Jack was set up. The Security Council let him take the plans on purpose, to get him out of the way." There was an icy pause, and then, "As I'm sure you're well aware, Senator."

Treacherous blood rushed to Crawford's face and his heart thudded loudly. *The Security Council let him take the plans on purpose*… How did Jackson know that? Was he guessing? Was he bluffing?

But the Senator was unfazed. "Nonsense." He turned away, anger masking his agitation and easing Crawford's flush of anxiety. Perhaps Kinsey was a better player than he'd realized. "General Woodburn, have these…people…taken away."

With a nod, the General ordered Major Lee into motion. The Major looked like he was chewing nails, but didn't hesitate. *Good little soldier-boy, do your duty.* To his credit, Lee did the dirty work himself. "Dr. Jackson, please come—"

"I'm not done," Jackson growled, shaking off the hand Lee had rested on his arm and advancing on the Senator. "You have no idea what you're getting into. The Kinahhi are using you! The *sheh'fet* is just the start, just a foothold here."

Lee stiffened at the term 'foothold', eyes snapping to Kinsey. The Senator simply shook his head. "Do you have any evidence, Dr. Jackson? Anything to back up your paranoid theory?"

Teeth grinding together, Jackson shook his head. "Not yet. But—"

"Daniel Jackson is correct," Teal'c chimed in. "There is much dissent and suppression upon the Kinahhi world. Your alliance with them is foolhardy. And dangerous."

Kinsey turned on him in one of those flashes of temper for which the man was notorious. "My alliance," he snapped, "is the first time we've gained anything – anything! – useful from this program."

Amen to that, Crawford thought.

"You are mistaken," Teal'c observed, but Kinsey bulldozed over him.

"And it'll be a cold day in hell before I start taking advice on the fate of this planet from an alien with a track record of mass murder!"

The Jaffa didn't respond, his face darkening. For a long time no one spoke. At length, Major Lee touched Jackson's arm again. "Sir, please come with me."

Jackson didn't resist, but his furious gaze didn't leave Kinsey. "This isn't over," he warned. "I'll never let this rest."

A sardonic smile twisted the Senator's lips. "What you'll never do is set foot on this base again, Dr. Jackson."

Daniel shrugged indifferently. "There are other ways."

Huge mistake, Danny-boy. Jackson didn't play the game nearly so well as Kinsey. *Never show your cards.*

The Senator took an eager step closer. "Be careful, Dr. Jackson. Be very careful." With that he turned on his heel and marched through a gaggle of lackeys who melted out of his path, reforming seamlessly to trail behind him as he left the room. It was over.

Crawford stepped off the end of the ramp, the click of his shoes on the floor the only sound in the room. "If I were you," he said, as he headed past Jackson, "I'd enjoy the vacation." He permitted himself a thin smile. "It might be your last."

There was no answer, but as he left the gate-room he heard Major Lee's muttered words behind him, followed by the muted scrape of combat boots on concrete, and recognized it as the sound of victory. SG-1 had been broken. A new era was dawning at the SGC, and he intended to be a part of it.

A big part.

CHAPTER ELEVEN

Dusk was creeping into nightfall, and through the window George Hammond watched as the trees at the end of his yard became silhouettes against the deepening blue of the sky. Above them a few stars shone, pinpricks of distant promise, but their bright sparkle did little to lift his dour mood.

He hadn't moved from his chair near the window since he'd returned home this afternoon, escorted from the base by his own men. For their sakes, he hadn't made a scene. They were still following orders, even if he couldn't.

"I'm sorry, Senator, but I refuse to do that."

Those had been the words that had sealed his fate – and the fate of others – the proverbial straw that had broken the camel's back and given Kinsey the excuse he needed to finally push him out of the SGC. What that meant for the fate of SG-1 he could only imagine, but his imagination was vivid. It haunted him as he sat in the dark, second-guessing everything he'd done since Jack O'Neill had returned, battered and bruised, from Kinahhi all those months ago. Try as he might, Hammond couldn't think how he might have acted differently.

As for this last crisis, he'd literally had no choice. There was no way on God's green Earth that he'd order Colonel O'Neill and Major Carter to be handed over to the Kinahhi. He simply couldn't do it. But in refusing, he hadn't saved them. He'd failed them, and now no one stood between Kinsey and his people at the SGC.

Desperate anger twisted in his gut, eating him alive. Everything he'd worked for, everything he'd built over the past seven years, had been torn away. Losing a limb would have been less painful. His fingers curled into fists where they rested on the arms of his chair, and he had to resist the urge to simply hit something. He was too old for such outbursts, but never in the last forty years had he ever—

Someone rapped loudly on the door and Hammond found himself sitting bolt upright. After a moment the urgent knock came again. The house was in darkness; he doubted this was someone hawking life insurance. Pushing himself to his feet, Hammond strode through the dark living room, turning on lights as he went. Pulling open the front door, he stopped in surprise at the sight of the man in front of him. "Major Boyd."

The young man nodded, glanced over his shoulder, and said, "Sir, I'm sorry to bother you at home but…" His face said it all – he looked like he'd been hit by a truck. Hammond could identify.

"Come in, son."

"Thank you, sir." Stepping inside, the Major glanced around once and then fixed his eyes on Hammond. He looked strained, his face pinched beneath his tan. No surprise, given what he'd been through. "Sir, I thought you should know what's going on back at the base."

Fearing the worst, Hammond led the young man into his living room and waved him toward a chair. Boyd looked like he could use a seat. Hell, he looked like he could use a drink. Turning to his liquor cabinet, Hammond said, "I'm afraid I have a good idea what's going on, Major."

"They've sent Colonel O'Neill and Captain – Major – Carter off-world, sir. To a prison, I heard."

Even though he'd known it was inevitable, the fact hit like a punch. They'd done it, they'd actually done it. With a dull thud that set the glasses tinkling, the whiskey bottle came to rest on the counter. The incongruity sickened him; here he was, pouring himself a drink, while two of his best people had been shipped off to an alien jail because he couldn't save them. Had they put up a fight, he wondered. Had they looked for him, and found him absent? Had they believed themselves abandoned?

No one gets left behind. Jack O'Neill didn't have a monopoly on that sentiment.

When Boyd cleared his throat, Hammond realized he'd been silent for too long. "I know," he said quietly, pouring two generous glasses. "Senator Kinsey told me that was his intention. When I refused to hand them over, he had me relieved of command." He picked up both drinks and turned around. "When did it happen?"

"A couple of hours ago, sir."

He nodded. "Were they harmed in any way?"

Boyd shook his head. "Not that I heard, sir. Although Chris Lee said it got kinda tense for a while." His face creased with puzzlement. "Sir, people say that Colonel O'Neill stole the technology that brought us home. They say that the rescue mission was unauthorized. Is that true?"

With a nod, Hammond crossed the room and handed Boyd his drink. "It's true, Major." It felt like a confession. If Jack had played by the rules, everything would have been different. And not all for the better.

Boyd digested the fact silently, staring at his untouched whiskey. "So no one else was coming after us?"

"SG-10 was declared MIA five years ago, Major." It was a tough admission. "I'm sorry."

"So, if it wasn't for SG-1 we'd be dead by now?"

Or perpetually lingering on its brink. It was an uncomfortable truth for the General to hear. "Yes, that's correct."

Boyd looked shaken, and Hammond wondered exactly how much sleep the man had gotten since his return. "Have you been home, son? Have you seen your family?"

"No, sir. I—" He paused and frowned down at his hands. He was clutching the whiskey glass with white fingers. "It's been over five years for them, sir. I'm afraid—" Sudden emotion smothered his words and with a shaking breath he lifted the glass to his lips and downed its content in one go. He sat very still for a moment, staring at the empty glass. And then he looked up, haunted but in control. "General, it's not just Colonel O'Neill and Major Carter."

The swift change of subject dealt the second blow. Hammond had been expecting it, but it was no less severe for that. "Tell me."

Boyd sat forward in his chair. "Teal'c is under local confinement on base, but I've heard rumors of Groom Lake, sir."

Area 51. Hammond remembered Crawford's blatant threat, and it turned him cold. God only knew what they'd do to Teal'c. Forcing words through tight lips Hammond said, "And Dr. Jackson?"

"House arrest, sir. He's been barred from the base."

And that was just the start. Kinsey was no fool – he wouldn't leave Daniel Jackson at large. The man was a walking encyclopedia of the Stargate program, and he'd never be intimidated into silence.

"Sir?" Boyd stared up at him. "This is all happening because they came after us."

Carefully, Hammond took a seat. "It's not your fault, Henry. They knew what they were doing."

To his surprise, the young man nodded. "I know, sir. But that doesn't change the fact that we owe them. Big time."

Hammond sipped his whiskey, relishing the transient fire in his throat as he appraised the soldier sitting before him. He was young in years, but not in attitude. Over the past couple of days he'd lost five years and gained a lifelong obligation in return. He'd seen an officer under his command die a horrible death and known that, if it hadn't been for the bravery of SG-1, he too would have died screaming in the inferno that had incinerated Lieutenant Reed. That was a powerful debt, one that couldn't be ignored. One that transcended the niceties of playing by the rules.

"We can't leave them there, General."

"No," Hammond agreed quietly. "We can't."

Sam Carter stepped from the icy disorientation of the wormhole and stopped. A small contingent of Kinahhi soldiers, immaculate in gray, were lined up behind the defensive shields they employed in their gate-room. Beyond them stood three others dressed in the flowing robes of the Security Council, the silver cascade of hair marking one of them as Tamar Damaris, their leader.

Suddenly the Colonel came stumbling from the Stargate as if he'd been pushed, just managing to keep his balance as he staggered to a halt. He looked furious, dark eyes glittering dangerously. If he'd had a weapon, Sam would have taken cover. For a moment he glared at the gate, as if he could see right through the event horizon and back to Earth. Then he snatched his gaze away and glanced around the Kinahhi gate-room. If he was looking for a way out, good luck to him.

As the rest of their Kinahhi escort emerged, Sam found herself unceremoniously shoved into motion, down three steps and toward the waiting soldiers.

O'Neill was at her side, hands flexing, testing the strength of his bonds. "I see the welcome committee's here."

"Yes, sir." As she spoke, the troops moved aside to allow Councilor Damaris to approach. She was as imperious as Sam remembered, regarding them both with cold contempt. And yet there was something else in her eyes, an eagerness Sam hadn't noticed before. Damaris looked like a hunter about to make the kill.

"Colonel O'Neill," the Councilor said. "I did not expect to see you on Kinahhi again."

"Yeah. I heard that."

She smiled, a slight parting of her thin lips. "You are a resourceful man." Her attention shifted to Sam, as incisive as a knife. *Cutting through flesh with a hot, searing pain...* Sam shook the unbidden image away, but not before the Councilor's elegant eyebrows had risen slightly. "And Major Carter. Strong-minded as ever, I have no doubt."

Sam was about to reply when the Colonel stepped forward. "Yeah, great. Whatever. Let's cut the bullshit, shall we? I know what happened, Damaris. I know you set us up."

What? She glanced at the Colonel but his attention was fixed on Damaris. A flicker of alarm lit the Councilor's eyes, swiftly extinguished like a spark falling into water. But it was enough to confirm the Colonel's accusation. They'd been set up. *But how? How the hell...?*

"Your lies won't work here, Colonel." The Councilor said. "We have ways of discerning the truth that you cannot understand."

"I leave the understanding bit to Carter," the Colonel replied, taking another step forward. The soldiers shifted uneasily, weapons rising. He ignored them. "Just tell me one thing – did you murder Quadesh?" Damaris flicked an urgent look over Sam's head and gave a barely perceptible nod. "I mean, you knew he'd given me the plans," the Colonel carried on. "Did you kill him too? Did you—" A savage blow to the head dropped him to his knees.

"Sir!" Sam spun around, trying to protect him from another blow. A tall, hard-muscled soldier stood with the butt of his weapon raised, eyes fixed on the Councilor. Waiting for his next order.

Blood was running freely from a gash above the Colonel's right eye, and he sagged sideways, on the brink of passing out. At a signal Sam didn't see, the soldier raised his weapon again. "No!" she yelled, forcing herself between him and the Colonel. "Stop, you'll—"

"Break off!" The barked command came from the direction of the Stargate and halted the soldier's weapon midair.

With a tense look at Damaris he stepped back, lowering his weapon. Sam instantly dropped to the Colonel's side. "Sir?" He was white as chalk, blood dripping steadily onto the floor from the gash above his right eye. "Sir, can you hear me?" No response – he was clinging to consciousness by his fingernails. She glared at the soldiers surrounding them. "Someone help him!"

No one moved. Damaris watched them coldly, and yet behind her hard eyes fear lurked. The Councilor was afraid of the truth, afraid to let her own people hear it. Sam's gaze fell on another man who was watching them silently from the lip of the Stargate. The man who'd ordered a halt to the beating: Commander Kenna, Damaris's right-hand man. Or so Sam had thought on their first visit. But there was something in his face now that looked like dissent. Or rage. Whatever it was, Sam sensed she could use it. "Please," she said, "help him."

Kenna fixed his gaze on Damaris as he said, "Chief, call a Medic." Then he pulled a cloth from his pocket, walked down the steps from the gate and handed it to Sam.

Carefully, she pressed it against the Colonel's bleeding head. "Thank you."

Kenna didn't reply. Instead, in a loud voice, he said, "I apologize, Councilor Damaris, for the rash behavior of my officer. He will be punished."

Punished? Sam glanced up at the man, who blanched but remained stoic. Hadn't he been acting on Damaris's orders?

"As you wish," came the restrained reply. Yet it was laced with ice; it seemed that Damaris was less than happy with the charade, but apparently unwilling to say more. At least, not in public. "Have the woman held in Plaza 323," she said frostily, turning on her heel. "When Colonel O'Neill has been treated, transfer them both to Tsapan."

Tsapan? Fear caught in Sam's chest. She'd glimpsed horrors there, but it was what they hadn't seen that frightened her most. Standing next to her, Commander Kenna shifted slightly. His jaw twitched as if with the effort of restraint, but all he said was, "Yes, Councilor."

Letting out a slow, steadying breath, Sam returned her attention to the Colonel. To her surprise, his eyes were open and they met hers with dour understanding; Sam had no doubt their minds were running parallel. *Clutching white fingers in the dark, coming out of nowhere…*

How the hell were they going to get out of this one?

The night air was cool and fresh in his lungs. Daniel embraced the sensation. It tasted like freedom. No doubt it was entirely psychological, but the air in his apartment seemed stale and stifling. Out here, at least, he could taste the mountain breezes.

He was the lucky one.

Teal'c was locked up on base, and God only knew where Jack and Sam were. If they were even alive. His fingers tightened around the cold of the railing that ran around his balcony, as if the sensation could counter the ache in his chest. He'd never felt so powerless, so unable to help his friends. He had no phone, no internet, no way to contact anyone. And the guys outside the building – and the one outside his door – ensured there was no escape. He'd briefly toyed with the idea of climbing out, either from the balcony up to the roof, or down to the ground. But even for someone like Jack the climb would have been near impossible. For Daniel, suicidal. And he hadn't reached that point. Not yet.

But the knowledge that his friends were out there, in desperate trouble, and that there wasn't a damn thing he could do to help them, was making him frantic. He felt it building inside, a suffocating pressure. He wanted to scream his rage out into the silent midnight city, to wake the people up to the injustice being perpetrated in their name. To show them the danger lurking in the heart of Cheyenne Mountain, in the minds of men like Kinsey, driven by fear and ambition to destroy everything that made humanity worth fighting for.

He had to get out. He had to *do* something. He couldn't just—

A noise, as unmistakable as it was out of place, cut through Daniel's frenzy in an instant. A zat. Someone in the street below had fired a zat! Heart racing, half in hope and half in dread, he leaned out over the balcony. He could see nothing. Cautiously, he crept back into the apartment. It was silent, and he suddenly wished he had a weapon. Glancing around he saw a kitchen knife, but quickly dismissed the idea. A zat he could cope with, he could even handle a P90 if he had to – but knives really weren't his style. Besides, if the intruder had a zat, Daniel would never get close enough.

Stomach twisting unpleasantly, he moved to stand by the front door. His view through the peephole was obscured by a burly guard. Daniel pressed his ear against the wood. After a moment he heard footsteps approaching and a muttered exchange of words, quickly followed by an electronic fizz and the thud of someone slumping hard against the door. Backing up, Daniel braced himself, half expecting the door to burst inward. NID? Kinsey's own guys? The Kinahhi?

Fingers itching for a weapon, he grabbed the nearest thing to hand – a bronze statue of Kali – and hoped the goddess wouldn't be offended. They called her the Destroyer, after all. Hefting its weight in both hands Daniel waited. And then—

Someone knocked on the door, three soft, urgent knocks. Heart hammering, he crept closer. Through the peephole, now unobstructed, he could see a baseball cap. Could be anyone. The knock came again, louder now. Figuring any kind of action was better than nothing, Daniel reached for the door handle and pulled.

Two men almost fell through, one out cold and the other…

"General Hammond?"

The General's grin was positively impish. "Thought it was about time we got back in on the action, Dr. Jackson."

Half an hour later, Daniel found himself standing in the Cheyenne Mountain Zoo's deserted parking lot, freezing his butt off as he tugged on his guard's over-large uniform. The guard himself, in nothing but his underwear, lay trussed up on Daniel's bed, probably just waking from the close range zat blast General Hammond had inflicted. Daniel smiled at the image, and tried to imagine how *that* would read in the official report. Jack would have a field day. If he ever got to read it. If he wasn't already—

"Major Boyd will be waiting for you inside the base," Hammond said, his crisp tones a welcome intrusion. "He'll take you to Level 17, where Teal'c is being detained. From there, head straight to the gate-room." He smiled, a glint of white teeth in the overwhelming darkness. "You've overpowered the night crew in the control room before, I'm sure you can do it again."

Daniel grunted. The last time they'd pulled a stunt like this, on the way to take out Apophis's *ha'tak*, everything had been different. He pulled the belt tight around his waist; his borrowed BDUs were about two sizes too large. "That was four years ago, General," he said. "And we had Jack and Sam with us."

"You've come a long way in four years, Dr. Jackson."

Which was true, he guessed. Back then he'd still flinched every time he fired a weapon. Now he was practically a card-carrying member of the NRA. He shuddered at the thought. "So, where are we headed? The Tok'ra?"

Hammond sighed, his breath misting in the cool air. "I don't see that we have a choice, despite the fragile state of our alliance. Besides, Jacob Carter should be told what's happened to his daughter."

"If we can find him." And what were the odds of that? Even if they did find Jacob, what were the chances of the Tok'ra having a ship to spare to take them to Kinahhi? "It's not like we have much time," Daniel said aloud. "The Kinahhi don't have prisons, General."

Hammond sucked in a sharp breath. "What?"

"Whatever they do to their prisoners, they don't lock them up," he said, reaching down and pulling on the BDU jacket. "The Kinahhi I spoke to didn't even understand the word, and I don't think it was an issue of dialect or idiom."

Hammond tugged his coat closer against a sudden, biting wind. "Then you're right, we don't have much time. But other than the Tok'ra, I'm at a loss. We can't contact the Asgard…"

The General's words drifted away as Daniel's thoughts took a different path. "Actually," he said, "we don't need either of them."

"If you're thinking of using the Stargate to reach Kinahhi, Dr. Jackson, I'm afraid it's impossible. The Kinahhi gate-room is too well guarded and—"

"I know that, General," Daniel waved the notion away. "We can use the *tel'tak* we stole from Baal's fortress. The one we used to rescue Boyd. It's still on P3X-500. "

Even in the darkness, Daniel could see the skeptical crease of the General's forehead. "According to Colonel O'Neill, it was barely flying when you landed."

"It'll get us there," Daniel insisted, fishing his borrowed ID card out of a pocket and looping it around his neck. "And it's our best shot, General." The odds were long, they both knew that. But when had the odds ever stopped them? "If we don't find Jack and Sam soon…"

Gravely, Hammond handed Daniel a cap. "I wish I could come with you, son."

Pulling the hat on, Daniel tugged the bill down low over his eyes. As disguises went, he'd had better. But it would have to do. "The SGC needs you here." He lifted a wry eyebrow. "Without being overly dramatic, the whole planet needs you here, General. We have to find out what the Kinahhi are doing. And you have to stop Kinsey."

"I intend to, Dr. Jackson," Hammond assured him, as quiet and as adamant as the shadowy mountain that loomed above them. "I intend to."

With a nod of acknowledgement, Daniel opened the door of an old Pontiac; his guard's car, requisitioned like the uniform. With luck, in the dark, it would get him through the external checkpoints. If it didn't, he had the zat on the passenger seat. Whatever happened, he refused to fail. He cast a final glance at Hammond, the General's solid shape dwarfed by the empty night and the vastness of the crisis they faced. On impulse, Daniel extended his hand. "Good luck, sir."

Hammond clasped it firmly. "You too, son. And Godspeed."

CHAPTER TWELVE

The courtyard where Sam found herself imprisoned was identical to the 'guest quarters' on their previous visit to Kinahhi. Low white buildings surrounded an empty plaza, dark doors opened into small individual rooms. Or cells. Even last time it had felt like a prison. Doubly so this time. The fact that her hands were still bound didn't help.

Above, the planet's large, cool sun was sinking toward the horizon. The air was warm enough though, and the sun's pale yellow light cast long shadows across the white stone floor. Sam glanced at her watch – 0200 hours on Earth. No wonder her eyes felt gritty and her limbs leaden. But she was too wound up to try and sleep. She hadn't seen the Colonel for three hours, not since he'd been hauled away from the gate-room, slumped between two Kinahhi, his face and shirt bloody.

Her foot tapped an unconscious staccato against the flag-stones, drumming out her anxiety. It was a tell, and she stopped as soon as she realized what she was doing. There were men on the flat roofs above her, pacing and watching; she refused to give them anything. But the image of the Colonel crumpling under the savage blow was persistent, and she knocked her head back sharply against the wall to try and dislodge it. *Think about something useful.*

Studying the buildings around her, she tried to assess their chances of escape. Pretty slim, with guards posted on the roofs. Not to mention that last time they'd snuck out they'd had ropes and free hands. *And maybe they let you get away?* The thought crawled into her mind like a worm boring into an apple. *Maybe it was all a setup.*

That's what the Colonel had said before they'd beaten him into silence. She felt sick. Had they been dancing to the Kinahhi tune all along, and not realized it? But why? What could—

The tramp of booted feet coming closer broke the still evening. Sam rose, heart thudding. Had they come to take her to Tsapan?

Her fingers curled into fists, itching for her absent weapon, and she swallowed hard. She'd be damned if she'd let them see her fear.

At the far side of the plaza, through the narrow passage that was the only way in or out, three men approached. Two Kinahhi, and – thank God! – the Colonel. He'd been cleaned up and seemed steady on his feet, though his face still had a grayish hue. Once she'd assured herself he was okay she took note of the men with him. Commander Kenna led the way, his weathered features as unreadable as always, and a younger soldier followed behind the Colonel. Apparently the kid hadn't mastered the Kinahhi poker face – his gaze darted from side to side in nervous agitation.

Sam stepped forward, trying to figure out what was going on. "Sir?"

O'Neill shrugged but said nothing, and it was Kenna who spoke. "You may rest here tonight," he said shortly. "Tomorrow you will be taken to Tsapan."

"And then what?" The quiet question came from the Colonel.

Kenna made no answer, but pulled a heavy knife from a sheath on his leg. Involuntarily, Sam took a step back and felt the wall behind her. *Damn it!*

With a quick glance between them, Kenna motioned toward their wrists. For an instant, Sam hesitated, long enough for the Colonel to step forward. He held his arms out and with a swift slash Kenna cut his bonds, then turned to Sam. Eyes fixed on the blade, Sam held out her wrists and watched the knife slice through the plastic cuffs as if through butter. Or flesh.

"Commander Kenna?" The young soldier's voice was a squeak of alarm.

"Even the *khaw-kar* must eat," Kenna said calmly. He looked up, straight at the Colonel. "Let it not be said that the Kinahhi are cruel."

O'Neill cocked an eyebrow. "Yeah, wouldn't wanna say that."

A flicker of irritation tightened the Commander's eyes. "I will have a meal sent to you," he said, turning away. "You should rest."

"You know Damaris set us up, don't you?" the Colonel called to Kenna's retreating back. "She told you to let us escape that night. Right?"

The Commander faltered, coming to a slow stop. "I have done what I can."

"They're going to kill us." O'Neill said the words softly, as quiet and certain as a knife at an unsuspecting throat. "You can help us."

Kenna looked away, his face fracturing with a sudden, brief repugnance. "I have done what I can," he insisted. "You carry your own fate, Colonel O'Neill."

"And who carries yours, Commander?"

This time there was no answer. After a moment the soldiers were gone, and they were alone in the silent courtyard.

The Colonel turned, rubbing at his chafed wrists. He looked as grave as Sam had ever seen him. "So…here we are again."

Sam nodded. "Sir? What the hell's going on?"

A summer breeze blew across the side of the mountain, cooled by the night and carrying with it the scent of pine as Daniel hiked toward the access hatch hidden amid the brush. He'd pulled off the road and hoped the car wouldn't be spotted until daylight. If all went according to plan, he'd be off-world long before then.

Hampered by his fragile shoulder, Daniel twisted the lock and heaved open the massive iron hatch with a grunt. The muscles in his one usable arm burned with the effort. Beneath him the ladder fell away into darkness. Sixteen levels to climb down. Not easy at the best of times, but with his shoulder still healing it would be tough. If the joint dislocated again… He dismissed the thought and flicked on his wrist-light. Climbing over the lip of the hatch his boots hit the ladder, sending a dull chime down the long shaft beneath. Daniel winced; it sounded loud enough to alert the entire base. But no one came running.

With a deep breath, he reached over to pull the hatch shut on top of him. The angle and gravity weren't on his side and it barely moved, his shoulder screaming in perfect harmony with his back as he stretched to reach the cover. Daniel growled a curse and tried again, pulling with all he had, willing the hatch to move. Slowly it did, lifting up towards its apex. For an instant it balanced precariously and then plummeted down like a falling rock. Heedless of the wrenching in his shoulder, Daniel slithered down the ladder as the hatch slammed just inches above his head. Any closer and his skull would have cracked like an egg.

Clinging to the rungs, Daniel gasped for breath until the pain receded along with the echoes reverberating through the access shaft. Eventually, all he could hear was the sound of his own breathing, fast and ragged. All he could see was the little pool of yellow cast by his wrist-light, dimly illuminating the ladder's rungs and the concrete walls beyond.

"Okay," he whispered. "Time to go." Like Orpheus, descending into the Underworld, he began to climb down through the bones of the mountain in search of his lost friends. He just had to remember not to look back. Or down, come to that.

They'd moved inside once the sun had set, the Kinahhi night air cooler than Sam remembered from their previous visit. Five months later, she guessed; it had to be a different season. Kenna had been true to his word and sent a meal, which they'd both made a half-hearted attempt at eating. Neither were hungry.

They're going to kill us.

The Colonel's words floated silently between them, a mute acknowledgement of what the dawn would bring. It was nothing they would ever discuss aloud, of course. Admitting defeat wasn't something they did, not ever.

"So you think Damaris knew Quadesh stole the plans all along?" Sam asked, from where she sat on the end of the room's narrow bed, legs crossed beneath her. It was as good a subject as any.

Colonel O'Neill nodded. He was propped against the wall, taking up the other end of the cot and toying with a piece of spiced bread. His face was sickly beneath the bloody gash over his eye. The headache had to be brutal, and they had no meds with them. They had nothing but the clothes on their backs. "It's Daniel's theory, and it fits," he said quietly. Then he looked up, intense in the gloom. "There's something else too."

Not that it really mattered now. "What's that?"

"Crawford said something." The Colonel's lips tightened angrily. "He said we weren't meant to come back."

For a moment, she was confused. "From here?"

"No. When we went after Boyd."

The truth hit her like a truck. "Oh my God, they designed the device to fail."

With a heavy sigh, the Colonel rose and walked over to the small window. In the moonlight Sam could see his face, taut from more than pain. He blamed himself. "Crawford told Damaris why I was after their technology, and she gave me exactly what I wanted."

"But with a fatal flaw," Sam added quietly. He flinched, and she added, "You couldn't have known, sir."

"Couldn't I?" He turned back to her. "Even Daniel was suspicious. But I—" He cut himself off, fingers clenching with the effort of restraint.

"We all wanted to believe it would work, sir. And it did. We saved SG-10." All but Reed. An incongruous, shameful bubble of relief abruptly burst on the surface of her mind. The device had been designed to fail; Reed's death wasn't her fault. "We did it, sir. Against the odds, as it turns out."

"It was always against the odds, Carter."

"So was escaping the consequences," she reminded him. "And we all knew that too."

"But not this!" A flash of anger sent him pacing. "A reprimand for you, maybe. A court martial for me. But this?" He reached the far wall and gave it a desultory kick. "This is exactly what Kinsey wants. Crawford, that rat-bastard…"

Rising slowly, Sam took a cautious step closer. "It's not your fault, sir."

He gave a harsh laugh. "Oh, yes it is, Carter. It's all my damn fault. I should've known better, I should never have taken those stupid plans. Or gotten the rest of you involved. Or—"

"Or saved Henry Boyd?"

"Damn straight," he snarled. "It's not worth the price."

"No. You're wrong."

Breathing heavily, he glared at her. "What?"

"You're wrong. Because if you hadn't taken those plans, if you hadn't done everything you could to bring SG-10 home, then—" She stopped herself, habitual restraint holding her back. *Damn it, just say it.*

"Then what?" Beneath the angry rasp there was a plea, a need to hear some vindication after all. It was enough to keep her talking.

"Then you wouldn't be the man I thought you were. Sir."

He shook his head. "Carter, I'm not—"

"Yes," she insisted quietly. "You are."

He stared at her, a silent interrogation, digging for a truth she couldn't admit. Not even to herself. Sam held her ground and at last he moved away, back to the window and stared out into the moonlit plaza beyond. He looked pensive, but something in his eyes hardened. Resolve; the indomitable tenacity that had always been the bedrock of SG-1. "Daniel and Teal'c will come after us." He said it softly, like an article of faith.

"Yes, sir." If there was anything left of them to rescue. Dawn was only a few hours away, and then... Her mouth felt dry, heart laboring painfully.

"Come on." He turned away from the window and raked a hand through his hair. "Let's get some rest."

It made sense, though Sam didn't hold out much hope of sleeping. Despondently, she turned toward the door and her own room – cell – but he stopped her with a hand on her arm. "No, stay. I'll take first watch."

She almost smiled at the guarded look in his eyes. "Yes, sir." Close, but not too close; it epitomized so much about their complex friendship. As the Colonel settled himself against the wall, watching the door, Sam curled up on the bed and closed her eyes. She could hear his breathing, slow and steady as the—

Clutching white fingers in the dark, coming out of nowhere...

Her eyes flashed open. It was going to be a long night.

The cell was small and poorly lit, but as he sat cross-legged upon the bed, Teal'c encouraged the room to expand within his mind. He allowed the walls to retreat, the ceiling to rise and the floor to fall until he was suspended in a vast, white space. It was empty now; no other consciousness shared this place. And for half a heartbeat he felt loneliness. How perverse, to miss the mind of the demon that he had borne for so long. It was an insidious reminder of the peculiar nature of Jaffa slavery; their masters were without and within. The battle must be won on many fronts before the Jaffa people could ever be truly free. But it was not—

A metallic clunk shattered his sanctuary, collapsing it in a flare of claustrophobia. Heart racing, Teal'c rose to his feet. The walls of the cell pressed in around him as he watched the door open. Instinctively he readied himself, weight moving forward onto the balls of his feet, fingers flexing in search of a weapon that was absent.

Two men in uniform entered, but they did not bear a meal. Nor did they summon him. Instead, the door was carefully closed before either man spoke. As the lock clicked, one of the two men turned around and pushed the cap back from his face. "Hello, Teal'c."

Elation surged. "Daniel Jackson!" He could not prevent a smile from reaching his lips. "It is good to see you."

His friend grinned. "You too." He indicated his companion. "We're getting outta here."

Glancing at the other man, Teal'c recognized him immediately. "Major Boyd."

"Teal'c," the young man nodded, nervously eyeing the door. "We should hurry."

Perhaps. But the man was ill at ease, and Teal'c could not trust him as implicitly as he did O'Neill. "Where are we going?" He directed the question to Daniel.

"Back to P3X-500. And from there to Kinahhi, to find Jack and Sam."

Teal'c inclined his head. "I assume this mission has not been approved by General Woodburn?"

His friend's eyebrows rose. "Ah… Not exactly."

"Then you intend to take the control room by force?"

From behind his back, Daniel Jackson pulled a *zat'ni'katel* and offered it to Teal'c. "It's the night shift," he said, consulting his wristwatch, "for the next half hour. That's only three people on duty."

Teal'c did not take the weapon. "If I am seen armed in the corridors, we will not reach the control room, Daniel Jackson."

"Then how—?"

Teal'c held out his arms, wrists together. "Bind me."

There was a moment of confusion as Boyd and Daniel exchanged a look. Then Daniel returned the *zat'ni'katel* to the waistband of his pants and pulled a flex-cuff from a pocket in his vest. "Subterfuge," he said, looping the cuffs over Teal'c's wrists and pulling them tight. "I like it."

"When we reach the entrance to the control room," said Teal'c, "release me."

"Oh you bet," Daniel nodded, pulling his cap down low. He turned to Major Boyd. "You're going to have to do the talking. I'll keep my head down. If anyone asks we'll say Teal'c's being transferred to Area 51."

"A believable story," Teal'c agreed. Then he addressed Major Boyd. "You will need to disable the guard outside the door. He will not release me without orders to do so."

A curt nod was Boyd's only reply, but a tightness about the eyes told Teal'c that the thought of firing on his comrades in arms – even with a *zat'ni'katel* – did not sit easily with the Major. For that, he had Teal'c's admiration. Without further conversation they took their places, Major Boyd in the lead, Teal'c behind and Daniel at the rear. As Boyd opened the door, Teal'c suppressed his instinct to fight or to run, and attempted to adopt the demeanor of a prisoner.

"Hey!" came the protest from outside the cell. "What're you doing? You can't take—"

The blue fire of a *zat'ni'katel* at close range danced across the limbs of the guard as he fell to the floor. Major Boyd winced, but said nothing and Daniel Jackson dragged the airman into the cell. "He's fine," he assured them, his fingers resting lightly on the fallen man's carotid artery. It was characteristic of his friend, Teal'c observed, that he would not only notice Major Boyd's unease but take it upon himself to assuage it.

Standing, Daniel Jackson tugged his cap lower. "Come on," he said. "Let's get outta here." In the blink of an eye he had switched from compassion to pragmatism. The former was innate, the latter learned. It had been a necessary evolution, Teal'c thought as they headed down the corridor, and yet he regretted the passing of the youthful innocence he had once known in his friend. But while men such as Ambassador Crawford were alive in the world, such innocence could not long survive. It was another charge to lay at the door of the man and his political master. And Teal'c intended to ensure that their day of reckoning would come. And come soon.

The Kinahhi dawn was cast in hues of tangerine and apricot as the planet's huge sun crested the horizon. From where he lay on the cell's narrow bed, Jack watched the light brighten the court-yard, giving its austere white an unaccustomed warmth. Shame it didn't have the same effect on the Kinahhi people.

He sighed, and rolled onto his back. He'd given up chasing sleep hours ago – the prospect of imminent death did that to a guy – and contented himself with savoring the silence. There wasn't enough silence in his life. Always racing, always rushing to stay one step ahead of the bad guys. Never time to simply be. Except when he was fishing. Now *that* was silence…

Sitting on the floor, back against the wall, Carter was equally riveted by the dawn. She looked tired, and he doubted she'd slept. How could she? Fear crawled beneath her stoic façade, like woodworm eating at her from within. And not just her. He felt it too, the sly paralyzing panic. It could cripple you faster than a gunshot, and he should know. How long had he hidden in the cold, damp darkness of Baal's palace instead of going after her? Too long. If he'd gotten there sooner…

He dismissed the memory with a shake of his head. It didn't matter now. Hanging in there, that's what mattered. He returned his attention to Carter. Bleak as stone, she stared, unseeing, into the sunlight.

This wasn't the first time they'd faced certain death, but usu-ally they had a fighting chance. Time for Carter to deploy that vast brain of hers and figure out a solution. But this time there was no miracle waiting to happen. They were locked up, unarmed, on an alien world with no way home. Hammond wouldn't be send-ing backup, and despite the unbending faith he had in his team, the odds of Kinsey letting Daniel or Teal'c within a mile of the Stargate were slim to none. And time wasn't on their side; Carter knew that as well as he did.

It was as close to hopeless as it got, and that was the problem. Without hope, you gave up. You sat braced against the wall, star-ing at the rising sun and waiting for them to come and take you away. *Staring at the opposite wall of the topsy-turvy cell, waiting for the sound of their boots as they came to take you back there, over and over and over…* Yeah, he knew what it was to despair. And he wouldn't let it happen again. Not to himself, and not to Carter.

"I've been thinking." His words sounded loud in the dawn silence, even though he'd kept his voice low.

Carter turned her lifeless eyes on him. "Sir?"

"Those creatures that attacked us on Tsapan?"

She shivered slightly, grimacing. "What about them?"

"I think maybe they escaped from…whatever is on Tsapan."

Drawing her knees up to her chest, she wrapped her arms around them and propped up her chin. Something flickered in her eyes, a spark not quite extinguished. "Meaning we could escape too?"

Exactly. A little positive thinking, Major. "We've gotten out of tight spots before." He paused. "Just last week, actually. Collapsing building, black holes…"

A faint smile touched her lips. "Is this a pep talk, sir?"

"Maybe." He sat up and ran a hand through his hair. "Are you feeling peppy?"

A soft chuckle escaped, and she was about to answer when the sound of booted footsteps rang across the courtyard. Carter was on her feet in an instant, skittery as a cat.

"Easy," he said, also rising. She was breathing hard, fear creeping in. He could feel it too, fluttering at the edges of his mind. This was it. They were coming for them. *Gut and legs liquid with terror he let them haul him through the doors, and out into the bright corridor beyond…*

"Sir, we can't just let them kill us."

Hell no!

Clutching white fingers at his throat…

Panic rippled through his mind in purple waves, stifling breath and suffocating reason.

Don't let them take you alive! His finger squeezed the trigger and he saw the man fall. He saw Teal'c fall…

Get a grip. The fear was irrelevant; action was everything. He pushed past the memories and the stifling band of pressure around his chest. "Carter, we have no weapons, no—"

"So?" She paced to the door and back, glancing out of the window. "We take theirs. Fight. At least go out fighting instead of…of…"

"Of what?" Through the window he saw half a dozen Kinahhi standing at attention in the middle of the courtyard. A single set of footsteps was approaching the door, but he couldn't see their owner. It didn't matter anyway. "Carter, we don't know what they're going to do to us there."

"They're going to kill us!" she protested. "You said it yourself."

So he had, testing the Kinahhi Commander. Kenna hadn't given much away, but he hadn't denied it either. "People try to kill us all the time, Carter."

She shook her head, anger rising and control slipping. "I can't believe you're just going to let them—"

"Hey!" He snapped a note of command into his voice. End of the line or not, discipline was paramount. And he knew exactly where panic got you. "I'm not giving up here. We have to wait for better odds."

Pissed, Carter subsided, but the protest didn't leave her eyes. She opened her mouth to speak again, just as someone knocked sharply on the door.

They *knocked*? *You are cordially invited to your own execution.* "No one's home!"

Carter snorted. Dark and dry, but it was a laugh nonetheless. Better. Clearing his throat, Jack whispered, "You know what they say: it's not over till the fat lady sings."

"The fat lady, sir?"

He shrugged. "Or in this case, until Crawfish screams like a cheerleader."

A bleak smile twisted her lips, and then the door swung open. Jack held her gaze for a beat longer, watching her fear knot itself into courage. *There is no courage without fear.* Teal'c had never spoken a truer word. Carter gave him a slight nod, and on that unspoken signal they turned together to face the man who entered.

"Come," Commander Kenna said calmly. "It is time."

CHAPTER THIRTEEN

The corridors of the SGC felt alien and unfamiliar as Daniel trailed Teal'c toward the elevator that would take them down to the gate-room. Without his glasses his vision was blurred, although with his head down he couldn't see anything more than his boots tramping on the gray concrete. Tramp, tramp, tramp.

As they passed a cluster of people – he didn't look, couldn't see faces – he heard someone mutter *Teal'c* in a tone of disbelief. There was tension in the air, like the oppressive heat of a summer thunderstorm. Heavy and brooding. No one would take kindly to Hammond's removal, nor to the fate of SG-1. But if they did nothing else, these men and women would follow orders. He knew that much about them. For better or worse, they did what they were told. It was their strength, but at times like this Daniel considered it a weakness too.

At last Boyd stopped, and Daniel glanced up to see him hitting the elevator call button. Edging closer, keeping his head ducked, he murmured, "So far so good."

Teal'c nodded, and there was a spark in his eyes that looked like humor. Daniel raised an eyebrow in a silent question, but the Jaffa simply shook his head. Behind them, footsteps echoed.

"Crap!" Boyd whispered. "It's Crawford."

Daniel's hand strayed toward the zat hidden under his vest. But this far from the gate-room, the odds were impossible. He could hear the muted drone of the Ambassador's voice now, too far away to make out words. Daniel's gaze darted back down the corridor, but without his glasses everything was blurred. There had to be somewhere to hide. Somewhere to—

Ping! The elevator doors slid open and, mercifully, the car was empty. Not daring to breathe, Daniel stepped inside with Teal'c all but diving in after him. Boyd slammed a hand on the controls just as Crawford's words began to coalesce into meaning.

"...test subjects seem to be having some trouble in—"

The doors slid shut, cutting him off. "Thank God." As the car trundled into motion, Daniel blew out a nervous breath and looked over at Teal'c. He stood before the doors, wrists still bound, with that hint of a smile playing across his face again. Jaffa humor...

"Teal'c?"

He turned, eyebrow cocked.

"What's so funny?"

Henry Boyd glanced between them. "Something's funny?"

"Apparently."

"It is nothing you would find amusing, Daniel Jackson."

With Jack and Sam in the hands of the Kinahhi, Hammond out of the SGC and Kinsey after their blood, Daniel could readily believe it. "Try me."

Teal'c shrugged and raised his wrists. "Chewbacca."

Daniel blinked. "What?"

"You've seen *Star Wars*?" Boyd asked, incredulous.

"Many times," Teal'c assured him. "Our current situation is not dissimilar."

There was a long silence as the elevator continued its rapid descent. Daniel cast a glance at Boyd, who simply shrugged in disbelief. Aliens were one thing, Daniel supposed, sci-fi fans were something else entirely. One and the same, Jack would have said. *Would say*, he corrected himself. No past tense.

Boyd shifted nervously, fingers flexing around his holstered weapon. "Hey, they were talking about doing a new movie, weren't they?" His eyes flitted between Teal'c and the floors counting down as they dropped further beneath the mountain. "Whatever happened with that?"

Teal'c redirected his attention to the elevator doors, face settling into its customary deadpan. "Let us not speak of it, Major Boyd."

Swallowing a smile, Daniel moved to stand at his friend's side. Level 26 morphed into Level 27. "It should be pretty quiet down here this time of night."

Teal'c agreed with a slight bob of his head.

"We'll take out the control room staff, then I'll dial while you two secure the gate-room," Daniel said. "With luck, it'll be empty." He fished his glasses out of a pocket, and slipped them back on – at this point, vision was more important than anonymity.

The elevator stopped. Level 28. "Good luck," Boyd said softly.

"You too. And thanks. Thanks for doing this."

Boyd dismissed it with a shrug. "You guys came after my team when no one else did, Dr. Jackson. We owe you one."

"Yeah, well, we appreciate it." Given all that Boyd had been through, this went above and beyond. It reminded him painfully of Jack. *No one gets left behind.*

The slight judder of the doors opening cut into his thoughts and— A babble of noise rushed into the elevator... the corridor beyond was teeming with people! "Uh-oh."

So much for empty.

Boyd's hand jabbed at the close button, but Teal'c stopped the doors. "This is our only chance."

He was right. Their escape would soon be detected, and they wouldn't get a second chance. "Come on," Daniel urged, leading them out into the busy hallway. "Let's go."

Doing his best to avoid eye contact, Daniel led Teal'c and Boyd through the corridor. Although a couple of curious looks slid their way, no one spoke or interfered. But then a flurry of activity approached from the direction of the gate-room. Above the clipped military voices drifted a Kinahhi lilt, which explained the late-night activity; someone had come through the gate.

Teal'c heard it too. "Daniel Jackson..."

"I know." He cast around the narrow corridor, spotting a door a couple of yards up to his left. Storeroom? Backdoor to the armory? He had no idea. Seven years, and he'd never been in the damn room. But there was no time to hesitate. Seizing the handle, he twisted and pushed at the door. Out of the frying pan... He ducked into darkness and was hit by the distinctive aroma of antiseptic. Medical store! Made sense for Dr. Fraiser to keep a few supplies close to the gate-room, and he sent her a silent thank you. Teal'c and Boyd swiftly followed him inside. In the hall the Kinahhi voices grew louder, accompanied by the familiar drawl of Senator Kinsey. Despite the risk, Daniel couldn't resist leaving the door ajar as the party drew close.

"I am personally overseeing the deportation program, Councilor Athtar," Kinsey was saying. "But it will take some time to convince..."

Daniel stopped listening, his jaw dropping open in shock. There was a ghost walking at the Senator's side. Athtar, Kinsey had called him, but Daniel knew him by a different name. Quadesh. The man who'd given Jack the Kinahhi plans; the man who'd apparently blown himself and the Security Council to smithereens.

Turning away from the door, Daniel blinked in the shadowy room. His mind was reeling. Quadesh had told Jack he was a dissident, opposed to the Kinahhi security state. They'd assumed he'd been killed for his beliefs, yet here he was haunting the corridors of the SGC as a representative of the government. What the hell was going on? "I, ah," he rasped, "I think things just got worse."

"How so, Daniel Jackson?"

He paused, trying to work through all the ramifications. There were too many and they were too wide-reaching, but one thing was certain. "I think the Kinahhi have a sarcophagus."

What exactly that meant, he had no idea. Yet.

Commander Ebrum Kenna did not look back as he led the prisoners toward the shuttle that would take them to Tsapan, but he could feel the eyes of the man – O'Neill – stabbing like daggers into his back.

You can save us. If that was truly what the Tauri thought, then he was a fool. He could no more save them than walk on the surface of the sun; to try would mean death. And not only his own. He had a son to consider. A father's disgrace would condemn Esaum.

Yet he saw in O'Neill's face something of his own. The man was a leader, his features marked by responsibility and loss. And Kenna saw no deception there, no threat to Kinahhi, whatever the Security Council might say.

Kenna had lived with politicians his whole life, he knew expediency when he saw it. If O'Neill and the woman, Carter, posed a threat it was to the Tauri, and therefore not his concern. He pitied them their lot, and doubted they deserved it – but he could not help them. As he had told O'Neill, they carried their own fate.

In the courtyard beyond Plaza 323 the transport was already waiting, its doors gaping and lined by a short rank of his own

men. They didn't move as he approached, already at perfect attention. He expected nothing less. With a nod to his second, Chief
Saulum, he turned and faced the prisoners. Their hands had been
tied once more, but both stood with straight shoulders and raised
chins. He admired that; neither would meet their end in supplication.

"It would help," O'Neill said in a quiet voice that somehow
sounded as hard as iron, "if we knew what was going to happen."

There was dignity in the request, and Kenna found it impossible to resist. "I believe it is not painful," he assured them. O'Neill
didn't react, but the woman's eyes narrowed as she processed the
information. "You will be joined with the *sheh'fet.*"

"Which means…?"

Of course. They knew little of Kinahhi ways – an ignorance
he was sure Damaris wished to preserve in her allies. A flutter of
disquiet accompanied the thought, and he shook the feeling away.
Such sentiments were dangerous. "Your minds will be absorbed
by the *sheh'fet.*"

"If that translates as 'sucked out with a straw'," O'Neill replied,
squinting through the morning sunlight, "you should know that
there's no way in hell we're gonna let that happen."

The idiom was lost on Kenna, but the defiance was clear to
all. He could not let it pass unanswered. "You have no choice,
O'Neill. You have been judged guilty—"

"There was a trial?"

"—and sentence has been passed." He paused, his discomfort
rising and threatening to become conscious thought. "I am sorry,"
he said, in an attempt to defuse his internal conflict. "But there is
nothing I can do."

O'Neill met and held his gaze. "Yeah. Right. Just following
orders, huh?"

"I am doing my duty."

"Are you?"

"You committed a crime—"

"To save four of my people!" O'Neill snapped. "And Damaris
knew all about it. She set us up, and you know it." That much was
true. It had been necessary, Damaris insisted, for the sake of the
treaty – for the sake of Kinahhi. And he had believed her. To do

otherwise was impossible.

O'Neill stepped closer, his dark, alien eyes seeming to see right through the Commander. "What are you afraid of?"

He could not answer and hurriedly schooled his mind and face to vacuity lest it betray him. "I serve Kinahhi."

"My country right or wrong?" O'Neill shook his head, a meager gesture, tight with anger. "That's bull."

"The *sheh'fet*," the woman said abruptly, thoughts racing through her eyes. Despite their more normal color, Kenna was shocked by their flagrant openness; had she stood before him naked he would have felt more comfortable in her presence. Suspicion, fear, sudden comprehension; all were blatantly on display. "Quadesh said Tsapan is where they send the dissidents." She turned her disturbing gaze on him. "If you question your leaders, that's where you go. Right? To the *sheh'fet*."

A void. A blank white space in his mind. "Enough," he said abruptly, turning away. "Saulum, escort the prisoners. I shall pilot myself today."

His chief stepped forward. "Yes sir." He didn't question Kenna's decision to pilot, and the Commander gave no explanation. If it served to remove him from the presence of the troubling prisoners, then so be it. Determinedly, he thought no more about them and fixed his inner eye on Esaum and home.

I serve Kinahhi. And while Kinahhi was safe, so was his son.

The corridor beyond the storeroom where they were hiding had been silent for at least five minutes. Daniel peeled the cover back from his watch, the Velcro rasping loudly and making him wince. "Fifteen minutes till the morning shift. It's now or never."

"Now gets my vote," whispered Boyd.

"Indeed." Teal'c flexed his arms, clearly pleased to be free of the cuffs.

Pulling the spare zat from his belt, Daniel handed it to his friend. "Control room, then gate-room."

There was nothing else to say, and silently Daniel led them out into the hall. Weapon raised, he crept along close to the wall until he reached C corridor. He listened, heard nothing, and slipped around the corner. All was quiet and he broke into a swift jog, keeping his footing light. By the time he reached the base of the narrow steps leading up into the control room his heart was racing – and not with the effort of running. This was it. If they failed, it was all over. For them, Jack, Sam and – if Kinsey and the Kinahhi had their way – the SGC. Maybe even the world.

Hugging the wall, Teal'c took the other side of the stairs and paused. Without Jack to give the signal, it fell to Teal'c. Three, two, one— *Go*.

Teal'c went first, barreling into the control room like a soundless whirlwind, Daniel on his heels. In two shots, half the people in the room were down.

Daniel fired at Sergeant Harriman, grimacing as the man fell spasming in a shimmer of electrostatic. Boyd took out a young woman Daniel didn't recognize.

"Sorry." Daniel winced guiltily as he stepped over Harriman's prone body to reach the gate controls. Why did it have to be Harriman? Was he on duty 24/7? "Go!" he hissed at Teal'c and Boyd. "I'm dialing."

"Daniel Jackson…?" The query in Teal'c's voice drew his gaze from the computer.

"What?"

Teal'c indicated Boyd, who stood tautly watching the door, and raised an eyebrow. Daniel understood. Boyd had done enough. He'd just lost five years of his life, no need to risk spending the rest in jail. Or worse. With a scant nod, he turned back to the controls.

"Dr. Jackson?" Boyd hit the floor with a dull thud, convulsing with the aftereffects of Teal'c's zat blast.

"Get down to the gate-room and—" Sirens started to blare. "Damn it!" Daniel slammed in the final coordinates and backed away, needing to see the gate start moving before he dared leave. "Teal'c, go!" After an eternity, the Stargate began to spin and Daniel took the stairs two at a time, barely ahead of the thundering footsteps coming down the corridor. The defense team deploying.

"Close the doors!" he yelled at Teal'c, who'd taken up position next to the blast doors. Daniel skidded in just as the room was sealed, but outside he could hear shouting. It wouldn't take them long to get through. Together, he and Teal'c raced to the foot of the ramp, attention split between the blast doors and the slowly spinning Stargate. Did it always move so damn slowly? Four chevrons locked. Three to go.

"Someone is in the control room."

Daniel's eyes snapped up. He recognized Colonel Dixon and the rest of SG-13. Damn it, what were they doing there? They'd abort the dialing sequence; they'd have no choice.

Behind him, another chevron locked – the fifth? – and Dave Dixon looked down, right at Daniel. He didn't say anything, just watched. Then his lips moved and two of his team peeled off and disappeared. The gate kept turning.

After a moment, the blast doors opened and two members of SG-13 stalked into the room. Beyond them, Daniel could see Major Lee holding a group of confused looking airmen at bay, but he paid them little attention; his eyes were locked on the two soldiers walking slowly toward him, P90s raised and aimed, coming to a halt at the foot of the ramp. He knew them both: Captain Richard Bosworth and Senior Airman Simon Wells. Behind him, the sixth chevron locked.

"What's going on?" Bosworth asked.

The zat in Daniel's hand felt heavy, and his wounded shoulder throbbed like hell. Could he raise the weapon and fire before Bosworth pulled the trigger? Would Bosworth shoot at all? SG-1 had pulled his team out of the fire more than once.

"Don't screw around, Jackson," Bosworth barked, urgent now. "What's going on?"

Daniel glanced at Teal'c. His zat was already raised. Possibly they could do it and escape with their lives. Or possibly not. He took a deep breath and said, "We're going after Colonel O'Neill and Major Carter." Sometimes, the truth was the most effective weapon of all.

Bosworth didn't seem surprised. "With two zats?"

"If we have to." He glanced down at the weapon. "We didn't have time to stop by the armory."

Without lowering his gun, Bosworth looked briefly back at Dixon. The Colonel nodded, and Bosworth turned back to face Daniel. "Our P90s are loaded and there's extra ammo in our vests. But you'll have to shoot us to get them."

Daniel blinked. "What?"

His voice was drowned by the sudden whoosh of the Stargate

engaging. Its light flickered over the faces of Bosworth and Wells, reflecting on the heavy glass that shielded the control room. Through it, Daniel could see Dave Dixon watching them without expression.

"You've got about sixty seconds before Woodburn gets here," said Bosworth. "And the video surveillance cameras are rolling, so you'd better make it look good."

For once in his life, Daniel found himself speechless. He hadn't expected this, not from the rule-bound military. He knew the risk they were running – if the truth ever got out, their careers would end in disgrace and prison-time. "Thank you." It was all he could muster, all his dumbfounded astonishment would permit. Then he ducked and fired, praying it looked like the act of a desperate man. It wasn't far from the truth.

Bosworth fell, Wells collapsing at his side in an arc of blue fire. Daniel jumped off the end of the ramp, unclipped Bosworth's P90 and snatched his ammo and a Beretta for good measure. Teal'c did the same to Wells. Shouts came from outside the door as Daniel stumbled toward the gate, clutching the weapons to his chest. At the top of the ramp he turned and saw Dave Dixon lift his hand in a brief farewell. And then Daniel flung himself into the wormhole and let it shred him to pieces.

CHAPTER FOURTEEN

The Kinahhi transport skimmed across the ocean, the bright glitter of sunshine on the waves as hard and uncompromising as diamonds. Sam knew it should have looked beautiful, but she was seeing it through a shroud. Her own shroud.

They're going to kill me. The truth was sickening and inevitable.

Teeth clenched, she forced herself to concentrate, to take in her surroundings. They were inside a Kinahhi transport ship, identical to the one they'd 'borrowed' for their first trip to Tsapan. Three guards stood watching them, weapons slung across their chests. They didn't seem to be expecting trouble; it would take them a good fifteen seconds to fire by Sam's reckoning. You could do a lot in fifteen seconds.

The cockpit door was closed, which seemed odd. Had she been Commander Kenna, she'd have wanted an ear – if not an eye – on her prisoners. He clearly trusted his men, but more than that, she suspected he was trying to distance himself from herself and the Colonel. Something about them disturbed him. What, she couldn't quite tell.

The ship banked slightly, causing the Kinahhi to shift their stance as a wider expanse of ocean rose up into view. And suddenly, ahead of them, Sam could see the sweeping towers of Tsapan. Her heart lurched; her life was ticking away in minutes now. Fear made her fingers tingle, churning in her stomach. Doggedly, she ignored it, refusing to let it choke her reflexes. *You're not dead yet. Anything could happen. Focus.*

The rainbow colors of the floating city gleamed like jewels. Once a gaudy monument to Baal's power and wealth, it was now used by the Kinahhi for their own dark purposes. Corruption corrupted. There was a strange irony to that. Evil and beauty entwined.

Tearing her morbid gaze away, Sam forced her attention back to the inside of the ship. The Colonel sat opposite her, face tight and eyes distant, assessing the risks and looking for a way out. It was reassuring. For a while back there she'd thought he'd given up. After all this time, she should have known better. He'd fight till the end – the question was, what were they fighting?

You will be joined with the sheh'fet.

What the hell did that mean? Nothing good. That much she'd managed to discern, even through the customary reserve of the Kinahhi; Commander Kenna had been afraid. And if he was afraid…

The Colonel cleared his throat softly. Sam looked over and saw that he was watching her. Intently. Then his fingers began to move, slowly and clearly. *Go left. On three.* Holy crap, *now*?

She tried to keep her face neutral, but he must have seen her surprise because an eyebrow lifted, clearly saying, *You got a better idea, Major?*

She didn't. He was right, the odds of success here were the best they'd get. No backup, a limited enemy force, and if they succeeded they'd have a getaway car. With a slight nod, she told him she'd understood.

He turned back to the window, apparently pensive, but Sam kept her eyes fixed on his hands. She knew him; the tourist impersonation was all for show. Sure enough, after less than a minute, he gave the signal. *Three.* She tensed, glanced over and eyed her target. *Two.* Slowly she straightened, the balls of her feet pressed to the floor. *One.* Her fingers were fists. *Go!*

Sam bolted to her feet and charged the Kinahhi who stood guard to her left. Her head plowed into his solar plexus, and he doubled over. Keeping low, she spun and kicked out, landing her foot against the jaw of a second guard and sending him sprawling.

A third man came toward her, weapon locked and loaded. Sam tried to dodge out of his sights, but there was no room. "Sir!"

A grunt distracted her. The Colonel had his bound wrists around the neck of one of the Kinahhi, using the cuffs like a garrote. Fingers scrabbling against O'Neill's arm, the Kinahhi was gasping for air. "Drop it!" the Colonel yelled at the advancing soldier. "Drop it now."

He paused, gaze flicking from O'Neill to the gray face of his struggling comrade. The Colonel didn't look much better than his hostage. He could be ruthless when he had to, but it didn't mean he enjoyed it. "I said *drop it!*"

Hesitantly, the man lowered his weapon.

"Carter, take it."

She stepped forward and seized the gun. "Sir, I—"

A hand wrapped itself around her ankle, and yanked. With a cry she fell backward, head cracking against the wall. A rainbow spiraled across her vision, pain ricocheted through her skull. And then something cold and hard pressed against her forehead.

"Let him go." The words were slurred and broken.

Sam opened her eyes and stared along the barrel of a gun toward the swollen face of the man she'd drop-kicked. His jaw looked broken, and he was pissed as hell.

So was she. There were worse things than death, and having her mind sucked out by a straw – as the Colonel had so graphically put it – was one of them. Especially if it meant that the Kinahhi would have access to all she knew about the Stargate program. When it came right down to it, this just might be plan B: a bullet to the head would be fast and painless. Better still, there'd be nothing left for the Kinahhi to suck out. To her left, the Colonel was watching. He was thinking the same thing; she could see it in his eyes as they lifted to meet hers. There was no decision there, only conflict. "Sir…"

He held her gaze a beat longer, then abruptly released the Kinahhi soldier. The man pitched forward, but Sam's attention was still fixed on the Colonel. For a moment she saw apology in his eyes, then his whole face shifted in alarm. The gun hadn't moved.

"*Kelimmaw.*" The voice was a rasp of raw anger, the cold metal pressing her head back against the wall. "He's already dead."

Daniel stumbled out of the wormhole with an armful of weapons, slipped on the short set of steps and skidded down to land on his ass in the dirt. Behind him, Teal'c stepped out of the gate with enviable elegance. As the wormhole evaporated into nothing, his gaze came to rest on Daniel with mild curiosity.

Not bothering to move, Daniel squinted up at his friend. The sun was bright here, and he didn't have any sunglasses. "That was close."

"We must assume they will redial," was all Teal'c said, trotting down the steps and heading straight for the *tel'tak* they'd abandoned here just a week earlier. Had it really been only a week?

Scrambling to his feet, Daniel clipped on Bosworth's P90, tucked the Beretta into his belt, and began stowing the clips as he jogged after Teal'c. "Let's hope Dixon slows them down." Although, God knew, he'd done enough already.

Daniel's grateful thoughts were forgotten as they drew closer to the *tel'tak*. He hadn't paid much attention to the ship after they'd limped in to land. Coming back hadn't crossed his mind. He'd been more concerned with his dislocated shoulder, Teal'c's gunshot wound, and Jack's uncharacteristic fatalism. But now he saw the black streaks of bubbling metal scarring the hull and a myriad other dents and twists that spoke of use and abuse. "Teal'c?"

The Jaffa stopped on the threshold and turned. "Daniel Jackson?"

"This will fly, right?"

Teal'c didn't answer, simply stepped up into the ship and disappeared. After a moment, Daniel followed. The *tel'tak* smelled of ozone and blood, a nice memento of their previous trip. Heading toward the controls, he saw the place where Teal'c had fallen, an abandoned field dressing frayed at the edges and dark with rusty brown stains. How much more blood would be spilled, he wondered, before this was over?

Dropping into the co-pilot's seat, he watched Teal'c make a careful study of the controls. Deciding not to disturb him, Daniel glanced out the window. Scoured with grit and dirt, it was murky, but clear enough for him to see the Stargate standing amid hazy ruins.

Suddenly he was filled with a nostalgic longing, as acute and poignant as lost love. God, how he wanted to be able to simply wander through the crumbling history of this world, to discover its secrets with nothing but discovery on his mind. But years ago his fate had taken a different path, a bloody path of war and conflict. It was nothing he'd ever looked for, nothing he'd ever wanted. Yet somehow he had found himself out here, fighting for the future instead of studying the past.

The thought came with a mixture of pride and loss. He wouldn't trade the past seven years for anything – he'd discovered unimaginable wonders, shaken every perceived truth about humanity's origins, and touched the faces of their ancient past. Yet he'd never again be the man he once was, and part of him regretted the loss of an innocence that had— "Uh-oh."

Teal'c looked up. "Daniel Jackson?"

"Now's probably a good time to test those engines." Daniel kept his eyes locked on the revolving Stargate. "I'm betting they didn't send Dave Dixon after us."

Jack stared, transfixed, at the gun wrinkling the skin on Carter's forehead. Half of him wanted to jump the guy, the other half whispered that this might be the best way out for her. Better than the alternative. *His weapon dipped. He'd killed her before, once. He knew he could do it. He'd killed her to save her...* "Don't."

The word slipped out unchecked and the Kinahhi soldier's head whipped around. "He was my friend."

"I'm sorry." Jack recoiled from the memory of the man's death throes, his feeble struggles as he tried to cling to life. It shouldn't have killed him, Jack knew how far to push it. Perhaps the Kinahhi were built different? But such was life. Such was death. What else was there to say?

On the periphery of his vision he could see Carter, coiled with tension. She looked like she was about to pounce. "Easy, Major."

"Sir…"

"Silence!" The weapon jerked toward Jack, tension rising.

Long and lean, it reminded him of a shotgun more than anything else. He wondered what it fired: projectiles, plasma, something new and funky? Maybe he'd get a demo.

"What kind of animal kills with its bare hands?" spat the Kinahhi. "Do you take pleasure in it? Do you—"

"Chief!" The bark came from the door to the cockpit, resonating with outrage. "Explain."

The soldier started, but didn't lower his guard. His narrow face quivered with momentary unease, however. "The prisoners attempted to escape, Commander. This one murdered Chief Saulum." He paused, nose twitching in disgust. "With nothing more than his own hands."

Carefully, Jack shifted his gaze to Kenna. He stood in the

doorway, staring at the carnage. Cold fury lurked behind his eyes, and when they came to rest on Jack they were sharp as broken glass. "Saulum was my friend," he said icily. "He had a wife, and two children."

Goddamn it. He didn't need to know that – which was precisely why Kenna had told him of course. The familiar wash of guilt broke over him, and he welcomed the pain. This wasn't the first father, son, lover or brother he'd killed – even if it proved to be the last. The fact that he still felt guilty at least meant he was human.

Refusing to back down, Jack held the Commander's angry stare. "I'm sorry." He meant it, and if Kenna was the soldier Jack had taken him for, he'd realize that. Eventually.

The Commander said nothing, his gaze dipping to the sprawled figure. He was silent for a long time, then lifted his head. The look he shot Jack was stony. "Damaris was right," Kenna hissed, "you are a threat. Brutal, as merciless as the Mahr'bal."

Huh? "Who?"

Kenna ignored the question, turning to the guard who was covering them. For an instant he thought the Commander was going to give the order to fire. But instead he said, "Shackle them, hand and foot. We are approaching Tsapan." His eyes slid back to Jack, bright with anguish. "This time, I shall have no compunction. You deserve the fate you carry, Tauri."

Maybe, Jack conceded silently. *But Carter doesn't.* Evading Kenna's intent scrutiny, he turned and glanced in her direction. To his surprise, she just gave him a wry shrug. *Better luck next time, sir.*

It was almost enough to provoke a smile. Nothing like a little hand-to-hand combat to get the adrenaline pumping; the panic he'd sensed in her earlier had been blasted away like cobwebs, replaced by the gritty resilience he'd so long admired. *Next time.*

Yeah, there'd be a next time. He had no doubt. And if Carter believed it too, then things were definitely looking up.

A rattle of P90 fire streaked across the bow of the *tel'tak* as its engines spluttered to life. It was a warning shot. Teal'c chose to ignore it and pulled hard on the controls. He felt the ship respond, lifting at his request and banking into a steep climb. Almost a century of experience had attuned his mind to that of any ship, and he sensed the cadence of its flight as if it were an extension of his own physical form. He could feel the weakness of the engines, hear their death rattle as they struggled to lift the ship beyond the insistent pull of the planet's gravity. They were teetering on failure as he coaxed the frail ship into the air, overpowering the engines to keep them from stalling. "*Bradio!*" he muttered, under his breath. "*Bradio.*"

"It's SG-2," Daniel Jackson called, peering out the window at the men firing ineffectually below them. "They're worse shots than I am."

Teal'c permitted himself a moment's amusement at his friend's self-deprecating humor. "I do not believe they intended to hit us."

Sitting back in his chair, Daniel Jackson cast Teal'c a sideways glance. "Kinsey's not going to be happy."

"He is not."

A smile toyed with his friend's lips; perhaps he was enjoying the prospect of the Senator's anger as much as Teal'c. But then he sobered and said, "They'll guess where we're going, and they'll warn the Kinahhi."

Teal'c inclined his head, relaxing now that the ship had stabilized its climb; the stress on the weakened engines was dropping. "The *tel'tak*'s stealth device will enable us to evade their detection." He paused, considering whether to voice his greater concern. Such discussions were usually reserved for O'Neill, but in this case he had little choice but to trouble the mind of Daniel Jackson. "Have you considered how we might locate O'Neill and Major Carter once we arrive on Kinahhi?"

A silence followed, and when it was broken Daniel Jackson was somber. "Well, we know the Kinahhi don't have any prisons, and I can't see them keeping Jack and Sam in the guest quarters for long. Which leaves..." His voice drifted into despondency.

"What does it leave?" Teal'c prompted quietly.

"Tsapan. Jack said it's where the Kinahhi send their political prisoners. But what happens to them there..." Daniel Jackson shook his head and stared out the window. Gray, wispy clouds shredded past them as they tore through the edges of the planet's atmosphere. "I do not believe," Teal'c said, unsure if his words would give comfort or pain, "that the Kinahhi would swiftly execute O'Neill and Major Carter."

His friend nodded in bleak agreement. "No, they're too valuable for that. They know too much about the SGC, about the Stargate—" A sudden flare of anger brought Daniel Jackson's fist down hard on the arm of his seat. "What the hell is Kinsey thinking? He's just handed the Kinahhi the key to everything we know about…about…*everything*!"

"O'Neill and Major Carter will not reveal any information that could damage—"

"Yes they will." He said it with such vehemence and such certainty that Teal'c was startled.

"I do not believe—"

"You're wrong," Daniel Jackson insisted hotly. "Everyone breaks in the end, Teal'c. That's the point of—" He stumbled over the word, and after a moment continued more quietly. "That's the point of torture. And if the Kinahhi have a sarcophagus…"

Teal'c understood his meaning, but had more faith in the strength of his friends. "O'Neill is a formidable warrior, as is Major Carter. Neither would ever surrender information that would harm—"

"It doesn't matter." Daniel Jackson waved away Teal'c's assurance with an irritated gesture. Teal'c found himself wondering why he was so certain of their friends' fallibility. But to ask felt like an intrusion, and so he held his silence. Into it, Daniel Jackson spoke again. "We know the Kinahhi have other methods." He took his glasses off and rubbed a hand across his eyes. "We know they can 'read minds', at least to some extent. Who knows what other technology they have?"

That was a fair point. Teal'c returned his attention to the window. The dark void of space filled it now, and far below the nameless, alien world glowed with the soft amber of rock, dust and slow desiccation. "Whatever the situation on Kinahhi," he said, "we must retrieve O'Neill and Major Carter swiftly."

At his side, Daniel Jackson sighed. "If we're in time."

The air in the small office crackled with anger and recrimination. It was as heavy as gasoline fumes, and twice as explosive. Crawford kept a low profile, trying to blend into the gray of the concrete wall and happily allowing the hapless General Woodburn to bear the brunt of Kinsey's attack. What else were the military for, if not to stand in the line of fire?

"This is supposed to be the most secure military base in the whole damn world, General!" Kinsey ranted. "How is it possible that you let these people escape?"

Woodburn's chin lifted higher, his eyebrows climbing like furry caterpillars into his hairline. The image amused Crawford, but he was careful not to let it show. Gravity and concern were all he wanted Kinsey to see in his features.

"I believe they had inside help, sir," Woodburn said, not for the first time. "It is the only explanation."

Kinsey shook his head, a gesture of weary resignation, like a parent scolding a child for an oft-repeated crime. It was as phony as everything else about the man, but Crawford studied the gesture with interest and filed it away for later use. *Always learn from the best*, his father had once told him.

"As I've said all along," the Senator sighed, "Stargate Command has become too incestuous, too far removed from the oversight of proper authority. There is no respect for chain of command. In fact, there's a distinct disrespect and distrust of anyone outside this base."

Rising from behind General Hammond's heavy mahogany desk, Kinsey began to pace the cramped office. "I want an investigation, I want names and I want heads on spikes!" He paused, his voice dropping into a menacing rasp. "And if I don't get them, General, rest assured that yours will be the first head that rolls."

Woodburn didn't flinch. "I suggest, Senator, that I begin the investigation by interviewing General Hammond. He is likely to know the ringleaders of an operation such as this."

A slow smile spread over Kinsey's face, and Crawford had to give Woodburn credit for playing to the Senator's weak spot. "Yes. Hammond," said Kinsey. "Have him brought in. If anyone knows what's going on here, it's him. He's been incubating this nest of corruption for years."

Abruptly, the smile faded and Kinsey's eyes came to rest sharply on Crawford. "As for the ringleaders," he said, face scrunching in renewed irritation, "no doubt they're the ones who escaped through the Stargate. Dr. Jackson and the alien, Teal'c, must be the instigators." Crawford blinked, unsure of why he was being pinned by the Senator's cold stare. Surely Kinsey couldn't suspect him of being involved? Anxiety rippled up his spine, tightening across the back of his skull. Should he say something? Should he— "Crawford, go back to Kinahhi. Explain what's happened, and apologize. No doubt Jackson is planning some sort of rescue attempt, and our allies must be forewarned."

Relief blanked his mind, and Crawford was obliged to answer simply with a nod. Schmooze with the Kinahhi? He could do that. Oh, he could certainly do that. Confidence renewed, he found his voice. "I shall make it clear where the blame lies, Senator."

Kinsey grunted. "And offer any help they might need to capture Jackson and the alien – men, arms, anything. But," he raised a finger, wagging it like a school teacher, "tell the Kinahhi that Jackson and Teal'c are mine." The wagging finger curled into a fist. "And I will personally ensure that they never, ever make trouble for us again."

"Yes, sir," Crawford agreed eagerly. It would be his pleasure to deliver the errant members of SG-1 into the Senator's hands and, with luck, that final gift would cement him forever to Kinsey's side. From there, the White House was only an election or two away. Vice President Crawford had a certain ring to it, but he had to confess President Crawford sounded better.

All in good time, he reminded himself as he obediently left the room. Indeed, with the *sheh'fet* on their side, it was simply a matter of time. He smiled as he headed toward his office to make the necessary preparations for his visit to Kinahhi. The future was looking bright, even if he was stuck in the dark, windowless entrails of Cheyenne Mountain. But not for much longer, not for much longer at all…

CHAPTER FIFTEEN

The last time they'd entered Tsapan it had been dark, the empty streets ghostly with shadows and the sounds of wind and crashing waves. This time, the creeping decay of the city was more visible and somehow more forbidding than the shadows of the night.

Sam stepped with difficulty from the transport ship and out into the cold sea air, tangy with ocean salt. Heavy shackles chained her legs together, and she was glad of the thick boots that protected her ankles from their bite. The sun was low in the sky, glinting off peeling gold and refracting through shattered windows in tall, disused towers. Like a crumbling castle from a children's fairytale, with no happy ending in sight.

"Could do with a coat of paint," the Colonel said as he jumped down and thudded onto the stone floor of the landing platform. The dark metal of his handcuffs clanked dully as he moved, and he shifted his wrists under their weight.

Sam smiled slightly at the comment. He still had hope. She could see it, although their situation was growing more desperate by the moment. If they could just get away, Tsapan would provide a rabbit warren of hiding places. O'Neill was squinting up and around, most likely making the same assessment. But they were surrounded by wary and angry Kinahhi soldiers who'd give them no room to run. And then there were the shackles…

The last to leave the ship was Commander Kenna. He studiously avoided looking at either herself or the Colonel, and moved instead to stand with his back to them. Waiting. For what, Sam didn't know, until she heard the rounded tramp of marching feet. The Commander had called for reinforcements. Not really surprising, given their antics on the shuttle. But with more troops coming to escort them, it cut down any chance – slim as it already was – of escape.

"Carter?" The Colonel moved closer.

"Sir?"

His gaze was fixed on the stairs at the far side of the landing platform, where the sounds were growing louder. "Not looking good."

"No, sir."

He cast her a fleeting look. "You okay?"

Not really, but that's not what he needed to hear. "We just need to give Daniel and Teal'c some time, sir. Hold out until the cavalry arrives."

The first rank of soldiers came into view, in perfect step and armed to the teeth. "We have to resist," the Colonel ordered. "Whatever happens, Carter, we can't tell them anything about the SGC."

"I know, sir." Although she suspected, as the Colonel must, that the Kinahhi had ways of extracting information way beyond their knowledge. The *sheh'fet* was no toy.

The soldiers – at least twenty – had crested the steps, and Commander Kenna strode forward to meet them. The stiff sea breeze whipped away the words Kenna spoke to his men, but three of them broke rank and headed into the transport – no doubt to retrieve their fallen comrade – while the rest surrounded herself and the Colonel.

"Move out!" Commander Kenna barked. The heavy chains made it hard to walk, but the sharp jab of a weapon in her back kept Sam moving as fast as she could. The landing platform gave way to the wide stairway, flaring out at the bottom toward a shadowed plaza that might once have been beautiful. The remains of a dry fountain stood in the middle, stray rays of sunlight glinting on the ragged patches of gold leaf that clung to a crumbling statue at its center. It was a woman. Some consort of Baal's, perhaps?

At her side, O'Neill was still scanning their surroundings. Assessing, remembering, planning. As if reading her mind, he quietly murmured, "We'll get out of this, Carter."

She nodded. "Just like always, sir."

"Getting old for you, Major?"

She shook her head, and began to negotiate the stairs. "Better than the alternative, sir."

That provoked a brief smile, but he said no more as the

Kinahhi soldiers herded them down into the shadows of Baal's former palace, toward a fate Sam didn't dare imagine.

The hum of the ship's engines was the only sound in the *tel'tak* as it streaked through the blur of hyperspace toward the distant world of the Kinahhi. Daniel stared blindly through the window, half-dozing in the co-pilot's seat. According to Teal'c, the journey would take about six hours – if the engines held out that long. Compared to the vast reaches of the galaxy, six hours represented little more than a hop, a skip and a jump, but to Daniel's mind, stretched thin with worry, it felt like an eternity.

A lot could happen in six hours. Jack and Sam could already be dead. What else the Kinahhi might do to them, he refused to contemplate. His mind was clouded by brutal images – visions and sounds that echoed through his nightmares. It was a colorful enough palette to sketch any number of atrocities, and he refused to allow it free reign. He was doing all he could for his friends, and to torment himself with his imagination served no purpose at all. This, at least, was better than standing on his balcony, raging at the stars. But the waiting was intolerable, the waiting and the unknown. He shifted in his chair. "Teal'c—"

"It is now three hours and fifty-four minutes until our arrival."

"I was going to ask if you wanted to get some sleep."

Teal'c turned, eyebrow rising. "There is still an hour left on my watch, Daniel Jackson."

"I know," Daniel yawned. "But I can't sleep anyway, so you might as well."

After a long, considered look, Teal'c nodded. "Very well." He rose, but before he left the cockpit he clasped Daniel's shoulder. "The situation is grave," he said. "Yet I believe all will be well."

Daniel didn't reply. Teal'c had demons of his own, yet he, at least, had never seen Jack O'Neill break at the hands of a monster. He'd never heard those screams, wretched and hopeless. He'd never been forced to watch, forbidden from interfering, until he could stand it no longer. Daniel didn't remember much from his time among the Ancients, but he did remember the agony of indecision, the weight of disapproval stacked against him.

Their concerns are not ours, intercession is forbidden. Death is the fate of the unenlightened.

Over and over...

It had weighed like a millstone around his neck, every scream, every silent appeal in his friend's tortured eyes, dragging him deeper and deeper. Inaction had been impossible, simply impossible. Sometimes the rules had to be broken.

Just like now. The thought that his friends were suffering, while he sat helplessly aboard the *tel'tak*, burned like an old wound reopened. *Death is the fate of the unenlightened.* He squirmed in his seat, and the minutes dripped by like water from a slowly leaking faucet. *Intercession is forbidden.* Screw that! He had to act. He had to *do* something, or he'd go crazy and—

"Daniel Jackson?"

Startled, he sucked in a breath. "Sorry, I, uh..." He sighed and pushed himself to his feet. "I'm okay. The sooner we get there the better."

Teal'c bowed his head, the expression in his eyes indicating that he understood more than he was revealing. "Indeed."

The city of Tsapan, Jack figured out, was constructed in layers – the surface brightly lit with sunshine and the lower levels increasingly dark, gloomy and stinking of decay. They'd been walking for at least half an hour, always downward, the stairways growing narrower and slicker as they went. Rivulets of water seeped down the walls, cutting passages through the green slime that coated the roots of towers sprouting up all around them. How the Kinahhi found their way, he had no idea. The place was a labyrinth. And murky too. The sunlight, golden blades of light with little power and no heat, rarely reached these depths and the air was dank and chill. The sound of the ocean was closer too, and he guessed they had to be approaching the base of this floating city. How far, he wondered, was it from the sea? And how far was the coast? Swimming distance? He glanced down at his shackles and gave up that idea, at least for now.

At his side, Carter tramped along in stoic silence. The sense of panic he'd seen in her earlier was gone, bottled up and replaced with a ruthless determination to survive. Not healthy, perhaps, but essential. If her experience in Baal's fortress still plagued her, she had it under control. So much the better. Dr. McKenzie could keep his head shrinking; there was nothing like a little action to clear the mind. If the debacle on the shuttle had done nothing else it had steadied Carter.

A rough hand on his back nudged him to his left, toward another, narrower, set of stairs. Water trickled over the steps in a shallow stream, splashing like a rock garden waterfall. "Elevators out of order?" he said, to no one in particular. "You call maintenance, but they never come—"

"You joke?" Commander Kenna asked from behind him.

Surprised, Jack turned around. The Kinahhi officer was watching him curiously. There was still anger in his eyes, but it was tempered with something else. Indecision? Uncertainty? He's seen it before in the man's face. "Never say die."

Kenna remained impassive. "Are you not afraid?"

"That's not really the point, is it?"

Kenna stepped closer. "Is it not?"

"Well, you know what they say," Jack hedged. "*Feel the Fear and Do It Anyway.*"

A repressed snort of laughter from Carter undermined the gravitas of the moment. Kenna shot a look between them. "Do you mock me?"

Carter shook her head. "No, I'm sorry." With a look, she urged Jack to say more. But what? Damn it, where was Daniel when you needed him? At his helpless shrug, Carter tentatively took over. "The Colonel's right, we believe that fear is not something to…fear. Right, sir?"

"There is no courage without fear," Jack agreed, silently thanking Teal'c for the homily. After a moment he added, "You have nothing to fear, but fear itself." He glanced at Carter. "Got any others?"

With a subtle roll of her eyes, she fixed her attention on Kenna. He recoiled slightly from her gaze, and Jack wondered what he saw to spook him. "Does that surprise you, Commander?" Carter asked curiously.

Still not quite meeting Carter's gaze, the Commander said, "We prefer security here on Kinahhi. Safety, tranquility. And peace."

Carter's face lit up with understanding, one of those moments that usually prompted a half hour of animated explanation. She glanced at Jack as if willing him to read her mind.

Not a chance. "Major?"

Instead of answering him, she turned back to Kenna. "The *sheh'fet* makes you feel safe, doesn't it?"

The Commander shook his head. "No, it *keeps* us safe, Major Carter. Without it… There are still those who peddle terror."

"The dissidents," said Jack, failing to keep the anger from his voice. A dissident bomb blast had nearly buried Daniel under a ton of rubble, and had cost at least one mother the life of her child. He could still taste the dust-laden air, thick as grief in his lungs. And Councilor Quadesh, killed for his beliefs, an unwitting pawn of the Kinahhi Security Council. Everyone was afraid.

Kenna acknowledged the point, but his attention was still focused on Carter. Carefully, he said, "Fear can be a formidable weapon."

"Yes," she agreed, layering the word with meaning. All of a sudden, Jack had the horrible sensation that he was missing half the conversation.

"Yet you are not afraid?" Kenna pressed, with a note of disbelief. "The people of your world do not know fear?"

Carter shook her head. "No, that's impossible. But we— When terror is used as a weapon, we believe that the only defense is to refuse to be afraid."

"And you can accomplish this feat?" His gaze darted between them dubiously.

"Not always, " Carter shrugged. "But we try. We find that when you let fear control you, you end up making some very bad decisions." A fleeting look at Jack told him where her mind had turned – toward the Jaffa on the roof of Baal's fortress. She shook the memory away, chin lifting. "Fear is an enemy of real peace."

For an instant longer the Commander held her gaze, then turned away sharply. "Fear is indeed an enemy of peace." He spoke in a voice loud enough to carry. "And on Kinahhi, we are fortunate to be shielded from those who would have us live in fear. The *sheh'fet* protects us." He gestured to his men, all conversation with Carter apparently over. "Proceed."

With nothing else said, Jack found himself prodded down the narrow staircase. He fell in at Carter's side, the steps allowing no more than two abreast and offering them a semblance of privacy.

As they clanked slowly down the stairs, he murmured, "What was that all about?"

She kept her eyes on the wet, slippery steps, but in a low, excited voice, said, "I think he was talking about more than the dissidents, sir. The way he was looking at me... I can't be sure, but I think when he said fear was used as a weapon he was talking about the Security Council."

Hope beat a sudden tattoo in Jack's chest. "Are we talking about a little dissent of our own here, Carter?"

She nodded. "It's possible, sir."

It was a chink in the enemy armor. A small one, but better than nothing. If – and it was a big 'if' – they could convince the Commander to cross the line and help them... Jack had seen Teal'c do it many years ago, renouncing his god to fight for the freedom of his people. But the situation on Kinahhi was far less clear cut. Kenna might have as much to lose as Teal'c, but what did he have to gain?

Jack considered the question as he descended into the cold depths of Tsapan, squinting up once to see the tops of the derelict towers closing over the last patch of blue sky. He shuddered as the shadows settled around him, damp and stale, and clung to Carter's words like a golden thread of hope.

"Here," a soldier barked, stopping them outside a pair of large, industrial looking doors. Water ran freely down the alleyway in which they stood, seeping into Jack's boots.

Carter shivered, whether from cold or fear he couldn't tell, and he edged half a step closer. "And they promised us a five star resort," he murmured. "There's not even an ocean view."

Commander Kenna moved to stand in front of the doors. "Within is the *sheh'fet*," he said, regarding them both intently. "What say you now?"

Carter's chin jutted defiantly. "I say you'd better open the doors."

You go girl! Jack met Kenna's surprised stare with a nonchalant shrug. "You heard her."

Still watching them keenly, face alive with expectation, the Commander stepped aside. Behind him the massive iron doors swung open.

CHAPTER SIXTEEN

General George Hammond had insisted on wearing his uniform, as neatly pressed as it had been every day of his four decades in the service, when he was escorted back into Cheyenne Mountain. He could only guess at the reason for his summons; Major Lee had been silent on the subject when he'd called at the General's house that morning. But Hammond suspected it had something to do with the escape – successful, he hoped – of Dr. Jackson and Teal'c.

Now he stood inside an elevator as it fell rapidly through the heart of the mountain, his hands folded behind his back and keeping a resolute silence. Until he knew for certain that his team had gotten away, the less he said the better. The elevator slowed, then stopped, and the doors opened onto the familiar corridors of the SGC. The scent in the air – a trace of ozone from the Stargate mixed with the institutional aroma of canteen food and polished boots – hit him with all the force of memory and he had to smother a sharp pang of regret. This place was no longer his home.

With a nod, he indicated that Major Lee should lead the way. Hammond expected to be brought before Kinsey, but to his surprise the Major turned in the direction of Colonel O'Neill's office. He dared not hope that Jack had returned, and determinedly dismissed the thought. SG-1 were good, but not that good.

Outside O'Neill's office, Major Lee stopped and knocked. Hammond noticed, with a wrench, that the Colonel's nameplate had been removed.

Because you let Kinsey hand him over to the enemy, a little voice whispered.

But he lied to me!

And you didn't protect your people.

I had no choice.

Didn't you?

There was no silencing his inner conflict. He'd been rehearsing it compulsively since the day Kinsey threw him out of the SGC, but it would be unwise to dwell on it now. There were other matters at hand. Nevertheless, the idea of anyone but O'Neill in that office felt like an affront, and Hammond found his hackles rising as an unfamiliar voice called out, "Come."

Lee opened the door, standing aside as the General stepped into the room. The desk, usually a study in barely contained disorder, was neat and empty. Behind it sat a man Hammond didn't recognize, but the stars on his uniform revealed his identity. "General Woodburn?" Hammond couldn't mask his surprise. What was the man doing hiding in Colonel O'Neill's office?

Woodburn didn't stand. "Leave us, Major," he said. A quiet click of the closing door was the only reply to his order as the General fixed a steady gaze on Hammond. Woodburn was a bluff looking man, wiry white hair streaked with gray, adding a touch of wildness to the pressed battle dress uniform he wore. A man of action, Hammond guessed immediately, uncomfortable behind a desk. This was no politician, and that gave him hope.

"General Hammond," Woodburn said, rocking back in his chair. "I have a problem."

Hammond folded his arms across his chest. "I can't say I'm sorry to hear that."

"No," the man agreed, "I'm sure you're not." Standing, he stepped out from behind Colonel O'Neill's desk, shaggy eyebrows contracting into a frown. "At 0400 hours this morning, Dr. Daniel Jackson and the alien, Teal'c, fought their way into the gate-room, disabled a number of my men, activated the Stargate, and left Earth."

"Did they?" Hammond said it without a flicker.

"We presume they have gone in search of Colonel O'Neill and Major Carter."

"I would say that's a good bet, General." Hammond paused. "But, as you say, *you* have a problem. How does this concern me?"

Without a word, Woodburn picked up a paper from the desk. "This is the report from the man on guard outside Dr. Jackson's apartment last night." He produced a pair of narrow reading glasses from a pocket and, perching them on his nose, began to read. "At 0115 hours, I was approached by a short, stout man wearing a baseball cap. I couldn't see his face and assumed he was one of the elderly residents returning home late. But then I realized he had a zat, and before I could raise the alarm he shot me."

Short and stout were a fair description, Hammond supposed, reigning in another smile. But *elderly*? He offered Woodburn an innocent look. "What's your point, General?"

"My point," Woodburn said, allowing the paper to flutter onto the desk, "is that Jackson and Teal'c couldn't have pulled this off without help. And you're the prime suspect."

"If I were involved," Hammond observed, "you could hardly expect me to admit it."

Woodburn stared at him, his sharp eyes drawing tight. "I guess Kinsey's right," he said at last. "You really have lost all respect for the principles of—"

"Senator Kinsey," Hammond snapped, his control starting to slip, "doesn't give a damn about principles, let me tell you that. What he's doing here with this alien technology is—" Woodburn's start of surprise derailed Hammond's thoughts. He nodded slowly. "So, he hasn't told you about that then?"

Recovering, Woodburn retreated behind the desk. "My brief is to clean out this base," he said gruffly, "and to return it to a proper level of discipline and accountability."

"Ask Kinsey what's happening on Level 17," Hammond urged. "Ask him about the *sheh'fet*, about the prisoners being transferred onto the base. Better still," he added after a moment's thought, "don't ask. Find out for yourself."

Woodburn frowned, conflict knitting his brow. "My brief is to—"

"To hell with your brief!" Hammond growled, leaning across the desk. "Remember your oath, General – to protect the Constitution from enemies, both foreign and domestic. Kinsey's playing with fire, and the only thing standing between it and the rest of this planet is the SGC." Lowering his voice, he added, "Why do you think he wanted me out of here?"

Silence.

Stepping back, Hammond took a deep breath. "Colonel O'Neill and Major Carter are good people. Kinsey has sent them to their deaths on Kinahhi. Does that sound like the principles of the United States Air Force?"

Woodburn frowned, his craggy features shadowed in the ill-lit room. He was uncertain, that was for sure. Confused. Hell, who wouldn't be, walking into this mess?

"Start digging," Hammond pressed. "Find out the truth yourself, if you don't believe me. But whatever you do, don't just sit there. We're the last line of defense, General. And as a good man once said, the barbarians really are at the gate."

From orbit, Kinahhi was a rainbow world. The bright blue of wide oceans collided with rich greens on one continent, and dark, dusky reds and ochre on the another. A few clouds scurried beneath them, but it was a world bathed in the light of its massive, cool sun.

"It's funny," Daniel said, studying the planet below. "I guess when we arrive someplace through the Stargate, I always imagine the whole planet being just like that one little corner." He sat back, watching as Teal'c brought the ship into a declining orbit. "I mean, anyone who'd arrived through the Antarctic gate would think Earth was an ice planet!"

Teal'c raised an eyebrow, apparently less than impressed by Daniel's observation. "The Goa'uld ensure that populations do not grow to threatening levels on the worlds they control."

"That makes sense, I guess."

"Which means," Teal'c continued, "such civilizations as exist on these worlds are indeed clustered around the Stargate."

"But on the worlds where the Goa'uld have lost their power…" Daniel peered out the window as their ship skimmed low over parched land, ragged mountains eroding into dusty plains. "I guess no one lives in this— Wait!" Stretching out for miles were the bones of a city. An ancient city, crumbling away into the sand. But from this height he could see causeways, roads, the foundations of massive structures. "Wow," he breathed. "Would you look at that…"

Teal'c spared a momentary glance from the ship's controls. "It appears to be an abandoned city, Daniel Jackson."

"Oh yeah," he nodded, feeling the familiar itch to get down there and touch it all. "But look at the scale of it. It's huge. I mean, we're talking about something the size of…I don't know, a big city. A *big* city." Nose pressed against the window, he tried to drink in the details. The roads were wide and paved. Some of the buildings still stood tall and elegant, their rounded outlines almost organic in design. The itch turned into a tingle of familiarity, as if he were poised on the cusp of making a hugely important connection. Damn, what he wouldn't give for five minutes in those ruins!

Teal'c cast him a sideways glance, as if reading his mind. "I believe it is unlikely that O'Neill or Major Carter are being held within the remains of this city."

"Yeah." Daniel sank back in his seat, repressing his compulsive desire to explore. "I know. I don't think the Kinahhi are even on this continent."

"No," Teal'c agreed. "There are no signs of technology. We must search the other continent."

Within a matter of moments they had crossed the ocean and were skimming across verdant green plains toward a distant white glitter. "Kinahhi," Daniel breathed, almost as astonished as he had been at the lost city. "Look at the size of it!" Small habitations – villages? Towns? – merged together until, as far as the eye could see, there was nothing but the square, white buildings Daniel remembered from their first visit to this world. "It takes up half the continent."

Lower now, Daniel caught sight of Kinahhi ships skimming over rooftops, like insects buzzing around a soda can. Too many to count. "You're sure our shields are working?"

"If they were not," Teal'c observed, "we would already have been detected."

Good point. "Let's hope they last all the way to Tsapan."

"I believe they will," Teal'c replied, gesturing through the window. "Look."

Following the direction, Daniel saw it, glittering like a pharaoh's jewels above the ocean. The sight tightened the knot in his gut, dread and anticipation mixing in a volatile brew. Somewhere, down there, Jack and Sam were hidden beneath the extravagant beauty of the city. He refused to think how they might be suffering. Now that the waiting was over he banished everything but the present from his mind. "I'll go get ready," he said, swinging out of the co-pilot's seat and darting into the cargo hold.

"Hang on guys," he muttered, as he pulled on his tac vest and double-checked his P90. "We're coming to get you."

The stench was the first thing that hit Jack as the doors opened. Rank and putrid, it reeked of unwashed bodies – and worse. For a moment his mind slipped, catapulted back to the four months he'd spent in that stinking, Iraqi jail before—

"Urgh!" Carter recoiled, nose wrinkling.

Jack shot Kenna a black look. "Civilized."

The Commander flinched at the rebuke, but didn't comment. "Follow," he said, leading the way.

With gritted teeth, Jack followed, Carter falling in at his side. If it had been gloomy outside, inside was worse. Makeshift lamps were strung across the ceiling like rancid Christmas lights, thick cables trailing toward a noisy generator. "There's no power down here," Carter murmured. She sounded like she was breathing through her mouth.

Kenna led them along a narrow corridor, as damp and cold as the alley outside. At its end, the light was brighter. And the stench was worse.

"What the hell is this?" Jack growled.

"It is the price we pay for our security." Unsteady with doubt, the Commander's reply drifted back to him through the darkness.

"Is it worth it?"

There was no answer. But they were almost at the end of the corridor now, and it opened up into a wide, round room. Kenna's bulk blocked his view, and Jack found himself hanging back. Carter, too, slowed to a halt. Behind them, their escort bunched up and he could hear the rapid, nervous breathing of the soldiers. "You know," Jack muttered, "I really don't want to know what's in there."

Kenna turned, silhouetted by the dim light from the room beyond. "Colonel O'Neill, you must—"

"Nah," Jack shook his head. "You know, I don't think so. I appreciate the tour. Really. It's been great." He backed up a step. "But I think we'll just head to the gift shop now."

The Commander said nothing, his face lost in shadows, but he gave a slight nod. A hand seized Jack's arm, the contact triggering claustrophobia and panic like a touch paper. With a furious grunt he spun around and brought his cuffed fists up under the soldier's chin. The man dropped with a satisfying thud. Carter lashed out the moment he struck, but chained as they were it was a futile gesture of defiance. The butt of a weapon crunched against the back of his skull, and he fell to his knees through a cascade of stars. The cold water soaking his pants kept him focused, as rough hands dragged him back to his feet and held him there.

"So, you do know fear?" Kenna's face was close to his, voice quiet and intense.

Jack spat a mouthful of blood onto the floor. It was the only answer he would give. Out of the corner of his eye, he saw Carter struggling uselessly against two men holding her arms. A dribble of blood leaked from a cracked lip, but otherwise she seemed okay. For now.

Without another word, Kenna turned away and walked into the room beyond. Jack was pushed into motion after him, heart racing as the stench of human misery washed over him with sickly warmth.

CHAPTER SEVENTEEN

With as much grace as their damaged ship could muster, Teal'c landed it in a vacant courtyard under the soaring spires of Tsapan. Its engines hummed, spiking from their usual frequency with alarming regularity, reminding him that their power was failing. If he left the stealth device armed, their chances of regaining enough velocity to escape the planet's gravity would be slim. If he did not, however...

"Did you hear that?" Daniel Jackson was craning his neck in an endeavor to see the sky. "I thought I heard something."

"A Kinahhi transport, perhaps?" If such a ship were to pass over the uncloaked *tel'tak* then they would lose any chance of escape. Teal'c's fingers hovered over the control, then withdrew. He would leave the ship hidden and hope they returned before the engines were entirely drained of power. Indeed, if they did not return by such time, it was likely that they would not return at all.

Standing up, he turned to face his friend. Daniel Jackson wore the expression of nervous anticipation Teal'c had seen on the faces of countless young warriors, yet in this man it was tempered by experience. There was no bravado to the eagerness, merely the unvoiced hope that they would see their teammates once more. "Are you ready, Daniel Jackson?"

"As I'll ever be."

"The *tel'tak* will not remain cloaked for more than a few hours," Teal'c told him as they walked together to the ship's hatch.

"Then I guess we'd better hurry." Determinedly, Daniel Jackson hit the controls and jumped from the ship.

Teal'c followed, breathing in the salty tang of sea air as the cold wind battered at his face. Behind him, the hatch disappeared into nothingness and they were alone in the center of a derelict courtyard. He glanced at his watch, setting the alarm for three hours. Much beyond that and the *tel'tak* would never leave orbit. Next to him, Daniel Jackson was scanning the dark edges of the courtyard, looking for an exit. "That way?" he said, pointing. "Looks like it goes down."

Teal'c had no reason to object and with a resolute stride headed out across the plaza. "Stay in the shadows," he advised as they reached the walls of a high tower, "so that we are not seen from above."

Daniel Jackson glanced up hurriedly. "Come on," he said. "And keep your eyes out for anything that looks like writing. Maybe Tourist Information put up a map, huh?"

Perhaps, if fortune were flowing in their favor. But of late, Teal'c thought bleakly, fortune had blessed the enemy.

At first, Sam couldn't understand what he saw in that large round room. She blinked, trying to make sense of the tangle of bleached limbs and flickering technology. Then she made out the faces – mouths stretched into silent screams, eyes wide and sightless, sunken into the leathery features of the almost-dead.

Bile rose in her throat. "Oh God…"A hand clamped around each arm, fingers like a vise, pulling her forward. "No!"

She hated herself for hissing the denial, hated sounding so afraid as the soldiers dragged her toward that obscene heap of machine and perverted humanity. But the sight turned her stomach, leeching heat from her body until she was clammy with disgust and terror.

Like a monstrous spider's nest, the thing held its victims, drilling into their minds with silken threads that spread across each temple and wormed under pallid skin. Iron clamps trapped limbs, tearing through the tattered remains of clothing. There must have been fifty, sixty – a hundred – souls lost in that tangle of dying flesh and merciless technology. "No…"

"Kenna!" The Colonel barked the word, short and brittle with rage. "You sonofabitch. What the hell is this?"

The Commander stood with his back to the hellish scene, his nose flaring with revulsion. His eyes betrayed him, though. Sam saw self-loathing in their depths, and fear. Fear of what lay in this room. "The *sheh'fet*," was all he said.

Her mind was sluggish with shock, but Sam forced it to work. The *sheh'fet*? From a single point in the ceiling an elegant lattice fanned out, curving in an intricate design and glowing with a faint violet light. Each delicate curlicue ended in a vulgar, metal bolt. Two technologies rammed together. From those iron bolts cascaded the tangle of wires that entrapped the wretched victims – of which she would soon be one. Thrusting the thought aside, she said, "This is how it works, sir. The *sheh'fet*. How it reads minds." She turned to Kenna for confirmation. "It harnesses the power of the human mind, uses it to interpret complex human emotions. To discern a threat."

A slight movement of the head was all the corroboration she got, but she hardly needed more. She was closer now. The stench was overwhelming, and she had to fight the urge to gag. Turning her head away, she breathed through her mouth.

The Colonel was doing the same at her side, his chest rising in short, shallow breaths. "When I get my hands on Crawford…"

"I'll be right behind you, sir."

A sudden, crushing pain in her right arm made her gasp; one of the metal clamps had tightened around it. *Shit!* Another bit into her right leg, and she tried to yank herself free in a burst of involuntary panic. The vise only tightened further.

"Carter." The Colonel was watching her. His own limbs were also trapped, sinewy metallic cables trailing from the vises back into the spider's nest. "Fight it," he ordered her. "Don't give a god-damn inch."

"No, sir." Following orders – she could do that.

One of the Kinahhi men released the shackles that had bound her arms and legs as a soft metallic hiss filled the air. Stepping hurriedly back, he cast Sam a swift look. She saw pity in his pale eyes, and it made her shiver. For a moment, she and the Colonel were alone, both held tight by the *sheh'fet*. He looked at her steadily. *Fight it, Carter.* She heard the words as clearly as if he'd said them. *Fight it!*

And then suddenly she was moving, yanked backward and up by the brutal machine that had seized her arms and legs. She was being sucked into the heart of the *sheh'fet*. She screwed her eyes shut, recoiling as soft leathery skin brushed against her hands and face. Foul breath, and worse, washed over her, and somewhere above she could hear the vociferous cursing of the Colonel. She barely dared open her eyes when the movement stopped, but fifteen years in the field had taught her the value of tactical information.

However bad the situation, it was always better to know *exactly* how bad.

Cautiously, she peeled open an eyelid. A face, stretched into a voiceless scream, stared at her sightlessly from no more than four inches away. Its faint breath was putrid, lips peeled back from decaying teeth. With a shudder Sam turned her head, looking past emaciated limbs and out into the room beyond. She was about ten feet from the floor, her arms and legs both pulled viciously behind her and something hard – she dared not imagine what or who – dug into her back. The Kinahhi Commander stood watching, his gaze darting to a place a couple of feet above her. Colonel O'Neill, she guessed. Kenna seemed tense, arms folded across his chest. Waiting. Waiting for the worst. What that might be, she could only—

Something crawled across her face. Spidery trails of fire, tracing along her cheek and up toward her temple. She flinched away, closer to the cadaverous face next to her, and squeezed her eyes shut. The sensation was all over her face now, burning like acid. Burning deeper, into her skin. Through her skin. Into her mind. Burning... But not acid now, something else. A knife, digging deep, scraping around in her mind, tearing it out. The pain seethed, burning and scraping and digging. Every moment growing more intense, more powerful. Filling her mind until the pressure fractured her skull and the molten pain exploded through the cracks.

Sam felt her mouth contort into a scream of despair. But she heard no sound. Heard nothing, felt nothing but a blaze of agony blasting through her mind, liquefying memory and pumping it out into a fathomless river of savaged consciousness. Her memories joined those of a hundred minds ripped bit by bit from their human husks.

Fight it. Somehow, the Colonel's words came to her through the fire. *Don't give them a goddamn inch.*

I can't... The pain overwhelmed everything. The fire scorched it all away. No one could fight this.

Fight it! Brutal, uncompromising, his order floated in the maelstrom like a life raft. She clung to it with the last shreds of her sanity.

Daniel trailed a hand along the damp walls as they descended into the depths of Tsapan. His previous visit had been shrouded in a blinding headache, but this time his mind was clear and he could sense the ambience of the city as if it were a living thing. Opulence, extravagance, and death. Tsapan had known them all, layered one atop the other; the Kinahhi inhabitation of the city grafted over the decaying remnants of Baal's occupation. He'd had a chance to familiarize himself with the Kinahhi script while back on Earth and saw it now scrawled on many of the walls. Signposts, mostly, in this city of alleys and steep, endless stairways.

His fingers brushed over a raised pattern as he passed, and Daniel stopped. The shape of the cartouche was familiar. "Teal'c," he called softly. "I might have found something."

Teal'c retraced a few steps. "What have you found?"

"A sign." Daniel peered closer and wished he had a flashlight. "It's Kinahhi, the script is a type of cuneiform, although far more sophisticated. It says, roughly, 'This way Judgment lies'."

Teal'c raised an eyebrow, awaiting further explanation.

"Judgment," Daniel explained, glancing up at his friend, "or, in Kinahhi, *sheh'fet*."

Studying the narrow stairway, Teal'c readjusted his hold on the P90 he carried. "That path offers little cover, should we be attacked from above or below."

Daniel had to agree. "But it's the best lead we have."

"The *sheh'fet*," Teal'c reminded him, "is nothing more than a security checkpoint."

Nodding, Daniel returned his attention to the cartouche. "You're right, but here," he pointed to the inscription, "the word *sheh'fet* is, in effect, capitalized. As if to imply not 'a *sheh'fet*' but 'the *Sheh'fet*.'" He straightened, shivering slightly in the chill air. "Do you see what I mean?"

The blank look on his friend's face provided a silent answer.

Daniel peered down the shadowy stairway. "Jack and Sam are here as prisoners, to be judged. Right?" Teal'c acknowledged the point with a bow. "If it's nothing else," Daniel continued, "the *Sheh'fet* – capital 'S' – is a place of judgment."

"I see." Teal'c shifted the gun in his hands again, perhaps missing the reassuring weight of his staff weapon. "Let us hope," he added in a low voice, "that it is not also a place of execution."

Daniel said nothing as he followed Teal'c down the narrow

stairs. Up above, the wind whistled between the towers, their tops glittering brightly in the morning sunlight. Yet here, far below, all he felt was the damp chill of dread.

"Fall in," Commander Kenna barked, his voice cutting through the mesmerizing horror of the *sheh'fet* and pulling his men back to their senses. Resolutely, they returned to marching formation, eyes fixed straight ahead. Most were grateful, he suspected, to be escaping the charnel house – and happy to forget the price Kinahhi paid for its security. "Move out." His men obeyed with alacrity, but Kenna hesitated before following. His gaze was drawn to the faces of the aliens by some emotion he dared not explore.

Major Carter's features were contorted into a grimace, as if frozen mid-scream. Her eyes were screwed tightly shut, limbs rigid. He could tell she was fighting, he had seen many try. None succeeded, and he believed their torment to be greater while they struggled against the inevitable. Weaker minds succumbed faster, and soon became insensible to their own suffering. So much the better for them.

"Oh…*God*…" The strangled cry came from above, startling the Commander from his thoughts.

O'Neill! He thrashed in his bonds, head battering from side to side. How was this possible? Could his mind be so strong? Kenna had never seen anyone resist the *sheh'fet* enough to utter a single word. Taking a step closer, he stared at the man. O'Neill's face was wretched, the tendrils of the machine worming beneath his skin, and yet he moved, he spoke. He— *opened his eyes.*

Kenna stumbled back in shock, almost losing his footing. Dark, alien eyes stared at him, full of hatred and pain. O'Neill's lips moved, as if he would speak, but then he was seized in an agonized spasm, back arching and eyes rolling. His face stretched into the familiar rictus and for the first time Kenna tasted the true horror of the moment. He was watching the man die. A good man, a soldier.

He killed Saulum…

A soldier. Fighting for his people, fighting for his life. Kenna had done as much in the name of his country. He had done worse. And this man, this soldier, did not deserve such a fate. Worse than the death of beasts bred for meat. Oppressed by sudden, heartsick shame, Kenna turned and fled. He fled from what he had done, from what his people were doing. He fled into the darkness of Tsapan and knew that there was no light to be found. No escape from the horror at the heart of his world.

Daniel's feet were wet. Not for the first time in the past seven years, he wondered how it was possible for the Air Force to be able to construct a ship as complex as the *Prometheus*, and yet be unable to supply a boot that didn't leak.

With a sigh he squelched on, keeping his attention locked on Teal'c. It was darker down here, in the pits of Tsapan's belly, and he didn't plan on getting separated from his friend. In this maze of decay, it would be—

Teal'c stopped suddenly, raising a hand to signal silence. Carefully, Daniel crept forward. He could hear it too; someone was coming up the steps. More than someone. Half a platoon, at least. Smooth walls lined the alley – no doors, no escape – and nothing but a turn in the stairway hid them from view. "This isn't looking good."

"It is not." Teal'c's eyes ranged higher, scanning the tower walls until he raised an arm and pointed. "There."

It was a small, dark window. And it was at least twelve feet above the stairs. "There's no way we can—"

"If we do not, we will be captured." Teal'c's dark eyes were intent. "I will not allow that to happen."

Daniel raised an eyebrow. "Unless you're planning to grow wings…"

"Follow," Teal'c said, taking the stairs two at a time until he stood beneath the small window. Below them, the marching sound grew louder. Bracing his back against the wall, Teal'c formed a cradle with his hands. "You must stand on my shoulders, Daniel Jackson."

Squinting up at the broken window, Daniel had his doubts. But, as Teal'c had pointed out, they were short of options. However, the real question on his mind was, "How will you get up?"

His friend's face remained inscrutable.

"Teal'c?" Daniel folded his arms, stubbornly ignoring the approaching soldiers. "I won't leave you here."

"If one of us escapes—"

Daniel shook his head. "Nope."

With a frown, Teal'c looked away, then back at him. "Very well. I did not suggest this, as it will hinder the speed of our escape. But, if I were to climb first…"

"You could pull me up after you. Sounds like a plan."

Teal'c looked unconvinced. "If the soldiers arrive before I am able to—"

"Then I guess we'd better hurry." Nudging him out of the way, Daniel braced himself against the wall and cradled his hands as his friend had done. "Come on, let's go."

With a final, serious look, Teal'c settled his foot in Daniel's hands. "O'Neill would not approve this plan."

"Sure he would," Daniel grunted, as Teal'c heaved himself up. The effort of supporting the man's weight yanked at the wrecked tendons in his left shoulder, shooting hot bolts of pain into his neck and down his arm. He grimaced. "No one gets left behind, right?"

Teal'c didn't answer. His other foot landed on Daniel's right shoulder, and he pushed up again. The hard sole of his boot bit into Daniel's collarbone, cold water soaking through his shirt as he staggered under the uneven weight. Damn, he was heavy! "You need to cut out the donuts," he hissed, wincing as Teal'c's other foot landed on his injured shoulder.

"I can reach the window!" There was triumph in Teal'c's voice, and suddenly the weight was gone. Daniel ducked out from beneath his friend as, slowly, Teal'c hauled himself up, feet braced against the slick wall of the tower, arms bulging with effort.

In the distance, Daniel heard a sharp bark. "Teal'c, hurry!"

Grabbing hold of the window frame, Teal'c braced one knee on the sill and then elegantly dropped out of sight into the dark room. Daniel edged closer to the wall, watching the stairs disappear around the corner. Waiting. Was there time? Teal'c could get away, and he'd have a good chance of finding Jack and Sam. Better than if—

"Daniel Jackson." Teal'c was leaning out of the window, one arm extended. But just as he spoke, the first ranks of soldiers turned the corner. With a shout, they started running up the stairs toward him. Their time was measured in seconds. "Climb!"

Daniel hesitated. "Go, you can—"

"Do not make me return to retrieve you, Daniel Jackson!"

Having no doubt his friend would do just that, Daniel took a couple of steps back – as far as the cramped stairway would allow – and ran, propelling himself into the air. His fingers clasped Teal'c's outstretched arm around the wrist, but the shock of the impact sent pain, like hot needles, driving through his left shoulder. Breath exploded from his lungs in a grunt of agony, but he held on. *Can't let go. Can't let go!* Feet scrabbling against the wall, he felt Teal'c start hauling him up like a sack of grain.

"This is insane!" he hissed, both hands wrapped around Teal'c's arm.

His friend couldn't answer. The tendons were standing out in his neck, face contorted with effort. Suddenly an explosion hit the wall, showering them both with grit.

"Halt!" a voice shouted from below. "Move no further!"

Daniel looked up, right into his friend's eyes. There was no question. Teal'c kept pulling. Another explosion hit, nearer this time.

"I said *halt!*"

But the window was getting closer, he'd almost made it and—

A hand seized his ankle and yanked. The extra weight was too much for Daniel's weak left shoulder; with an agonizing wrench it slipped out of its socket. His scream was unstoppable, holding on impossible. He let go.

"Daniel Jackson!" Teal'c seized his other arm with both hands. "Climb!"

Nausea clawed at his throat, the pain graying the edges of his mind. He couldn't focus, couldn't hear above the sound of blood rushing in his ears. Consciousness was ebbing away, he was falling backward… "No!" He kicked out, felt his boot connect with a head. There was a grunt, and he was free. "Teal'c," he slurred through the pain. "Pull!"

How long it took, he had no idea. Eternity. A few seconds. It all blended together into a red stream of pain, accompanied by angry shouts. A bright blast. Stinging grit in his eyes. And then rough hands seized his shoulders and he was dragged forward into damp, decaying darkness.

CHAPTER EIGHTEEN

The pain was unbearable, like fire or acid burning into his mind. Acid and daggers. Bright white light… *Oh God, not there. Not there again.* The memory surfaced and was swallowed. Washed away. No, this pain wasn't white. It was red. Fiery red, scorching, obliterating. He could feel its heat, as if standing before a blast furnace. From a distance. A fire, streaming past. Like lava. *Lava streaming down the sides of the mountain as the moon bled to death, annihilating everything. Swallowing the Stargate, the kids, Carter—*

He jerked awake. Not there. He wasn't there either. His eyes opened, the stench of putrefaction and human degradation filling his mouth and nose. His arms and legs were pinned out, like a lab rat's. But his mind was clearing, the pain was receding. Acid neutralized. *Cooperation will be rewarded.* He cursed silently at the memory, pushing it back into the singed, tender parts of his mind. He felt raw, as if he'd left his brain out in the sun for too long. But he was okay, he knew it instinctively. He was himself. And if he was okay…

"Carter?" His voice sounded weak, and he cleared his throat. "Carter?"

Nothing. Turning his head, he tried to get a visual on her, but all he could see were the sinewy, half-dead faces of his fellow captives. He gritted his teeth, but didn't shy away. He'd seen death before, many times. His head was filled with images of humanity's inhumanity, and he filed this one along with the rest. Deal with it later. Or never. Whatever worked. What mattered now was getting the hell out of Dodge.

"Carter?" he called again, pulling fruitlessly at the metal clamps that held him in place. *Damn it, why wasn't she answering?* He hoped – prayed – that she'd gotten out already. Maybe she'd gone for help? *Yeah, right. Gone for help where, exactly?* Even his stubborn optimism had its limits. "Carter!" He yanked at his bonds again, but they were immovable and just bit deeper.

There was no way he was going anywhere unless—

With a sharp metallic click the pressure on his arms and legs was gone. He had half a second to think *Cool!* before he started falling. The ten-foot drop was cushioned by numerous limbs, iron clamps and bits of meaningless machinery, and Jack hit the stone floor with a grunt. Today was just full of surprises.

Pushing himself into a low crouch, he glanced around cautiously. The room was empty, except for the victims of the Kinahhi's life-sucking fortune-telling machine. No soldiers. No guards. Who'd want to stay here anyway, watching people die like this?

Slowly he rose, wincing at the sharp pain in his right knee. He had no idea why he'd been released, although he half suspected Kenna was responsible. "Carter?" he called her name again, still hoping she'd already been freed. But there was no reply – in truth, he knew her too well to think she'd leave him trapped in that thing. At least, not if she had a choice.

Keenly aware of the sound of his footfalls in the quiet room, he started to circle the *sheh'fet*. If she was still trapped in it, he had to know. He had to get her out. He didn't see the faces or the skeletal arms and legs; they passed by in a blur of nameless, shapeless revulsion. He wasn't looking at them, he was looking for something else. Someone else. The green of her uniform, torn and bloody beneath iron clamps, her hair falling lank against an ashen face, screaming in silent horror… "Carter!"

She was ten feet above him, back arched and mind lost. Thin red tendrils, like a spider's web, traced her cheeks and temple, spilling out and looping through the tangle of wires and cables, up into the vastness of the machine. Destroying her. Killing her.

He looked around for something – anything – to use to free her. There was nothing. Screw it. Doggedly blind to everything he touched, Jack climbed up the human machine. "Carter!" he barked, reaching past another rigid body to slap her face. "Come on, Carter. Snap out of it." Nothing. Not a flicker. Desperate, he turned his attention to the clamps on her arms. They wouldn't budge but were attached by cables no thicker than his finger. He grabbed one and pulled, yanking it ferociously, trying to break it. Nothing.

Perhaps if he could wake her? Shifting closer, ignoring the feel of clammy skin against his face, ignoring the putrid breath of the half-dead creatures that surrounded them, he reached out tentatively to touch the gossamer threads that had invaded her mind. "Crap!" He recoiled, the pain sharp as a bee sting. But not nearly enough to stop him. Ignoring the biting pain, he grabbed the spider's web and pulled.

Carter's scream curdled his blood. It was agonized, inhuman, and it didn't stop. He jerked back, lost his footing and slid down the side of the *sheh'fet*. His boot grazed the face of one of the other lost souls, thin blood beading where the skin was torn. Jack backed away, horrified. What had he done to her? Carter kept on screaming, desperate as a trapped animal. And then the alarms started to wail, so loud he clamped his hands over his ears. Every damn soldier in the city had to be on his way!

Logic told him he had to leave. Go hide, come back later when he might have some chance of pulling her out of the nightmare. It went against everything he believed in, but he was soldier enough to do the right thing. Whatever the cost.

"Fight it!" he yelled, backing toward the door. "Fight it Carter. I'll be back. I swear to God, I'll be back."

And with that he turned and ran, out into the decaying city.

Sirens wailed, a mournful note of warning loud enough to block out all thought. Teal'c crouched low beneath the window, shielding Daniel Jackson from the masonry blasted free by the energy weapons of the Kinahhi. His friend was unconscious, his left shoulder twisted once more from its socket. Teal'c cursed silently. He should have insisted that Daniel Jackson flee alone.

Beneath the window the soldiers still lingered, although the noise of the sirens masked their movements. It mattered little, for the alarm called all in Tsapan to alert. The Kinahhi would hunt them, and the advantage of familiarity in this alien city was all theirs. One thing was certain; he had to remain ahead of his enemy. Taking care to protect Daniel Jackson's shoulder, Teal'c carefully lifted him and rose to his feet. The burden was not inconsiderable. Unsure of the floor's strength, Teal'c stepped warily through the damp room and approached the door.

The corridor beyond was empty and dark, and he could discern a staircase leading downward. It was the direction in which he needed to travel, despite the likelihood of the Kinahhi waiting at the bottom. For a moment, he hesitated. But time was running away, like warm sand through his fingers, and soon the shield hiding the *tel'tak* would fail. The engines would have insufficient power to break free of the planet's gravitational pull, and escape would be impossible.

Shifting the limp form of Daniel Jackson over his shoulder, Teal'c pulled a *zat'ni'katel* from his waistband and headed resolutely down the stairs.

The rough and ready lights looping down the corridor led Jack back to the iron doors through which he and Carter had been dragged only hours before. Bracing a shoulder against cold metal, he heaved them open and gratefully slipped out into the fresh air beyond. But the stink of the *sheh'fet* still clung to his clothes, reminding him of what – and whom – he'd left behind. As if he could forget.

Cautiously, he studied the cramped staircase. Vast towers rose up on each side, gaping black windows staring down like blind eyes, concealing secrets. He wondered if they concealed snipers too. Moving as quietly as possible, sticking to the shadows, Jack began to climb the stairs and tried to formulate a plan.

First he needed a weapon, which meant taking out a couple of Kinahhi the old-fashioned way. Then he needed to find out more about the *sheh'fet*, and to figure out a way to free Carter. The memory of her scream echoed in his mind, mingling in his memory with the wail of the sirens that still rang through the empty towers. Was she still screaming too?

Refusing to contemplate the answer, he kept climbing. Up ahead, the stairs turned and he slowed, flattening himself against the wall and peering carefully around the corner. His caution was justified. A little knot of soldiers stood staring up at a small, broken window in one of the towers. Their weapons were at the ready, and even from this distance Jack could see the scorched evidence of weapons fire around the window frame. Someone was up there. Or something. *Clutching white fingers in the dark, coming out of nowhere...* White, gristly fingers. Skeletal limbs. Cadaverous faces. Now he knew what they were, those things that had attacked him and Carter last time they'd visited Baal's pleasure dome. Escapees. Or rejects. Or survivors. Others, like himself perhaps, spat out by the machine. Only he'd been lucky; he was still human.

Repressing a shudder, he forced himself to focus on the half dozen Kinahhi ahead. He figured he had a couple of options. Retrace his steps and find a way around them. Or take them out. He had no weapon, which meant disarming at least one of them in the cramped confines of the stairway, then taking out the others – at short range, hopelessly outnumbered. As plans went, it sucked.

He ducked back around the corner. He needed to get off the stairs, to find an alternate route. There were no doors in the smooth walls of the towers, but there were windows. High windows.

Thoughtfully, Jack studied the wall. Its smooth surface was cracking, rivulets of water seeping beneath and swelling the plaster into crumbling blisters. With one finger he tested it, pulled a clump away to expose rough stone beneath. Over the years he'd done his fair share of free-climbing and if there were enough cracks in the crumbling brick face... The closest window was a dozen yards back down the steps, perhaps twenty feet up from the ground. A short climb, but a nasty fall onto the steep stairs below.

"Better not fall then," he muttered to himself, jogging down the stairs. He quickly removed his boots and socks, tied the laces together, and strung them through a belt loop. The bite of the icy water made him grimace, but without climbing shoes, bare feet would have to do. As long as they didn't go numb from the cold.

Rubbing his hands against his shirt to dry them as best he could, Jack studied the wall. There were a couple of patches of exposed brick, others of rotting plaster that looked treacherous. Twenty years ago, he thought ruefully, it would have been a breeze. But the universe had been a different place twenty years ago, and not all for the better.

Flexing his fingers, he spotted his first hand hold and reached for it. The stone was damp but coarse beneath his fingers, providing enough traction to pull himself up. Feet braced on the sliver of an edge between two exposed bricks, he let everything but the climb drift free from his mind and contemplated the next move.

"Ow! Holy— Goddamn, ow!"

Daniel shot upright, clutching at his arm, dizzy, disoriented and in pain. "What the hell…?"

A firm hand seized his arm. "Do not move, Daniel Jackson. You are well."

Teal'c? Vision blurred – why was his vision blurred? – Daniel peered through the darkness. A wailing noise, droning and muted, pulsed in the distance. It sounded like the keening of mourners. Confused he shook his head. Sunshine filtered into the room, indistinct shafts of light cutting through shuttered windows, glinting in Teal'c's eyes and making them glitter. "Where are we?" His memory was as blurred as his vision. The last thing he remembered was climbing…

"We are within a tower on Tsapan," said Teal'c slowly, his gaze roving restlessly around the room. "Your shoulder slid from its socket while you attempted to scale the building."

Ah. Yes. Daniel winced. "Right, it's all coming back to me now." Unfortunately.

"I took the liberty," Teal'c added quietly, "of resetting the joint while you remained unconscious." He paused for a moment. "The pain has roused you, however."

"Ya think?" He blinked again, rubbing at his misty eyes. Which was when he remembered he'd taken off his glasses. He fumbled for them in his pocket, relieved to find them still in one piece. Thank heaven for small mercies. Straightening the arms with his teeth, he slid his glasses one-handed onto his face. The world snapped into focus, and he realized they were sitting in a small room that would have been elegant once. The rotting remains of fabric sagged from the walls, graceful furniture lay scattered and broken on the floor. "Now what?"

Teal'c studied his face carefully. "Are you able to walk, Daniel Jackson?"

Good question. The pain in his shoulder was intense, radiating out in waves down his arm and across his back. Even breathing was difficult. Not that he had any intention of mentioning the fact to Teal'c. But his bravado didn't make him a fool. "My arm needs to be strapped."

Teal'c considered the problem for a moment. Then, with a rapidity and efficiency born of decades on the battlefield, he tore a strip from the hem of his shirt. Silently he unzipped the front of

Daniel's tac vest and, as carefully as possible, removed it. Even the slight motion sent agony shooting down Daniel's arm, but he gritted his teeth and made no sound. Fashioning a basic sling from the material, Teal'c tied it around Daniel's neck, then slid the tac vest back over Daniel's good arm. Wrapped around his injured arm, and zipped firmly shut, it did a good job of immobilizing the shoulder.

"Not bad," Daniel approved.

Standing, Teal'c offered his hand and pulled Daniel to his feet. The world spun queasily for a moment, but Daniel willed it to stop and forced a smile. He hoped it didn't look too sickly. "I'm okay."

Despite the skeptical lift of an eyebrow, Teal'c let it slide. 'Okay' was a relative term, and in this context they both knew what it meant. "I believe there are Kinahhi soldiers searching the building," said Teal'c, changing the subject. "Shortly after we escaped, the sirens began."

Sirens. That explained the noise. "Because of us?"

"Perhaps. The Kinahhi certainly know we are here. We cannot linger."

"No," Daniel agreed. "So, which way?"

"I had hoped," said Teal'c, "that you would know better than I."

Daniel shook his head. "Your guess is as good as mine. But... down? We need to get back to that staircase."

"Agreed."

Moving past him, Daniel was almost at the door when Teal'c stopped him with a hand on his arm. "Daniel Jackson?"

He turned. "Yeah?"

"There is another matter." Teal'c looked at his watch, face serious. "There is little over an hour remaining before the shield cloaking the *tel'tak* will deplete the power supply to such an extent that escape from this world will no longer be possible."

Daniel considered the information, sharing a long look with his friend. "I'm thinking," he said quietly, "that we're not leaving here without Jack and Sam anyway."

Satisfaction settled over Teal'c's face. "I concur."

"Good." Turning back toward the door, Daniel straightened his shoulders as best he could and said, "So let's go find them."

CHAPTER NINETEEN

Ambassador Crawford stood in the large, airy office belonging to Councilor Tamar Damaris and took a deep breath. Beyond the tall windows, pale gold sunlight glittered against the drab buildings of Kinahhi. It lent the place a transient beauty; even the plainest of women looked lovely in the right light.

At one of the windows stood Damaris herself, mind clearly preoccupied. The news he'd brought from Earth had not been well received, and she was endeavoring to recover her composure before resuming the conversation. At length she turned back toward him, her colorless eyes sharp but veiled. "And you say these men escaped no more than a day ago?"

Crawford inclined his head. "Yes, Councilor. They were traced to a world we designate as P3X-500, where they retrieved a stolen alien vessel. It is likely that they are on their way here."

"I confess myself surprised that such a thing might happen," Damaris said coldly, moving away from the window. "Were they not held in detention?"

An awkward question. "They were. However, we believe they were assisted by those within the SGC unsympathetic to our treaty." When Damaris's eyes narrowed, he hastily added, "You may be assured that the culprits will be apprehended and removed from the base entirely."

"It is a little late, is it not, for such precautions?" Her smooth brow contracted briefly. "I understand why Senator Kinsey was keen to be rid of these troublesome people. However," she offered a thin smile, "if they attempt to land their vessel on this world, we will detect and destroy them."

Crawford couldn't help but start. *Destroy?* "I believe Senator Kinsey wishes to—"

"This is our sovereign territory," Damaris interrupted curtly. "Intruders entering without permission will be destroyed."

"As is your right," he assured her, ignoring a cold squirm of doubt in the pit of his belly. The Kinahhi were a ruthless people, but that was no concern of his. Which brought him to another subject. "Senator Kinsey has asked me to pass on his thanks for the technology and expertise you have provided in regard to the *sheh'fet*. The test is proceeding well."

Relaxing slightly, Damaris nodded. "Yes, it is. We will soon be ready to expand the prototype. And in return…" Her head cocked to one side. "Has Senator Kinsey made any progress on the subject of our payment?"

Payment? His confusion must have been evident, and he cursed himself for being taken by surprise. "I— Ah, he hasn't—"

"The deportation program," Damaris prompted. "We have fulfilled our end of the contract, Ambassador, but have yet to receive any felons in return. Excepting Colonel O'Neill and Major Carter, of course."

Crawford stared, entirely derailed for the first time in many years. "I hadn't— Forgive me, I'm not privy to the Senator's dealings on that matter, Councilor." *Felons?* One of the Kinahhi had mentioned the idea, but he'd thought it an idle comment. Deporting prisoners to Kinahhi? There was no way the electorate would buy that! What the devil was Kinsey thinking, promising such a thing? The Councilor's suddenly suspicious gaze made it imperative for Crawford to cover his confusion. "I will certainly pass on your question to the Senator and provide you with a speedy answer," he hedged. *Damn it, if Kinsey thinks he can cross these people…* He forced a smile, but knew Damaris didn't buy it. She'd always been able to read him like a book.

"No," she said quietly, softly. "That will not be necessary. You can—"

A man abruptly burst into the room, eyes wild with panic. "Councilor!" he blurted, heedless of Crawford's presence. "The *sheh'fet*! There's been a disruption, the alarms are—"

"Silence!" Damaris snapped the word like a whip.

The intruder's mouth snapped shut with an audible click, his eyes fixed on Crawford. Tension filled the room like an electrostatic charge; Crawford could all but feel his hair standing on end.

Calmer, Damaris raised her voice and called, "Chief Officer, please come in."

A young, cold-eyed soldier appeared in the door, saluting

sharply.

"Escort the Ambassador to the guest quarters," said Damaris, with a hasty wave of her hand. "He will be staying with us."

Crawford blinked. *What?* "I— That won't be necessary, Councilor. I must return to Earth and discuss—"

Damaris ignored him, turning to face her anxious aide and talking to him in a very low voice. A strong, determined hand landed on Crawford's arm. "This way, please, Ambassador."

He tried to pull away, but the soldier didn't relent. "Let me go! You can't keep me here!"

"I believe we can," Damaris replied, sparing him hard look. "We will continue our discussion another time."

Standing his ground, he demanded to know the truth. "Am I your prisoner?"

"Not at all, Ambassador." She smiled with all the charm of a gecko. "You will be free to return home – as soon as we begin to receive payment for our services."

A hostage! Stunned, Crawford found himself pulled into motion by the Kinahhi soldier, his mind reeling. He, Ambassador Bill Crawford, right-hand man of Senator Kinsey, was being held hostage!

Heart thudding with fear, he was dragged from the room on shaky legs. A hostage? This was crazy. Kinsey would go insane. It would destroy the whole treaty, it would— *It would make him a goddamn hero*.

He smiled, despite his erratic, panicking heartbeat. There was nothing the electorate liked better than a bona fide hero... And once Kinsey got him the hell outta here, sent in some of those crack troops the SGC was always boasting about and taught these skinny aliens what happened when you messed with the US of A, then the world would be his oyster.

Former hostage, Bill Crawford. Hero. President Elect. His smile strengthened. *Watch out Washington, here I come!*

It was always halfway up that the real fear set it. Too far to jump back down, muscles beginning to burn with the effort, and utterly vulnerable. One slip... Jack fixed his mind on the next move. *Left, a small gouge in the exposed brick*. Focus. He stretched, fingers finding purchase and pulled up.

Once he was inside the building he'd stop to rest, figure out what to do next. Get himself armed. Damn, but he was thirsty though. If only he had some water.

He found a corner with his right foot, but his knee was protesting wildly. He pushed up again, fingers reaching for an inadequate sliver of brickwork. Heart pounding.

Don't fall!

His fingers slipped, he scrabbled for something else. A rough patch of plaster. It crumbled beneath his touch. Something else! A crook of stone, just below the window. Too far to lunge. His right hand started to tremble with the effort of maintaining its tenuous hold, his right knee screaming.

He was going to fall! If he could just reach the window…

It was quiet in the tower as Teal'c led the way down the spiraling staircase. His senses heightened by darkness and adrenaline, he caught every sound. The sigh of a breeze through broken glass, the slow drip of water. The creak of a distant door opening.

He froze, lifting a hand to halt Daniel Jackson.

"What?" his friend whispered.

Teal'c didn't answer, he just listened. Muted voices, their words unintelligible but the pattern of speech that of orders given and received. Then footsteps ascending. "Soldiers," he murmured.

"That's not good."

"It is not." Teal'c cast around for ideas. Many doorways led off from the stairway, but the Kinahhi would be foolish not to search them as they passed. "We must be ready to fight."

Daniel Jackson nodded. "You'd better take this," he whispered, indicating the P90 strapped to his tac vest. "I can't use it with one hand. I'll use the zat."

Below them, the footsteps drew nearer and the sharp slam of a door being kicked open reverberated up the stairwell, confirming Teal'c's guess. Each room would be searched. But they had time to prepare. "This way," he said quietly, opening a door and peering inside the room. Broken furniture was scattered across the floor. It would provide scant cover from the blast of a Kinahhi weapon, but at least it might afford them the element of surprise.

"We must be cautious," Teal'c warned his friend as he quietly closed the door. "In such confined surroundings—"

A faint grunt drifted through the shattered window.

Daniel Jackson's head snapped around. "What was that?"

"Perhaps they are attempting to scale the building?" If they faced attack on two fronts, they would have little chance of success.

Daniel Jackson moved warily toward the window and pressed himself flat against the wall. Cautiously, he peered out. His eyebrows shot up and a wide, astonished smile split his face. "You're not gonna believe this!"

He was clinging to life by his fingertips. Literally. His feet fumbled for purchase, the safety of the shattered window no more than a stretch above him if he could only get a foothold. Sweat beaded on his forehead, trickling down his face despite the damp chill. His hands were sweaty, trembling with the effort. He couldn't hold on, couldn't make it.

Yes you damn well can, O'Neill! Get your ass up there, you useless piece of—

Growling, he jammed his grazed and bruised feet against the crumbling stone, willed them to find a ridge, anything, to brace himself. There, under his left foot. Something, barely something. But his right hand was slipping anyway, and if he didn't move now...

Using the scarce leverage under his foot, he pushed up and threw himself at the window. Plaster crumbled beneath his weight, his foot slipped, scraping down the brick. His fingertips grazed the windowsill but he couldn't grab hold. He hadn't made it. He was falling!

No!

And then a strong hand seized his wrist, fingers like iron, wrenching his shoulder but holding him firm. Saving him. Gasping for air, Jack squinted up at his savior, and found himself staring into the troubled face of Commander Kenna.

"Damn it," Daniel hissed, pulling away from the window. "They've got him."

Orders drifted up the stairs, accompanied by the brief sound of a struggle. A heavy weight fell to the floor. Jack? He'd looked battered and bruised, clinging to the wall like a bug in a storm.

But he'd been close enough for Daniel to glimpse the look of utter defeat when Jack recognized his captor. "We have to get him out of there." Daniel skirted the overturned table and headed toward the door. "Come on, let's go."

Teal'c seemed to hesitate. Considering the odds, perhaps. But it was only momentary. His face hardened and he took hold of his weapon with both hands. "I will secure the stairway," he declared as Daniel pulled open the door. "Follow me."

Like a giant, stealthy cat, Teal'c crept out of their hiding place. The sounds of voices were clearer now, and Daniel thought he could make out the dry tones of Jack. Which meant, at least, that his friend was conscious. So far so good. Sticking close to the wall, Teal'c slipped silently down the stairs, Daniel on his heels. Another turn in the spiral hid the soldiers from view, and Teal'c slowed to a halt. Silently he motioned Daniel to stay where he was, while he slowly edged forward. Daniel barely dared to breathe, expecting an explosion of gunfire at any moment. The Jaffa stopped – the cat had sensed its prey – then gestured for Daniel to follow.

His strapped shoulder threw his balance off, but Daniel refused to let it hold him back. Drawing his zat, he moved to crouch behind Teal'c. Below them gaped a door, the faint sunlight drifting from the room beyond illuminating the dark stairs.

"Tie him," a voice snapped.

"Open your eyes, Kenna!" It was Jack, spitting tacks. "You know what's going on. That...that *thing*! That's how you protect your people? You're worse than those bastards planting the god-damn bombs! You're—"

The soft thud of fist-on-flesh cut off his words. "Silence."

What thing? Jack's voice had dripped with disgust, horror even. *What had he seen?*

"Tie him." Again, the same order. There was a scuffle; Jack had to be putting up a fight. The soldiers were distracted...

Teal'c pounced, fast and silent. In two steps he was down the stairs, hiding on one side of the door. Daniel was on the other, heart racing, and struggling for breath against the pain in his shoulder. But he gave Teal'c a swift nod – *I'm okay.* In reply, his friend's fingers started the count down. Three, two, one.

Go!

As one, they burst into the room. Teal'c's P90 dropped three men, two more fell to Daniel's zat. "Jack!" he yelled. "Get down!"

Teal'c opened fire on the remaining three soldiers. One of them managed to raise his weapon, its energy bolt searing past Daniel's face and blasting a hole in the wall behind them before Teal'c took the man down. Only one Kinahhi was left: the Commander. His weapon was raised, attempting to cover both Daniel and Teal'c. He looked pissed. "Stay back!" he snarled. "Or your friend will die."

"You will die first." Teal'c stalked closer, gun aimed at the Kinahhi officer.

Kenna mirrored the gesture, hard eyes meeting hard eyes. "I am prepared for my death. Are you, alien?"

Oh please. Sometimes there was only so much macho posturing Daniel could handle. He raised his zat and fired. Kenna crumpled in a spasm of blue light, and lay still. Teal'c cast him a thwarted look, lifting an eyebrow.

Daniel shrugged. "What? I thought we were in a hurry."

A low laugh suddenly filled the room. Jack was pushing himself to his feet, staring at his friends with astonishment and a rare, broad smile on his face. "Guys..." He took a quick look at Kenna's inert body and carefully stepped over it, shaking his head and still grinning. "Guys!" And suddenly, Daniel found himself wrapped in a firm – and quite painful – hug, being thumped repeatedly on the back. "How the hell did you get here?"

"Ah!" Daniel winced. "Ow! Shoulder."

Abruptly, Jack let go and took a hasty step back. He cleared his throat and turned to Teal'c. A slight twitch of an eyebrow warned him not to repeat the enthusiastic welcome. Jack contented himself with a manly pat on the shoulder. "Damn, I knew you'd come after us. Carter said you would. She—" And suddenly his grin dissolved.

Daniel frantically scanned the room. "Where is she? Where's Sam?"

"She's—" A shadow darkened his bruised features. "She's inside the *sheh'fet*."

Inside? "What do you mean?"

Jack just shook his head, yanking free the boots that dangled from his belt. "It's a machine. It's—" He cut himself off, meeting Daniel's gaze with a desperate look. "It's killing her, Daniel. And I don't know how to get her out."

CHAPTER TWENTY

George Hammond had been surprised by the request – that was how it had been phrased – from General Woodburn to stay on base during the investigation of the escape of SG-1. Hammond knew the man had no power to order him to remain, short of having him arrested for his part in the affair. But there had been something in Woodburn's eye – almost a knowing look – when he'd made the request that had instantly piqued Hammond's curiosity.

His curiosity, however, was not answered until the small hours of the following morning. At 0300 hours precisely, a swift rap on the door of the guest-quarters woke him. Groggy, he crawled out of bed and dragged on some clothes. If there was trouble afoot, he at least wanted to face it with his pants on. "Come in."

The door opened to reveal General Woodburn, who smoothly slipped into the room. His gruff face was guarded and lined with uncertainty. "I apologize for waking you," he said in a low voice. "But, as you suggested, I've been doing some digging."

The news hit like a splash of cold water and woke Hammond fully. "What did you find?"

"You're right, there's something going on here." Woodburn sighed, walking further into the room. "Over thirty prisoners have been transferred to the base, under no authority I recognize. And Senator Kinsey has barred all access to Level 17."

"That's where he's testing the Kinahhi *sheh'fet* technology."

"Alien technology?"

Hammond grabbed his shirt from the chair. "According to SG-1, it allows the government of Kinahhi to read the minds – the intentions – of its citizens. They use it as a kind of—"

"Thought police?"

Hammond raised an eyebrow. "That's the implication. Kinsey's keeping the details to himself."

"And you believe this is a threat to Earth?"

"Look, we don't know what the Kinahhi want," Hammond

admitted. "For all we know, this is how they take over a world. It might not be fast, but we've dealt with patient races before." He paused, and when Woodburn didn't answer, added, "Would you want to live in a world where the Joint Chiefs can read your mind?"

"No." It was a firm, swift answer. After moment, Woodburn continued in a lower voice. "I haven't been able to access Level 17. Truth is, I don't know who to trust on this base."

He was astute, Hammond conceded that much. Over the years, he'd come to pride himself on his ability to judge the measure of a man. His gut told him that General Woodburn was sound. "You can trust me."

With a slow nod, Woodburn appeared to come to a decision. "I want to take a look in that room, General. I have no one to send in my place, and you know this base as well as anyone."

If he was suggesting what Hammond thought he was suggesting... "Do you think a couple of old desk-jockeys are up to the job?"

A brief smile answered him. "Who's old, General?"

Hammond snorted a quiet laugh and held out his hand. "I like your style," he said. "And call me George."

"George?" Woodburn clasped his hand in a strong grip. "Shaun."

So much for Kinsey's attempt to circumvent the integrity of the Air Force. When it came down to the wire, there was a thin blue line standing between Earth and those that would threaten its survival. A line that men like Kinsey, behind their safe Washington desks, couldn't hope to comprehend. Usually it was defended by the men and women of the SGC's field units, but today it was Hammond's turn to step up to the plate. He hoped he could do his people justice.

With a nod to Woodburn, he headed for the door. "Let's get to work."

Is this an out-of-body experience? The question filled her mind as she drifted somewhere outside herself, and yet within at the same time. Half in, half out. There was pain too, but distant now. The fire that had burned her mind was far away, like a river on the horizon. She could feel its heat, knew it was scalding her body, but didn't feel the pain. *Am I dying?*

She didn't want to die. There were so many things she hadn't done, so many lives she hadn't led. *No one dies and wishes they'd spent more time at the office.* Who'd said that? Her Dad? Daniel? She couldn't remember.

"The tendrils are damaged." The voice came from far away too, unfamiliar and harsh. "Someone pulled them free."

"The woman?"

"No, impossible. See? Her arms are bound."

"Then the man tried to free her."

The man tried to free her. What did they mean? The Colonel, perhaps. But he was trapped in this horror too.

"Will they re-implant?"

"No." The harsh voice spoke again. "See? They are already being absorbed. But," something touched her face. She knew it, yet could hardly feel it. Almost as if she were watching, while her eyes remained shut. "On the left, they are intact. She is still connected."

"Is that enough?"

A pause. Uncertain. "I do not know. For now, we will leave her. When the *Kaw'ree* arrive, they will know."

The presence moved away, the voices becoming more indistinct. "The Commander thinks the man will make another attempt to free her."

"If he does, he's a fool." The harsh voice was angry now. Angry and triumphant. "He won't escape a second time."

Escape? Could it be the Colonel? A beat of hope floated into her dislocated mind, drifting on memory. *What was it he always said?*

No one gets left behind.

Running footsteps and a barked order echoed through the empty tower as distant flashlights pierced the darkness with bright, white blades. The chase was on.

"In here," Jack hissed, ducking through a doorway into a room crisscrossed with light seeping through its boarded up windows. "Get down."

Daniel and Teal'c followed, crouching behind him. All eyes were on the door, all weapons raised. All ears on the alert for pursuit. No one spoke, and in the darkness the only sound Jack could hear was Daniel's labored breathing; a nasty mixture of pain and exhaustion. *Your fault*, a small voice reminded him. *He wouldn't be here if you hadn't got your hands dirty. None of them would.*

He shifted and smothered the guilt. There was a time and a place for wallowing, and this wasn't it. "They're moving away," he breathed, focusing on the noises drifting through the abandoned building.

"They are moving downward," Teal'c added, lowering his weapon and relaxing a fraction. But his eyes fixed on Jack's with a knowing look.

Kenna was a smart guy, he wouldn't waste his resources on a search when he knew exactly what Jack would do next. "They're falling back to the *sheh'fet*."

With a stifled groan, Daniel turned until his back was against the wall and slowly slid to the floor. Eyes closed, he looked like he could sleep where he sat. He was probably already dozing; Daniel had long ago learned the knack of catnapping. Jack saw the same exhaustion in Teal'c, if better masked, and made a decision. "We'll rest for ten." Easing himself to the floor next to Daniel, he sank into a moment of deep fatigue. But he didn't close his eyes. He knew exactly what was facing him if he dared to drift toward sleep – tortured, cadaverous faces, stretched into silent, animal screams. The sound of Carter's inhuman howl, the pain contorting her face. And the stench of that place, the degradation and cruelty. He'd seen a hell of a lot of distasteful things in his time, but that—

"Jack?"

He almost jumped at the sound of Daniel's voice. "What?" *Damn it, focus O'Neill.*

"How did you get out?"

"Huh?"

Daniel was watching him with those shrewd eyes of his. "How did you get out of the *sheh'fet*?"

It wasn't a question Jack had considered, although he probably should have. He frowned and shrugged. "It just let me go."

Daniel's eyebrows lifted skeptically. "It let you go?"

"I didn't do anything," Jack assured him. "They strapped me in. And then—" He recoiled from the memory of that tidal wave of pain, refusing to examine it too closely. "It hurt. A lot. And then it didn't. Next thing I know, I'm wide awake and the damn thing just drops me."

He dragged one of the Kinahhi weapons onto his lap and began to examine it. Keeping his mind busy helped. No dwelling. If he could just get the stench of that place out of his nostrils…

"I knew you would fight it, O'Neill." Teal'c sounded satisfied, as if some kind of point had been proven. "Most likely your resistance to the device is what set you free."

Jack didn't reply and noted that Daniel's gaze darted away from him. He tried not to imagine what Daniel was thinking, although he had a good idea. Daniel knew the truth, better than anybody. Everyone broke in the end. And this time there'd been no resistance at all, just an overwhelming inferno of pain blasting through his mind like a blowtorch. If it hadn't simply stopped… Clearing his throat, Jack resumed his study of the Kinahhi weapon. "I don't think so, Teal'c." He ran his fingers along the firing mechanism, getting to know its shape and form. "Carter's still in there." Screaming, burning, dying. *Don't think about it.* His voice thickened. "She'd fight as hard as anyone."

There was a moment's silence, then Daniel spoke. "Maybe…" He paused, frowned, and rubbed at his injured shoulder. "Maybe there was something about you that it didn't like?"

There, a pressure point on the gun. Carefully Jack raised it, aiming away from Daniel and Teal'c. "Maybe I'm too dumb for it?" His forefinger tightened on the trigger. "Or maybe—" A short, red bolt of energy spat from the muzzle, blasting a neat hole in the wall. He winced at the noise and lowered the weapon. "Maybe it didn't like my sense of humor."

Teal'c gave an unimpressed lift of an eyebrow; it was clear he didn't approve of the impromptu weapons test.

Jack shrugged. "I found the trigger."

"That is fortunate," Teal'c replied dryly. "For now we shall require its use."

Ha-ha.

Jack stood, his feet sore from the climb. Not as sore as his dry throat, however. "Either of you guys got some water?"

Daniel shook his head. "We, ah, kinda left in a hurry," he explained. Then, indicating the P90 at Jack's side, added, "We only got the weapons courtesy of SG-13."

"Dixon?" That was unexpected.

"Long story," Daniel sighed, pushing himself awkwardly to his feet.

He grimaced as he moved, and Jack guessed his shoulder was a hell of a lot more painful than he was letting on. If it came to a fight... A creeping sense of dread ran icy fingers over his skin. "No Tylenol either, huh?"

Daniel just shrugged one shoulder, and tried to look like it didn't matter.

"Let's get this straight," Jack said, slinging the Kinahhi weapon over his shoulder, and stooping to pick up the P90. God, it felt sweet in his hands. But his disquiet didn't abate. "We've got no water, no food, a junker of a ship and only a couple of rounds of ammo?"

"And no backup," Daniel helpfully added. "And unless we get back to the *tel'tak* in about half an hour—"

"Twenty-seven minutes," Teal'c corrected, consulting his watch.

"Right. Twenty-seven minutes, then we'll have no way off the planet other than through the Stargate, which is in the center of the Kinahhi military compound and—"

"Ah!" Jack silenced him with a swift lift of his hand. "I get the picture." And it was a bad picture. Extremely bad. Worse than he'd realized, worse than he'd let himself believe. He suddenly found his chest tight, breathing short and painful. The walls of the small room seemed to crowd him, overwhelmingly claustrophobic.

Jack flexed his fingers around the P90, trying to draw comfort from its familiar weight. But there was none to be had. Truth was, going back for Carter would be insane. Kenna was no fool, he'd have the *sheh'fet* crawling with men. It was the perfect, irresistible trap. He'd be waiting for them, a spider in the web. And Carter was the bait.

"Damn it," he muttered, drawing a curious look from Daniel. He'd be a goddamn fool to walk into that ambush. And he'd be worse than a fool to lead an injured, insufficiently armed team into it.

No one gets left behind.

Bull. They had no supplies, no backup, no ammo. No water. Daniel was injured, they were all exhausted. The whole damn Kinahhi military were after them and in less than half an hour they'd have no way off the goddamn planet. Retreat and regroup. It was the only strategy that made sense.

But it's Carter.

Undead faces in living cadavers, rotting where they lay trapped, seeped like sin from his memory. To leave her there to die like that, to rot and— *No, never.* But—

I was sick to my stomach when I found out you were still alive.

The voice from the past was loud, and poignant as hell. Frank Cromwell. The man who'd left him behind, the man who'd left him to rot in a stinking Iraqi prison.

Someone dropped a dime on the incursion. You got hit, you went down.

The man he'd hated for a decade.

I made a judgment call to save the rest of the team.

To save the rest of the team. When it came to bitter, goddamn ironies… *I can't make that call,* he protested to a heedless universe. *Give me another option!*

But there was no answer.

"Jack?" Daniel's voice sounded troubled, as if he could see the path of Jack's thoughts. Knowing Daniel, he probably could.

Turning away, Jack edged closer to the door. "Get your stuff," he growled. "We're moving out."

Councilor Damaris gazed from the window of the shuttle as it circled once around the ornate onion dome that crowned the tallest tower on Tsapan. It was the only place in the city where she customarily set foot, and it was always with trepidation. But under the circumstances, she had little choice.

With practiced ease the pilot guided the ship into the small landing bay within the tower, and after taking a moment to collect herself, Damaris rose and stepped out. Around the courtyard's three walls ran a cloister, overshadowed by stooping arches that kept their secrets to themselves. Thus she was greeted only by silence. None of the denizens would appear, she knew, until the shuttle had left. Without looking back she listened to the quiet hum of the engines and sensed the emptiness behind her as the ship retreated. Sunlight filled the void, designed only to deepen the shadows within the cloistered walls.

A slight breeze caught her white gown, and she smoothed the fabric with both hands as she waited. Before long her escort revealed himself, emerging from the arcades as though he were a shadow himself. He was one of the *Mib'khaur*, selected to serve the *Kaw'ree*; a slight man, draped in dark velvet. His sunken eyes and hairless head gave him a skeletal appearance, and Damaris repressed a shiver as he bowed slightly before her. "Councilor Damaris," he murmured, "the *Kaw'ree* have been expecting you."

Of course. "Under the circumstances it could hardly be otherwise."

Another bow, and he turned away. She followed as he led her through the cloister, toward the Sanctum of the *Kaw'ree:* the guardians of the *sheh'fet*. This was her third visit to Tsapan, and her most urgent. Escape from the *sheh'fet* was impossible. Such a thing had never occurred, and its portent was disturbing. If news of such defiance were allowed to spread, if the people were to consider the *sheh'fet* fallible... The thought did not bear exploration. But the *Kaw'ree* would explain it all. They would explain this impossibility.

Her guide stopped before the carved wooden doors of the Sanctum, turned, and bowed a final time before retreating back down the corridor. Ignoring the flutter in her stomach, Damaris rapped on the heavy door. Her knock seemed to raise little sound, yet the door swung open on silent hinges and she was bidden to enter the room beyond.

The domed ceiling swept up above her, decorated in rainbow colors, depicting scenes she could not interpret. Scenes from Kinahhi's past, before the fall of the false gods and the rise of the world she knew. But here, in this halfway house, sat the remnants of those days. A bridge between past and present; a link to a history even more ancient than Tsapan. The nine men and women watched her, their eyes bright as stars against the robes they wore, their sallow skin riddled with scarlet tendrils that radiated from their temples, threaded down their necks and disappeared beneath the black velvet of their robes. The *Kaw'ree*. She bowed low, out of respect and fear. So close, she suspected they could see her thoughts hanging in the air before them.

"You are afraid," a woman's voice said. "You are afraid of the Tauri."

Straightening, Damaris nodded. Denial was impossible in this place. "They are unpredictable, their minds powerful. The one who has escaped is a danger to Kinahhi."

"We saw his mind," another replied, a man. Smooth skinned and softly spoken, he was the youngest of the *Kaw'ree*. "He is strong-willed, volatile. Fascinating. But we could not hold him."

Damaris looked between them, confused. "Why not? Is his mind so strong?" Stronger than the *sheh'fet*?

"Not stronger than the *sheh'fet*," the young man rebuked her. "But his blood is tainted. He is Mahr'bal."

Impossible! "He is not from this world!" she protested. "How can he be Mahr'bal?"

The woman spoke again, turning her bright eyes on the Councilor. "That is a question we cannot answer. We have searched the mind of the Tauri woman, but of this she knows nothing." A slight confusion flickered through her eyes. "Yet she has strength, great strength, and great knowledge."

"Knowledge we cannot access."

Cannot access? "Is she too tainted? Are they both Mahr'bal?" Frustration curled unpleasantly inside her chest. If all Tauri were incompatible with the *sheh'fet*…

"Her link was damaged," the woman replied. "The man – O'Neill – attempted to free her."

Yes, of course. "Can you restore the link? She has information I must have. The Tauri have much to teach us, and this one knows more than most about their defenses, their leaders…"

The young man raised his hand. His skin was almost translucent, and she could see crimson strands fanning out along his fingers like the fragile roots of a plant. "We may. The link is not broken, merely damaged. In time, we will subdue her."

Hope eased the Councilor's frustration and she breathed more easily. "That is well." After a moment she added, "There are two more aliens on this world. Dr. Daniel Jackson, a Tauri, and Teal'c – known as a Jaffa, servant of the Goa'uld. When they are captured, they will be joined to the *sheh'fet*. They too, have valuable knowledge."

A hungry smile touched the colorless lips of the woman. "From Dr. Jackson, I believe we will learn much. I glimpsed his mind as he passed through the *sheh'fet*; it is rich and deep. I shall enjoy—" She cut herself off, but the desire in her eyes didn't fade as she hissed in two quick breaths. "Yes, I shall enjoy Dr. Jackson."

Despite herself, Damaris felt a chill at the sight of the woman's hunger and turned her gaze back to the man. He looked scarcely less avid. "It will not be long," she assured them. "Even now, my men are in position – when O'Neill and his friends attempt to free Major Carter, we will have them all."

"Yes," the young man agreed, resting his head against the back of the tall chair, eyes drifting shut. "You will."

The others, all nine *Kaw'ree*, emulated him. They seemed balanced on the point of extreme pleasure or pain. Balanced, but not falling. Waiting, anticipating. Hungering.

Damaris took it as dismissal and, with a last bow, left the room in relief. But her thoughts were no less confused than when she had arrived. O'Neill was Mahr'bal? If the *Kaw'ree* said it was true, then she could not question it. But how was it possible? He was not of their world. Unless…

She stopped dead in the corridor. Could he be a spy from beyond the Cordon? Was there more deceit here than she knew? If the *Kaw'ree* could not invade his mind, had he been able to deceive the *sheh'fet* in other ways? As the Mahr'bal did, concealing their thoughts in darkness? Fear swiftly turned to anger.

Colonel Jack O'Neill must be eliminated.

And the truth about him had to be discovered. With Carter's link to the *sheh'fet* damaged, there was only one other Tauri within her grasp. Only one who could begin to answer her questions. A cold smile of satisfaction reached her lips: Ambassador Crawford.

Perhaps he would prove more useful than she had first imagined?

CHAPTER TWENTY-ONE

Jack stalked up the stairs. For a moment Daniel just stared in disbelief, then he darted up after him, taking the steps two at a time and heedless of the wrenching pain in his shoulder. "No!" he hissed as soon as he was within reach, grabbing Jack's arm and yanking him to a halt. "You can't do this."

"I'm making a judgment call, Daniel," Jack growled. "We can't get her out. If we try we'll all end up trapped in that thing."

Daniel shook his head. "You don't know that."

"Yes. I do." He tore his arm free and kept striding up the stairs. So much for reasoned argument!

Daniel didn't follow, and behind him Teal'c came up the stairs to stand by his side. At the last moment, when he was almost swallowed by the shadows of the staircase, Jack stopped. "I gave you both a goddamn order." It sounded like he was spitting glass.

Teal'c shifted, clearly disturbed. He seemed uncertain and conflicted –it wasn't an expression often seen on the man's face. But he didn't say anything, and Daniel fixed his attention on Jack.

"Actually," he said calmly, "you can't give us orders anymore, Jack. Kinsey relieved you of command, remember?"

There was an icy silence. And then, "Daniel—"

"Just because you feel guilty about getting us into this," Daniel pressed. "It doesn't mean that—"

"Daniel!" Jack stepped down a couple of stairs, moving back into the murky light. His face was all hard angles, his eyes flat as stone. "That's not what this is about." He looked at Teal'c. "You know I'm right."

Teal'c was torn, but eventually he bobbed his head. "O'Neill is correct, Daniel Jackson. We are not equipped to mount an effective rescue of Major Carter at this time. And the Kinahhi are surely awaiting us."

Daniel couldn't believe what he was hearing! "We've been through worse. We've taken on bigger odds than this. We've—"

"It's a trap!" Jack snapped. "It's a goddamn trap, Daniel, and I won't lead you into it."

"But it's Sam!"

"I *know*!" His voice cracked as he spat the words, and for an instant Daniel glimpsed what lay beneath: a blizzard of self-recrimination, pain, loss, duty and honor.

Jack sucked in a breath, under tight control. "Daniel, it's bad enough that they're sucking Carter's brain out. If they get you too…" He left it hanging, fixing him with a long, serious look. "*You* don't even know everything you know." He frowned. "If you know what I mean."

The unease Daniel felt when confronted by the black gap in his memories rolled in like thunder clouds. "You mean, about the Ancients."

"Among other things."

Daniel held his gaze, then deliberately dropped it to the P90 Jack held in one hand. "I'm willing to take the risk. And if it came down to it," he said quietly, "I'm sure you wouldn't let them get me."

A brief flash of anger widened his friend's eyes. "Daniel—"

"You'd do the same for Sam."

Jack flinched – obviously he'd already considered the possibility. But all he said was, "It's not a question of risking our lives. God, if that was all—" He stopped, chewing unspoken words, and cleared his throat. "There's more at stake here."

"We must warn the Tauri," Teal'c agreed. "Even now, Senator Kinsey is constructing a *sheh'fet* at Stargate Command. If we do not return with the information O'Neill has gleaned, then we cannot prevent the Kinahhi from establishing a hold upon Earth."

Earth. Damn it, Teal'c was right. They were both right. But, God, it felt so wrong. The fight drained out of him, replaced by a rising tide of grief. "I can't believe we're leaving her behind."

"She'd understand." But Jack's voice was rough, as if he barely understood himself.

The mournful drip, drip of water against stone was the only sound in the heavy silence. It reminded Daniel how dry his throat felt, how empty his stomach. "We shall return," Teal'c insisted. "We shall return in greater numbers and free her."

Jack gave a short, tight nod. "The bastards won't know what hit them." But they were only words, a hollow reassurance. Daniel could see the truth in his friend's empty eyes; Jack believed they were leaving Sam to die. And it was tearing him apart. Daniel held his gaze, and for once Jack didn't look away. He was searching for something. Absolution? Some recognition that he'd made the right choice, that they understood why he was breaking their Golden Rule?

"Come on," Daniel said quietly, heading up the stairs. "Let's go bring in the cavalry."

The stench of the *sheh'fet* surrounded him, moist and cloying, clogging his nose even though he was careful to only breathe through his mouth. Commander Kenna stood with his back to the machine – if that was the right word – and kept his eyes locked on the arched doorway of the single entrance into the room.

Ten of his men surrounded the *sheh'fet*, another twenty lurked in the corridor that led out into the dank streets of the lower levels. O'Neill's friends had taken him by surprise in the tower; they would not do so again. Yet, they were clearly planning their attack carefully, taking their time before returning. He approved of the tactic – sometimes caution was a soldier's best ally – but he found himself surprised. O'Neill had struck him as the reckless type, the kind of man who led from the heart and not the head. Perhaps he'd underestimated him? O'Neill was resourceful, that was without doubt. More than that... Kenna stole a look at the *sheh'fet*, his gaze turning irresistibly to the alien woman tangled in its web. More than that, O'Neill had escaped.

Such a thing was unprecedented.

Kenna had not believed that the mind survived intact. But if O'Neill could escape several hours after being joined... An involuntary shiver turned the Commander cold as he watched Major Carter. Her face was slack now, only half traced with the scarlet threads of the *sheh'fet*. O'Neill had tried to free her, so they said. Kenna could imagine the man's frantic efforts, and his ultimate failure. No commander worth the rank easily left his men behind, and he doubted O'Neill was any different. Which was why he knew the Colonel would be back. O'Neill wouldn't leave her here, of that Kenna was certain.

A slight noise outside wrenched his attention away, gun rising and heart pounding. Then silence fell. Without lowering his sights, Kenna carefully approached the doorway. "Report," he ordered.

"All correct," came the response.

But the feeling of unease didn't dissipate. The waiting was always the hardest part. Moving back from the door, he once more found himself staring at Major Carter.

This time she was staring back.

"*Hadad!*" Kenna hissed. Around him his troops started, weapons lifting. Expecting the fight. "Stand down," he growled, irritated by his own discomposure. "Man your posts."

Reluctantly they turned away, but Kenna saw many a significant look pass between them. They'd seen the woman's eyes, they knew she lived. It shook many certainties to the core. Slowly, Kenna approached, forcing himself to hold her disturbing gaze. *Help me.* Her lips moved silently, cracked and dry. *Help me.* The plea was in her eyes. Louder than any voice, it spoke right into his mind. *Help me!*

Sickened, he turned away. She didn't know what she asked. He was just one man, he could do nothing for her.

You can help us! O'Neill had believed the same. But they knew nothing of Kinahhi. They knew nothing of his life, or his son's. Besides, it would soon be over. She could not last much longer, and when O'Neill and the other aliens were also in custody...

There was nothing he could do. He was just one man.

The city was deserted. Nothing but the occasional call of a stray seabird echoed through its streets as Teal'c followed Daniel Jackson and O'Neill through Tsapan's fading shadows. And yet he could not dislodge the sensation of eyes, peering out of the dark windows that surrounded them, watching every step they took. The feeling crept along his spine, tensing his shoulders and tightening his grip on the P90 he carried.

Ahead of him, Daniel Jackson stopped suddenly and glanced up. He, too, could feel the danger.

"Keep moving," hissed O'Neill. His weapon, Teal'c noted, had the safety off and was ready for use. But he did not look around, nor did he stop. Constant activity was always O'Neill's cure for emotional disturbance.

With great effort, Daniel Jackson resumed climbing the seemingly endless stairs. He clutched his injured arm close to his body, and Teal'c suspected that pain and exhaustion were pushing him toward the limit of endurance. Indeed, the muscles in Teal'c's own legs burned from the long trek up from the bowels of Tsapan, and his throat was parched enough to make the pools of murky water scattered through the city's streets seem as appealing as a flowing spring. Without a symbiote to counter any microbial infection, it would have been unwise to indulge – yet the need for water, food, and rest was increasingly pressing.

Up ahead, O'Neill stopped and dropped into a crouch, raising his hand to halt them. They were approaching the top of a wide flight of stairs, above which lay the plaza in which the *tel'tak* was concealed.

"We're going to be fish in a barrel crossing that courtyard," O'Neill murmured, as Teal'c and Daniel Jackson drew closer.

"If there's anyone up there."

O'Neill squinted at the buildings surrounding them. "Oh there's someone up there. Kenna's a fool if he hasn't got every approach staked out." He turned around to face them: "On the plus side, they don't know our ship's up there."

"They may believe we are seeking an alternative route to rescue Major Carter," Teal'c agreed. "In which case, they will not attack until they believe themselves confident of our plan."

"Yeah, well, once they see the ship they won't hold back," O'Neill said, returning to his scrutiny of the buildings. "We've got five minutes before—"

A distant cry of surprise drifted through the city, as dissonant as the tolling of an alarm bell. O'Neill tensed, listening hard. No one breathed. Then Teal'c sensed movement in a window behind them and to their right. "Get down!" A red bolt of laser fire exploded into the wall inches away, spitting gravel into his face. Then another. And another. "We are discovered!"

"Ya think?" O'Neill yelled, grabbing hold of Daniel Jackson's arm and yanking him into motion. "Get to the ship! Now!"

As O'Neill dragged Daniel Jackson up the stairs, sheltering as much as possible against the walls of the city, Teal'c returned fire. The rattle of his P90 was satisfying, but he longed for the power of his staff weapon.

"Damn it!" O'Neill barked, skidding to a halt at the top of the stairs and pulling Daniel Jackson down behind him. The *tel'tak* was in clear view – the shield had failed – and a knot of Kinahhi clustered around the entrance to one of the buildings, firing at will and cutting off their approach.

"There are more behind us, O'Neill." Teal'c fired in short bursts down the stairs. "We cannot delay."

"You go," O'Neill decided. "I'll cover you. Daniel, on my six. Get the damn thing in the air, T, and come back for us."

Teal'c appraised the cluster of Kinahhi blocking their way and exchanged a short, significant look with O'Neill. "Hold your position."

O'Neill nodded. "Yeah. And no dawdling."

As Daniel Jackson pulled free his *zat'ni'katel*, and O'Neill positioned himself against the corner of the building and raised his weapon, Teal'c prepared to run the gauntlet. "On my mark," said O'Neill, settling the weapon against his shoulder. "Three, two, one. Mark."

Gunfire exploded. The rattle of the P90 and the electronic zing of the zat filled the air with carbite, static and ozone. Laser fire scalded through the hazy light, blasting fragments of rock and dust up into the air. And into the heart of the battle Teal'c started running...

It was like being in two places at once. Half her mind was filled with noise – with voices and thoughts and desires and pain and joy – a flood of consciousness too huge to comprehend. It surged through her like a flood, a ceaseless flood of information too powerful for the delicate vessel of her mind. But above that, as if floating on the surface of the torrent, she somehow managed to cling to a shred of sanity. A window onto the outside world.

Sam opened her eyes. She could see Commander Kenna staring back at her as if she were a ghost, and watched him turn away in disgust. But not disgust at what he saw, she realized – disgust at himself. His thoughts were almost audible: *How can I permit this?*

Startled, Sam turned her eyes away. The tormented faces of those dying in the *sheh'fet* were all around her, but she ignored them. Instead, she studied the room, the round, windowless room. One way in, one way out, and that was guarded by a ring of soldiers braced for attack. Her lips moved, instinctively pulling toward a triumphant smile. Rescue was on its way.

Suddenly she heard footsteps. She couldn't move her head to see where they came from, but they were running and growing louder. "Commander!" a breathless voice barked as Kenna turned to face the newcomer.

"Report."

"They've got a ship!" the voice gasped. "An alien ship. They're trying to leave, Commander!"

An alien ship? Sam struggled to process the information. *They're trying to leave?*

"How many men up there?" Kenna sounded spooked. Instinctively, Sam knew the price of failure would be high. And not just for him. For his son too.

How do I know about his son?

"Twelve Squadron, sir. They've called for backup."

The Commander seemed satisfied, if not confident. "What about the ship? Why wasn't it detected?"

The soldier frowned. "Sir, apparently it was— Invisible, sir."

Cloaked! A tel'tak, something small enough to land on Tsapan. Hope stirred. *Daniel and Teal'c. It had to be. But why are they leaving? God, they can't leave me like this!*

"Invisible?" Kenna frowned and started moving toward the doorway. "They must be stopped. Tell Twelve Squadron to use any means necessary."

"Sir?" The soldier seemed surprised. "Are we not ordered to return them to the *sheh'fet*?"

Kenna paused, and Sam sensed his indecision. He was afraid, mortally afraid for his son. For Esaum.

How do I know that?

A fleeting look came her way, barely perceptible, but Sam felt it like hot breath against her neck. Kenna was repulsed by his own inaction. So conflicted, he was ready to snap. "No," he said at last. "Shoot to kill."

Somehow, it felt like defiance.

Laser blasts were coming from everywhere at once, every single window. Daniel returned fire as best he could, but nothing stopped the relentless assault. "There's too many of them!"

"Keep firing!" Jack dropped an empty plastic clip and fluidly slid in the new one. It was the last. "Teal'c's almost— *No!* Damn it." Jack was on his feet, about to dart out into the battle.

"What?" Daniel scrambled upright, but dared not take his eyes from the enemy. "What happened?"

An angry burst of gunfire answered him. "He's down. Teal'c's down."

"Where?"

"I can't see him. I saw him go down." Another burst of gun-fire.

"Now what?" Daniel figured they had two choices; surrender or die. Of course, for the Kinahhi, those probably amounted to much the same thing.

Jack spared him a fleeting glance, half apology and half regret. "We run for it."

Run for it? The *tel'tak* was out of reach, across an infinity of death and destruction. The odds of either of them making it were slim to none, and they both knew it. This was the end. "Just like Butch Cassidy and the Sundance Kid, huh?" The end of every-thing.

Jack grunted. "You're thinking of Harry Maybourne."

"Bonnie and Clyde?"

"Daniel…!" Anger and anxiety mingled with other emotions in the heated look Jack flung at him. Gratitude, affection, friend-ship. Regret. Things they'd never talked about and never would. It was a fleeting, silent farewell, and it cut to the quick.

Having no voice or time to answer, Daniel simply moved to stand at Jack's side. They'd face the end head on, shoulder-to-shoulder, just like they'd faced everything over the past seven years.

Jack turned his eyes to the smoke-shrouded silhouette of the *tel'tak*. "Let's do it."

CHAPTER TWENTY-TWO

Yelling his defiance, Jack charged into the fray. All thoughts were swamped by the adrenaline-high of battle, by the overwhelming, primal desire to survive. Every sense alive, clear as crystal. He raked the enemy with gunfire as he sprinted. Daniel was behind and to the right, the electronic fizz of his zat crawling over the Kinahhi, silencing their weapons. But more kept coming. Reinforcements. Too many.

Keep firing.

He could see Teal'c now. His right leg was bleeding, but he was moving, doggedly crawling toward the *tel'tak*. Never giving up. Never, ever—

A shaft of white-hot pain clipped Jack's shoulder, spinning him as he fell hard onto his right knee. He felt it blow, and cursed in pain and anger. Sonofabitch, goddamn sonofa—

"Jack!" Daniel was covering him. "Get up!"

"Go!" he shouted, nauseous with the pain. He wasn't going anywhere.

"Jack!"

"GO!" He fired again, dropping three men. "Daniel, get the hell outta—"

The bloodcurdling scream came from up high, where a man was falling, flailing to his death, from one of the tall towers. For a moment, all eyes were on him. Then the chill cry came again, but not from him. He hit the ground with a bone-shattering splat, just as a face appeared in the window above. A white, inhuman, insane face. Clutching fingers gripped the shattered window, skeletal limbs pulling the creature to perch like a gargoyle on the edge. Raising its head, it screeched again.

And was answered. Another cry rang out from behind them. Then another, closer, closer to the ground.

"What are they?" Daniel breathed, both horrified and fascinated.

The Kinahhi were in panic, backing away from the towers

and into the center of the plaza. Their weapons were pointing up, down, everywhere. Someone was shouting orders, or yelling for backup – Jack couldn't hear the words.

From another window, much lower down the tower, another face appeared. Ragged hair hung from its cadaverous head, lips parted over decaying teeth. Despite the blazing agony in his knee, Jack backed up. He'd seen these faces. The creature screamed its own inhuman cry. *Like Carter. Just like Carter...* And then it pounced, flying like a monstrous, twisted bird through the air to land on the Kinahhi. They fired, and blood splattered from its white skin, but it didn't seem to care as it tore into the Kinahhi soldiers with all the ferocity of vengeance and hatred.

And then the others came, spilling from windows and doors in a frenzy of desperate, dehumanized retribution. The Kinahhi were swamped, screaming as they died.

"O'Neill!" Teal'c, his face glistening with a sheen of sweat, had hauled himself upright against the *tel'tak*. This was their chance.

"Help me," Jack ordered Daniel, grunting with the pain in his knee as Daniel hauled him to his feet. "Run."

Between his blown knee and Daniel's dislocated shoulder, it was more of a hobble, but they were moving. And no one was firing at them. Screams and howls echoed off the towers, eerie and insane. *Like Carter, just like Carter. That's what she'll become.* "No." He'd die himself before he let that happen.

"Jack?"

"Keep going." But his vision was starting to gray out. Blood oozed from the hit he'd taken to his arm, the pain in his knee cramped his gut into nauseous spasms. Stubbornly, he clung to consciousness, willing himself to move. They had to survive, they had to come back. His sight was tunneling, blood pressure falling. He could feel it drop, making his ears ring and his head dizzy. *Keep going, keep going...*

"O'Neill." Teal'c's firm hand gripped his shoulder as he fell into the *tel'tak*.

"Go," Jack whispered, sliding to the floor, mind spiraling away into darkness. "Teal'c, just go."

"This is it," General Hammond announced, breathless and

dripping with sweat from the long climb. Beneath him, on the ladder, Woodburn wasn't in much better shape.

"Twenty years ago…" he gasped.

Hammond managed a rueful chuckle, but saved the rest of his breath to turn the heavy wheel on the access hatch. The loud grating sound made him wince, and he stopped. Had they been heard? He strained to listen over the thudding of his laboring heart and the rasp of Woodburn's breathing.

Nothing.

He kept turning until the seal gave way and the door cracked open, letting a flare of light into the darkness of the access tunnel. Again, Hammond stopped and listened. All was quiet beyond. Exchanging a *here-goes-nothing* look with Woodburn, he pushed open the hatch and climbed out.

The corridor was empty, but Hammond could hear the distant sound of footsteps as Woodburn emerged and closed the hatch behind him. "So far so good." He glanced up and down the corridor, making a swift calculation. He'd never gotten further than the checkpoint Kinsey had established outside the dedicated 'testing room'. But they'd come out behind the checkpoint, and Hammond knew there was a back door. All they'd need was a little luck. "This way," he murmured, heading along the silent corridor.

Two days ago, this place had been home. Now it felt like enemy territory. Kinsey had stolen it from him, stolen his friendships, his people and his home. But not for long. Hammond would get it back. He'd get it all back.

Including SG-1.

Councilor Tamar Damaris sat once more behind the desk in her office, watching the man who stood before her. Or, perhaps, slumped would be a more appropriate description. Commander Kenna's shoulders sagged, his dirty, scratched face was pasty beneath its weathered skin, and his eyes were alive with indecorous emotion. He appeared distressed and unbalanced, which was unsettling in a man of his age and experience.

"And where is this alien vessel now?" she asked. "Did your men track it?"

He shook his head. "For some distance, yes, Councilor. But

then it... It disappeared, from sight and from our sensors. I believe it must have left orbit." He frowned, as if uncertain of the truth of his words.

Damaris's eyes narrowed. The Tauri obviously possessed technologies greater than they had admitted, and the deception irritated her. "I find it hard to believe," she said acidly, "that the one-hundred men you had stationed on Tsapan could not restrain these three aliens."

The Commander's chin lifted, nostrils flaring in anger. "We had them cornered, Councilor. But the Outcast—"

"The Outcast!" she spat in disdain. "Your men were defeated by animals, Commander? Perhaps you had better rethink your training practi—"

"They are not animals!" Kenna snapped back. His eyes flashed, almost as wild as those of the Tauri. "They are..." He hesitated, one hand drifting up to the scratches on his face. "They are no longer human, but they fight with human guile and strength. And rage."

Uninterested, Damaris rose and walked to the window. "I do not understand why the *Kaw'ree* insist that they be allowed to live."

Kenna offered no answer, but she could feel his disapproval burning like the heat of the sun on her back. She was not used to such insolence, and it frightened her more than she was prepared to admit. Carefully, she turned around and studied his face. "You have failed me, Commander." A flash of fear rippled across his features, but was soon swallowed by the darker tide of his rising anger. At that moment, she knew that Commander Kenna could no longer remain in Kinahhi. Neither could he be sent to Tsapan; she had no wish to spread the dissent she saw festering in his eyes by allowing his men to witness his absorption into the *sheh'fet*. But there were other ways to neutralize him.

She returned to her desk and sat, hands folded before her. "Report to the Cordon, Commander Kenna. You are to relieve Commander Lah'hag, and remain there until recalled."

"But my son—"

"Your son," she replied coolly, "will transfer to Tsapan and serve the *Kaw'ree*."

"But he's only seven years—"

Damaris wove threat through her voice like steel through silk. "Do not provoke me to be less generous, Commander. The *sheh'fet* is always eager for new blood, and your son – Esaum? – shows much promise."

Ashen-faced, the Commander bowed: "My honor is to serve Kinahhi," he muttered in a hollow voice.

Damaris permitted herself a smile. "Yes," she replied. "I'm sure it is."

The need for water and to pee were becoming pressing issues, not to mention the cramping agony of her muscles, staked out like a lab rat awaiting vivisection. If the guys didn't turn up soon...

On the plus side, her head was clearer. The tumult of information stampeding through her mind was more distant, and she had the distinct impression she was disconnecting from the machine. The left side of her face burned, but it was mild compared to her other discomforts. And nothing compared to the nagging fear that no one was coming after her.

No one gets left behind. Good in theory, but not always possible.

She closed her eyes and tried to listen more closely to the cacophony in her head. If she concentrated, she could sense things, pick out detail amid the chaos. Right now, she could sense deep anxiety. Shock. As if something basic had been attacked, certainties overthrown. She wasn't sure if she was listening to the mind of one man or a hundred, and yet there was a familiarity to the thoughts. They reminded her of Commander Kenna. Could he hear her, she wondered? *Help me.* She sent the message out as best she could. *Don't leave me here. You can help me.*

There was no time to listen for any kind of response, however, for at that moment two dark-robed figures entered the room. Their faces and hands were filigreed with scarlet, their eyes as dark and deep as the ocean, and their minds... They slammed into hers with such force that she jerked back against the restraints, gasping for breath.

"She is strong," said one. A young man, Koash he had once been called, but no one had used his name for years.

"Yes," agreed a spindly woman – Elessa – watching her with hunger. "These Tauri are not like the Kinahhi. Their minds are richer."

Koash stepped closer, peering up at where Sam hung suspended in the *sheh'fet*. "And yet the one called O'Neill is Mahr'bal." She felt his mind in hers, pressing, searching. "She does not understand me," he said, turning away. "Yet she feels that O'Neill is important."

"Perhaps if we bring her to the tower?" Elessa suggested. "A closer contact would provide the answer. If it is true that the Mahr'bal exist beyond Kinahhi…"

She said no more, but Sam could feel the shiver of revulsion that accompanied the thought. *Rats. Hundreds of diseased rats, crawling all over each other in a dirty, abandoned hovel.* Disoriented by the image, she tried to shake it away and found herself staring into the fathomless eyes of the strange woman. "Who are you?" Her voice was cracked and dry, but it was loud enough to be heard.

Elessa's eyebrows shot up. "You speak."

"I can tap dance too. You gonna answer my question?"

Koash turned back to face her. "Do you need to ask the question, Major Samantha Carter?" He smiled thinly.

Kaw'ree. The alien word was familiar, she understood its meaning as clearly as if it were English. *Leaders.* "You control the *sheh'fet*."

Koash nodded. "We are the Guardians of the Kinahhi. We keep our people safe."

Safe? If she'd had the energy, Sam would have laughed. "No," she croaked through her parched throat. "You don't. You enslave them." She looked deliberately at the dying faces around her. "You're monsters."

"And you are a fool."

Sam shook her head. "No. You know I'm right – you can read my mind."

Koash exchanged a brief, startled look with Elessa, but didn't answer. After a moment they left the room together, their dark robes rustling in the silence. But she'd sensed their surprise. Surprise and something more. Fear? She didn't think they'd been expecting her defiance, and that meant some part of her still remained her own – separate from the *sheh'fet*. It was enough to give her hope, and to keep her fighting.

Score one for the SGC.

Daniel could tell something was wrong, and he'd be the first to admit that he was no expert in the intricacies of *tel'tak* design. The ship was shaking like the wreck he'd driven as a freshman, reminding him vividly of the night it had ground to a halt ten miles out of town and never moved again...

"Daniel?" Jack's eyes drifted open. He lay sprawled on the floor, his right sleeve dark with blood and his face ghost-white. "What's going on?"

"Ah, we're having a little trouble leaving orbit."

Even semi-conscious Jack had an instinct for the tactical. "Pursuit?"

"Yeah. Teal'c had to re-engage the cloak or they'd have shot us out of the sky, but now we can't—" The shaking intensified, rattling Daniel's teeth together.

"I am attempting to reach escape velocity," Teal'c yelled from the cockpit, glaring at the controls as if he could intimidate them into cooperation. "Stand by."

The ship banked and Daniel started sliding back against the far wall of the cargo hold. Jack joined him in an undignified heap as Teal'c forced the screaming engines to their maximum. With a wince, Jack sat up. In the thin light from the window his face looked colorless, and Daniel was convinced that willpower alone kept him conscious.

"Come on," Jack whispered under his breath.

Through the cockpit window Daniel saw the clouds scatter. The air was blue and bright and clear and— A loud bang clapped through the ship, followed by an ominous moment of silence. The engines had stopped.

"Oh crap."

And suddenly they were dropping, like an elevator in freefall. Daniel's stomach leaped to somewhere near the ceiling, and Jack was yelling. "Teal'c!"

There was a muted whine, and then another miserable clunk. Teal'c spun out of his chair, clinging to its back to support his injured leg. "I cannot reinitialize the engines!"

Jack tried to stand, grabbing hold of Daniel's arm for support. Together, they struggled upright. "Tell me we have escape pods!" Jack yelled.

"There are three left," Teal'c shouted. "But—"

"What?"

"I do not know where we are. All the ship's systems are malfunctioning. If we are over an ocean..."

The image of the coffin-like escape pods plummeting beneath the waves, entombing them forever, provoked a wave of claustrophobia. Daniel sucked in an involuntary, deep breath.

Jack cast him a quick look. "Only one way of finding out."

And no other choice. Together they lurched toward the escape pods, wrenching open the doors and all but falling inside.

"Go!" Jack urged. "Get the hell outta here!"

As the door slid shut inches away from his face, Daniel calmed his breathing and tenaciously thought about hilltops and wide open spaces. He ran his fingers over the familiar controls – how often had he been in one of these things? – and found the failsafe manual release. In his mind he could hear Jack barking the command. *On my mark. One, two, three. Mark!* Daniel triggered the release and felt himself falling backward, whooping like a kid on a roller coaster as he plummeted toward the ground, or the ocean, or whatever else fate had in store...

CHAPTER TWENTY-THREE

It could have been the middle of the night or the middle of the afternoon. Sam had long ago lost track of time, her mind drifting between its two spheres of consciousness, sinking beneath the buffeting waves of a thousand voices and thoughts, then floating to the surface and staring through her gritty eyes at the reality of her imprisonment.

And then they came. Two men, robed in black like the others, but without the filigree of scarlet on their skin. They came to stand before her, talking too quietly to hear. She sensed something from them, however. Unease, disquiet – a sense of shaken faith. And then she'd started to move.

The clamps around her limbs snaked from the *sheh'fet*, pushing her past the dying faces and bodies of the others until she hung suspended above the floor. Reality sharpened, and she forced herself to focus. The pain in her arms and legs, her parched throat and acid-burned face all anchored her to the present, dulling the eternal whispering. "What's happening?" she managed to scratch out.

There was no answer as she was slowly lowered to the ground. Her legs sagged as the clamps released her, and she hit the floor in a crumpled heap. *Now what?*

A cup was pressed to her lips, and she drank greedily of a cool, bitter liquid that burned in her chest and made her cough. Arms hooked beneath each of her own, and she was pulled upright and dragged into motion. She tried to walk, but her muscles were cramping with lack of use and refused to respond. Her whole body felt clumsy and uncoordinated, as if it weren't quite her own. *Maybe it's not?* Even her mind, always so crystal clear, was foggy and indistinct. It was hard to concentrate, so easy to get lost in the endless chatter that deafened her thoughts, but she refused to let it wash her away. *Fight it*, the Colonel had ordered. *Don't give them an inch.*

Her body might be beyond use for the moment, but her eyes

at least were working. If she could do nothing else, she could try to understand where she was being taken – and how the hell to get out. At first it was too dark to see much, and she recognized the damp, ill-lit corridor through which she and the Colonel had been marched so long ago. At the end loomed massive iron doors, and she remembered them too, and the stench that had almost knocked her over. Funny that she barely noticed it now, although she suspected it clung to every strand of her hair and every fiber of her clothing.

Expecting to go through those doors again, Sam was surprised when her escort slowed and stopped some twenty feet away. One of them muttered something she didn't catch, and then to her surprise a section of the wall slid to one side, revealing the inside of a bright, clean elevator.

Still sagging between the two men, Sam was hauled inside and her stomach flipped as they began a swift ascent. Up was good, she figured. Up meant ships and fresh air and escape – if she could only force her sluggish body to respond. She closed her eyes and focused on moving her legs. It was an arduous process, almost like operating them through a crude remote control, but at last her feet were under her body and she could push herself up to stand.

It earned her a shocked stare from her companions, and she met it with fierce triumph. "Where are we going?" Even her voice sounded stronger, despite being filtered through a sandpaper throat.

"To the *Kaw'ree*," the man replied, eyes so wide they almost took over his narrow features. "They wish to examine you in detail."

"Examine—"

"Say no more," the other man trilled nervously, jittery as a bird. "It is not permitted."

Sam cast him a penetrating look. "You're afraid of them, aren't you?"

He shook his head. But his thoughts were clear to her, almost as if she could feel them herself. "You're afraid of them and— And of me." *Outcast! Dissenter. Wormwood. Destroyer.* The impression was so powerful she gasped, stumbling back. "You think I'm here to destroy you?"

The man just stared straight ahead. But he couldn't hide his thoughts from her, they blazed like an angry torch, alight with a single word. *Law'ayg.* Stranger. "Look," she said, mind reeling from sudden insight. "We're not here to destroy you, or your people. You don't have to be afraid, you can—"

A sharp slap across her face silenced her. "Say no more, Outcast," the other man hissed at her. He was furious, she could feel it rolling off him in waves like heat. "Your lies do not deceive us."

"I'm not lying, I'm—"

Another slap. "Silence. The *sheh'fet* does not lie; you have been judged."

Judged? If she'd been in better shape, she might have put up more of a fight. But her head was spinning, her body still frustratingly uncooperative, and at that moment the elevator slowed rapidly, the slight g-forces buckling her knees as the doors slid noiselessly open.

She was yanked into motion before she had time to get her feet under herself again, and stumbled to stay upright. Beyond the elevator was the kind of opulence Sam imagined had graced the city in its heyday. The gilt of Goa'uld architecture abounded, augmented by the weight of solemn Kinahhi tastes. The lighting was low, heavy drapes masking some of the familiar Goa'uld designs, and once they passed a window that glowed with the burnt orange of a fading sunset. *Couldn't be the same day we arrived, could it?*

They approached the end of the corridor and two carved wooden doors. One of her escorts – the man who had struck her – released her arm and moved to knock respectfully. After a moment the doors slid open and Sam was tugged forward. She shook off the hand that clutched at her arm. "I can walk."

Chin high, she forced her rubber legs into what she hoped was a confident stride, and led the two frightened men into the massive chamber beyond. Its domed glass ceiling glinted in muted shades, struck by the dying rays of the sun, refracting subdued rainbows throughout the room. And beneath it, on a dais, sat nine men and women, slender even by the standards of the Kinahhi, their alabaster skin traced with red fire and their eyes dark and knowing. The *Kaw'ree.* Among them were the two who had visited her in the *sheh'fet*, Koash and Elessa.

Koash rose from his chair and stepped forward. "Welcome, Major Samantha Carter."

She didn't reply, her attention caught by his chair. It was throne-like, and clearly very old. Wires and cables ran from it up towards the ceiling, their smooth lines and curlicues reminiscent of the *sheh'fet*. Whatever technology this was, it wasn't Goa'uld. An invention of the Kinahhi themselves, perhaps?

"You intrigue us," Koash continued, stepping carefully down from the platform. "We would examine your mind more closely."

"Having trouble getting into the corners?" Sam said. "Your machine not working right?"

Koash was unperturbed. "Your mind is different to ours, cruder perhaps."

She gave him a flat look. *Insults?* He must really be struggling. "Stronger," she countered. "Less diffident. More resistant." She could see the truth of it reflected in his eyes and wondered if the *sheh'fet* was a two-way street. "I know what you're thinking," she said aloud, and watched for a reaction.

A flutter rippled through the eight *Kaw'ree* still seated, and Koash straightened his narrow shoulders. Behind her she heard a stifled gasp from her nervous escort. "If we are to merge with the Tauri, we must know your minds better," Koash told her. "Understand how they work, their structure. In deconstructing your mind, Major Carter, in finding all your secrets, we will learn much."

Merge with the Tauri? What the hell did that mean? A sudden fear turned her cold at the thought of Kinsey's blind, greedy trust in these people. She pushed the thought away; there was nothing she could do about that, not yet. Focus on the now. "If you could pull my mind apart," she told Koash coldly, "you'd have done it already."

A slight smile touched the man's colorless face and he extended a hand to her face. "Your companion disrupted our connection," he said, brushing icy fingers across her temple. "But we will re-establish it, and dig deep."

"But he got out, didn't he?" she shot back. "Colonel O'Neill escaped." She jerked her head toward the men behind her, "You can't control us like you can them."

"Not yet," he agreed. "But the rewards of conquest will be…"

He shivered in anticipation, licking lightly at his thin lips. "The rewards of penetrating your mind will be immense."

Sam shrank back, but refused to back down. "I'll fight you all the way."

"I'm counting on it," Koash replied, stepping closer, his cool breath misting across her face. "But if you resist too strongly…" He smiled, staring right into her for an instant before turning away sharply. "Bring him."

Sudden panic flared up. *Him? Who? Not the Colonel! Damn it, no…* A small door at the side of the chamber opened, and two Kinahhi soldiers stepped through. Between them scurried a bedraggled, terrified looking man in a crumpled suit. Sam could hardly believe her eyes.

"Crawford?"

Koash's face was unreadable. "If you resist us, Major Carter, he will suffer the consequences of your defiance."

The Ambassador fixed her with rheumy, fearful eyes. He looked as though he'd been crying. Like she gave a damn. Arms folded, she turned back to Koash in triumph. "Wow, you really don't have a clue do you?" He was taken aback and her spirits rose. He couldn't have gotten it more wrong. "You can send that bastard to hell, for all I care. I'm not telling you a damn thing."

In the distance she heard Crawford whimper. It sounded good.

Jack wasn't sure if it was the blood loss, the pain or the force of the impact that left him woozy and faint as his escape pod finally stopped rolling and came to a bone-jarring halt. At least he was on dry land – got to look on the positive side of things. With a grunt of effort he found the mechanism to open the damn coffin, cast a quick prayer toward no one in particular and activated it.

After an eternal moment of nothingness there was the sharp hiss of a pressure seal breaking and the door cracked open. *Yes!* Air – hot and dry – seeped inside, accompanied by the faint light of dusk. With his good leg, he pushed the door up and open, then struggled to sit up.

In the twilight, he could see little. Just a blur of orange and— No, it wasn't the encroaching darkness. Rocks, sand and some distant piles of rubble. "Oh, for crying out…" They'd landed in a goddamn desert!

He flopped back down, was rewarded by a jarring pain in his arm, and cursed. Loudly.

"Jack?" The distant voice, half-hope and half-curiosity, belonged to Daniel. At least he was alive, but how long he'd stay that way in this godforsaken dust-bowl was a completely different question.

Struggling to sit up again, he watched Daniel picking his way through the rocks, studying the ground as if something utterly fascinating lurked beneath the dirt. Frankly, unless it was a cold beer and a burger, Jack couldn't give a rat's ass what Daniel was looking at. "Teal'c?" he asked, as Daniel drew closer.

"Over there," came the distracted reply, accompanied by a vague waving of his arm. "He's looking for signs of, ah…" Daniel was gone, crouching down and brushing away at the sand. "Look at this," he said. "The scale is just astonishing. How does something like this just disappear? I mean, we're talking about something advanced enough to—"

"Daniel!"

He peered over the rims of his dusty glasses. "Jack?"

"What are you *doing*?"

Daniel considered the point for a moment, then shrugged as if it were obvious. "Looking at the ruins."

"Ruins?" He gave an exaggerated look in all directions. "It's a desert, Daniel. As in *deserted*. As in *we are totally screwed*!"

Nodding absently, Daniel turned back to scraping at the ground. "You're right, we're probably screwed. But it's not a desert." He frowned. "Well, it wasn't always a desert." Even through his exhaustion and pain he managed to look awestruck. "It's a city, Jack. A huge, ancient city."

"Does it have water? Food? Medical care?" Damn it. "A way back to the Stargate? Another ship?"

With a grimace, Daniel stood up and offered Jack his hand. "Abydos looked like an empty desert when we first arrived."

Jack let himself be pulled to his feet – foot, rather, since his blown knee refused to take an ounce of weight – and squinted into the dusky evening. "You think people could live out here?"

"Why not?" Daniel said. "They obviously lived here once. Old habits die hard."

"But it's a desert."

"So was Abydos."

Jack cast him a sideways glance, trying to decide if Daniel believed what he was saying or was just looking for hope. He couldn't tell, but decided it didn't matter. They were still alive, and back on Tsapan he hadn't thought they'd get this far. He offered Daniel a smile, "Good shooting, Sundance."

Daniel accepted the compliment with a lopsided shrug, and then nodded off into the distance. "Here comes Teal'c. Maybe he's seen something."

"Burger King, with any luck."

Teal'c limped toward them, each heavy footfall raising clouds of orange sand into the amber night. From his flat expression Jack knew there was nothing in sight but sand, sand and more sand.

"We must wait for dawn," Teal'c said as he drew closer.

"Not even a Starbucks, huh?"

"It is difficult to see in this light."

"Right," Jack agreed, although the chances of civilization springing up from the dust in the morning were slim. He shivered and realized it was getting cold. "Let's see if there's anything in the escape pods to burn," he decided, wishing there was something to drink. Anything. "And we should all get some shut-eye."

It didn't take long to rip out everything combustible from the escape pods, and soon all three were huddled around a meager, smoking fire. With the aid of Teal'c's knife, Jack tore a strip from the bottom of his shirt and let Teal'c bind it tightly around the laser wound in his arm. Just a scratch, but it would fester without a sterile dressing and antibiotics. Septicemia made such a nice counterpoint to dehydration and starvation.

He did the same for Teal'c in return, staunching the blood seeping from his leg wound. It was all they could do, and he knew damn well it wasn't half enough. Without a miracle, it would end here. His eyes moved to land on the Beretta Daniel had holstered at his side. It would be easy enough, almost painless, if it came down to that. His eyes lifted and he found himself skewered by Daniel's sharp gaze. He didn't flinch, just gave a slight shrug, and Daniel nodded. They understood each other.

"Let's get some rest," Jack said quietly, his voice rasping with thirst. "I'll take first watch. Then Teal'c, then Daniel."

Without another word his friends settled themselves on their backs and stared up at the alien stars. Jack just gazed into the ugly blue flames of their fire, turning his last moments in the *sheh'fet* over and over in his mind.

I'll be back. I swear to God, I'll be back.

Could he have done more to free her? Should he have stayed on Tsapan? Had he made the wrong call, abandoning her only to see the rest of his team die slow, pointless deaths in the middle of nowhere? He had no answers. But one thing was certain – he'd be damned if his promise to her proved to be a lie. There had to be some way out of this. All he had to do was find it.

The Commander's office was on the second floor of the tatty building at the heart of the compound. The air was cooling at last, but the heat of the day had left Kenna irritable and low. Standing at the open window, he stared out into the cloudless night of this strange, alien place to which he'd been banished. *I'm so sorry, Esaum.* The compound was bathed in a sickly yellow light. It did little to penetrate the rich darkness of the desert, and failed utterly to compete with the bright white lights that roved across the Cordon and glinted on the jagged wire curling along its length.

Beyond that lay chaos. The badlands, crisscrossed by ever-growing numbers of lawless vagrants, living in poverty they were too idle to remedy. Or so the official line went. Clasping his hands behind his back, Kenna stared as if he could penetrate the night. He'd only been beyond the Cordon a handful of times, but the hollow features and hopeless eyes of those who clung to the border, desperate for the handouts from Kinahhi, had haunted his dreams. Until recently.

Now, another face kept him awake at night. Esaum, his little boy. Kenna went cold, thinking of him in the hands of Damaris or the *Kaw'ree*, and was ashamed of himself for letting his son down so badly. He should have known better than to question, than to listen to the dangerous words of O'Neill. What right did he have to risk his son for the sake of his own petty compunctions? The *sheh'fet* was evil, but he'd rather see the Tauri woman in its clutches than his son. It was a cruel truth, but honest. If there only were some way to regain the trust of the Security Council, to allow him to bring Esaum home…

A door squeaked open in the security hut and one of his men ran across the courtyard, a paper flapping in his hand. It did not look like good news. Swallowing a harsh sense of dread he turned and braced himself. After a minute he heard booted feet hurrying down the corridor, and then an abrupt rap on his door.

"Enter."

A young soldier hurried inside. "Sir," he reported breathlessly. "We have a report from Tracking Station 36."

Thirty-six? That was off-shore, on one of the islands. "And?"

"They report a ship, sir. The alien ship, crashing into the Mibsaw Sea."

Kenna felt the stirrings of hope. "Any report of survivors?"

The soldier shook his head. "No sir, but—" He frowned down at the paper he was holding, then handed it over to the Commander. "Three smaller vessels were also detected before the ship crashed, right at the edge of 36's range."

"Some sort of emergency evacuation devices?" Was there no limit to O'Neill's resourcefulness? The man must possess a dozen lives.

"Possibly, sir. They can't confirm it, but they think they must have crashed somewhere beyond the Cordon." He took a breath, slowing his speech as the urgency lessened. "Given their trajectory before thirty-six lost them, sir, they may have landed in Arxantia itself."

"Is that so?" The heart of the Mahr'bal. A harsh, uncompromising land. If they survived the crash, they would not live long in such a place. But if he could find them, return with them to the Security Council in triumph... Hope, a distant dream mere minutes ago, beat louder in his chest. "Send in Chief Officer Lahat to see me immediately," he ordered, "and rouse the watch. I shall lead the hunt myself."

The young man's eyes shot wide open. "Sir? You're going to—"

"Find them," he confirmed, searching through his predecessor's desk for one of the rudimentary maps of Arxantia. He looked up at the still staring soldier. "Go, man. We move out within the hour."

The boy turned and fled, but Kenna paid him no mind. His blood was flowing fast, eager for the fight. "This time, O'Neill," he said quietly, "I will have you. And your life will buy that of my son."

CHAPTER TWENTY-FOUR

"For the love of God, what is this?" George Hammond breathed, staring out through the two-way mirror into the room below. A dozen men lay on gurneys, teeth bared in a grimace, with cables trailing from their heads toward a central device of undoubtedly alien design. A doctor whom Hammond didn't recognize drifted between them, checking vital signs and making notes on the charts dangling from each bed.

"Some kind of medical experiment?" Woodburn guessed. "I thought you said this was a security technology."

Hammond frowned. So he'd been told by O'Neill. Was it possible that the man had lied about more than the plans he'd planted among Crawford's belongings?

"Look at their faces," Woodburn carried on. "Is that some kind of rash?"

It was hard to tell. The red spiderwebs that covered the cheeks of each man looked raw and painful, yet... Hammond peered more closely. Were they attached to the cables? "How many men have been brought onto the base?" he asked, turning away from the experiment and casting his eyes around the small observation room.

"Over thirty," Woodburn said.

"So where are the others?"

"They must be being held somewhere else. Maybe," Woodburn frowned, "maybe it's some kind of bio weapon."

Hammond shook his head, spying a neatly labeled filing cabinet and crossing the room toward it. "If it were a disease," he said, "the doctor wouldn't be in there with them."

"Depends on how it's transmitted," Woodburn pointed out.

Hammond conceded the point with a grunt as he tried one of the drawers in the filing cabinet. It was locked. "You know—"

"...start transporting them as soon as we have received the additional *sheh'fet* checkpoints." The voice came from the corridor outside, its familiar drawl making Hammond's hackles rise.

Kinsey.

"Senator," said another, in the lilting accent of the Kinahhi. "Our treaty specifically requires the exchange of subjects before we expand your *sheh'fet*. It is, after all, a question of trust."

There was a pause, and Hammond moved quietly to the door, barely daring to breathe as he peered into the corridor. "It is not as simple as that," Kinsey complained irritably. "I can't just— There are procedures. Not everyone takes the same view of the criminal underclass. I can't just hand them over without doing the right paperwork."

Criminal underclass? Was he talking about giving the Kinahhi American prisoners? What the hell for?

"That," said the amber-eyed Kinahhi, "is not our concern. The treaty has been signed." He moved his head to one side, lowering his voice, "If you cannot honor our agreement, we will be forced to station an administrator here at Stargate Command, to ensure that our conditions are met."

"You have no right to—"

"Right?" The Kinahhi man smiled. "Senator, don't you understand that there are no such things as rights? Only power."

"Don't you threaten me, Ambassador." Kinsey's ice-chip eyes narrowed. "I don't take kindly to threats. You'll get your prisoners when I'm good and ready to send them through that gate and not before. In the meantime you'll watch your attitude on my base and—"

"*Your* base?" the Kinahhi interrupted, the smile falling from his face. He raised a hand, and dropped it with a slashing gesture.

The power went out. Everything was pitched into solid, black night.

God in heaven! Behind Hammond, through the observation window, a sickly violet glow cast the faces of the prisoners in a hue of death. It was the only light left shining. A Kinahhi light. *What have you done?*

"We can be great allies," the Kinahhi man said through the blackness. "We can give you all the power you desire, Senator. But we will not be crossed. Deliver the test subjects to Kinahhi within the day, or we will find another puppet to fill your shoes."

There was no answer, no sound in the thick darkness of the

corridor until, after a moment, the power came back on. Hammond squinted in the sudden glare, and saw Kinsey do the same, his face an unpleasant mottle of red anger and white shock. The Kinahhi Ambassador had disappeared and, after cursing vociferously, Kinsey turned and stalked away. In the silent observation room Hammond and Woodburn breathed a sigh of relief.

"You were right," Woodburn whispered. "This is a foothold situation."

"And more advanced that I'd realized," Hammond agreed. "They must be in the computer mainframe, we've seen that before, which means—"

"They have control of the Stargate." Woodburn's face hardened. "I'll lock down the base, contact the President. And to hell with Kinsey."

Hammond shook his head and checked that the corridor was clear. "Come on, let's get out of here," he said, slipping out into the empty hall. "It's not that easy," he added as they walked. "What if the Kinahhi send an army through the gate? Or something worse? We can't show our hand too soon. Besides," he cast a look at Woodburn, "if we're going to start a war, I'd rather fight it in their backyard than ours."

"What are you saying?" Woodburn asked, slowing as they approached the access hatch through which they'd arrived. "Send an army to Kinahhi? They'd never let us get past their gate-room. The security is—"

"Not if they know it's an army," Hammond pointed out. "But if the army is dressed in orange jump suits…" Carefully, he opened the access hatch and stepped inside, onto the ladder.

"You mean disguise our men as prisoners?"

"That's exactly what I mean." He started climbing down, wishing he was twenty years younger. Wishing he had his best team at hand to send into the fray. "We deploy a team to secure the Kinahhi gate-room for as long as possible, to give you time to go over Kinsey's head and clear out this mess at the SGC without interference from Kinahhi."

Above him, Woodburn was already breathing heavily. "I'd have to get volunteers. Men willing to go against the express orders of the Senator—"

"Consider me your first," Hammond said.

"You?"

Hammond laughed at the incredulity in the man's voice. "I'm still a good shot, General. Besides, I have friends on Kinahhi, good friends. And I want to make sure they get home in one piece." He refused to consider the possibility that it was already too late.

The clang of booted feet on the ladder was the only sound as they continued their slow descent. Eventually Woodburn said, "Then the mission's yours, George."

Hammond smiled in the darkness. *General, you have a go.*

The air was clear, right up to the stars, sucking every scrap of heat from the desert floor. The fire was long gone, a stench like burning rubber all that remained of its miserly heat, and Jack could feel the cold sinking deep into his bones. His teeth had stopped chattering and he suspected the blood had frozen in his arm, keeping it from bleeding further.

Daniel sat next to him, pressed up close, on watch, while Teal'c lay on his other side trying to sleep. But there wasn't enough heat to share in the barren, unsheltered night, and Jack was beginning to wonder how many such nights they could survive. If the clawing thirst didn't get them first. Sleep was impossible. Everything was—

Daniel tensed.

"What?" Jack rasped.

"I see something." Stiffly, Daniel rose and stared out into the darkness. "Lights."

Teal'c sat up, helping Jack to his feet – foot. "I, too, can see them," he confirmed, raising his hand to point. "There."

Bobbing in the distance snaked a short procession of flickering yellow lights. Moving closer. "Take cover," Jack said quietly, nodding toward the gutted escape pod behind which they'd built their fire. "Help me over there, Teal'c."

Gritting his teeth against the swelling pain in his knee, he slid down behind the pod and raised his P90. He had half a clip left, max. Daniel and Teal'c settled themselves either side of him, close enough that he could feel Daniel's arm shaking where it brushed up against his. From the cold, no doubt. His own fingers were so numb he could barely feel the trigger.

"You know," Daniel said, as they watched the weaving lights advance, "shooting at these guys is probably not the smartest move."

"Who's shooting?"

"I'm just saying… We're freezing our asses off in a desert, with no water, no food, and no way out of here," said Daniel. "Whoever they are, how could they make things worse?"

Plenty of ways, Jack thought bleakly, but all he said was, "Just keep your eyes open."

At some distance from them, the lights stopped moving. It was hard to tell what they were. Searchlights a mile away, or flashlights at twenty feet? It didn't help that there was no noise. Jack settled his weapon firmly against his shoulder, ignoring the flash of pain from his right arm. Perhaps whoever carried those lights hadn't made them yet? It was dark, their fire was long gone, and if they just kept quiet… He reached out and placed a restraining hand on Daniel's arm, just to make sure.

The silence stretched long, biting cold cramping each muscle. Jack was just wondering if they were all suffering from some kind of shared hallucination when a clear, lilting voice spoke. "*Amici vel inimici?*"

Huh? It sounded kinda familiar, but the accent was thick and strange. He turned to Daniel, but all he could see of him was a flicker of yellow light dancing against the lenses of his glasses.

"Ah," Daniel hesitated, "I think it's, um… You won't believe this."

"What?"

"Ah, he said 'friend or foe?'"

"Well, that depends," Jack replied, "on who the hell they are." After a moment, he added, "Ask them."

Carefully, Daniel stood, arms spread wide. "My name is Daniel Jackson, and this—"

A man stepped forward, holding a light close to his face. He was young, little more than a kid, dark-skinned and bright eyed. "Dan'yel Jak'sun?"

"Ah, yeah. That's right. And this is Jack O'Neill and Teal'c. We're from a place far away, and we're looking for a friend – *amicus. Amica.*"

"You talk in the tongue of our enemy," he said. "And yet you are not Kinahhi."

"No," Daniel agreed, stepping around the escape pod. "No, we're not. We're from a place called Earth. Far, far away." He cleared his throat. "Ah, do you have a name?"

The man eyed him carefully, then straightened in pride. "I am Atella, of the *Arxanti*. You stand in Arxantia, our home."

Daniel shrugged slightly. *No idea.*

The kid, Atella, watched him for a moment and cautiously added, "The Kinahhi name us Mahr'bal."

The reaction was instant. Daniel's eyes went very wide, and he fixed a smile on his face – the kind of smile that promised trouble. Sliding a look toward Jack, he said, "That would be what the Kinahhi call their dissidents."

Or terrorists, in the language Jack spoke. Out of the frying pan... But if doing a deal with the devil was what it took to get his team home alive, then so be it. He pushed himself upright, doing his best to hide his crippled leg. "Look," he said, keeping his weapon neutral but ready. "We need to get back to Kinahhi. They're holding a friend of ours in a place called Tsapan, and—"

"Sa'mantha Kah'tur?"

Jack's weapon snapped up. "How do you know that?"

Atella smiled. "The Arxanti know many things."

"Like how to get her out of there?"

The kid said nothing. He looked over his shoulder, toward his men lurking in the shadows, before returning his attention to Daniel. For someone so young, he had remarkable composure. "You are injured, Daniel Jackson." He took another step closer and encompassed them all with a single look. The thick cloak he wore against the desert night was tattered and old and his boots, wrapped around his legs, seemed little more than strips of animal skin. Very primitive. "You are not clothed for Arxantia. If you remain here, you will die."

"Then help us get back to Tsapan and—"

Atella turned. "Follow, as best you can," he said, and set out with a long-legged lope across the freezing desert. "Alvita Candra awaits you." Soon the small procession of lights started to move, snaking off into the darkness. To Jack it looked like their only hope, slowly fading away.

He flung a brief look at his friends. "Anyone have *any* idea how they know about Carter? And who – or what – is Alvira Candarella?"

"It's a name," Daniel said quietly. "Alvita Candra. A woman's name. As for how they know about Sam…" He shrugged.

"Perhaps they are in contact with the Kinahhi?" Teal'c suggested. "It is possible that our names and descriptions have been circulated in order to more speedily apprehend us."

"Maybe." Jack wasn't convinced. Carter hadn't escaped, after all. At least, not as far as he knew…

"We have little choice but to follow them, O'Neill," Teal'c pointed out carefully. "They at least have water and food."

"Yeah."

Atella had been spot on; if they stayed out in the desert they wouldn't last long. And besides, Jack hadn't sensed any threat from these guys. There'd been no posturing, no waving weapons around – in fact, no intimidation at all. The kid hadn't even been armed.

"Not exactly what you'd expect from the kind of people who bomb women and children," Daniel said, staring out after the lights. Must have been reading Jack's mind.

"No," Teal'c agreed. "However, I have come to distrust much that the Kinahhi have told us about their world."

"You said it, T." Never believe anything you can't see with your own two eyes. "Daniel." Jack beckoned him closer. "Give me a hand. Teal'c, take point – and don't lose them. I wanna know exactly what these guys know about Carter, and how they know it."

Teal'c nodded, and disappeared silently after the train of lights. Jack squinted out into the darkness with a grimace. It was going to be a long night.

Daniel moved close enough for Jack to loop an arm around his shoulders, flinching slightly at the weight on his dislocated shoulder.

"Sorry," Jack muttered.

"It's okay." He was lying, but what choice did they have? Then Daniel cleared his throat. It sounded like something unpleasant was trying to get out, and Jack wasn't sure he wanted to hear it.

"Ah, Jack?"

"Daniel?"

"There's something you should know."

He didn't answer straightaway, letting Daniel take his weight as they began to hobble forward. When they'd established an ungainly kind of rhythm he grated out, "If you're gonna tell me you forgot to tape *The Simpsons* now's not a good time."

Daniel's eyes were fixed on the wil o' the wisp lights leading them deep into the ruins and dust. "Mahr'bal," he said at last. "I could be wrong, but... Well, I'm probably not."

"About what?" Damn, it felt like his entire knee had swollen to the size of a football, each jarring limp dislodging something else inside the joint.

Daniel cleared his throat. "Ramses the second called himself Mahr-B'l," he explained, "which is generally taken to mean, ah, champion or upholder of..." He paused, then in a quieter voice finished, "of Baal. Mahr means upholder, supporter if you like. Mahr'bal."

Jack stopped. "Are you saying these guys are Jaffa?"

"No," Daniel shook his head. "No. Like I said the first time we were here, I don't think Baal has a presence on Kinahhi. It must be some kind of historical holdover." He gave a slight shrug, causing them both to list a little to the right. "In fact, it's significant that Atella called himself *Arxanti* – which, incidentally, is of Latin rather than Canaanite derivation, obviously denoting an entirely different linguistic origin."

"Obviously."

"It's possible that the Kinahhi call Atella's people Mahr'bal as some kind of tag, dating back to their overthrow of Baal." He nodded, apparently agreeing with himself. "It makes sense, when you think about it. It's an attempt to link the enemy to an idea which, in essence, is the antithesis of modern Kinahhi identity."

"Oh yeah," Jack agreed, gasping as his foot hit a large stone, jarring his damaged knee into scarlet shards of agony. He sucked in a breath. "*That* makes sense. When you think about it..."

"In addition," Daniel mused, "it effectively masks the true identity of your opponent, thus allowing you total control over how they are perceived by your own people. It's the ultimate propaganda, in a way reminiscent of the Roman evisceration of Carthaginian culture after—"

"Daniel!"

"What?"

"Your point?"

"Oh." He nodded. "Well, I thought you should understand the significance of the name. Just in case."

Jack grunted in response. "Yeah, you're right. I should." Not that it changed anything. Teal'c was right, they had no choice but to follow these strange people, who seemed to know far more about SG-1 than SG-1 knew about them. He hated it when he was out of options. "Keep your eyes open. If there's trouble brewing, I want to know about it."

Daniel snorted softly as they hobbled back into motion. "Let's just hope we don't have to make a run for it."

"Sit," Koash instructed, waving his scarlet-traced fingers toward the large chair.

Sam regarded it with suspicion. It was clearly alien, and she doubted it was Kinahhi. There were some kind of controls on its arms, and a plate that seemed designed for a hand. Like a palm reader. "What is it?" she asked, folding her arms over her chest and refusing to move.

"It is a seat of learning," Koash told her. "A powerful weapon."

"Weapon?"

"Against dissent and chaos. It helps us read the truth in men's minds."

A faint violet light deep within the chair gave it a ghostly glow, and Sam saw thick Kinahhi cables connecting it to the nine chairs that stood on the dais in the center of the room. "This is how you access the *sheh'fet*," she guessed. "It acts like a kind of buffer, filtering the thoughts so you can only read the ones you want. Right?"

Koash didn't answer. "Sit," he repeated.

"I don't think so." The cacophony of sound that had overwhelmed her in the *sheh'fet* had sunk to a distant roar, and she had no intention of—

Strong hands seized her from behind, and her aching and abused body was slow to respond as she found herself flung into her chair. Cuffs whipped around her wrists and ankles, strapping her in place.

Koash drew nearer, stooping so that his narrow face was close to her. "I wish to know about O'Neill and the Mahr'bal."

"You'd better ask him then. I don't know anything."

"You know O'Neill. That is enough. We will find the answers that we seek, and if you resist…" His cruel eyes moved deliberately to where Crawford was huddled in a miserable heap against the far wall. "I know you, Major Samantha Carter," his gaze returned to her face. "I have felt your mind. You will not let another suffer in your place."

She didn't look away, beckoning him closer with a twitch of her head. He bent nearer, eager to hear. With a smile, Sam butted him hard in the face. Koash jerked back with a cry, hands cupping his nose as blood seeped between his fingers and dripped to the floor. "Go to hell!" Sam spat, and from the corner of her eye she saw Crawford staring at her in open-mouthed shock.

Score two for the SGC.

By the time the ragged settlement came into view, the pale light of pre-dawn was painting a thin strip of white gold on the horizon. A scant dew had settled on the rocks and sand, and Daniel eagerly licked the moisture from his lips. At his side, Jack hobbled in silence. His face was past gray, turning almost transparent in the morning light and aging him twenty years. He hadn't spoken for hours, and Daniel wondered if he was even aware of where they were. Nothing but utter determination not to give up kept him on his feet, but even that was wearing thin. Their pace had slowed to a crawl.

In the fragile light ahead he saw the dark shape of Teal'c silhouetted against the horizon, waiting.

"Almost there," Daniel croaked through a dry, raw throat.

Jack said nothing, just kept walking. And then, out of nowhere, Daniel saw people approaching all around them. Noiselessly, they materialized out of the pre-dawn gloom and he drew Jack to a halt. "Company," Daniel whispered.

Jack lifted his head, brown eyes stark against his ashen face. His lips moved, as if he were about to speak, but no sound came out.

"Daniel Jackson." The voice, young and strong, belonged to

Atella, who approached with a glint of admiration in his eyes. "I did not believe you would make it so far." His attention turned to Jack. "This one is unwell."

"Been worse," Jack scratched out, surprising Daniel.

Atella nodded, as if he believed him entirely. "Come, let my men aid you now."

Silent as shadows, two Arxanti moved in and supported Jack between them. Daniel almost staggered at the sudden loss of his weight, and Atella reached out to steady him. "I would learn more of your people, Daniel Jackson. You are brave and strong."

Daniel mustered a smile. "I'll be happy to tell you, Atella. But first, if you have any water…?"

"Come," Atella said, by way of an answer. "We will share what we have."

The encampment into which they were led was an eclectic mixture of tents and crumbling buildings, a civilization built into the ruins of one much older and much greater. Tantalizing glimpses of ancient writing caught Daniel's attention as he trudged between the ragged shacks, watched the whole time by a gaggle of wide-eyed, skinny children. These people were dirt-poor, scratching a subsistence out of the sand. Could they really be the dissidents so feared by Damaris and the Kinahhi? Of course, poverty bred anger, and anger bred violence. It seemed to be one of the universal constants of human history, wherever in the galaxy it was played out. A depressing thought.

"Here," Atella said at last, stopping before one of the largest structures in the settlement. A long awning stretched out from the crumbling ruins of a building, serving as a kind of veranda beneath which Daniel could see the welcome flicker of flames and the hustle of movement. He ducked beneath the awning and found himself amid scattered carpets, blankets and cushions. A fire burned in a battered brazier that gleamed like a treasured possession. Beyond that stood the wall of the old building, its open door leading into a room brightened by a light so steady it couldn't have been natural.

"Your friends are within," Atella told him, brushing past Daniel and leading him onward. "Come, there is water and food."

Stepping carefully over the carpets, Daniel followed Atella into the room. It was bigger than he'd imagined, and a soft light emanated from a strip that ran around the wall. It was oddly familiar. Electricity? How was that possible? More threadbare carpets and cushions covered the floor, but the walls were smooth. Not stone. He moved closer, to touch one. Not plaster. Almost metallic...

"Daniel?" Jack croaked. He lay propped up on a pile of cushions next to Teal'c, waving ineffectually at one of Atella's men, who was trying to examine his blown knee. "Tell him not to touch!"

Crossing the room, Daniel joined them. "Maybe he can help." He eased himself to the ground with a grateful sigh. God, it felt good to rest.

Jack cast him a skeptical look. "Unless he has a shot of morphine up his sleeve, Daniel, I doubt it."

Atella was watching them, his curious gaze darting between both men. "Fortus is a skilled healer, Jack O'Neill. Let him help you."

"Ah, look, no offence. I just—"

"Your prejudice against cultures different from your own does you a disservice, O'Neill," observed Teal'c. "Even among the Tauri, are there not many different forms of medicine?"

"Sure," Jack agreed sourly. "Crystals, leeches, voodoo-dolls. Aroma-goddamn-therapy. I prefer the kind that actually works. So if you—"

"If we are to rescue Major Carter," Teal'c cut in, "we must seek what help we can." He cast a pointed look at Jack. "Unless you are able to walk, Daniel Jackson and I will be forced to leave you here when we return to Tsapan."

Jack was about to protest when a commotion at the door attracted all their attention. Three women entered, each carrying a tray, stepping lightly over the carpets to set their burdens on the floor. Atella bent and picked up a tall cup from one of the trays, offering it to Daniel. "Water."

Daniel glanced over at Jack. They had no purification tabs, but it was either this or dehydration. With a shrug, Jack gave his permission and Daniel took the cup gratefully and lifted it to his lips. The water tasted pure and sweet, cool and perfect as it slid around his dry mouth and down his parched throat. He drank, and drank.

"Not too much," Jack cautioned. "You'll make yourself sick."

After a year on Abydos, he knew that all too well and lowered the cup. Teal'c and Jack were both taking restrained sips at drinks of their own. "Thank you," Jack said to Atella, without a hint of sarcasm.

"Indeed," Teal'c added. "We owe you a debt of gratitude."

Atella bowed in acknowledgement. "Our water, at least, is plentiful and pure. A gift of our ancestors. But our food…" He gestured to the few dried fruits and hard looking loaves of bread the women had provided. "You are welcome to what we have, but it is little."

"Looks great," Jack enthused, picking up a fruit and biting into it.

Daniel mimicked him, and the taste wasn't bad. A little musty, but sweet. Almost like dates. "It must be hard to grow food out here."

"It is the price we pay for our freedom, Daniel Jackson," Atella replied, sitting cross-legged before them. "The Kinahhi do not trouble us here."

"Speaking of," Jack said, taking another sip of water. "Where exactly is here?"

"Arxantia," Atella replied. "The city of the Arxanti."

"Yeah," Jack agreed. "And that would be how far, roughly, from Tsapan?"

"A great distance," Atella assured him gravely. "I do not know. You would have to cross the Mibsaw Sea."

Jack glanced over at Daniel, eyebrows raised. "Sea?"

"I believe," said Teal'c, "that this city is located on a different continent than the city of the Kinahhi."

"*Continent*?" Jack groaned. "You gotta be kidding…"

"Teal'c is correct," said Atella. "This is not the land of the Kinahhi." He scowled suddenly and spat on the floor. "Yet they treat it as their own, plundering our heritage."

Jack wasn't listening, his head sinking back into the cushions, one hand pressed over his eyes. "A different *continent*?"

Daniel had flown over it on their arrival, the vast ruined city spread out like an ancient map and calling to him with a siren song.

"I don't suppose you guys have a Stargate?" Jack asked, sitting up straight again.

Atella looked blank.

"Chappa'ai?" Daniel suggested.

"I do not know these words," Atella apologized, pushing himself to his feet. "And dawn is upon us. My watch is complete, and I must rest. As must you." He glanced at them all and his gaze arrested on Jack. "Allow Fortus to treat your wounds, Jack O'Neill. Only a fool rejects aid in this land."

Jack gave a nod, but whether it was of agreement Daniel couldn't tell. Atella seemed to take it as such, however, and with a respectful bow turned and left. "He speaks the truth, O'Neill," Teal'c observed.

"Yeah, yeah," Jack sighed wearily, beckoning the man, Fortus, over. He was of middle years, his black hair streaked with gray, and his face wise.

"He looks like a doctor," Daniel said quietly.

"I prefer the look of Fraiser."

Daniel smiled but didn't answer as Fortus drew closer and crouched. From his belt, he pulled a sharp knife.

"Whoa!" Jack yelped. "You're not chopping the damn thing off!"

Fortus raised a curious eyebrow. "I must see your injury, friend," he said. "I need to remove the clothing on your leg."

"Oh." Jack cleared his throat and relaxed slightly. "I see. Okay."

With a nod, Fortus sliced the fabric of Jack's BDUs. Daniel winced at the sight of the swollen, purpling knee. "Ouch."

"Yeah," Jack agreed. "Look, if you can strap it or something. Trust me, I've done this before, it's gonna need surgery and—"

Fortus touched Jack's leg with a light finger. "There will be some pain," he said after a moment. "But I can cure this wound." He looked up. "If you will permit me."

"Cure?" Jack cast Daniel a *what-the-hell-does-he-mean?* look.

"How?" Daniel asked curiously, casting half a glance up at the weird lighting in the room. Why did it seem so familiar?

Fortus rose and moved to the back of the room. Another light suddenly switched on, illuminating a narrow alcove where Daniel glimpsed a square box with something glowing in its center. Then Fortus obscured his view, withdrawing a dull silver disk from above the box. He hefted it in one hand and turned back toward them. The light in the alcove shut off, hiding what lay within. "The *remem* cures many wounds, if the eye of the healer can understand the injury," he said, moving back to Jack's side. He held the disk out, strong fingers gripping its rim. A soft violet light began to glow at its heart and he turned to Teal'c. "Restrain your friend."

"What?"

Teal'c placed a firm hand on Jack's shoulder.

"Hey!"

"All will be well, O'Neill."

"Yeah, I— Ow!" As the violet light touched his knee, Jack arched back against the cushions, biting off a scream. "Holy crap," he hissed. "Oh, *God...*"

Daniel's eyes widened. "Look at that..." The brutal swelling was receding, even the scars from previous injuries seemed to fade.

A sweat of concentration stood on Fortus's brow. Finally, with a gasp, he withdrew the device and sagged back on his haunches. He was breathless. "You drew much power," he said after a moment. "More than—"

"He has lost consciousness," Teal'c said, studying Jack's slack features with guarded concern.

Fortus nodded. "This is to be expected. He will sleep and feel better for it." He turned to Daniel, head tilting to one side. "And now, your shoulder...?"

Ah.

CHAPTER TWENTY-FIVE

The sand glistened in the morning heat, a heat Commander Ebrum Kenna could already feel through the walls of the aging transport ship. But he ignored the discomfort, satisfied at what he saw below. Tracks in the sand, from the impact of three smooth capsules that lay cracked like the discarded eggs of some giant bird.

"This is it," he told the pilot. "Land here."

The ship dropped smoothly, and the capsules grew larger until Kenna could see the ornate designs they bore, oddly reminiscent of Tsapan. Where had O'Neill acquired such technology? The answer would have to wait. For now the Commander's single objective was to capture his prey and secure the freedom of his son. His men were ready, armed and alert. Although the search had been protracted, and dawn had long since crested the horizon, they showed no weariness. They knew better than to dare.

With a barely perceptible bump the transport landed and its door slid open. Hot, dry air hovered on the threshold, barely beaten back by the ship's cooling system. "Secure the area," Kenna ordered, "and report any evidence of what has occurred here. But stay alert. This is Mahr'bal country, every fold in the land may conceal the enemy." He met the reserved, neutral gaze of his men with pride. These Tauri, with their overt feelings and passions, would be no match for the stoicism of the Kinahhi. He nodded his approval. "Move out."

The sun had reached its zenith, its brilliance magnified by the wide, white ruins that spread across the desert as far as Teal'c could see. Heat shimmered between them, reflecting up from the ground in waves.

At his side, Daniel Jackson mopped at his brow with his sleeve. "Hot," he murmured, unnecessarily.

"Indeed."

They walked together, following in the eager footsteps of Fortus. Teal'c's hand moved to the wound in his leg, now no more than a ragged slice through his clothing. Daniel Jackson, rotating his formerly injured shoulder as if for the simple pleasure of the movement, was equally well healed. And pleased with the result.

Neither of them had slept long after the intense – and admittedly painful – process, but their wounds had been superficial. O'Neill, however, still slept. The knee and arm wounds, Teal'c suspected, were not the only injuries O'Neill had sustained – who knew what damage the *sheh'fet* had inflicted? O'Neill had volunteered no information.

Teal'c was still uneasy with his choice to leave O'Neill alone and sleeping amid an untried people, but he had been reluctant to wake him when Fortus had returned to their room, with an urgent summons for Daniel Jackson to meet with their tribal shaman.

"She can tell you of your friend, of Sa'mantha Kah'tur," Fortus had insisted.

Teal'c had sensed no malicious intent from the Arxanti, nothing to make him suspect them. If he was mistaken, the blame would follow him to his grave. But he believed O'Neill would have wished him to accompany Daniel Jackson, to glean what they could of Major Carter's situation.

"Here," said Fortus, stopping abruptly and indicating a steep trail that lead underground. "Alvita Candra is within."

Teal'c eyed the entrance dubiously. "This dwelling does not appear entirely stable, Daniel Jackson."

His friend laughed. "What does around here, Teal'c?"

"You will come to no harm," Fortus assured them. "There is no danger of collapse, or we would not permit Alvita Candra to reside here."

Daniel Jackson clasped the man's arm. "Thank you," he said. "Ah…is there anything we should know before we meet her? Any sign of respect we should make?"

"None but the common courtesy you would extend to the seers of your own people, Daniel."

He nodded gravely and said, "Right. Let's, ah, go."

With their boots slip-sliding on loose sand and gravel, Teal'c followed Daniel Jackson as he scrambled down and into the blessedly cool shade below. A large stone lintel marked the mouth of a short tunnel, seeming murky after the sun's glare. As they walked through it, Daniel Jackson reached out to touch a pattern on one of the walls. "There's art here," he murmured. "Quite sophisticated."

"This would not be the first great civilization to have been destroyed by the Goa'uld," Teal'c observed.

"True," Daniel Jackson agreed, "but—" He stopped as they reached the end of the tunnel. Before them opened a round room, lit by shafts of sunlight that lanced through cracks in the ceiling and cast jagged spots of light on the sandy floor. Dust motes danced and all was quiet.

Daniel Jackson stepped into the room, Teal'c on his heel. After a moment, he spoke. "Hello? I'm Daniel."

"Daniel Jackson?" A young woman's voice drifted from among the shadows and sunlight. "You are as I have seen you."

Teal'c turned toward the sound and saw a lean girl emerge from the edges of the room. Her mass of hair hung in broken curls, falling all around her shoulders and partly obscuring her face. But beneath her wild mane he saw bright, intelligent eyes, and they were fixed on Daniel Jackson with an expression of awe and reverence.

"Have you come to fulfill the prophesy?"

"Ah… The prophesy?" Daniel Jackson cleared his throat and threw a helpless look at Teal'c. He had no answer.

"To lead the Arxanti out of the desert, and to lay low our enemy."

"Oh." Daniel Jackson grimaced, taking a step closer. "I'm sorry, whoever you're expecting, it's not me. I—"

"But you have walked with the Angels!" Alvita Candra exclaimed, tossing her hair over her shoulder. The face beneath was beautiful and fiery. "I have seen it."

"Angels?" Daniel Jackson shook his head. "I'm sorry, I don't understand."

Alvita Candra regarded him carefully, her disappointment clear. "The spirits of our ancestors, Daniel Jackson." After a moment, she turned her back on him and walked away. "Come. I will show you."

They followed, weaving in and out of the shafts of sunlight until they stood in the shadows at the back of the room. Alvita Candra lifted her hand, and a polished dome the size of a table appeared out of the darkness. "A gift of the ancestors," she said softly. "The *auspicium*. Through it, the past, present and future of my people can be seen. Watch."

Under her touch, the surface of the dome misted and cleared. Within, as though modeled to perfection, Teal'c saw a vast, gleaming city of white and gold, rising up from the blossoming desert and glittering in the morning sun.

"Beautiful." Daniel Jackson's eyes were wide as he bent to look more closely.

"Arxantia," Alvita Candra breathed, proud and sad. "As our ancestors knew it." She waved her hand over the device again and the city collapsed before their eyes, the flash-fire of staff cannons crumpling its towers and decimating its gleaming boulevards.

"Baal," Teal'c hissed.

"The gods of the Kinahhi were cruel," Alvita Candra said. "But not so cruel as their people."

The image shifted. The city lay in ruins, as they saw it now, victim to the encroaching desert. Within its walls Teal'c saw people move, a ragged, starving army colliding with the military might of the gray-clad Kinahhi. A massacre.

"There were too many of us, said the Kinahhi. They could not feed us, could not admit us to their world. And so they left us to die here, among the ruins of our city, even as they stole the gifts our ancestors had left behind. We fought them, but their gods had left them powerful weapons of destruction and we had nothing but the fire in our hearts."

Alvita Candra moved her hand once more, and the image faded to a steady violet gleam. She lifted her chin. "But we did not die. We remain, and we grow strong. Our ancestors gifted us with pure water, that we may live and grow what little food we can. And we endure, waiting for the day the Angels will return and lead us out of the desert."

Daniel Jackson rose. "I'm sorry," he said. "For what's happened to your people. But I'm not who you want me to be. I'm not one of your ancestors or—"

"I have seen your mind, Daniel Jackson," Alvita Candra insisted. "I know what you are."

He frowned. "I'm sorry, I think you're mistaken. You can't have—"

"You passed through the *sheh'fet* in Kinahhi, did you not?"

He frowned. "I— Yes. Yes, I did. How do you know that?"

Alvita Candra smiled. "What the Kinahhi call the *sheh'fet* once belonged to my people. Our enemy stole it, and now twist it to their own purpose. But they do not know that with the *auspicium* we can see into its very heart. Thus, I saw your mind and know that you have walked among the Angels."

"And you can see Sam?" Daniel Jackson asked. "Samantha Carter, our friend."

Alvita Candra's face grew solemn. "I have seen her. But she is lost to me now."

Lost? Teal'c felt a sudden pain in his chest, grief denied. It could not be. "Lost, how?" he asked, his first words to the woman.

She turned her bright eyes on him. "I do not know, Teal'c of the Jaffa. Her mind is no longer within the *sheh'fet*. I can say no more than that."

"Then I choose to believe that she yet lives."

Alvita Candra bowed her head. "A wise choice, ancient one."

Daniel Jackson cleared his throat, in a transparent attempt to hide his sudden amusement. "Can I," he said, covering his lack of decorum. "Can I use it?" He was gazing at the *auspicium* as if it were an oasis. "Perhaps I could try to find Sam, to communicate with her?"

"You may try." Alvita Candra appeared curious, as if testing a theory. It made Teal'c nervous. "Touch the *auspicium* and open your mind."

Daniel Jackson reached out gingerly, as if expecting a trick, and touched the shimmering dome. There was no sizzle of a force shield to throw him across the room – all that occurred was the slow fading of the dome's light. "What happened?" His friend's disappointment was obvious.

"Only the Arxanti are able to use such gifts, Daniel Jackson. They are intended for us alone." She ran her hand over the surface of the dome, reigniting its light. "Even when the Kinahhi steal them and pervert them to their own purpose, they can never truly understand the gifts of the Ancients."

A beat of silence followed her last word. Daniel Jackson blinked, jaw dropping slightly. "Ah, I'm sorry, did you say

Ancients?"

Alvita Candra smiled. "The Ancients, yes. Our ancestors."

Daniel Jackson exchanged a startled glance with Teal'c and looked back at the softly glowing device in sudden understanding. "*Arxantia*," he breathed, as if a thousand jigsaw pieces were slipping into place all at once. "Latin-based. Or, rather, Ancient-based. *Arx*, fortress, *antiquus* – ancient. Arxantiqua, or, with a little allophonic shift, *Arxantia*. Ancient Fortress."

Teal'c lifted an eyebrow. "This is most significant, Daniel Jackson."

Alvita Candra smiled in triumph. "Then you do know of the Angels! The spirits of our ancestors. I knew the *auspicium* could not be wrong."

Daniel Jackson was thoughtful. "We call them the Ancients," he said quietly. "And, uh, yeah. I know a little about them."

"You have walked among them," Alvita Candra insisted, darting around the *auspicium* and seizing Daniel Jackson by both hands. "And you have come from beyond the stars, to fulfill the prophesy."

"I—"

"I have *seen* it!" Her mass of curls shrouded her face as she bent to kiss his hands. "You will lead us out of the desert, and bring truth to our enemy. My people have waited generations for your arrival, Daniel Jackson. You cannot abandon us."

Daniel Jackson just stared at Teal'c over the top of her head. Teal'c could see the conflict his friend felt, his desire to help these people warring with the more pressing need to return to the SGC. And to save Major Carter.

Help! Daniel Jackson pleaded voicelessly. But Teal'c had no aid nor answer to offer.

Jack woke slowly, drifting up from a deep and restful sleep into a leaden body that felt as though it hadn't moved for hours. He blinked in the bright sunlight that sliced through the doorway and raised a heavy hand to rub his eyes. Gradually, he became aware of voices chattering away, one in particular sounding extremely animated. And extremely familiar.

Pushing himself upright, he saw Daniel sitting not far from him in deep conversation with Atella and the Doc, Fortus. Daniel was gesturing like some kind of mad conductor with an orchestra on the loose and—

Gesturing. With *both* arms?

Jack studied his blown knee, realizing his leg lay perfectly straight. Tentatively he tried to bend it. No pain. None whatsoever. And that probably hadn't happened once in the last five years. His arm, too, felt fine. The skin beneath the ripped sleeve of his shirt was smooth and unbroken. There wasn't even a scar.

He felt a presence beside him, and looked up to see Teal'c crouch at his side. "You are well rested, O'Neill."

"Yeah." He indicated Teal'c's wounded leg. "You too?"

The Jaffa nodded. "The Arxanti possess technology of great power."

"Yeah, I'm getting that." He yawned, and glanced over at Daniel. "What's going on there?"

The slight lift of one eyebrow gave away Teal'c's affectionate amusement. "Daniel Jackson has made a discovery of great importance."

"What discovery?"

"I believe he would wish to tell you himself."

"Does it get us outta here?"

Teal'c sobered and stood up. "Perhaps"

Perhaps was better than 'no' at least. With a grunt of effort Jack pushed himself to his feet, silently marveling at the lack of complaint from his knees. Or his back. All in all, he felt better than he had in a good long time. Which only made his memory of Carter, trapped in that brain-sucking torture device, that much more painful. He checked his watch and grimaced. He must have slept the whole day. "Daniel!"

His friend turned, beckoning to him from across the room. "Jack. You won't believe this. Come here."

"I shall scout the area, O'Neill," Teal'c offered quickly, eyeing the door with obvious desire. "Before the sun sets."

Jack nodded his agreement. But impatience was pounding in the back of his mind, like a headache waiting to pounce. How long had they left her there? Would there be anything left to rescue? His instinct was to just act, to do something – anything! But he kept it in check. Forcing himself to relax, to look for opportunities even in the most unlikely places, he stepped over the ragged carpets and approached Daniel. "Teal'c said you found something."

"Oh yeah," Daniel grinned enthusiastically. "This is incredible, Jack. This whole place is…it's an ancient city. As in *Ancient* city."

"As in the glowing octopus variety?"

A flicker of irritation crossed Daniel's face. "No. Older, before they ascended." He pointed at the wall. "Look at that, the lights – the whole city. They have technology, Ancient technology. Like the healing device." Suddenly Daniel was on his feet, grabbing Jack's arm and dragging him across the room. "Look, check this out. It's a little hard to see, but I think you'll recognize it."

With a frown, Jack peered into the dark alcove at the back of the room. "What? In here?"

"Just look."

He leaned closer. A bright light came on inside the alcove, illuminating a large, square box. Familiarity nagged at the back of his mind, and not in a good way. "Daniel, tell me this isn't a zombie machine."

There was no answer, and when he turned his head Daniel was staring at him in astonishment. "What?"

"Do that again."

"Do what again?"

"That. With the light."

Jack straightened, glancing up at the light. It switched off. "What thing?"

"That thing."

"I didn't do anything."

"Move closer again," Daniel urged, pushing him forward. "Closer to the alcove."

With an impatient sigh he leaned in, and, sure enough, the light came on. "Sweet. A motion detector. You know, I once knew a guy who had these things installed in his apartment, and if you were sitting watching the game you'd have to keep waving at the ceiling to stop the lights from—"

"It's not a motion detector," Daniel interrupted. "At least, it doesn't work for me. Or Teal'c. The Arxanti say only they can use the 'gifts of the Ancients' because…"

"Because?" Jack stepped back from the alcove and the light

switched off.

"Because they believe they're descended from the Ancients."

Oh please. "Yeah, well," Jack muttered, "as far as I know none of my grandparents glowed in the dark. Must be a coincidence." He squinted back at the alcove. "You didn't answer my question about the zombie machine."

Daniel was still looking at him oddly, but after a moment he collected his thoughts and began to babble excitedly. "Oh, yeah. You're right, it looks exactly the same as the healing device Dr. Lee and I found in Honduras. Only," he tapped at the alcove with one finger and a fizz of blue energy scattered through the air in front of them, "it's shielded, to prevent it's, ah, more negative effects from damaging the population."

"How reassuring." Jack lowered his voice and hissed, "Daniel, the last time we came across one of those things you were nearly scalped by a dead guy!"

"It's what cured us, Jack," Daniel said. "It's what keeps these people alive out here. According to Alvita Candra—"

"Who?"

Daniel waved an impatient hand. "Alvita Candra. Their seer, wise-woman."

Old crone, in other words. "Right."

"According to her, the Kinahhi refuse to allow them to leave the continent. There seems to have been some kind of conflict, perhaps an uprising, a generation or so ago. The Kinahhi erected something they call the Cordon – ah, imagine the Berlin wall only a hundred times longer – and since then the Arxanti haven't been allowed to leave. They're trapped, Jack." He lowered his voice. "You've seen what it's like out there. This climate… Even with the healing device, their people are dying. There's hardly any food, no infrastructure… And we've seen how the Kinahhi live."

"That's rough," Jack agreed. But it wasn't his concern. "This… Cordon? It's manned by the Kinahhi?"

With a frown, Daniel nodded. "Yeah, of course."

"How far is it?"

"I don't know. Why?"

Why? "Because if the Kinahhi are there, then they have transport. And we need to get outta here and back to Tsapan, and then—"

"Jack!" Daniel protested. "We can't just walk away from this."

Oh, here we go... "From what, Daniel?"

"From what's going on here."

"And what's that? Exactly?"

"Genocide."

Jack turned away. "It's not our war, Daniel."

"But they're dying!" Daniel grabbed his sleeve, yanking him to a stop. "Come on, Jack, how can you even—"

"O'Neill!" Teal'c's voice boomed from the doorway.

It sounded like trouble. "What you got?"

"Kinahhi soldiers," Teal'c reported. "At least fifty, well armed."

Atella and Fortus were on their feet, agile as cats. "Take the women and children to the sanctum," Atella ordered, and with a nod Fortus slipped away. Atella's eyes came to rest on Daniel. "The Kinahhi have never ventured so deep into Arxantia in my lifetime."

"They're after us." Jack stepped forward, flinging a look at Daniel, who was watching him expectantly. *It's not our war.* Except now they were dragging Atella's people into their own squabble with the Kinahhi. It sucked.

"We cannot allow them to capture us, O'Neill," warned Teal'c, as if guessing the path of Jack's thoughts. "Everything depends upon our returning to the SGC."

"I know." He looked at Atella, not much more than a kid wrapped in rags, with a belly full of anger fueled by a lifetime of oppression. It felt like exploitation. "Your men ready to fight?"

There was an eager light in the kid's eyes. "We have prayed for the chance to spill the blood of our enemy," he said. "Today will be glorious."

Like hell. "Get them ready," Jack said. "And tell them to do exactly what I say."

Atella nodded and ran from the room, leaving Jack alone with his team. "For the record," he said, stalking toward their small pile of weapons, "I'm not happy about this."

"The desire for freedom burns bright in all men, O'Neill," Teal'c told him, retrieving his P90. "They want to fight."

"They're kids," Jack replied, as he holstered a zat. "They have no idea what they're doing."

"Do not be so sure." Teal'c fixed Jack with a pointed look. "They know what it is to be enslaved. More so than you, O'Neill. They know the value of freedom."

"And they have a right to fight for it," Daniel added.

Jack slung the stolen Kinahhi weapon over his shoulder with a grunt. "They're going to die for it too," he said bluntly. "And not just them. You think Damaris and her crew will let them get away with this? The tanks will be rolling in before they've buried their dead. Believe me."

Daniel opened his mouth to respond, but at that moment Atella appeared again in the doorway. "O'Neill, they come."

With a final glance at his friends, Jack led them out into the long shadows of dusk, unable to shake the feeling that he was about to fire the first shot in a war.

In the flat desert, there was little in the way of cover for Commander Kenna's men. He had scouts ranging ahead and to each side, to warn of the enemy's approach, but despite that he felt the silence like a weight around his neck as his phalanx of soldiers marched through the decaying streets of Arxantia.

Some said the city was haunted by the ghosts of its former denizens, that the very ground had been poisoned by death and turned into the wasteland upon which he now trod. But the Commander did not deal in superstition, he dealt in facts. In this case, the facts were that the tracks of O'Neill and his two accomplices led right into the heart of Arxantia, apparently following behind a small troop of the Mahr'bal. It was equally apparent that at least one of the Tauri was severely injured.

Good, he told himself. And yet... Despite everything, he felt a niggling respect. To trail O'Neill like a pack of dogs trailed wounded prey somehow seemed undignified. Kenna would have preferred a fairer fight rather than a—

"Commander." Chief Officer Lahat was pointing toward one of the returning scouts, climbing up a ridge that had obscured their view of what lay beyond. With a lift of his hand, Kenna stopped his men and waited.

"Contact, sir," the scout reported with a salute. "A shantytown. Straight ahead. The Tauri tracks lead right into it."

Wounded prey seeking safety. Kenna found himself unexpect-
edly disturbed by the image, and dismissed the scout with a curt
nod. Then he turned to Lahat. "Surround the village. Enter on my
mark. And, remember, the Tauri are to be captured alive."

"Yes, sir." The Chief saluted and moved away. Behind him,
Kenna saw his men fan out to either side, moving watchfully
through the ruins of the ancient city. He advanced with them,
dropping low as he crested the rise. In a shallow bowl of a valley,
lay the shabby encampment. It nestled against some of the more
intact structures in the city. He saw no movement among the flapping fabric of the tents, and guessed that their approach had been
detected.

*Are you there, O'Neill? Are you injured? Are you rallying this
tattered army against us?* There would be no escape this time.
The sticks and stones of the Mahr'bal would be no match for the
Kinahhi army, even with O'Neill at their head.

At a signal from Lahat he knew his men were in position.
Kenna answered for them to hold fast; they would wait until
nightfall and then descend like the thunder of Re'ammin himself
to claim their prize.

CHAPTER TWENTY-SIX

A strap held Sam's head tight against the back of the chair, and on either side of her stood a black-robed figure. *Mib'khaur.* The name came to her unbidden – the Chosen. Chosen to serve the *Kaw'ree.* Although she couldn't move her head she could see a glint of silver, the lethal curve of a blade stark against black velvet robes. Security, or sacrifice?

Her attention shifted to the man standing before her. Koash. His nose was swollen and bloody, probably broken, and he glared at her with eyes as sharp as the dagger held by the *Mib'khaur.* "If you will act like an animal," he told her coldly, "then you will be treated as such."

Sam snorted a humorless laugh. "You mean worse than being stuck in the *sheh'fet*? Where I come from, we don't even treat animals like that."

Koash's gaze drifted to Crawford, who still sat hunched against the wall. "And yet you would condemn this man to such treatment?"

"He's the reason we're here," she said flatly, refusing to feel guilty. If anyone deserved that fate... *No one does*, a treacherous voice whispered. *Not even him.*

Koash smiled, a thin stretch of his lips, as if he'd heard the murmuring of her conscience. He probably had. "Let us see." He moved closer, lifting icy fingertips to her temples. "Let us see the truth you hide about the Mahr'bal, and your people."

"There is no truth about—" She gasped. A sensation like cold maggots crawled under her skin, something hard slammed into her mind and strong, merciless hands gripped each side of her head.

Obey, a voice hissed inside her head. *Let me in.*

She bucked in the chair, but the grip on her mind only grew stronger. Crushing her. It shook her physically, and then another vicious blow knocked her sideways until she lay sprawled on the floor.

A figure stood over her, cloaked and featureless. *Death?*

It laughed. *Worse. I am the sheh'fet, and you will hide nothing from me.* With one impossibly long arm it reached down and curled skeletal fingers around the fabric of her shirt, lifting her up into the air and pulling her closer to the empty space that should have been its face. *Tell me of O'Neill. Of the Mahr'bal.*

"There's nothing to tell," she spat.

A single ivory finger, its nail blackened and decaying, pressed into the center of her forehead. *You lie.*

"No. I—"

A shattering blow threw her across the room so hard she felt herself splinter into a thousand tiny pieces...

"Captain Samantha Carter reporting, Sir."

A bony claw dug into her shoulder, blood seeped through her dress uniform.

Show me, *whispered a voice, darker and more frightening than death.* Show me where he is...

Stars shone brightly in the cold, black sky, a sliver of moon cutting like a blade and offering no light. A good night for battle, Teal'c thought, as he looked around at the shabby, malnourished men who had poured from their wretched dwellings, eager to strike a blow against their oppressors. He could see the hunger for retribution in their drawn faces, see the longing for justice burning bright in their eyes. But as he studied these men, some barely older than boys, others old before their time, he began to share O'Neill's view of the situation.

This was no army.

Next to him Daniel Jackson stood staring up at the crumbling buildings around them, lost in thought. And a little further off, O'Neill was in urgent discussion with Atella. Even from this distance, Teal'c could hear his conversation.

"Weapons," O'Neill was saying, gesturing to the P90 he held in one hand. "Any kind of weapons?"

Atella shook his head, but did not seem perturbed. He stooped and picked up a sizable chunk of stone. "This," he said, "is our weapon. Arxantia."

O'Neill was shaking his head in frustration. "No. You don't get it. You can't— You can't throw stones at these people! They have guns. Lots of guns." He raked a hand through his hair and blew out a breath. "Just— Wait here."

Teal'c clasped his hands behind his back, bracing himself as O'Neill stalked over to where he and Daniel Jackson stood waiting.

"This is hopeless," O'Neill hissed. "They don't have any kind of weapon. Nothing! Not even bows and goddamn arrows."

"So much for the terrorist theory then, huh?" Daniel said, not moving his gaze from the buildings above them.

O'Neill scowled. Teal'c could see him weighing the odds, judging right and wrong. A Jaffa in service to the Goa'uld would not hesitate to use these people for their own defense, if for no other purpose than to mask their escape. But O'Neill was different. "It's going to be a slaughter," he said quietly. "We can't drag them into this."

"What choice do we have?" Teal'c asked. "We are surrounded."

O'Neill squinted out into the night, deliberately avoiding looking at either of them. "If I surrender—"

"No," Daniel Jackson objected instantly. "Jack—"

"It'll buy you guys some time," he insisted. "Get to the Cordon, find yourselves a ship, and get off this damn planet. Get back to the SGC and tell them what the hell is going on here."

Such bravery, while typical of O'Neill, was impractical. "The Kinahhi know we are here, O'Neill. Your surrender will not prevent them from razing this settlement in order to find us."

"I'm the one they want," he insisted. "I escaped and—"

"Colonel O'Neill?" It was Atella. "Forgive the interruption, but... There is no need to fear. The Kinahhi can not harm us here."

O'Neill appeared to be swallowing a reply, but Daniel Jackson spoke. "How do you know that, Atella?"

He shrugged. "All the Arxanti know as much."

"Yeah," O'Neill snapped, eyes scanning the dark horizon. "But I'm betting the Kinahhi don't."

Atella smiled fiercely. "They soon will."

"Jack, it's possible..." Daniel Jackson began, but at that moment Teal'c saw movement high up in the ruins.

"O'Neill!" He barked, grabbing his friend's arm as a bolt of scarlet laser fire streaked through the night. The side of the building exploded, throwing them to the ground and scattering them with debris.

"Damn it!" O'Neill growled. All around them the night sky erupted with streams of blood-red energy. "Too late."

Atella stared up in shock. He had never seen such a thing, Teal'c surmised.

"All will be well," he whispered to himself. "Arxantia will protect us."

"Like hell," O'Neill cursed.

Teal'c was inclined to agree.

"Move in!" Commander Kenna gave the order, leading his men down into the shallow scoop of land. To his left, he heard the telltale whine of the alien weapon, and watched the dancing blue energy fell one of his men. The sensation had been unpleasant, he remembered, but not harmful. An odd kind of weapon. *A civilized weapon…* He shook the thought away and tightened his hold on his own shotgun. There was no room for sympathy or mercy; the life of his son was at stake and nothing in his world was more important.

In the ruins now, he could see scurrying figures. Thin limbs, the hushed whispers of panic, as the Mahr'bal scuttled through their encampment. Hard to imagine these people having the intellect to plot the atrocity at Libnah that had massacred so many Kinahhi. But that had been a generation past. By the look of things, the Mahr'bal were now barely able to clothe themselves.

Another blue flash lit up to his left, followed by the rattle of the Tauris' more lethal projectile weapons. Kenna turned toward the sound.

A large pillar rose up before him, its surface smooth and less damaged than the rest of the city. Ducking behind it, he watched as his men tightened the noose around the settlement. There was no way out for O'Neill and his friends. As his soldiers moved past him, Kenna slid around the pillar to take the lead.

Suddenly he became aware of a soft, violet light gleaming against the ruins all around him. The pillar where he'd stood was glowing.

His men stopped, looking around in confusion.

And then a scream of abject terror echoed through the night from the far side of the valley. "*Êdimmu!*" someone shrieked. "*Êdimmu!*"

The ghosts of the departed...

"What the *hell* is going on?" Violet light washed the city, painting everyone in grisly shades of gray. And people were dying; their screams sounded like they were being ripped limb from limb. It made his skin crawl. "Daniel?"

"Arxantia," Daniel breathed, awestruck.

"What?"

"The city," he replied, slowly standing to take it all in. "Atella was right. It's protecting them."

Jack shifted until he was sitting with his back to the wall, his P90 at the ready. "How?"

"I have no idea."

A quiet sound to his right announced the arrival of Teal'c, his skin like ebony in the strange light and the brand of Apophis gleaming silver. "An invisible force is attacking the Kinahhi soldiers," he reported, dropping into a crouch next to Jack.

"Invisible?" Jack sighed. "Sure, why not."

Teal'c's face betrayed his disquiet. "I have witnessed several Kinahhi fall to the ground as if under attack, yet I could see no attacker. After some time, they become still."

"Dead?"

"I do not know."

Invisible aliens? Wouldn't be the first time. "I don't like this," Jack decided. "What if—"

Daniel suddenly stiffened. It was as if every muscle had contracted and only his eyes could move, growing wide and horrified. "Oh *God*..." The words crawled out of a throat tight with terror.

"What?" Jack was on his feet, weapon leveled. At nothing. "What do you see?"

Daniel was shaking, his face drained of color. "They're coming."

"Who?" Jack couldn't see a damn thing. He did a slow three-sixty, but there was nothing. Nothing! "Where?"

"No!" Daniel screamed and staggered backward, hands flailing at his face. "No! What have they done to you? No!" He fell to the ground, writhing. "Sha're, don't!"

Crap! "Teal'c!" Jack barked, trying to pin down Daniel's thrashing body. "Cover us and—"

"*Heelksha.*" Teal'c whispered, voice hollow, eyes fixed straight ahead. His mouth dropped open in fear. "*Na-ney!*"

"What?" *Damn it!* "Teal'c! Focus. Come on, there's nothing there."

But Teal'c was backing up, trapped against the wall. "*Na-ney!*" He yelled, frantically trying to ward off something. "*Na'noweia si'taia!*" And then he was running, vaulting over the wall and fleeing through the ruins like the devil himself was on his tail.

"*Teal'c!*"

"No!" Daniel shrieked the word, back arching, eyes rolling. "*No!*"

With a desperate glance at the darkness swallowing Teal'c, Jack abandoned his weapon and grabbed Daniel's shoulders, shaking him hard. "Wake up." Daniel's face was white, ghostly in the violet light of the city, his body rigid. "Wake up, damn it.," Jack hissed. "It's not real! Wake *up!*"

Daniel's breathing was barely a ragged wheeze, his lips gray. And then he collapsed, like a puppet with its strings cut, blood trickling from his mouth.

Oh God, tell me it wasn't real. Jack's fingers searched Daniel's throat for a pulse. *Please…*

Flashes of imagery raced before her eyes. Snapshots. It was dark. Night. A ruined city. She saw Daniel, dead and bleeding. *No!* Teal'c, screaming in terror. Confusion, despair. She felt them. Were they her own feelings, or his?

Then a face she didn't recognize, hollow-cheeked but triumphant. *Mahr'bal.* The name was spat out, vile and dripping with fear. But that was not all… there was another name buried beneath layers of time. *Arxanti.*

Mortal enemy.

"You're afraid of them," she realized, her voice echoing in the void of her mind. "You think they can destroy you."

They have killed your friends.

"I don't believe you," she whispered.

Teal'c, back arched, and teeth bared. Ashen in the first light of dawn. Not dead, please not dead.

"You're lying. This is all a lie!"

He is Mahr'bal. O'Neill is Mahr'bal.

"No."

Are there more like him? How many? A sliver of fear sliced through her chest at the thought. But not her fear – it came from outside. From the vast, brutal mind that held her in a vise. *Will they come to Kinahhi? Will they seek vengeance?*

"I don't know!" she shouted until her throat was raw. "I don't know who they are!"

Her mind was being squeezed, ready to burst. The pressure and pain were enough to shred her sanity. *Tell me!*

A scream ripped from her throat. "I don't know!"

Then a fist, hard as iron, slammed into her head, and everything went black.

CHAPTER TWENTY-SEVEN

The orange jumpsuit was a little tight across the chest, a little long in the leg, but other than that it did its job just fine. It hid the tac vest Hammond wore, hid the zat strapped to his leg, and, most important, made him invisible.

He stood at the foot of the Stargate, in line behind Dave Dixon and the rest of SG-13, just to the right of Henry Boyd, Captain Watts and two dozen more volunteers – all dressed in the same prison garb. Behind him, in the control room, Kinsey was observing the first shipment of 'prisoners' to Kinahhi. That Kinsey could consider trading human beings like chattel made Hammond's blood boil. His fingers curled at his side, and he deliberately flexed them.

Without warning, the Stargate began to spin and the first chevron locked in place. From the corner of his eye, he saw movement; one of the Kinahhi soldiers lining the room was staring at him. There was something Hammond recognized in the man's eyes and he gave a slight nod. The Kinahhi looked away uneasily, shifting his hold on the weapon he carried. But Commander Kenna had worn the same expression of doubt many months back, when all this had started, and Hammond decided to take it as a hopeful sign.

As instructed, the men in front put on a good show when the wormhole erupted into the room. No one was going to win an Oscar, but their 'shock' was enough not to draw attention. The Kinahhi detached themselves from the wall and took up formation around them. "Proceed up the ramp," someone ordered, his speech heavily accented. "Do not be afraid, you will not be harmed."

Like hell. The faces of the men Hammond had seen attached to the machine up on Level 17 were still fresh in his mind. It was time to put an end to this, and the Kinahhi were about to bite off a hell of a lot more than they could chew. As the line ahead shuffled forward, Hammond stepped up onto the ramp. Adrenaline pumped hard, taking a decade from his shoulders and bringing a fierce smile to his lips. He tried his best to hide it, but it felt good to be going into action again. It felt good to be going after his people.

He took a quick look at the intense face of the man who walked at his side. Henry Boyd had insisted on volunteering for the mission, determined to pay his debt to SG-1. Hammond understood him entirely.

Godspeed, he said silently, encompassing his entire team in the prayer. *And good hunting.*

In the first light of the desert dawn, Jack picked his way through the ruined city, scanning the dozens of sprawled bodies for the only one he cared about. Teal'c.

A low groaning echoed across the sand, the sound of the survivors. If that was the right word. He saw some of them, crouched with their hands over their heads, rocking on their heels. A night of horror had stripped them of their sanity, leaving little behind.

Sonofabitch. He tried not to think about Daniel, still out cold when he'd left him to the care of Atella. The kid had been mortified, shocked at what had happened. And confused. Jack could relate. He had no goddamn idea what was going on, or why he'd been the only member of SG-1 not to start shouting at thin air.

"Are they gone?" Fingers grabbed at him from behind a large block of stone, catching in the sleeve of his shirt. "Are they gone?"

"Yeah," he shook the hand off and backed up, trying to be gentle. Terrified, crazed eyes stared at him from a kid's face. "They're gone. You should…" *Hell, what?* "Go home," he said. "You should go home." He turned and kept on walking.

"Are they gone?"

Jack ignored the call and kept walking. He had to find Teal'c. What was left of him. Up ahead lay a body, dressed in the gray of the Kinahhi. Blood pooled under its head; the man must have fallen. Maybe bashed his own head in. *Goddamn it, what kind of people would invent a weapon like this?*

The sun was getting warm, even this early, glaring off the sand and making it hard to see. Atella had given him a strip of cloth to wear around his head, bandana style, but he missed his cap. And his shades. Lifting a hand to cut the glare, he peered across the endless sea of ruins. Suddenly there was a hoarse cry.

"O'Neill?"

He spun around, and there, close to the dead Kinahhi, crouched Teal'c. He looked wild, but not crazy. Not vacant.

"Hey buddy." Jack approached slowly. Teal'c held a large rock in one hand, red with drying blood. "What's up?"

"I saw…" Teal'c stared for a moment at the dead man, oblivious to the rock in his hand. "I saw *Heelksha*."

"Okay." That meant nothing. "I'm guessing…not a nice guy?"

Teal'c's eyes were still fixed on the body before him. "The gods of the underworld."

"Ah."

"They were bent on my destruction."

Jack blew out a breath and crouched a couple of feet away from Teal'c. "Yeah, about that. See, turns out there's some kind of…hallucination device out here. It's a weapon. Makes you see things." He studied the dead man, and the rock in Teal'c's hand. "Drives you nuts."

Teal'c's gaze wandered to the rock. He started, dropping it. With a dull thud it landed in the blood-damp sand. "I did not—"

Jack winced. "It was a brutal night, T. I'm glad you're okay." He hoped.

Staring at the body, Teal'c pushed himself to his feet. "I saw demons. Monsters." He looked over at Jack. "How is such a thing possible? I know these things do not exist, and yet—" He looked again at the bloody corpse. "Did I kill this man?"

Rising slowly, Jack shrugged. "I don't know. But they came here to kill us, don't forget that." When Teal'c didn't move, Jack stepped closer. "Come on," he said, "let's get back. Check on Daniel."

Teal'c's head snapped around. "Was Daniel Jackson also affected?"

"Oh yeah," Jack sighed. "He—"

"You!" The voice came from behind, shaking with rage. Turning, Jack found himself staring over the muzzle of a gun into the wild-eyed gaze of Commander Kenna. "What have you done to my men?"

Oh crap. Jack raised his hands. "It wasn't us," he said. "My people were affected too."

Kenna was jittery, as if expecting the hordes of hell to come bearing down on him at any moment. "It is of no matter," he said, tightening his hold on the weapon. "No matter. You live, and you will come with me." He jerked the gun in Jack's direction. "Disarm."

So not gonna happen. "I don't think so."

Kenna took a step closer, eyes desperate. "Drop your weapon." He pressed the muzzle into Jack's chest. "I will kill you if you do not."

Something moved behind the Commander. Like quicksilver the men of Arxanti were flitting through the ruins. Perhaps twenty of them. *Sweet.* "Here's an idea," Jack said. "You drop your weapon, and I'll persuade those guys not to kill you."

Kenna didn't turn around. He was too good for that. But his eyes widened, his face fracturing in anguish as he looked past Jack. They had to be surrounded. The Commander lowered his weapon, defeated. There was something in the man's face, a flash of utter distress, that Jack found hauntingly familiar. He couldn't put his fingers on why, but it was enough to disturb him.

He took Kenna's weapon and passed it back to Teal'c. The Arxanti were all around them now, in a large, rangy circle. From among their spindly figures, Atella watched through cold, hard eyes.

"It's okay," Jack said. "Why don't you guys round up the rest of the Kinahhi? Can't leave them out here."

Atella nodded, gesturing to his men. As silently as they had arrived, they slipped away into the growing heat of the day. Jack squinted up at the sun, still not far from the horizon but already hammering a hell of a lot of heat down onto the parched desert. "Let's get inside," he decided, nudging Kenna forward. The Commander stumbled, lost in misery.

"Despite what you may believe," Teal'c said suddenly, addressing his remark to Kenna, "there is no need to fear the Arxanti – the Mahr'bal, as you name them. You and your men will not be harmed."

"If you think I fear for my own life, then you are a fool," Kenna spat. "I would trade it in an instant for—" He bit off his words and said no more.

Jack cast a curious glance at the Commander. *Trade it for what? Or, more likely, who?* As they walked through the building heat of the morning, he watched the man's face. He looked crushed, but beneath the despair there was fury, desperate fury. A volatile mix. It had you clinging to the edge of reason, and God knew Jack had been there a time or two in his life. It was something he could use. All he had to do was figure out how...

Daniel woke from the nightmare to the concerned face of Fortus, the Arxanti doctor. His body felt stiff, muscles cramped as if they hadn't moved in an eternity, and all around baleful images pressed down hard, like black clouds that wouldn't lift.

"Are you well?" Fortus asked.

Stiffly Daniel managed to nod, but he couldn't speak beneath the oppressive weight of the nightmare. He'd seen Sha're, tortured and twisted into something unrecognizable. He'd seen his parents die, seen a lifetime of death and misery. And other images, barbaric deeds he could hardly comprehend. Images dragged from memories trapped inside his mind. A blackness, a place of utter darkness where the only light had been forever extinguished. Hopeless and desolate, it had felt like the future... He shivered.

"Daniel Jackson?" Fortus again, sitting back on his heels.

With huge effort, Daniel tried to give the man a reassuring smile. "What happened?"

Fortus frowned. He seemed nervous and unsure. "Arxantia," he said quietly. "She fought our enemy as foretold, but..." He paused. "But you and Teal'c also suffered, as if you too were our enemy."

"And Jack?" Daniel asked, rubbing at his aching temples. "Was he affected?"

"No." Fortus replied. "He has gone out into Arxantia, in search of your friend Teal'c."

At least that proved Daniel's theory. Somehow, Jack was connected to these people on a basic, perhaps genetic, level. If that was true, it suggested that not all the Ancients had ascended. Perhaps a few had survived long enough to witness – even encourage – humanity's second evolution? "I think Jack," he said, pushing himself upright, "might be genetically—" Fortus looked blank, and Daniel changed tack. "I think he might be Arxanti. Teal'c and I are not. We're…different. But not your enemy. We're—"

A shadow fell across the doorway and Jack stepped inside, face flushed with heat. Behind him came a severe-looking Kinahhi soldier, and after him Teal'c. Thank God.

Still shaky, Daniel stood up.

"Hey," said Jack, swiping a bandana from his head and mopping his face. "You okay?"

Daniel shrugged. "Been worse."

For a moment Jack stared, measuring the truth of his words, then he gave a slight smile. Satisfied. "Looks like they were right about the city fighting back."

"Must be some kind of automated Ancient defense system," Daniel guessed. "Designed to take out anyone who's not Arxanti." He looked over at Teal'c, who was escorting the Kinahhi soldier toward a pile of cushions at the far side of the room. Fortus was watching them with open hostility, but said nothing. "So, Jack… You weren't affected by it?"

"Nope."

Daniel lifted an eyebrow.

"What?"

He shrugged. "You don't think that's a little—"

"Daniel, I'm not an Ancient!"

"Ah, no. No you're not. But perhaps there's some kind of genetic link, or throwback to—"

"Colonel O'Neill." Fortus approached, stiff with indignation, voice pitched low but heated with anger. "Why have you brought that… That *scum* into our home?"

Unfazed, Jack glanced over at Kenna. The Kinahhi Commander was sipping from the cup of water Teal'c had provided but his mind was obviously elsewhere, trapped in some fear or memory that was twisting his features into hard lines of despair. "Because he can help us."

Chin lifting, Fortus demanded, "How?"

"He has a ship," Jack said. "And I plan on getting hold of it."

"You will leave Arxantia?"

"Yup. One of our friends is…" He faltered, searching for the right word. "She's a prisoner on Tsapan. We have to go back for her. And we have to get word to our own people, to warn them about the Kinahhi."

"Then it is as Alvita Candra foresaw!" Fortus stared at Daniel with hope shining in his eyes. "You will lead us out of the desert!"

"Ah, now, I didn't say anything about—"

Jack's words were cut off by a bitter laugh; Kenna was watching them. "You seek to retrieve Major Carter?" he sneered. "It's a fool's errand. She is already dead."

Jack went very, very still. When he spoke, his voice sounded like steel rasping against steel. "What?"

"She is dead!" Kenna spat at him. "Her mind is gone, she's just a shell, an empty, rotting—"

"Sonofabitch!" Jack was across the room in two strides, launching himself at the Kinahhi soldier. The water cup went flying, and Jack landed a solid punch on the man's jaw, sending him sprawling onto his back. "You sonofa—"

"O'Neill!" Teal'c darted forward, hauling Jack off of the man. "Wait. He lies, to bait us—"

"No," Kenna hissed, scrambling upright, fists raised. Blood seeped from a split lip. "It is no lie. I saw her. She is dead." There was a glint of madness in his eyes. He wanted this, Daniel realized. He wanted to fight. There was so much rage, so much impotent fury burning deep down. "You should have killed her when you had the chance," Kenna taunted, beginning to circle Jack. "Spared her the suffering. Allowed her to die as a human being, not an animal. Not screaming like an animal—"

Pushing past Teal'c in a flash, Jack landed another blow, sending Kenna stumbling backward. He lashed out, but Jack was faster, grabbing the front of the man's shirt and slamming him hard against the wall. "You bastard," he snarled, breathing hard.

He's going to kill him... "Jack!"

"You goddamn sonofa—" He pounded Kenna hard against the wall again. "You're a coward. A miserable, stinking coward." He backed off, sucking in a shaking, furious breath. "You killed her." His words were molten with rage. "You killed her, and how many others?"

Kenna said nothing, but his eyes... God, they looked like they were dying. Turning cold and gray and lifeless.

"How many?" Jack hissed. "How many have you strapped

into that damn machine? And for what? *Thinking the wrong damn thoughts*?" He grabbed Kenna by the shirt, yanking him closer. "How the hell do you live with yourself? You spineless piece of utter, utter—"

"I had no choice!" Kenna spat, thrusting Jack away hard enough to make him stumble.

"There's always a choice!"

Kenna laughed bleakly. "You know nothing of Kinahhi!"

"I know enough," Jack growled. "I know you've condemned hundreds – thousands – of people to death because you're too afraid to—"

"They have my *son*!" The words cracked like a whip, plunging the room into rigid, shocked silence. The only sound was Kenna's uneven breathing. "They have my boy."

Jack looked like he'd been hit by a truck.

It was a strange sensation to be crawling around your own mind, oblivious to yourself, but that was the only way Sam could understand exactly what it was she was doing. It was cold and misty, the distance fading into hazy oblivion, while a shimmering presence dominated the center of the room in which she sat – the room of her own mind. She could see it, a massive force filtering through the minutiae of her consciousness, looking for something.

The Mahr'bal.

She knew nothing about them, certainly nothing about any connection with the Colonel. Just as well; if she had known, there was no way she could have kept it from the invader.

Rising slowly to her feet, she turned around. There was nothing to see but mist. *Who knew my mind was so dull?* She began to walk, circling the iridescent force in the center. *Does it know I'm here? Does it know I'm alive?*

She remembered the vicious blow that had sent her into oblivion. *Perhaps I'm dead?*

Or perhaps not. It hardly mattered. She chose to put her faith in Descartes: *I think, therefore I am.* The gleaming presence, like refractions from a cut gemstone, was the only movement in the room. Tentatively she reached out to it, as if touching the surface of a rippling pond, and—

Fear. Danger all around. Invasion. Destruction.

She pulled back her hand, startled. What was that? Koash? Or the collective mind of the *Kaw'ree*, or the *sheh'fet*? Whoever it was, they were afraid, and she had been able to feel it. *Know your enemy.* Bracing herself, she tried again.

Danger! A fragmentary image assaulted her; Colonel O'Neill with his head trapped in the Ancient device that had downloaded their repository of knowledge into his mind. *Panic.* Then another image, not one she had seen before. A projection, a nightmare – the Colonel again, but this time seated in one of the *Kaw'ree* chairs. Blood seeped across the floor in pools, fire licked at the walls, and crazed half-human creatures danced around him in triumph. *The destruction of all things. The end of Kinahhi.* Another image. An army of wild, sticklike creatures pouring through the Stargate, led by the Colonel. At least, she thought it was the Colonel. But he was dressed in rags, and somehow barely human. A feral grin split his face, growling and insane. *The end of all things!*

With a gasp, Sam pulled her hand away, nursing it against her chest. Her fingers were red raw, as if burned, and she found herself shaking. What the hell was that?

The future.

The words boomed, and Sam covered her ears.

You see the future, if the Mahr'bal are not stopped. Help us… Help me. Koash. She recognized him now, talking directly into her own mind.

"I don't know anything about the Mahr'bal," she shouted back at him. "You must know that by now. You can read my mind."

There was a pause, and in that moment Sam understood the truth. He couldn't. At least, he couldn't read all of it, otherwise she wouldn't be standing here watching him sift through her memories. There was some aspect of her, some fundamental kernel of herself that Koash – and the *sheh'fet* – couldn't access. *Because they can't make it work*, she realized. *For some reason, they can't use it properly!*

Pulse racing with sudden excitement, she decided to test her theory. It would be a one-shot deal, and if it didn't work… Sam closed her eyes, focused her thoughts on what she was saying and built a mental wall around her true intentions. A shield, shimmering blue, standing between Koash and the truth she was hiding.

Carefully, with utter concentration, she reached out and touched his mind.

"These Mahr'bal... Are they monsters?"

They are as you see them.

"And the Colonel is one of them?"

He is.

Focus. Focus... "He abandoned me here." Cold. Angry. Afraid. "He could have saved me."

Such are the Mahr'bal. Without honor.

"But you..." Warm. Insinuating. Grateful. "But you saved me from that place. You brought me out of the *sheh'fet*."

His mind shifted, glittered before her. Preening like a peacock. *And I can keep you from it, Samantha Carter. If you will help us find him – find out all he knows of the Mahr'bal. Find out if there are others, beyond the Stargate.*

Flattery. Men were such slaves to their own egos. "He left me behind, I owe him nothing. But you saved me, Koash." His mind shivered at the use of his name, and Sam smiled. "Yes," she pressed, "I know you. I can see your mind..."

And I yours.

So you think. "Help me, Koash. And I will help you."

A bargain?

"An act of trust." If he could take what he needed from her mind, then he would have done so. But he couldn't, and they both knew it. "Release me from the chair, and I'll help you find Colonel O'Neill."

In the silence that followed Major Samantha Carter held her breath and waited.

CHAPTER TWENTY-EIGHT

Jack could feel Daniel's eyes on him, watching for a reaction. Waiting for him to fly apart, perhaps. It had been a long time now, the pain was old and familiar. But every so often it jabbed like a knife, as fresh and appalling as it had been the day he died.

They have my son! Damn him. Damn him to hell for having a reason.

"How old is he?" It was a carefully calm enquiry, giving away nothing. But Daniel knew, so did Teal'c, and they were watching him with guarded concern.

"Seven, now." Kenna whispered, his back to them.

Just a kid, just a baby.

Kenna's hands fell to his sides. "They took him three years ago, to ensure my cooperation."

Bastards. Jack felt a new wave of rage break over him, directed at the smug, sanctimonious face of Damaris that hovered in his mind. He didn't doubt she was capable of it, he'd seen the ice in the heart of that soulless bureaucrat the first moment they'd met. *We'll get her*, he promised himself. *We'll make her pay – for the kid, for Carter, for all of them...*

Into the silence Teal'c spoke. "My son, Rya'c, was once captured by my mortal enemy." His voice resonated with deep feeling. "It is an almost unbearable pain to suffer."

Facts, get the facts. "Where's he being held?" Unlike Teal'c, Jack could offer no consolation from his own experience. There'd never been any hope for Charlie. "Have you tried to get him out?"

Slowly, Kenna turned. "He was in a school, in Kinahhi. Well treated, or I could not have continued to— You don't understand. Had I tried to free him, they would have known it. To even think such thoughts..." He shook his head, "But after your escape from Tsapan, Damaris said she would send him to the *Kaw'ree*. I believe she sensed my...disquiet." His face dissolved into remorse. "My weakness has condemned my son."

Jack recognized it now, the bleakness in the man's eyes. It was guilt. He saw it every day in his own reflection.

"*Kaw'ree*?" Daniel prompted softly, a gentle distraction from the man's overwhelming despair. He always knew the right thing to say, it was a goddamn gift. "It means *leaders*, right? I thought the Security Council led your people?"

Kenna threw him a dark look, sucking in a steadying breath. "So they did, before the *sheh'fet*. But now, even they must bow before the *Kaw'ree*."

"Their own fear has enslaved them," Teal'c observed coolly.

"Literally," Daniel agreed, a gleam in his eye. *Do you get it?* he seemed to be asking. Jack didn't. "The *sheh'fet* was created to counter the threat from the Mahr'bal, right?" Daniel carried on, scratching through his memories. "There was an attack? On an outpost?"

"Libnah," Kenna replied. "You are correct, Daniel Jackson." His gaze moved to where Fortus stood watching the exchange with curiosity, and his face hardened. "Hundreds of thousands of my people were massacred at the colonial outpost of Libnah. After that, the Cordon was constructed and—"

"And thousands of *my* people were massacred. And have continued to die, from starvation and disease, in the fifty years since." The voice came from the doorway. It was Atella, leaning against the doorjamb, bright anger in his eyes. "Do not listen to the lies of this Kinahhi. His words are poison."

Kenna stiffened, bristling with generations of hostility. "Do you deny what happened at Libnah?"

Jack had seen the same reaction in countless hotspots around the world and blew out a weary sigh.

Atella languidly strode into the room. "They were on our land."

"Peacefully."

"Stealing our heritage," Atella countered, helping himself to a cup of water. "Stealing the gifts of our ancestors. Destroying our holy sites." He shrugged, circling Kenna as though he were prey. "You witnessed last night the anger of Arxantia. Libnah was no different. All this land is ours, and our ancestors protect it."

Kenna returned his attention to Daniel. He was tired, Jack realized, and a couple of decades older than Atella. Like Jack himself, Kenna had seen enough of the world to trust little beyond his own experience. "Libnah was not destroyed by ghosts, Dr. Jackson," he said. "Its people were poisoned: men, women, and children – my own grandparents among them."

With a grunt, Jack turned away from the entire conversation and paced to the far side of the room. Shades of gray, good and evil so entwined that no one was right and no one was wrong. And so many injustices perpetrated and suffered, on all sides, that no one could forgive or move on. A poisonous quagmire of ambiguity.

Behind him he heard Daniel speak. "It's possible that the city at Libnah had created some kind of bio-specific poison, to rid it of enemy occupation."

Possible. After what he'd seen last night, he'd believe anything. Jack leaned against the wall, relishing its cool feel against his back. The heat was rising, outside and in. Too bad the Ancients hadn't invented air conditioning. "What about the bombs?" he asked, drawing Atella's attention. "Does your city send them to Kinahhi too? To kill kids?"

"Bombs?" Atella shook his head, confused.

"Explosive devices," Daniel explained. "Designed to harm the people of Kinahhi."

"We are not responsible for any such attacks." His gaze slid to Kenna. "More is the pity, but you see how we live. We have no weapons, beyond Arxantia."

"Well, someone's planting them, Atella. And the Kinahhi seem to think it's you guys."

"It is not."

To Jack's astonishment, the answer had come from Kenna. "It's not?"

For an instant, the Kinahhi met his eyes. There was boldness there, daring. Almost a sense of wild relief. But then the Commander looked away, as if ashamed. "My unease with the direction in which our government has moved began some years ago," he said. "The *sheh'fet*, you must understand, was introduced shortly after the atrocity at Libnah. It was welcomed, because our people were afraid. We had never seen such destruction, and feared that our own city would soon become a target."

Fear can be a formidable weapon. Hadn't Kenna said that himself?

"But there were no more attacks. The people became complacent, and the *sheh'fet* was soon seen as an infringement upon their freedom." He grunted in disgust. "People have short memories, and no mind for strategy. Ten years is but a heartbeat in a war, Colonel. The Security Council knew as much. They refused to allow the *sheh'fet* to be dismantled. I agreed with them, but the protests became more vociferous, the calls became stronger even from within the Security Council, and so…" He took a deep breath, lifting his chin. "The decision was made by a few in the Council to demonstrate what might happen should our security be compromised by the withdrawal of the *sheh'fet*."

Holy crap. There was no question where this was going. Daniel was staring wide-eyed, Teal'c simply raised an eyebrow as if to say 'been there, done that, bought the Goa'uld T-shirt.' "You planted a bomb," Jack guessed.

Kenna nodded. "The intention was to demonstrate that a threat still existed, that it was foolish to dismantle the very thing that had secured our safety."

"But…?"

"It was too successful." His eyes flickered shut for a moment, as if he'd been struck by a sudden, unpleasant memory. "All protest died down. And thus, I am ashamed to say, such 'events' came to be considered an essential aspect of our security policy."

All protest died down? So Quadesh had been working for Damaris when he'd given Jack the plans. There were no dissidents; the whole thing had been a setup… They'd been taken for a ride from the very beginning!

Daniel was shaking his head in disbelief. "You're kidding me? You terrorize your own people, to keep them safe from terrorism? That's insane! That's… That's—"

"By the time I was sure of my beliefs, protest was impossible. Anyone who dares to question the Council is pronounced a dissident by the *Kaw'ree* — and sent to Tsapan. I learned to keep my thoughts to myself. For the sake of Esaum, my son."

"Tell me something," Jack interrupted. "That day in your gateroom, when the bomb went off and a bunch of your guys died.

Did you plant that too?" Was he that cold-hearted? That desperate to save his son?

Kenna's face hardened. "I did not. Councilor Quadesh acted without my knowledge. Had I known…" He shook his head. "The truth is, Colonel, had I known there was little I could have done for my men. They are not privy to the truth, and their 'sacrifice' is deemed necessary by the Security Council for the safety of our people."

"Isn't it always?" Jack grunted. "So what about Quadesh? Most politicians I know stay well behind enemy lines – they don't usually go blowing themselves up to prove a point."

"Ah…" Daniel said, "I guess I forgot to mention that he's not dead."

"Not dead?"

"Looks like they have a sarcophagus."

Jack fixed Kenna with a sharp look. "This true?"

"I do not recognize the name you use, but yes, there is a device that can restore life." He frowned, like a man at confession. "It is rarely used by any but the *Kaw'ree*; it seems that repeated use has adverse affects. However the *Kaw'ree* use it to prolong the life of those in the *sheh'fet*. If that can be called life."

Jack felt every muscle tighten in revulsion. *White agonizing dawn, over and over and over…* Except this was worse. To be trapped in that stinking hell forever, to die there and then come back again. Over and Over. *Oh God. Carter…*

"Unbelievable," Daniel was muttering, shaking his head. "This is just unbelievable. It's insane, it's like Orwell gone mad!"

"I do not find it so incredible," Teal'c replied. "Have we not witnessed the beginnings of such a situation on Earth?"

Jack's stomach lurched. "Kinsey."

Teal'c inclined his head. "Such tactics are not beyond him."

"No," Daniel agreed, tight-lipped. "No they're not."

Commander Kenna sighed. "Forgive me," he said, "but your Senator is a fool. The *Kaw'ree* will permit no one but themselves to control the Tauri *sheh'fet*, and, by extension, your world. It has much wealth, and we have an ever-expanding population."

Daniel started pacing. "We have to get back. We have to tell them all of this! Commander, if you come with us they'll have to believe you and—"

"I cannot!" Kenna recoiled, horrified at the suggestion. "My son... They would kill him." He glanced at Jack. "Or worse."

He knew exactly what that meant. Doom the kid to the same fate as Carter. *She is dead! Her mind is gone, she's just a husk, an empty, rotting—* His throat constricted, painfully tight. *Not now. Time for that later.* Or maybe not. Some things were best left undisturbed, buried forever. "Do you have a ship?" he asked roughly.

"You mean," Kenna waved toward the ceiling, "a transport? Or a boat?"

"A transport," Jack clarified. The only boats he liked were of the fishing variety.

"I do," Kenna replied, cautious now. "But I cannot allow you to take it."

"You're not exactly in a position to stop us."

Kenna flinched, as if to say, *What about my son? If you steal it, you condemn him...*

Jack ignored the awkward question in favor of pragmatism. "How fast does it go? Faster than light?"

"I am unsure of your meaning. It is a transport. It will take you back to Kinahhi, or Tsapan, but it cannot take you to your world. We have no vehicles capable of traveling to the stars."

"None?"

A slight twitch of triumph touched the man's face. "There is only one way off this planet, Colonel O'Neill – and that's through the Stargate."

In other words, it was impossible.

General Hammond stepped from the icy roller coaster ride of the wormhole into the Kinahhi gate-room. He was glad to find no welcoming committee; Councilor Damaris had sharp eyes, and he could not have preserved his anonymity for long. He tramped down the steps with the rest of his team, taking in the huge transparent shields and the cluster of Kinahhi soldiers who watched the 'prisoners' as if they were vermin.

The blast doors at the apex of the room were sealed, glimmering pale blue until the wormhole fizzled out. They were alone, at the heart of enemy territory. In front of him, Colonel Dixon rolled his shoulders, readying himself. His right hand hovered close to the 'pocket' of his jumpsuit, ready to pull out a concealed zat. Hammond did the same, waiting for the two Kinahhi behind him to walk down the steps from the Stargate.

Two behind.

Two up front.

Three behind each of the shields.

Ten men, and twenty of his own. So far the odds were on their side. At least, as long as those blast doors remained closed. Even as the thought crossed his mind, he saw one of the gray-clad Kinahhi move toward the doors. Dixon tensed, Boyd already had his hand on his weapon. It was time.

For the SGC, Hammond thought, heart pounding. *And SG1.* "Now!"

At his order, all hell broke loose. His men snapped into action, zat blasts exploded like the Fourth of July over Travis Lake, turning the air blue and ripe with ozone. A couple of red energy blasts from the Kinahhi scorched into the walls, and Hammond heard one of his men cry out. But in moments – battle moments, that compressed and stretched time interminably – it was over.

"Dixon, secure the door," Hammond shouted. "Boyd," he turned to the young man, "I want all the C4 strapped to the DHD and ready to blow."

"Yes, sir." He didn't flinch from the order, although, like everybody else, he understood its implications. The Kinahhi would never again set foot on Earth. Whatever it cost Hammond's team.

CHAPTER TWENTY-NINE

"There is a way," Daniel said, stepping from the relative cool of the ruins into the heat beneath the frayed awning. Jack sat on the ground, chewing on a piece of hard Arxanti bread and staring at the Kinahhi soldiers who were being corralled – with more care than Daniel had expected – into a scrap of shade at the center of the settlement. He was brooding.

"A way to do what?"

"To get home. To find Sam."

Jack didn't reply, just took another bite of bread. He probably knew what Daniel was going to suggest, but to hell with it, he'd suggest it anyway. "They want to fight, Jack – they've been waiting decades for this chance."

You will lead us out of the desert. You cannot abandon us. I have seen it.

"They deserve the right. Look at this place, Jack! The Kinahhi keep them here like animals. Waiting for them to die, while the Kinahhi live like kings."

"They've got no weapons, they're not trained to fight."

Daniel moved closer, squatting down and forcing Jack look at him. "Then we give them weapons. Give them the Kinahhi weapons."

"Are you kidding?" Jack shook his head in disbelief. "You're talking about starting a goddamn war."

"No," Daniel insisted. "The Kinahhi have already started the war. I'm just talking about giving these guys a fighting chance." Daniel's choice of words was deliberate, and it hit the mark.

Jack flinched. "It's not the same."

"Isn't it? Don't they deserve a chance, Jack? To fight back?"

Pushing himself to his feet, Jack took a couple of steps away, then turned, waving the piece of bread like an accusing finger. "We don't take sides in other people's wars, Daniel. You know that never ends well."

"So we don't take sides." Daniel nodded toward the blistering midday sun, toward the Kinahhi soldiers hunkering in the shade. "Let me talk to them. Kenna can't be the only one with doubts, maybe some of them will join us. Join with the Arxanti, and we can start something here. We can start—"

"A war, Daniel. A war is the only thing we'll start."

"No. We can start building bridges," Daniel insisted, warming to the topic. "Start building some trust." Jack cast him a skeptical look, but beneath it Daniel saw a glimmer of that fundamental core of compassion and optimism that ran through Jack like a vein of gold. He wanted to believe. "Don't they deserve to be able to fight for their freedom?"

Jack hesitated. "You really think you can pull this off?"

"I can try. Jack, what other choice do we have? We need these people. We can't get home without help." Daniel paused, lowering his voice. "We can't find Sam without help. And there's no one else."

Looking away, Jack squinted into the bright glare beyond the awning. Weighing the odds. God knew it was a tough decision. To risk starting a war to save his team. To save Earth. How many lives would be lost, Kinahhi and Arxanti? How many families torn apart? And Jack would take them all on his shoulders; he'd wear them like sackcloth and ashes. Daniel sighed, staring down at his scuffed, sandy boots. If there were any other way, any other choice…

Jack moved, his mind made up. "Do it. Talk to them."

Daniel glanced up. He'd won his point, but looking at Jack's grave features it hardly felt like victory.

Commander Kenna stood on an alien world, or so it seemed. He had climbed to the top of a large pile of rubble, and sat staring out over the Mahr'bal shantytown. The sun, hotter here than in his homeland, baked the ground and beat down ferociously on his exposed head and neck.

Below him, he could see his men – those who had survived the madness of the night. They sat hunched together in a small, shaded space at the center of the settlement, watched by curious men, women, and children. These people, he suspected, had never seen a Kinahhi man before. Just as his own men had never seen the Mahr'bal.

And they were not so different. The Mahr'bal had somewhat darker skin and eyes as brown as sun-baked clay, but they talked and laughed and tousled the heads of their children. In fact, he mused, they bore a striking resemblance to the Tauri, mirroring their broader faces and stocky build. Less elegant than the Kinahhi, perhaps, but no monsters.

He watched as one of the Tauri – Daniel Jackson, he believed – came to join his men. A peacemaker? Jackson sat, cross-legged, and began to talk earnestly, his hands gesticulating. Around him, the spectators drew closer, listening intently while a number of Arxanti women, all carrying round trays, moved through the crowd toward the prisoners. They were offering them water. Kenna held his breath as he watched his Chief Officer hesitate; all his men would emulate Lahat. But at length he lifted a cup from the tray, sniffed at its contents, and took a sip. A slight smile touched his lips and he murmured words of thanks that were lost in the distance. The act was repeated by all his men, a glimpse of hope in this dark day. Perhaps, in some far future, his world would not be tyrannized by fear and suspicion. Perhaps the *sheh'fet* could be torn down and his people could know peace and freedom.

Or perhaps those were merely the foolish daydreams of an old man who had traded in too many lies.

"They seem to be getting along." The dry voice was accented with a Tauri drawl. O'Neill.

Kenna didn't turn around. "They do. After last night I expected harsher treatment from the Mahr'bal."

A few stones skittered down the rubble pile as O'Neill moved closer and settled down next to him. The Colonel's head was covered roughly in some material of Mahr'bal creation, and one hand was lifted to shade his eyes from the sun. "You know, I don't think they knew what to expect last night either," he said. "This city might have belonged to their ancestors, but they don't know much about it."

"It must be very old," Kenna replied, surveying the vast sprawl of rubble.

"Ancient, in fact." O'Neill said the word with a wry twist of his lips that Kenna did not fully understand. The Colonel squinted out across the settlement. "It was here way before the Goa'uld showed up."

Kenna could quite believe it, looking at the ruins. "Our schol-ars dispute that," he said, without conviction. "But the Mahr'bal – the *Arxanti* – have always claimed this world belonged to them before the Kinahhi arrived." He was silent, allowing the dry des-ert wind to gust over his face, although it offered scant relief from the heat. "I believe," he said after a moment, "that my govern-ment has lied about many things. Not just the attacks by Mahr'bal dissidents."

O'Neill nodded, picked up a small stone and threw it at one of the distant walls. It hit the pale surface with a puff of dust and fell to the ground. "They lied to my people too," he said, choosing a second stone. "They set me up with the plans for the anti-grav device – Damaris set up the whole thing. Quadesh deserves a goddamn Emmy."

O'Neill's precise meaning was lost to Kenna, but he shared the Colonel's outrage. "I too was deceived. Five of my men died that day, by Quadesh's hand."

O'Neill tossed the stone into the air and caught it again. "The plans were designed to fail, did you know that?"

"So Damaris informed me." Kenna couldn't help but smile at the wry look on the man's weathered face. Like himself, Kenna realized, O'Neill did not always trust the men giving his orders. "You too have enemies among your leaders, Colonel. Your Sena-tor Kinsey wished to be rid of you."

O'Neill threw his second stone, as accurate as a laser shot, knocking a hole in the crumbling wall. "Yeah. I bet he did." He paused, fingers scraping through the sand seeking another pebble. "Look," he said after a moment, "I'll be frank with you, Kenna. I need to get back home. I need to get to the Stargate."

Kenna shook his head. "Impossible. You could never penetrate the complex without assistance or—"

"Then *help* me!" All pretense at casual conversation fell away, and the man's alien eyes glittered angrily. "Help me."

"I cannot. My son—"

"We'll find your son." O'Neill said it with such conviction, such utter faith that Kenna almost believed him. "You can come with us, both of you."

Kenna looked away. Such honeyed words were difficult to resist, but the Tauri knew so little about Kinahhi and the power of the *sheh'fet*. "You don't understand," he said. "We could never find him, never reach him before they knew we were coming. The *sheh'fet*—"

"Then we take that out first." O'Neill spat the words, lifting his arm to fling another stone at the ruins. It hit the wall with a sharp crack, sending a cascade of broken stone to the ground. "We blow the whole thing to hell. And everything—" He stopped, swallowing hard. "And everyone trapped in it." For an instant he was at sea, as if a sudden squall had knocked him off-course.

Kenna thought he knew why. "Including Major Carter?"

"Better than leaving her behind."

That was true. But what the man spoke of was impossible, incredible. To destroy the *sheh'fet*? Kenna found his heart beginning to race, his palms tingling with the possibility of striking the blow he had believed to be decades away. To destroy the *sheh'fet* and its power over Kinahhi… To free Esaum, to be able to bring his son home again! It was an intoxicating promise, but dangerous. So dangerous, he barely dared entertain the possibility. "You speak brave words, O'Neill, but you know little of Tsapan. It is well guarded, and—"

"I can do this," O'Neill insisted. "I can free your people. And mine."

A thrilling thought, but impossible. Or was it? "I cannot risk—"

"Yes," O'Neill insisted, rising angrily. "You can. You have to." All Kenna could see was O'Neill's silhouette, stark against the bright blue sky. He looked as immovable as rock, as intransigent as the desert. He held out a hand, as if to pull Kenna to his feet. "Help me. Help me free your people. Help me free your son."

The Commander stared at the offered hand, but did not move. Could he believe this man? Dared he place the life of his son in his hands? And yet… Had not O'Neill proven himself to be an intractable enemy, resourceful, unrelenting, and unstoppable? Had he not already done the impossible in escaping the *sheh'fet* unscathed? Kenna looked up, shading his eyes until he could see the man's intent face. *Help me free your son.* "What you intend," he told O'Neill at last, "is impossible."

The Colonel's eyes narrowed slightly, but otherwise he did not respond. Intransigent as the desert. He would never give up.

Re'ammin help me... Kenna grasped the man's hand. "But I have already seen you accomplish the impossible, O'Neill. If anyone can do this thing, then it is you."

With a nod O'Neill hauled him to his feet, seizing his other arm in a fervent grip. "We'll do it," the Colonel said fiercely, eyes hard. "We'll end this. For good."

It was impossible not to believe him.

Bill Crawford sat with his back to the wall, staring in numb horror at the scene playing out before him. Beneath the domed ceiling the rainbows were dying as dusk fell, and large, creeping shadows encroached from the edges of the room. But at its center, lit by a soft light of no visible source, sat Major Carter. She was strapped into some kind of alien chair, surrounded by the terrifying men in black robes..One of them had his hands pressed on either side of her head, rocking back and forth, mumbling like the freaks Crawford endured every night on the Metro.

He shivered and squeezed his eyes shut, wrapping his arms around his legs. *Kinsey! You bastard, why haven't you gotten me out of here?*

But in his heart, he knew the answer. He was expendable. Not worth rocking the boat for one little diplomat – after all, he wasn't the first Ambassador to go MIA through the Stargate. They must have procedures for dealing with such unfortunate mishaps. Maybe he'd get a plaque. *Here lies Bill Crawford, sucker. Rest in peace.* Or pieces, more likely. He'd seen the silver-bladed knives the freaks in the robes carried, could imagine them raised high and plunging into his chest. He began to shake, swallowing nausea. *Someone help me...*

"Wait!"

Crawford lifted his head, dreading what he might see. The black robes still hovered around Carter, studying her with rapt attention. But now she seemed to be awake. Her eyes were open at least, and she was staring at the man with his hands pressed against her head. His skin was translucent, blood-red veins – or something more sinister – drawing ugly patterns on his cheeks. His lips were moving soundlessly, and Carter was staring at him like she was crazy. Maybe she was, maybe they all were.

The other robed figures flapped around them like black moths around a flame, their gaze darting between Carter and the silently gibbering man. Abruptly he stood up straight. "She will help us," he said.

"Have you penetrated her mind?" It was a woman who spoke, trailing bony fingers across the side of Carter's face. "Have you seen the truth?"

The man hesitated. Few, perhaps, would have noticed it. But Crawford had spent a lifetime watching people, looking for their weaknesses.

"I have."

It was a lie. How interesting. From the sleeve of his robe, the man produced a curved steel blade. Crawford started, cringing back against the wall, eyes shut tight. Oh God, he was going to kill her. And then? And then…

He heard a slicing sound but no screams. Then another.

"What are you doing?" The woman's voice again.

Crawford opened his eyes. There was no blood or gore. The man was slicing through the ties that kept Carter in the alien chair. She was moving groggily, rubbing at her wrists, touching her face. With a shiver of revulsion Crawford realized that she too was filigreed with scarlet.

She was compromised. Somehow, they'd infected her. Made her one of them!

"She will assist us," the man insisted, helping Carter to her feet. With his other hand, he brushed her temple in a strangely intimate gesture. She didn't seem to resist. In fact she smiled.

"Thank you," she said, touching his cheek in return. Good God, what was this? Carter trailed her hand down from the man's face to his narrow shoulder, then caressed his arm. "And now, I will help you. What is it you need to know?"

The man stared at her, entranced. "You know."

"Of course," Carter smiled again. "Colonel O'Neill is at large, somewhere on your world. In league with these Mahr'bal?"

"So we believe."

She took his hand. "What does he want?"

"To destroy us."

"Will he bring the Mahr'bal with him?"

A fluster of fear shivered through all the robed figures. "Surely not!" cried one. "Here? Tsapan? They would destroy us all!"

Carter didn't turn away from the man before her, one hand entwined with his. "You're afraid," she said, her voice hardened slightly. "I saw an image – the Colonel sitting in one of these chairs. Is that what you're afraid of? What would happen?"

"Help us find him!" the man insisted. "As you promised. Help us to find him, before he comes here and destroys everything."

Carter flashed a wide smile that seemed to light the entire room, unfeigned and ebullient. "Oh, we'll find him," she insisted. "I think I can guarantee it."

Betrayal? Not long ago Crawford would have laughed at the notion; the famously loyal SG-1 fragmenting, saving their own skins at the expense of each other. But now…? Now he wanted to curse her. He needed O'Neill, he needed them all if he was going to get out of this goddamn—

She moved like a cat, slick and without preamble. One shoulder ducked, tucked into the man's gut, and suddenly he was flipping over to land in a crumpled heap on the floor. The silver dagger he'd been holding was pressed against his exposed throat, his head yanked back by the hand Carter had knotted in his hair. "One move," she shouted, "and he dies."

Crawford felt like cheering…

Alarms blared through the Kinahhi Stargate complex, urgent and unplanned. Councilor Tamar Damaris jumped from her desk in a manner most undignified, and irritably slapped her hand on the communicator. "What is this?"

The answer came in the form of her aide, Matan Tal, bursting through the door, his young face white with panic. "Councilor! We are under attack!"

"From whom?" There were no events scheduled for the next month. Surely she had not forgotten to—

"The Tauri!"

"*What*?" It had to be O'Neill, of course. Damn the man. Why could he not be caught? "Where is he?" And how had he infiltrated the security of—

"They came through the Stargate, Councilor," Tal babbled. "We have been betrayed! They came dressed as Tauri dissenters, destined for the *sheh'fet*, but they were armed…"

Shocked, Damaris dropped into her chair. "Impossible."

"It is true," the young man's voice fell, fearful and awed. "They have taken control of the Stargate and threaten to destroy the dialing device if we attempt to retake it."

"What do they hope to achieve?" It made no sense. "Kinsey is a vain, arrogant fool. But he is not so stupid as this."

Matan had no answer. "They have asked to speak with you, Councilor. They wish to know of the Tauri prisoners, O'Neill and Carter."

O'Neill and Carter? This attack, then, was not sanctioned by Kinsey. *He* wanted them gone. This must be the action of a rogue element. Damaris felt herself relax. In time, no doubt, the Tauri authorities would return to Kinahhi to retrieve their errant sons. All that was required was to keep them from damaging the dialing device, and to do that she simply needed to dangle hope before them.

"Have these sirens silenced," she told Matan. "And tell the Tauri that I will speak with them in due course."

His surprise was well hidden. "Yes, Councilor."

"All will be well," she assured him. "Let this event remind us of the value of the *sheh'fet*. Such disorder could never occur among the Kinahhi, and in time the Tauri will be equally civilized."

"Yes," Matan agreed vehemently. "May that time come soon, Councilor."

"Oh, it will. And when it does, the wealth of their world will be ours for the taking, Matan. We must be patient a little longer."

But not much. Kinahhi was about to complete its first step into interplanetary dominance. These troublesome Tauri would be pacified, and the Kinahhi people would know might and wealth never before in their planet's history.

She smiled. Yes, their patience would soon be rewarded beyond measure.

CHAPTER THIRTY

Jack stood leaning against the Kinahhi transport, watching Daniel lead his ragtag army out of the desert like some latter-day Lawrence of Arabia. He just hoped to hell Daniel knew what he was doing. Taking inexperienced kids like this into battle went against almost all of Jack's instincts – all but one: trust Daniel. Over the years he'd learned to compromise his pragmatism and to open his mind, a little, to some of the crazier ideas his friend liked to spout. And if Daniel told him these guys had to go to Tsapan, then he'd choose to take that leap of faith.

"Colonel O'Neill?" Talking about leaps of faith… Commander Kenna jumped down from the doorway of the transport. He too surveyed Daniel's army, no doubt picking out a few of his own men in the mix.

"Your friend is a persuasive speaker," he said.

"Yeah, silver-tongued."

"I did not think any of my men would wish to challenge the *sheh'fet.*"

Jack shoved his hands in his pockets. "Guess you're not the only one with doubts."

"Yes." The Commander said the word slowly, as if considering it for the first time. "Yes, perhaps you are right."

Clapping him on the arm, Jack turned to climb aboard the transport. At the last moment, Kenna stopped him.

"O'Neill."

"Yeah?"

"What I said this morning, about Major Carter."

She's dead! A wave of grief and anger swelled in his chest, tightening his throat. "What about it?"

Kenna looked away, squinting out over the desert. "I do not wish to give you false hope, but… I was not speaking the whole truth."

Jack froze – in stark contradiction to his overwhelming desire to seize the man by the throat and throttle the truth out of him.

"Meaning?"

"She still lived when I last saw her."

His fingers clamped around the doorframe as the world spun in giddy relief. He said nothing, couldn't find his voice, just stared, demanding more.

Kenna frowned. "Your attempt to free her had damaged her connection to the *sheh'fet*."

Meaning what? What?!

"She was conscious. I saw her open her eyes, I…" Kenna looked doubtful. "I thought I heard her mind, in my own, O'Neill. I thought I heard her talking to me."

Jack was breathing hard, as though he'd just run 10 klicks. "What did she say?"

"She asked for my help." He fixed Jack with a steady, unflinching look. "I am ashamed to say that I ignored her plea."

Bastard. Anger flared dark red in Jack's mind, until he remembered the boy. It faded, extinguished by a splash of older, deeper pain. "You did what you had to," he said gruffly. "I'd have done the same, for my son."

Kenna's face brightened. "You have a son?"

Damn it. "I did. He died."

The brightness vanished. "I am sorry, I…" The Commander trailed off. No one ever knew what to say, probably because there was nothing to say.

It wasn't the point anyway. "When was this?" Jack asked, snapping the Commander back into the moment. "When did you last see her?"

"More than two days ago," he answered. "O'Neill, you must be prepared. Much might have changed. The *Kaw'ree* intended to reintegrate her into the *sheh'fet*."

"Screw them, whoever they are." He jumped up into the ship. "Carter's alive. I know it."

Kenna was unconvinced, but Jack ignored him and turned to watch Daniel's army trailing through the desert. Suddenly, they didn't seem so pitiful. They looked young and strong, and full of potential. There was hope. He'd bring his team home, he'd rip the goddamn brain-sucking machine to pieces – with his bare hands if he had to – and then he'd take down Damaris, and Kinsey and Crawford. The whole craphouse of corruption was going to come crashing to the ground, and he'd be the one wielding the ax.

He glanced down at Kenna and found himself grinning. "Come on," he said, offering the puzzled man a hand up. "We've got some serious ass to kick."

"On your feet," Sam hissed, yanking the man to his feet. Skin and bone beneath the voluminous robes, Koash weighed no more than herself. Whimpering, he scrabbled upright.

Don't hurt me! How can you do this? It's impossible. You'll destroy us all. The barrage of his thoughts was constant, beating like hot wings against her face. They made it hard to think. *The others will come. They'll free me. And then you'll suffer, you'll suffer for eternity in the* sheh'fet...

An image flashed into her mind, startlingly intense. Gold inlay on the roof of a coffin, a lid of stone sliding back. A white light within, and the raving face of a cadaver leaping out like a grue-some jack-in-the-box.

"Sarcophagus!" Sam gasped and almost lost her footing. "Oh my God, that's how you keep them alive..."

"If you do not release me," Koash snarled, "you too will require its healing effect before long."

Dream on. She tightened her hand in his lank hair, edging the knife closer against the thin skin of his throat. "Move," she told him, keeping her eyes on the other *Kaw'ree* as she backed towards the door. He did, reluctantly, his pulse pounding half an inch from the blade of the knife. It seemed to take forever to cross the vast expanse of the domed room, but at last she felt the handle to the tall, wooden doors press into her back. "Open it," she ordered.

"Wait!" The squeal came from Crawford, scrambling to his feet at the opposite side of the room. "Don't leave me here!"

He was flanked by two Kinahhi soldiers, glaring at her in hor-ror-struck rage as she dragged one of their holy men out of the room by his hair. Slowly, one of the soldiers seized Crawford by *his* hair and yanked him to his knees. He obviously thought he could bargain. "Release the *Kaw'ree*," the soldier shouted.

Too bad Crawford's such an asshole. Sam kicked open the door and dragged Koash out after her.

"No!" Crawford yelled desperately. It was enough to make her flinch with guilt, but not enough to make her reconsider. She'd come back for him if she could, but otherwise… Better men had died off-world.

Another kick slammed the door on Crawford's wails, and she spun around and grabbed Koash by the arm. "Run," she told him. "Or I'll throw you out the nearest window. You understand?"

He blanched. *I hate you.*

"Yeah, the feeling's mutual." She pushed him, hard, into a staggering lope. "Now move it."

Ignoring the waves of outrage, Sam started running. Her first objective was to hide herself in the labyrinth of the city. The next was to find the rest of her team. She knew they were out there, as sure as night followed day. If she did nothing else, she'd find her team and get the hell off this nightmare world.

General Hammond paced behind the tall, transparent defense shields in the Kinahhi gate-room, watching his team train the enemy weapons away from the Stargate and toward the door. Beyond, he knew, gathered half the Kinahhi military – he'd glimpsed them when they'd ejected the Kinahhi soldiers who'd been guarding the room.

A sudden rap on the door startled him. Over at the DHD Boyd moved his hand to the detonator, while Dixon approached the door. He looked to Hammond for approval before he cracked open the door. A few words were exchanged, then Dixon stepped back and allowed Councilor Tamar Damaris to enter.

She'd come alone, and Hammond respected her for that – if little else. She glanced around as if surveying a pigsty. "General Hammond. I find myself unsurprised at your involvement with this…unpleasantness."

"I take that as a compliment, Ma'am."

"We can have little to discuss," she said, regarding Boyd and the rigged DHD with cool calculation. "Why do you wish to talk to me?"

"I think you know why."

"You have the advantage of me, General. Unless, perhaps, you wish to discuss terms for your surrender and reparations for the damage you have caused?"

She was playing for time, going for a long volley instead of a smash across the net. Hammond recognized her tactics, but was in no mood for games. "I want my people back," he said bluntly. "And I want them in one piece."

"Your people?"

"Colonel O'Neill and Major Carter."

"I'm sorry, General, but that's not possible."

His heart thumped, hard. "Why not? So help me, Councilor, if you've harmed them I'll—"

"You misunderstand," she assured him, mildly triumphant. "The truth is, it's not possible for me to return your people to you because they're no longer in Kinahhi custody."

They'd escaped! "Where are they?"

She smiled coldly. "All we know, General, is that their alien ship crashed into the Mibsaw Sea." She placed a comfortless hand on his arm. "I am sorry. No survivors were detected."

"Is that so?"

"I would not lie to you."

He laughed. "Well, you'll forgive me for not believing you, Councilor. Truth is, SG-1 have an uncanny habit of beating the odds." Her lips tightened, just slightly. It was enough to make him smile. "Better get comfortable out there, Councilor. It's going to be a long wait."

Without answering, she strode back toward the door. At the last moment, she turned around. "You realize that I cannot allow this situation to endure."

Hammond shrugged and indicated the DHD. "And I can't let you back to Earth, Councilor. Any of you. The deal's off, all I want now is my people. Once I've got them, we'll be gone."

She cocked her head, a flicker of surprise running over her usually guarded features. "You do not represent the Tauri. Senator Kinsey—"

"Senator Kinsey is a grade A fool. By now, he's out of the SGC and heading back to Washington with his tail between his legs." Or so Hammond hoped. He stepped forward, lowering his voice. "We've found you out, Councilor. You played your cards too soon. The Kinahhi will *never* set foot on our planet again. We'd rather die first."

"If that is what you wish," she snapped frostily. "Then so be it."

Hammond folded his arms. "We'll just see about that, Councilor." Or, as Colonel O'Neill might have said, *Bring it on*.

It was dark in the city, dark and damp. Only the thin crescent of a single moon cast a pale light that, in places, slipped down into the depths of the city where Sam crept. Far above, occasional lights gleamed amber or ocher, seeming to accentuate the darkness and dereliction of the rest of Tsapan.

It was an easy place to get lost. There were pros and cons to that, Sam reflected, as she dragged the shivering Koash through the narrow streets and alleyways. On the upside, no pursuit. On the downside, she didn't have a clue where she was or where she was going.

And she was exhausted. Her mind still raced with a thousand thoughts, her face still burned and when she touched it she could feel strange ridges and lines tracing across her temples and cheek. She was glad there was no mirror, afraid of what she might see. Had her face already disintegrated into the red-traced cadaverous features of those trapped in the *sheh'fet*? Or did she look like Koash, pallid as the moon, disfigured by the scarlet filigree that patterned his skin?

Not that any of it would matter if she couldn't find her team or get the hell out of this city of the dead and dying. But her leaden limbs struggled to keep moving, as if her muscles had atrophied, and at length she was forced to stop. "We'll rest," she panted, easing herself to the floor and dragging Koash down next to her.

He was watching her with hate-filled eyes, his fear like a stench in the air. Sam kept the knife, her only weapon, visible and pondered what to do next. Koash was a burden now, but how to get rid of him without risking him running back to his friends and giving her away? Her hand tightened around the hilt of the weapon, but she wasn't that desperate. If she'd had a zat, or something to tie him—

There was a sound, a mere hint of a whisper behind her. Sam spun to her feet, heart hammering as she peered into the darkness. Nothing. All was silent but for Koash's suddenly uneven breathing. He was frozen, like a cat sensing prey. Or, perhaps, the prey sensing the cat. His eyes were wide, tremors rippling along his skinny arms.

Outcast. She heard his thought, drenched in horror. He was staring past her, as if he could see through the impenetrable gloom. *They are coming. They are coming!*

"Who?" she hissed, backing up a step. His fear was contagious and began to squirm in the pit of her belly. "Who is coming?"

Another sound, the pat of flesh on stone. A footstep, behind her. Sam turned again, forcing her sluggish legs to work. The hilt of the knife grew slick in her sweating palm, and she longed for a P90, or a zat, or her team. Most of all her team, covering her six. "Who's there?" she called. "Show yourself."

Koash had crumpled into a shivering heap, arms over his head, whimpering. His mind was full of half-formed imaginings, bloody images of murder, flesh ripped apart. It sickened her, and she tried to tune it out, rubbing at the stinging ridges on her face, trying to blot him from her mind.

A shuffling, snuffling noise – breathing – came from behind her. All around her. She backed up against the wall of the narrow alley. "Who are you?" she called again. "Who's there?"

No answer. But then... *Oh God.* She saw a face, emerging bone-white from the night as if rising from the pits of hell. Thin, leathered skin hung in folds around sunken features, wild eyes staring from deep sockets, and a mouth stretched wide in a silent scream. Or in hunger.

Sam shrank back, trapped against the wall. Oh God, oh God... She knew that face. She knew that face!

Outcast! Koash wailed. *Outcast!*

Filaments of red, like fading blood vessels, covered the creature's skin. Lank, scrappy hair fell to its shoulders. *Clutching white fingers in the dark, coming out of nowhere...* It moved closer, its starving body limping into a shard of moonlight. Shreds of clothing still clung to it, only seeming to accentuate its emaciation. It sniffed the air, then lifted its head and let out a mindless howl.

Sam recoiled as pattering sounds of movement answered its call. They were coming. They were all coming.

And they're going to rip you apart!

She didn't know if the thought belonged to herself or to Koash. It didn't matter. She turned and fled, dragging Koash with her, running until her lungs burned. And it came after her, ravening like a mad dog. And behind it, the others came. Dead white faces, the decaying victims of the *sheh'fet*, driven beyond humanity, beyond insanity. And they were hungry. So very hungry.

They flew into night, the sun falling behind the horizon as swiftly as a tropical sunset. The cramped Kinahhi transport sank into the silence of a long-haul flight, passengers pretending it was night and trying to sleep, even though it was the middle of the afternoon. Of course, some people could sleep anywhere, anytime, Daniel thought sourly. Jack, for example, was slumped next to him, snoring softly.

A few emergency lights glowed close to the floor, providing just enough light for Daniel to be able to pick out the features of his makeshift army. It was still amazing to him that these people, so ordinary seeming, were direct descendents of the Ancients. Their history spanned millions of years, yet all but a fraction of it was lost in time, destroyed by the ages and new, hostile peoples – Baal, and the humans he'd brought as slaves to Kinahhi. Or Arxantia, as it had once been known.

"Soon, much will change." The voice belonged to Alvita Candra, who had come to crouch at Daniel's side. Her narrow face was difficult to see behind her cascade of wild hair, but her eyes shone bright even here. "The wheels of time turn backward. Can you not feel it, Daniel Jackson?"

Like a cold shiver down his spine, a sense of everything being in freefall, of the world turning upside down... He felt something alright. Jack would call it pre-battle nerves, piled on days without proper sleep and an adrenaline-high of illegal proportions. Alvita reached out and touched his face. "You sense it." She shivered. "And through you, I sense them. They are watching us. The Angels are watching us."

And for a moment, he was aware of them too. All around. Watching. Expectant. Waiting on the periphery of his consciousness.

Oma?

It was like walking through an impenetrable fog. If he could just reach out, just pierce the barrier between his mind and his memories... He started, disturbed by a sensation of utter emptiness, and suddenly the moment was gone. All he could feel was the warmth of Jack's arm resting against his own.

Alvita removed her hand, sitting back on her haunches. "You are a strange Angel, Daniel Jackson. A fallen Angel."

He laughed. "I hope not."

She tilted her head, eyes sliding past him to Jack. "And him? What of him? I have seen his mind too. He is of us, but different. He has not touched the Angels."

"Oh, I don't know," Jack murmured, eyes firmly closed. "I've touched my fair share of angels over the years."

Daniel swallowed a smile as he tried to answer Alvita's question. "Ah, we believe that your ancestors lived on many worlds beyond this one. And that some of us may, perhaps, have inherited a genetic…" He changed tack. "That is, that the blood of your ancestors may still run in the veins of some of us."

Alvita sat down, cross legged, her lean limbs moving with a grace Daniel decided it was best to ignore. It was difficult, though, when she rested her fingers on his arm and leaned closer, her breath brushing his cheek. "Such wonders you share, Daniel Jackson. So much you have to teach."

He cleared his throat. "Ah, yes… Well, I'd be happy to—"

"Sorry, kids." Jack opened his eyes. "School's out for the duration." He cast a glance at the young woman, then lifted an admiring eyebrow. "I'm Jack, by the way."

"I know," Alvita replied. After a moment, she added, "Your thoughts are more worldly than those of your friend."

Daniel slid an amused look in his direction. "Jack?"

"What? I didn't think anything!"

Alvita smiled, a flash of white against her dusky skin. "Worldly pleasures are no less blessed than those of the mind. I am not offended."

Offended? "Jack?"

"Right, well." Jack jumped to his feet, clearing his throat. "Think I'll just go check on the, ah… Oh look, there's Teal'c."

With that he was gone, picking his way across the crowded transport to where Teal'c stood gazing out the far window.

Alvita watched him for a moment. "Your friend is uncomfortable with his feelings, both shallow and deep." She tossed her head, sending her mane of black hair tumbling over one shoulder. For an instant, a split second, she was Sha're, and it hit him like a sucker-punch. "Are all your people so conflicted, Daniel Jackson?"

"No." Swallowing, he shook his head. "Yes. Probably."

She smiled. "Then perhaps there is something we can teach you. Something of peace."

"Peace," Daniel let out a breath, and the familiar pain of loss along with it. "I like the sound of that."

"Heads up!" The abrupt order came from Jack, back in command. It was the place, Daniel suspected, where he felt most at home. "I see the city." He turned from the window, Teal'c at his side. "Everyone, get ready. It's show time."

Alvita rose, as did Daniel. "Time is running backward, Daniel Jackson," she repeated. "And forward. Things will be as they once were and as they always have been."

Daniel dropped his hand to the zat strapped to his leg. "Just keep your eyes open," he said. "Things are gonna get rough."

CHAPTER THIRTY-ONE

Koash scurried ahead of her, black robes flapping as he half-fell down the narrow staircase, running blindly. Sam followed, heedless of where she went. Everything was dark down here, shadows on shadows, and from behind them came the constant sound of pursuit. Whooping howls, the slap of bare feet on stone, the rasp of hungry breath.

Her chest was on fire, she was gasping for air. Her heavy legs screamed for oxygen, rubbery and stumbling. How long since she'd eaten? Her reserves were low, her mind still shredded by voices and feelings and a thousand impulses not her own. A constant background chatter of insanity.

She was slowing, stumbled on a step and fell. But in an instant she was upright, skidding down the stairs, ignoring the graze to her leg and the throbbing in her ankle. They were coming, and they had no pity.

Limb from limb! Koash was screaming the thought. *They'll rip me limb from limb!*

The bottom of the staircase ended at a door. A trap! But they were out of options. Koash hesitated and Sam raced past him, pulling through the doorway. Perhaps they could hide?

No chance. The room was empty, merely a corridor leading to another door. Nowhere to stop, so she dashed through and out the other side. Nothing but stairs, leading up! *Up!* No choice.

On shaking legs, she began to sprint up the stairs. Koash was on her heels, whimpering now. And behind her they kept coming, they kept coming, until—

"*Khan'an!*" Koash shrieked, skidding to a halt and cowering against the wall.

Ahead, the way was blocked. White figures crawled toward them, like ivory spiders stalking the flies in their web. Sam spun around. More creatures poured from the corridor they'd just left, slowing now, pacing themselves. Slathering.

Koash flung his arms over his head and began to wail.

This was it, the end. God help her…

The doors slid open while the transport made its final descent, the fresh sea breeze a stark contrast to the dry desert air. Holding on with one hand, Jack leaned out as far as he could, relishing the cool wind and the adrenaline rush. All around him Tsapan's spires rose like bejeweled arms lifted in silent supplication. A whore of a city, begging for salvation. Too bad. It would get none from him – at least none that didn't come from the barrel of a gun.

Behind him, Daniel and Teal'c were gearing up; they both still had their zats, Daniel had his handgun, and Teal'c had a P90 with half a clip. Much like him. But there were Kinahhi rifles aplenty, courtesy of Kenna and his men. Enough for all the greenhorn kids to have one in their eager hands. Like popguns, he thought bleakly. Only they packed a bigger punch.

The image awoke disturbing memories of Charlie. He shook them away, leaning out further. The tug of the cold, damp air was insistent and, for an instant, he wished for a 'chute. The dive would be one hell of a rush in this city of spires and towers.

Slowly, the ship sank into the forest of buildings and the air stilled and stifled. The fresh breeze turned to dank chill, and Jack pulled himself back inside the transport. Recess over, time to get to work. Teal'c and Daniel were watching him without comment. They'd known him long enough to understand his insatiable appetite for a cheap thrill.

"What?" he asked, running a hand through his hair. Difficult to inspire the fear of God into the newbies if he looked like Krusty the Clown.

"You know," Daniel said, "I used to have this dog. Whenever he traveled in the car, he'd always stick his head out the window, right into the wind."

"Your point?"

Daniel shrugged. "I don't know. I guess I don't have one."

"Dogs are most intelligent animals," Teal'c observed mildly.

"Thank you!" Jack stooped to pick up his Kinahhi rifle, hefting it in his hands. No match for the P90, but beggars couldn't be choosers. "Dogs know how to have fun."

With a soft jolt, the ship came into land and the smile that had been hovering on Daniel's lips fell away. "Okay," Jack called to the hushed, nervous men. "You know what to do. Stay close, and watch your backs. Any trouble, holler. We only have one shot at this, so no screw-ups."

From the cockpit, Commander Kenna emerged, his weapon slung over one shoulder. "I'll take my men straight to the *Kaw'ree*."

"Yeah, go get your son," Jack agreed. "We'll handle the rest."

Kenna nodded. "Thank you."

"When you're done, get back here. If we're not already here, go. Come back for us. Got it?"

"I understand."

There was nothing else to say and with a couple of quiet orders Kenna leaped down from the ship, followed by five of his men. Within moments, they had disappeared into the night.

Jack turned back to his team. Behind them, the eager faces of the Arxanti blinked in the darkness, the bright eyes and wild hair of Alvita Candra among them. She too carried a weapon, holding it across her chest with both hands. On her back, she'd strapped a small pack.

"What's that?" Jack asked.

She smiled, lifting her chin. "An offering of peace."

Oh please. "Daniel?"

He shook his head slightly and shrugged. "I'll keep an eye on her."

Good enough. "Okay," Jack said. "Daniel, you're with me. Teal'c, cover our six." And with that he jumped down onto the wet stone of Tsapan, and headed off into the gloom. All he needed now was Carter, and he'd be damned if he left this place without her again.

Not this time.

They were coming at her from all sides. Fetid breath, clawing white fingers, ravenous eyes.

"Stay back!" She swung the knife in a wide arc. "Koash, close up."

He didn't move until one of the Outcast grabbed at his robe, tearing a handful of fabric from his back. With a screech of horror, he scuttled toward her on all fours, to cringe like a dog at her feet.

The creature lifted the black velvet to his face, sniffed it, then dropped it with a snarl. "*Kaw'ree.*"

Koash wailed, even his thoughts now an incoherent mass of horror and despair.

"Stay back!" Sam yelled again, keeping the knife moving. "Stay back, or—"

Strong, bony fingers seized her arm. She spun around, slashing down hard with the knife. The creature shrieked, pulled back. But not far. Another hand grabbed her shirt from behind and she lashed out with a kick. Soft flesh gave under the heel of her boot; one of the creatures crumpled to the ground. But another grabbed her sleeve. She hacked at it with the knife until a third caught her wrist and yanked her arm in the air. "No!" She kicked out with her feet, elbows, head. Everything. "Let go!"

Koash was screaming and screaming and screaming...

The weight of the P90 felt solid and comfortable in Jack's hands as he stalked through the streets of Tsapan. Third time's the charm, third time he'd been here and with any luck the last. Behind him flowed about fifteen Arxanti, surprising him with their stealth. He'd expected them to be gawping like tourists, but they were focused and silent. Even the girl. Woman. Whatever. She crept beside Daniel with the grace of a panther, a pleasure to watch. Not that he was watching.

He stopped, raising his hand for a halt. The tower housing the *sheh'fet* was a couple of blocks over; he recognized it from Kenna's description, its top lit up like a Christmas tree. Fancy. That's where they were holding Kenna's kid, but it was the basement of the tower that interested Jack. The *sheh'fet* was there, and so was Carter. If she was still alive. If not... Cross that bridge later, if he had to.

The low hum of a transport vehicle overhead cut into his thoughts. "Find cover," he hissed, ducking into the shadow of the building. The Arxanti melted into the darkness, all eyes turned on the ship as it skimmed overhead. Broad beams of light swept down through the streets, slicing the toes of Jack's boots. The Kinahhi were looking for someone.

Carter? He barely dared hope.

Silence followed in the ship's wake, but it wouldn't last long.

Above, Jack could already hear the hum of another aircraft. "Move out." A narrow alley ran between the two buildings opposite, heading in the general direction of the *sheh'fet*. And, more importantly, heading down. Down was good, down away from the search lights and into the depths of the city.

The alley was lined with doorways, some open, others welded shut by the elements. Jack kept his weapon raised, finger tight on the trigger. If they were attacked here, with no room to maneuver...

"O'Neill!" The sharp whisper came from the back of the rank.

He spun around. "What ya got?"

With his zat, Teal'c indicated one of the doorways. "Several of the Arxanti have entered."

You gotta be kidding... "Daniel!"

"I'll check it out."

"Just get them the hell outta there," Jack growled. "This isn't the goddamn city tour!" So much for not acting like tourists.

Tucking his zat into its holster, Daniel ducked into the doorway. Soft talking ensued, and Jack nervously backed against the wall. "Daniel?"

Just then an echo of marching feet reached them, bouncing off the towers. Could have been coming from anywhere. *Damn it!*

Teal'c crouched, weapon raised, covering one end of the alley. "Everyone down," Jack hissed, mirroring his friend. The footfalls grew louder but until Jack could pinpoint their location... "Scratch that. Everyone, get inside. *Now*."

The remaining Arxanti slipped quietly after Daniel into the room, while Jack and Teal'c closed ranks. The alley would be too narrow for the soldiers to pass through. His team would be safe, as long as they didn't draw any attention to themselves.

He gestured to Teal'c, and they both took cover in the doorway, each guarding opposite ends of the alley. The marching sounds grew nearer now. At least twenty men, he guessed. Maybe more.

Shifting his hold on his gun, Jack lifted it and looked down the sight. He had the perfect shot. With enough ammo, he probably could have held the alley indefinitely. But with half a clip...? He tightened his finger on the trigger and watched the first ranks of the Kinahhi hove into view, marching in perfect unison past the end of the alley. *No one sneeze.*

Behind him someone moved and Jack grimaced. It was too dark to kill anyone with a look, and a reprimand would only make things worse. The Kinahhi were still marching, knee-length boots clomping precisely, arms swinging. Weapons glinting in the scant moonlight. Passing them by, oblivious.

"What…?" Daniel whispered urgently, from the back of the room. "No, don't touch—!"

The room lit up like the Fourth of July. Lights, in every color, swirled down from the ceiling like a crazed disco, illuminating a shocked tableau. Daniel was frozen, reaching out to seize the back of Atella's shirt, while the kid stared in astonishment at the small, sleek device he held in one hand. For an instant no one moved – and then all hell broke loose.

"I said don't touch it!" Daniel cried.

"Shut that damn thing off!"

Daniel snatched the device from Atella's hand and the room was plunged back into shadows. Too late.

"The Kinahhi have made our position, O'Neill."

"Yeah, color me surprised."

Damn it. Damn it to hell!

"No!" Sam hissed as her back crashed into the wall, strong hands and arms pinning her there. Fingers seized her face, digging into her flesh, holding her immobile. She was breathing in short, rough gasps. The knife was pried from her hand and fell clattering to the ground, tumbling down the stairs. Too far to reach.

Limb from limb! Koash had curled himself into a ball, shivering with terror. His thoughts were barely coherent. *Limb from limb from limb from limb from limb from limb…*

The fingers around Sam's chin belonged to the first of the creatures who'd approached her. His eyes were still misted with madness, but he was studying her intently. Then his fingers moved, sliding up from her chin to her cheek. Sam repressed a shudder, tried to keep her face neutral. His touch was cold and leathery, a grim reminder of the *sheh'fet.* "Who are you?"

He didn't respond, but she could feel him tracing the ridges on her cheek. The scarlet ridges that matched those on his own face. "*Sheh'fet?*"

"Yes. I escaped." She forced herself to meet his eyes. "Like you."

He pressed harder against her temple, needle-points of pain driving through the trails of scarlet. A breath hissed over the decaying stubs of his teeth, and he closed his eyes. Suddenly a barrage of images flooded her mind...

It was dark. Night. They always came at night. His wife was screaming his name, 'Eytan! Eytan!'

Their daughter was sobbing, clinging to him. 'Papa!'

Elisha! Oh my baby, my sweet little girl...

A long dark journey of fear and pain. And loss. Down, down into the depths. And then the stench, the bowel-churning stench. The sheh'fet*. Dead faces. Not me, I can't be here. This is wrong. This is all wrong. Save me! Someone save me!*

The fire, the deadly fire and pain and madness. And darkness. Death. Sweet death, and memories of laughter...

But then the white light, the vile white light that heralded a terrible dawn. Back to living death. Over and over. A lifetime, too many lifetimes of suffering. And then confusion. Lost forever in this endless maze, consumed by hatred, wandering endlessly, trying to—

"No!" Sam wrenched her head from his grip, gasping with horror. A sob choked her throat. So much misery! His daughter, crying out for him. The pain felt like her own, so intense she could hardly breathe. Tears scalded her eyes, trailing down her cheeks and the creature – the man – touched one and brought it to his lips.

In a shaking voice, Sam said, "Eytan?"

He started in shock, crazed eyes wide. And then his hands fell away from her and he turned to the others. At a silent command they released her and stepped back, watching. Waiting. For what?

An expectant silence fell, broken only by the whimpering of Koash.

"Eytan?" Sam said again.

The creature – man – waved a hand toward the sky. *Bayith.* Home.

Sam felt her heart break. Did they know what they'd become?

"*Bayith*." The word rasped from the man's throat, filled with longing.

It was impossible. They could never go home, not like this. But she was in no position to turn down allies, in whatever form they came. "Help me find my friends," she said, swallowing the bitter taste of her deception. "Then we'll go home together."

"Fall back!" Jack yelled, as the Kinahhi pressed down the narrow alley. He opened fire and took out the first rank, then the second and then—

Nothing. Out of ammo. "Daniel! Take over."

They swapped places in the cramped room, Daniel's zat lighting up the alley along with the red bolts of Kinahhi laser fire. A burst hit the door frame, spraying them all with sharp fragments of rock. Jack dropped the P90, picked up the less accurate Kinahhi weapon and returned to the door. The enemy were closer now, tucked into a doorway halfway down the alley. If their commander was smart, which he probably was, he'd have sent half his team around to the other end of the alley. Wouldn't be long before they were under attack from both sides.

"Teal'c!" Jack shouted. "Any luck?"

"There are stairs," his friend shouted back. "They go up three flights, then there are no more. There is no way out."

What kind of house doesn't have a goddamn back door? "I'm open to suggestions," Jack hissed, ducking away from another laser bolt. "Anyone?"

Behind him, the Arxanti crowded together nervously, hands flexing on unfamiliar weapons. They were scared, he could smell it. "Teal'c, take the kids upstairs. Two at each window. We'll make this harder for them." At least they'd have something to do. A fighting chance, as Daniel had put it.

They clattered upstairs like kids home after school, and after a moment he saw their own fire raining down on the advancing Kinahhi, followed by an occasional whoop of success. *Enjoy it while you can.*

"Jack?" Daniel was moving to the other side of the doorway. "I think I just saw something."

"I'll bet you did," Jack breathed, taking Daniel's position. "Other end of the alley?"

"Yup." Daniel was straining to see through the dim light. "I've got them. Looks like half a dozen men, maybe more."

Too many. "I don't know how we're gonna get out of this one," Jack confessed quietly.

By way of an answer Daniel opened fire, and in the distance a man yelped and fell, convulsing, to the ground. "We'll make it," Daniel said. "We'll— Oh."

Jack didn't look around. "What?"

"Ah... It's jammed. The zat's jammed!"

Things were not looking good. Jack glanced over his shoulder as Daniel pulled out the Beretta, studying it as if it were a bad smell. "After this," he said dryly, "I'll be reduced to throwing insults."

Jack grunted. "We'll be lucky if—"

A barrage of laser fire blasted into their meager cover, coordinated and sustained. Rock flew in tiny pieces of molten slag, chunks of stone fell to the floor and shattered with explosive force. Daniel cried out, clutching the side of his head, blood welling between his fingers.

"Daniel!" Grabbing him, Jack yanked him out of the line of fire while the assault continued.

"I'm okay," Daniel insisted, wiping his bloody hand on his pants. "Shrapnel. It's just a scratch."

Not that it mattered much. The attack intensified, crimson streaks of fire reducing the door to rubble, darting into the room and exploding against the floor. They were coming, and there was no way out.

I'll be back. I swear to God I'll be back...

"O'Neill!" Teal'c thundered down the stairs.

"Over here!"

He was with them in two strides, keeping low. "The Kinahhi are advancing."

"I know. Teal'c, we have to—" Suddenly the ferocious assault stopped and the room fell into a ringing silence. The calm before the storm. Dust drifted from the ceiling like dry rain, pattering onto the floor. Through the shattered doorway Jack heard the crunch of feet over rubble.

"They are here, O'Neill."

I'll be back. I swear to God I'll be back...

With a crash, Jack overturned the round table in the center of the room and dropped to the ground behind it. His friends followed, bracing themselves in the sparse cover. "Give 'em hell."

He refused to let these bastards make a liar out of him.

CHAPTER THIRTY-TWO

66 They're definitely planning something, sir." Henry Boyd ducked back behind the transparent Kinahhi defense shield. "I can hear people moving about, sounds like they're bringing in some heavy machinery."

Hammond nodded. "I'd be surprised if they weren't, son." He consulted his watch. They'd been holding the gate-room for three hours. Not long enough yet for Woodburn to have picked the maggots out of the SGC. "We'll be ready for them."

"Yes, sir." Hands resting lightly on his weapon, Boyd kept his eyes fixed on the slim door at the apex of the gate-room. Through it lay their future. And maybe their end.

As he watched the young man, Hammond was struck by a sudden thought. "Did you ever go see your family, son?"

Boyd's gaze dipped to his boots. "No sir, I— I didn't know what to say to them. It's been so long. Five years. I've been dead for five years. What if Heather…? She might have moved on, and Lucy probably won't remember me. I just didn't know what to say…" He shrugged, and looked up. "Then I heard about what had happened to SG-1. There didn't seem any point in going home, only to… You know."

"When we get home," Hammond said gently, "you'll take some time off. As long as you need."

The man smiled sadly. "Yes, sir."

"We *will* get home, Major," Hammond assured him. "Never doubt that."

Boyd's gaze slid to the door, his ears open to the shuffling and banging from beyond. "Sir, there's a whole army out there."

Hammond nodded. "A whole army – and SG-1."

Boyd looked uncertain. "Sir, that Kinahhi woman said—"

"I don't care what she said. SG-1 are out there, and they have an uncanny ability to beat the odds."

"That's a lot of odds, sir."

"Yes, it is." He cast Boyd a sly glance. "But better odds than bringing your team out of that black hole, wouldn't you say?"

Boyd smiled again. "Yeah, I guess if I had to put money on—"

With a tremendous roar, the door to the gate-room exploded.

For an instant, Hammond was airborne. Then the ground came up to meet him with a crunch that punched the air from his lungs. An eternal moment of silence and shock reverberated through his mind, and then he was shouting. "Return fire!" He scrambled to his feet, shaking his head to clear it. "All units, return fire!"

Boyd was already on one knee, P90 rattling. Dixon was yelling, gesturing to his team as they darted through the smoke and the noise toward the gaping doorway.

"Hold your positions!" Hammond bellowed over the chaos. "We stand here. We stand here!"

And then he lifted his own weapon and began to fire. For God and country. And SG-1.

"Look at them," Sam grated, yanking Koash's head upright by his hair. "Look at them!"

His jaw was trembling, eyes wide as he stared at the group of Outcast gathered around them. They were hunkered down now, watching her with crazy, desperate eyes. Desperate with hope. She hated herself for using them, pretending she could save them from the hell they'd been thrown into, when the most she could offer was a swift death. Nothing could save these people, so far beyond salvation.

"Look at what you've done to them!"

Koash flinched away. "They are Outcast, dissenters—"

"They're people!" Or they were. She sucked in a furious breath, trying to keep control of her rage. "How many times?"

"What?"

"In the sarcophagus. How many times?"

Koash shook his head, recoiling from the answer.

She shook him hard, then slammed his back against the wall. "Tell me. Five? Ten?"

"Until there is no more use to be got from them," he hissed. "Until…"

"Until their minds are destroyed?" Sam felt sick. "You bastard. And then what? You just throw them out here to starve? Why not just kill them?"

"They are of the *sheh'fet*," Koash lifted a shaking hand to his head. "They are in here. To kill them would be—"

"Merciful?"

"Sacrilege."

"Of all the screwed up…" She let him go with disgust, and he slumped to the ground, clutching his torn clothes around him. "You're lucky I don't let them pull you apart. Limb from limb."

"You are appalled by us," he jeered, voice quavering between anger and fear. "Yet you are willing to manipulate them for your own purposes. Are we so very different?"

For an instant her mind was clouded by doubt and guilt. But it was a passing shadow. "If you have to ask that question, Koash, then you don't know me at all. You've created an abomination, and I swear I'm going to bring it down. All of it. No one else will ever, ever suffer like these people."

Koash began to shudder, shaking his head in denial. "You cannot, the *Kaw'ree* will never let—"

"It's over," she hissed. "I'll—"

A hand tugged at her sleeve, and she turned to see Eytan standing at her side. He was trying to speak, to form a word. His lips twisted, frustration making him twitch.

"Here," Sam said gently, and reached out to touch the *sheh'fet* marks on his face. At once he relaxed, and her mind filled with an image.

A battle. Red blasts of hot Kinahhi fire, seen from far above. From a high window. Many troops, scurrying like insects down a narrow passageway. But then a blue flame darted out from a dark doorway, sending the Kinahhi twitching to the ground. And a rattling-crack, over and over, followed. An alien weapon.

Sam's heart leaped. "It's them." Eytan nodded and capered. In pleasure? "Can you take me to them?"

He was nodding again, grabbing at her sleeve. She moved to follow, but at the last minute turned back to Koash. "Run," she told him. "Run back to your tower and get ready. The end is coming."

With that she turned and ran herself, surrounded by the leaping, scampering creatures of the *sheh'fet*. Her people. For she knew she was one of them, she was Outcast. And she would have revenge, for herself and for them all.

Face down on the floor, a boot crushing the side of his face, and his arms yanked behind his back, all Jack could see of Daniel was the top of his head. As for Teal'c, last time Jack had seen him he was going hand-to-hand with a dozen Kinahhi, swinging his empty P90 like a club. After that, Jack had had his own problems to deal with.

"You fight well, Tauri," one of the Kinahhi said. "You have killed many of my men."

"Glad you approve," Jack growled. "Want a rematch? See if you can do better?"

"We have done well enough."

With a rough tug, Jack was pulled to his knees. His jaw throbbed from the blow of a Kinahhi gun stock that had dropped him. But it wasn't broken, so at least he could talk. Some comfort. He briefly checked out their situation. Teal'c was trussed up like himself, his face bruised and blood seeping from a spectacularly split lip. But he was all there, and replied to Jack's silent question with tight nod. *I am well, O'Neill.* Jack could almost hear the words in his head.

Daniel, however, was still sprawled on the floor. His hands weren't tied, and he wasn't moving. Bad sign. Jack glared up at the Kinahhi commander, a thin, wiry creature with an icy expression. "Is he dead?" He kept it neutral, in hopes of getting an honest answer.

The man's attention flickered to Daniel without much interest. "No. Our orders were to capture you alive." He smiled nastily. "But perhaps he will wish that he were. You're to be returned to the *sheh'fet.*"

"I hear it's nice this time of year." *Sonofabitch.*

A sudden commotion on the stairs drew Jack's attention. Breathless with shock, one of the Kinahhi stumbled out into the room. He was white as a ghost and shaking. "Commander," he stammered. "It's… They're… Oh *Re'ammin* save us!"

"Control yourself, man!" the Commander ordered. "Give me your report."

"Yes, sir." The kid was still shaking, fingers curling and flexing. "They're… Sir, they're Mahr'bal! The Mahr'bal have come!"

The officer's head snapped back to Jack, color rising to red fury in his cheeks. "Mahr'bal?" he spat. "You dare bring Mahr'bal *here*? To Tsapan?"

Jack shrugged. "Kinda looks that way, doesn't it?" He gave a bright smile. "Lots more where they came from too. And, boy, are they pissed at you guys."

The flush of anger drained from the Commander's face, turning it chalky. "Bring them," he ordered the shivering soldier. "Bring them down where we may look at them. The *Kaw'ree* will know what to do." He nodded, as if convincing himself. "Yes, we will take them to the *Kaw'ree*. All of them."

The soldier disappeared up the stairs, and after a moment Jack saw the Arxanti being ushered down. With their wiry limbs and ragged clothes it was hard to see what had the Kinahhi so spooked. Among them was Alvita Candra, taut with indignation as she paced down the stairs. But when her eyes fell on Daniel she darted forward with a desperate cry. "Daniel Jackson!"

One of the Kinahhi grabbed her, his face twisted with fear and loathing. "*Keleb!*" he snarled, yanking her back.

She struggled against him. "Daniel Jackson!"

"Easy!" Jack cautioned. "Easy, he's just—" The butt of a Kinahhi gun came down on the back of her head, and she crumpled. "Hey! What the hell did you—"

"Alvita!" Atella fought his own guards, the rest of his men joining the revolt, lashing out and kicking one man down the stairs. "Alvita Candra!"

The Kinahhi crowded the foot of the steps, cursing and panicking, trying to hold back the frantic Arxanti. "Seize them!" the Commander was screaming. "Stop them!"

And then someone fired the first shot.

She was so tired, she couldn't keep up with this race through the endless, twisting stairways of Tsapan. Her legs were shaking with exhaustion, and she was light-headed with hunger.

Keep going. Almost there.

The Colonel, Daniel, Teal'c… It had to be them. She'd seen the zat fire, heard the rattle of a P90. It had to be them. But there'd been so many Kinahhi, and they were so far away.

Ahead of her, at the top of the stairs she currently was forcing her body to climb, she saw Eytan. She could recognize him now, the long hair, the stoop of his shoulders. He was waiting for her. With an effort, she lifted her hand and waved. Beneath it all, she thought as she sucked in another burning breath, there was a shred of compassion or humanity. Something left of the man he'd once been. For all its power, the *sheh'fet* hadn't destroyed that, not entirely.

At last she reached the top, her legs trembling with the effort. "Rest," she gasped, leaning against the wall, catching her breath. She didn't allow herself sit down; she doubted she'd be able to get up again.

Eytan watched her for a moment, then tugged at her shirt. He didn't understand her exhaustion. "*Mayray'ah.*" Friends.

"Yes," she smiled. "I know." With a desperate effort she let him tug her back into motion. At least they were on level ground here, a wide street that disappeared into the night beneath the empty towers of Tsapan.

A burst of gunfire split the darkness, not far away. A bloody flash. Sam's heart missed a beat.

"*Mayray'ah,*" Eytan insisted, tugging at her again. He wanted to run.

"Go," Sam gasped, forcing her legs to move. "Show me."

"Stand down!" Jack surged to his feet. "Atella, stand down!" A hand grabbed his arm where it was tied behind him, but Jack jerked his head back and felt it impact on something soft. A nose? He stomped down, found a set of toes, and with a howl his guard let go. Jack pitched forward, right into the Commander, knocking him to the ground.

The man scrambled back to his feet, shaking with outrage. Or was it fear? "Subdue them!"

More Kinahhi piled through the door, using their weapons like batons. "Atella!" Jack shouted. "Stand down. Stand dow—" A rifle butt smashed into his cheek, jerking his head sideways and knocking him to his knees.

"Kill them!" the Commander shrieked. "Kill the Mahr'bal, before they murder—"

An inhuman shriek lanced through the chaos like a blade of ice, silencing everything.

Oh crap.

The Kinahhi froze, weapons raised. The Arxanti cast wild looks at each other, full of fear and confusion.

Another shriek, this time closer. Definitely closer. And more than one.

"O'Neill!" Teal'c knelt at the opposite side of the room, hands still tied. He recognized the sound too.

The Kinahhi Commander spun toward the door, panicking. All around a horrified whisper rustled through his men. "Outcast! The Outcast are coming."

"Get out," Jack ordered. "Everyone get out, they'll slaughter us in here." He yanked at the cuffs that bound his hands, but they wouldn't move. "Untie us!"

The Commander's gaze darted between the door and his prisoners. "I am no fool, I will not—"

"You're a damn fool!"

"Untie us," Teal'c growled, standing up. "Or we all die together."

Behind him, Jack heard a soft groan. Daniel was pushing himself groggily to his hands and knees, head moving slowly from side to side. "What happened…?"

Thank God! "Daniel, untie—" Jack stopped. The stench. That horribly familiar stench oozed past his face, chilling him to the core. Breathing hard, Jack turned back to the door. Heart racing, he struggled back to his feet. "Daniel. Get up. Now."

A scream echoed down the alley, human and terrified, before ending in a sickening gurgle. Then he heard it, the soft slap of flesh on stone, the flutter of tattered clothing. And the stench filled the room with death and degradation.

Damn it, he refused to die like this. "Someone give me a god-damn weapon!"

Too late. A face appeared at the door, a devil's face, piteous and terrifying in equal measure. Lank scraps of hair fell over the red-raw acid trails of the *sheh'fet*. Jack could almost feel his own face burning in response, and suddenly the creature's eyes were locked on him.

He could hardly breathe for the stink and the fear. Someone behind him screamed – one of the Arxanti. So much for their revolution, so much for their glorious battle for freedom. Now they'd know the horror of war, and the futility of death.

From above came a scrabbling sound, like rats' claws on the floorboards. Teal'c looked up. "They are coming through the windows."

It was too much for the Kinahhi Commander. "Open fire!" he screamed in desperation. "Open fire!"

"Get down!" Jack barreled into Daniel, knocking them both to the floor as the room erupted into bloody chaos. The air burned with laser fire, turning red and smoky. Into it poured the demonic creatures, pouncing on the backs of the Kinahhi like wild animals, ripping, shredding, and shrieking.

"O'Neill," Teal'c crawled toward them. "Daniel Jackson, we must—"

A white, bony hand seized Jack's shoulder, yanking him around. With a curse, Jack pulled his arm free and scrambled away from the emaciated creature. It squatted before them, head cocked, face convulsing grotesquely.

"What's it doing?" Jack rasped. Damn, if only he had a weapon.

"He's watching you," Daniel whispered. Unbelievably, he sounded fascinated. "I think he's trying to communicate."

"Daniel!"

"No," his friend insisted, turning his hands palm up in a gesture of friendship. "He's not attacking. See? He's—" Daniel suddenly looked up, eyebrows rising. "Ah. Hello."

Following his gaze, Jack saw a ring of the creatures forming around them, all sniffing at the air hungrily. "What are they doing?"

Teal'c edged closer, doing a good job of hiding his repugnance. "Perhaps they know we are not Kinahhi and therefore do not attack us?"

"Yeah. Or perhaps they're just firing up the barbecue."

The alley was filled with death. Fallen Kinahhi soldiers lay sprawled on top of each other, and further down – she tried not to look too closely – Sam saw the Outcast huddled together, their backs to her. She didn't care to know what they were doing, and fixed her eyes on the battle-scarred doorway instead.

Carefully she picked her way through the debris. It was difficult on her rubber legs, they barely felt like they belonged to her. Hunger made her clumsy, and she was hugging the wall for support. Outside the door lay one of the Kinahhi, his throat ripped out. She averted her eyes and pulled the weapon from his dead fingers. It was better than nothing, although she'd have preferred the solid weight of a P90.

Dizzy for a moment, she took a deep breath. Then, cautiously, she eased herself around the corner, weapon leveled. Her eyes took a couple of moments to grow accustomed to the deeper gloom. To her left, crowded around the bottom of a narrow staircase, were a group of skinny young men, staring at her fearfully. One of them started, and half rose to his feet. Sam had no idea who he was or why he should recognize her. She just nodded, and he sat down again, returning to his task of cutting the ties that bound the arms of his comrades.

Turning away, Sam moved toward the small group of Outcast gathered at the back of the room. "Eytan?"

He was there, beckoning her closer. And then, as the Outcast made way for her to pass, she saw them. Her team. Battered, bruised and disarmed, they sat backed into a corner with their hands tied. But they were alive. Her legs almost gave out in relief.

"Carter?" The Colonel was gaping in astonishment, as if she were a ghost or a figment of his imagination.

"Yes, sir. It's me."

For a moment he just stared. "I've, um…" And then he shook himself, hiding everything behind an arid smile. "We've come to rescue you."

She laughed, but it sounded dangerously like hysteria, and then Daniel was on his feet and wrapping her in a hug that lifted her off the ground. "Sam! We thought you were dead."

So did I. She dropped her weapon and just held on to him. *So did I.*

CHAPTER THIRTY-THREE

Jack rubbed at his chafed wrists, while Teal'c wrapped a make-shift bandage around Daniel's bleeding head. It made him look like the Karate Kid. "Stylish, Daniel-san."

Daniel lifted an eyebrow, and wriggled his glasses onto his face. "So?" He glanced at Carter – Carter! – who was munching on a piece of dry Arxanti bread like a starving dog. "What next?"

"We can't stay here," Jack decided, eyeing the strange, snuffling creatures who were still watching them. He swore he could see hunger in their eyes. "We have to get down, to the *sheh'fet.*"

"Sir?" Carter's voice was muffled by a mouthful of bread.

He met her gaze and held it. "I'm going to blow the thing to hell." No argument.

"Yes sir. But there's a better way."

Ten minutes later Jack found himself climbing yet another interminable staircase, surrounded on all sides by Carter's tame monsters. And was it his imagination, or were they growing in number?

Outcast, she'd called them. But he knew what they really were, and he hadn't missed the telltale scarlet threads that marked her face too. Carter might not be sporting the zombie-look, but she was one of them. He could sense it, see it in the way they looked at her. The way they obeyed her. He wondered if she even realized that she seemed to communicate with them telepathically.

She was up ahead now, deep in conversation with Daniel. Jack let them talk, happy to hang back. What did he have to say to her anyway? Not much that was fit for public consumption, and as for the rest... There was a time and a place, and this definitely wasn't it. She was alive; that would have to be enough for now.

"O'Neill!" Teal'c had been scouting ahead and came loping down the stairs.

"What's up?"

"I have seen several Kinahhi transport ships arrive in the last few minutes," Teal'c replied. "I believe the garrison here is being reinforced."

Great. "Carter!"

She turned. "Sir?"

"How far? We've got company on the way."

"Nearly there, sir." She indicated a walkway that peeled off a hundred yards up to their left, ending at the base of a giant onion-shaped dome. "It'll be guarded."

"Figures." A soft light, one of the few in the city, filtered out through the dome, giving it a deceptively welcoming look. "And what's in there, exactly?"

Her face hardened. "The *Kaw'ree*. From there we should be able to use the *sheh'fet* itself to disable the whole system. More specifically, sir, you should."

He blinked. "*I* should?"

"Yes, sir. I think— The Kinahhi are convinced that you can destroy them, that you're what they call Mahr'bal." Her gaze drifted to the Arxanti ranging out behind them. "They're terrified of them."

"From what I saw in Arxantia," Daniel chimed in, "there's some kind of genetic component to their technology. You have to be genetically compatible to use it." He gave a long-suffering roll of the eyes. "Which, incidentally, is why we had that lightshow back there. Atella picked up the device, and it just activated. Like the light in Arxantia worked for you, Jack, but not me or Teal'c."

"Even if you're right," Jack said, striding up the stairs and waiting for the rest of them to catch up, "and I'm not saying you are, but *if* you're right, the ability to turn lights on and off without using my hands is not exactly—"

"Did not Alvita Candra declare that the *sheh'fet* itself was a device of the Ancients?" Teal'c, as always, cut straight to the point.

Jack fixed him with a hard stare. "She said that?"

Daniel rubbed at the bandage around his head, causing his hair to flop all over the place. "Yeah, she said they'd corrupted it."

"Of course!" Carter had that look in her eye, the one that generally preceded a long explanation. "I should have known. Sir, I'm sure you noticed the design differences between the center of the *sheh'fet* and the supporting technology? The power cables, the...ah...clamps..." Her voice cracked and broke.

"I'm sure *you* did," he said brightly, covering her momentary stumble. "And this is significant because...?"

"Because Daniel's right. This isn't Kinahhi technology. They can't use it properly, and that's why they're afraid of the Mahr'bal. They're afraid they'll take it back, and use it to destroy them."

Teal'c looked at the Arxanti, who followed them without fatigue or complaint. "Their fear is justified," he said. "The Arxanti are here to reclaim their birthright."

A holy war. Jack slowed as they reached the walkway, peering over the edge. The city disappeared below, lost in darkness. This high up he could taste the tang of salt in the air, the breeze washing away the stink of the *sheh'fet* – even with Carter's zombie army squatting all the way up the stairs, staring down at them like a flock of tortured, naked vultures.

The onion-dome was massive up close, towering above them like a giant, glowing...onion. Jack turned away; so much for poetry.

"Daniel." He glanced uneasily at the wild-haired Alvita Candra, who stood at the head of her ragtag militia. "I'm thinking we should keep the crusaders out of the temple. What do you say?"

Daniel frowned, the expression slipping into a grimace. "I don't know. This is their war, isn't it?"

"He's got a point, sir." Carter indicated her own private army with a slight nod. "Perhaps we should just let them loose?"

Cold. Jack didn't miss the cold rage behind her eyes, the desire for a kind of revenge she'd never be able to exact herself. "Carter? Who's in there, exactly?"

And what the hell did they do to you?

She shook her head and looked away. "Just an idea, sir."

"It would be a massacre."

"I concur with O'Neill," said Teal'c, coming to his rescue. "We require a more disciplined assault if we are to achieve our purpose and return in good time to the SGC." He fixed them all with a firm look. "Do not forget the Kinahhi already have a foothold among the Tauri. The destruction of the *sheh'fet* is not our primary goal."

"Not ours," Daniel agreed. "But it is for the Arxanti and for the Outcast. We can't stand in their way."

And for Carter?

From the corner of his eye Jack saw her studying the dome, so intently you'd think she could see right through it. Then he noticed the scarlet pattern on her face, disfiguring her pallid skin. Perhaps she really could see inside, or into the minds within? "We'll go in together," he decided, "all of us." For some reason, Carter's restrained smile of anticipation made him shiver.

"Once more unto the breach, huh?" said Daniel.

Jack shucked the Kinahhi rifle off his shoulder and into his hands. "Just watch your ass, Sundance."

They exploded into the vaulted room like water breaching a damn. First the Outcast, raving and hooting as they surged through the tall black doors, then the Arxanti, running on strong, sinewy legs with the grace of wildcats. And on their six, SG-1.

Laser fire felled the first ranks of the Outcast, and through the chaos of battle Daniel glimpsed a terrified line of Kinahhi soldiers. They fired, and fired and fired again. But the Outcast were beyond fear. Within moments the Kinahhi were overwhelmed, buried beneath a wave of unwashed, starving people dehumanized at the most basic level. *Reaping the whirlwind.* The screams were pitiful, gurgling with terror. He was forced to look away and found himself eye-to-eye with Jack. His friend looked faintly nauseous.

"I'm not putting this in the report."

"O'Neill," said Teal'c, pointing beyond the Outcast. "Look."

It was Sam. She was skirting the mob of creatures, crouched low. Hunting.

"What the—" Jack bit off the curse. "Damn it." Then he was moving, Teal'c on his heels. Daniel was about to follow when a warm hand took his.

"Daniel Jackson." It was Alvita Candra, gazing at him with a fervent light in her eyes that was almost disturbing. "Come. It is time for you to change our world."

He blinked. "For me to… *What*?"

"Come," she insisted, tugging him into motion. "Come. Only you can show our enemy the truth."

"Look, I'm sorry. I'm not him. I'm not one of your ancestors, I'm not here to fulfill your prophesy. I have to help my friends."

Her hand tightened on his. "You are more than you think, Daniel Jackson. Trust me. I have seen it."

Do you seek the truth, Daniel Jackson?

The voice in his head came out of nowhere. "Oma?"

Alvita Candra smiled. "Come," she said. "End this."

Shaking his head, disoriented, he let her pull him into motion. *Oma? Are you here?*

There was no answer.

Teal'c kept low as he followed Major Carter, O'Neill at his side. She was approaching a man, he realized. Several men. They were dressed in black robes and sat in several large chairs placed in a semicircle on a dais at the center of the room. The Outcast had gathered around the platform, swaying and flinching, snapping their jaws like wild animals. It was evident that they hungered for the lives of these men, but some force was keeping them at bay.

"Carter?" O'Neill hissed as they drew closer. "What's going on?"

"Koash," she replied, eyes fixed on a man who stood on the dais staring down at her. There was anger and fear and horror in his dark eyes, all of it aimed at Major Carter. "The *Kaw'ree*."

"Yeah. Right. Wanna try that in English?"

"They're the ones who control the *sheh'fet*, sir." Her voice was tight, as if speaking were difficult. "Those chairs give them access to all the minds trapped inside it. They control it all."

O'Neill's face hardened. "Then we take them out."

She nodded, breathing quickly. The weapon in her hand began to shake, her face twisting in sudden pain. "Sir..."

"Major Carter!" Teal'c moved to her side, exchanging a concerned look with O'Neill.

"I can't," she gasped. The weapon dropped from her hands. "I can't move."

Teal'c looked up, right into the face of the man she had called Koash. The scarlet veins on his skin stood out like trails of blood, and the murderous look in his eye was mirrored in all the white faces of the *Kaw'ree*. "They are doing this to you."

Major Carter moaned and dropped to her knees, her hands pressed hard against her head, fingers cramping to fists in her hair. Teal'c dropped to her side, offering what comfort he could. All around, the Outcast began to shriek and wail, flailing on the floor in agony. "Stop," Major Carter cried. "*Oh God, make them stop!*"

O'Neill stalked forward, gun raised and aimed. "Let her go. Right now."

"Lower your weapon," Koash said coldly, "or she will die this instant."

O'Neill didn't move an inch. "Then so will you. All of you."

Alvita Candra led Daniel toward a large chair set at the far side of the room. It seemed identical to those on the dais, apart from the ominous addition of ankle and wrist cuffs.

"What is it?" Daniel asked, circling the chair curiously. Its design was clearly not Goa'uld, the technology was too sophisticated. He glanced at the young woman. "Is this one of the gifts your ancestors left behind?"

"Yes." She reached out a hand and touched the chair lovingly. "It was stolen by the Kinahhi when my mother was a child." Her dark eyes met his. "It is the heart of the *sheh'fet*. And you must use it."

"Me? I can't. Maybe Jack can—"

"*You* must use it," she insisted. "Jack O'Neill has a different purpose. You are here to reveal the truth, Daniel Jackson. And, perhaps, to discover it for yourself." She held out her hand for him again. "Come, sit."

If this machine could truly penetrate his mind, could it perhaps dislodge the hidden memories of his time among the Ascended? He knew what Jack would say: *Don't touch it!* But Jack didn't have a big gaping hole in his memories, an entire blank year full of mysteries and wonders that were lost in an opaque fog. If this machine could somehow cut through all that...

He touched the arm of the chair, cool and smooth beneath his fingers, and felt a thrill of excitement. "What do I have to do?"

Carter gasped through gritted teeth. "Sir... The chair. You have to sit—"

"What for?" Jack's eyes dropped briefly from Koash to the strange chairs. They looked like some sort of weird-ass recliner, but there was no plasma screen TV. "Carter?"

He couldn't see her, but he could hear her ragged breathing. "To… destroy…" She stopped, crying out in pain.

But she'd said enough. "Sit in the chair, huh?" He kept his eyes fixed on Koash and saw a flicker of terror in the man's eyes. That told him all he needed to know. "Don't like the idea?"

Behind him Carter shrieked, a nerve-shredding repetition of her howl in the *sheh'fet*. Jack's resolution wavered; they were killing her! He took a step closer, keeping a tight rein on his anger. "Stop," he growled at Koash. "Stop right now, or I swear to God I'll kill you."

"You will not risk her." A sly smile touched the man's pallid features. "I have seen your mind, Colonel O'Neill. Albeit briefly. You would rather die than—"

In two bounds Jack was up on the dais with the muzzle of the Kinahhi rifle pressed against the man's thin chest. "Actually, I'd rather *you* die."

The apprehension Jack had seen earlier mushroomed into full-scale panic. "Go back!" Koash screeched. "Stand back!"

Jack let his gaze drift to the recliner of doom. "What? You don't want me to touch this thing?"

"Stand *back*!" The red veins criss-crossing his face bulged as if they'd burst. "Filthy animal—"

Carter screamed again, the sound abruptly cut short.

"O'Neill!" Teal'c sounded desperate. Jack's stomach twisted, hands tightening on the weapon. *So help me, if he harms her…*

He jammed the gun against Koash's chest. "Let. Her. *Go!*"

"You should have listened!" A toxic mix of fear and spite spread across the man's face and gathered into a terrible smile. "She's already dead."

It was like swimming through noise, as if his mind were floating through a cacophony as thick as water. Pain and fear sank to the bottom, cold and dank, while above drifted treasured memories of joy and happiness, a thin film of light covering the depths of despair.

Let them see you. The voice was Alvita Candra's, rich and dark in his mind.

"Who?"

The Kaw'ree.

"How do I—"

No need to ask. A giant fist seized hold of his mind, yanking him through the noise and the chaos like a shark hauled its prey. He tried to fight free, but it was impossible.

You are Daniel Jackson. Not one voice, but many. The *Kaw'ree*, he guessed.

"Yes."

You come voluntarily to the sheh'fet?

"I've come to show you the truth. About the Mahr'bal – the Arxanti. And the Ancients." He felt their unease as if it were his own, rippling in cold waves through his mind. "You don't need to fear them," he said. "They are not your enemy, the Ancients were a wise and—"

His mind was cut open as if with a slash of a scalpel. *We will see the truth, your lies will not hold here.*

"No lies," he gasped through the pain.

We will see. We will see everything, Daniel Jackson.

Twenty hands seized his mind, pulling it apart. Memories scattered like shreds of paper. His mom, holding him on her knee. Sha're's smile. Jack beating him at chess, Teal'c teaching him to fight, Sam asleep on his couch… A hundred, a thousand memories torn apart and discarded. "No!" He was losing everything, losing them all.

The pain was all over, inside and outside. His cells liquefying, drowning him. He was dying. Oh God, he was dying again. So much pain, so much sorrow. "I don't want to die!"

You must choose. Oma! *You must choose.*

Oma. Always watching. The bright light of salvation, leading to a new life. A new existence of light.

"I remember! I remember choosing."

And then floating. Watching. An endless wait, always seeing, never acting. Trapped in an agonizing paradox, at once omnipotent and powerless. He saw darkness too, evil unleashed and unchallenged. Frustration and fear. Anger and conflict. He knew something terrible, something he had to stop. But the others refused to intervene, refused to act. But *he* knew, if only he could tell—

No!

He was dropped, as if the hands who grabbed at him had suddenly been burned, and the fleeting memories shattered.

No, it cannot be.

Crumpled amid the chaos of his mind, Daniel struggled to cling to the truth he'd almost grasped, but it slipped through his fingers like sand. He screamed with frustration.

All around him rose the panicked cries of the *Kaw'ree*; they'd seen a truth themselves, something that had sent them fluttering like a flock of birds around a treetop, too afraid to land.

He ignored them, tuned them out, desperate to return to the half-memories that had promised so much. But they were fading, the fog was descending again. "Oma! Why won't you let me remember?"

Faintly, distantly he heard something. *Daniel!*

"Oma?"

Daniel! Stronger this time, a desperate plea for help. *Daniel!*

It was Sam.

"No, it cannot be!"

All nine of the *Kaw'ree* said the words together, like a horror-struck choir. And then all hell broke loose. All around Jack, the Outcast leaped up onto the dais; whatever hold the *Kaw'ree* had on them was broken. It was like feeding time at the zoo and the *Kaw'ree* leaped in terror out of their chairs.

A massacre was seconds away. The Outcast prowled the edge of the platform, hungry for revenge, herding the petrified *Kaw'ree* into its center. The white limbs of the Outcast were stark against the shivering black robes. "Help us!" Koash screamed. "Save us!"

Jack stared back at him, the man's cold words stuck like a blade of ice in his chest. *She's already dead.* His weapon fell to his side. "Why?"

"Have mercy…"

"You *killed* her!"

Koash's eyes were stark with horror. He knew the truth; he knew he'd find no mercy. Not after that, not ever.

Jack turned his back and listened to the man scream until the end.

CHAPTER THIRTY-FOUR

Daniel sprinted across the room, Alvita Candra on his heels. "Use the chair!" he yelled, dodging around the Arxanti warriors. "Jack, use the chair!"

Jack's face was like ice, his whole body rigid. Sam lay blue-lipped on the ground, her head resting in Teal'c's lap. But not dead. She wasn't dead!

"Jack!" Daniel skidded to a stop and seized his friend by the arm. "You have to use the chair, Jack. Use it to destroy the *sheh'fet* and free them."

"I don't know how—"

"You have to. It's the only way to save Sam."

The ice cracked. "She's dead."

"No," Daniel panted. "She's still trapped inside the *sheh'fet*. She always was. Jack, you have to destroy it."

Without hesitation, Jack leaped up onto the dais and threw himself into the nearest chair. It came alive immediately, flooding with a violet light and tipping right back in a way it hadn't done for Daniel. Or the *Kaw'ree*.

"Exactly what am I—" Jack was cut off when a slim metallic strip whipped up and around his forehead. His body stiffened, as if readying itself for battle, and his eyes closed. Beneath their lids, Daniel could see rapid motion. Jack's lips moved too, but no sound escaped. Suddenly, a burst of energy shot along the cable that attached the chair to the dais, detonating into the floor amid sparks of silver.

Jack frowned, as if listening intently. And then far, far away, from deep down in the bowels of the city there came a hollow concussion. It rippled like an earthquake through the tower, rocking it wildly. Daniel hunkered down as the room shook, shards of glass from its ceiling crashing like daggers to the floor.

As one, the Outcast screamed, batting wildly at their heads, shaking them, running in all directions as they fled the dais. Daniel's gaze shrank from the pile of black robes they'd left behind.

He dared not imagine what lay beneath.

"Daniel Jackson!" Teal'c's urgent voice drew his attention and he hurried over to Sam. Her back was arched, her face contorted into a grimace of pain. But she was very much alive. "Is he harming her?"

"No," Daniel insisted. "Just wait. It's okay." *Please God, let me be right about this.*

Suddenly the Outcast stopped screaming, and Sam slumped back to the floor, her face slack. Teal'c's hand darted to her throat, and he gave a slight nod of satisfaction. "Look," said Daniel, touching her cheek. The scarlet imprint of the *sheh'fet* was fading, its hold loosening. Her mind returning, or so Daniel hoped. He'd seen her inside, trapped and lost, driven from her body by the power of the *Kaw'ree*. But they were gone now, and Jack had destroyed the *sheh'fet* so she—

Another explosion rocked the tower, this one much closer. Then another, more distant. And a third. Teal'c looked up. "We must leave."

"Not yet. Let him finish."

"Daniel Jackson!" The animated voice came from the far side of the room, heavy with a Kinahhi lilt.

He spun around to grin at the sight of Commander Kenna striding through the open doors, with a small boy and at least thirty men in tow. "You've found him," Daniel said, rising.

Kenna looked like a man reborn, his face alive with relief and determination. He placed a firm hand on his son's shoulder. "I have. As well as more men willing to join with us."

"That's great. You—" Daniel staggered as yet another detonation jolted the tower. "You should get back to the ship."

Kenna's gaze slipped past him, toward Sam. His face darkened. "What of your friend? Does she live?"

"Yeah. She'll be okay."

The Commander closed his eyes in a moment of profound relief, then nodded crisply at two of his men. "We will assist you. The whole city has become unstable, we cannot—" He stopped abruptly, eyes fixed on Jack. "Colonel O'Neill is... What *is* he doing?"

Daniel followed his gaze. "Ah, he's destroying the *sheh'fet*."

"Then he *is* Mahr'bal?"

"Something like that."

As Daniel spoke, Jack's eyes snapped open and the silver band around his forehead slithered back into the headrest. Jack scrambled out of the chair, casting it a sour look as if it might reach out and drag him back into its clutches. "Whatever the hell that thing is," he said, jumping off the dais, "I never, ever want to sit in one again."

His gaze came to rest on Kenna, then the boy, and he opened his mouth to speak. But someone else cut him off.

"Sir…?" It was Sam, sounding groggy as Teal'c helped her to sit up. She rubbed her hands over her temples, shaking her head. "It's so quiet."

"It's gone." For a moment it looked like Jack might reach out and touch the fading marks on her cheek. But he didn't. "The whole, stinking mess, Carter. Gone for good."

She nodded. "How?"

"I blew a few fuses." His attention roved back to the chair. "Don't ask me how, because I don't know."

"And the people inside it?"

Jack's face darkened, and Daniel instantly knew he was hiding something. "They're free."

Sam just nodded again, not seeming to catch the deception Daniel had sensed. There was no time to press the subject, anyway. A Kinahhi ship roared overhead, spitting laser fire.

"Get down!" Jack bellowed.

A huge explosion shattered the dome above them. Daniel threw himself to the floor as splintered glass fell in a deadly rainfall, and all around the Outcast were wailing.

"The military will not allow us to leave," Kenna shouted. "They cannot permit the truth to reach Kinahhi."

"Screw that." Jack shot to his feet, boots crunching on broken glass. "We're getting the hell off this planet. Teal'c, Carter—"

"Sir, wait," Sam said. "The Outcast – we can't leave them here."

They were gathering around her now, disoriented and passive, as if all the fight had been drained from them. But still not human, thought Daniel. Still only husks of humanity. "We can't take them home, Carter," Jack said, dragging her into motion.

She pulled away from him. "Sir, I promised I'd help them."

Jack's silent answer was eloquent, but Sam wouldn't back down. "I won't leave them here."

Eyebrows raised, Jack repeated, "*Won't*, Major?"

"They saved my life, sir."

"And ours also, O'Neill," said Teal'c, brushing a shard of broken glass from his sleeve and sending it tinkling to the floor.

Jack's eyes narrowed. "*Et tu*, Teal'c?"

Shakespeare? Now he'd heard everything! "Come on, Jack," Daniel called. "No one gets—"

"Ah!" Jack cut him off with a sharp lift of his hand and started crunching across the floor toward the doors. "Just…don't. Okay? Don't say it."

Councilor Tamar Damaris stared at the paper in her shaking hands. The words seemed to slide together in a dance as impossible as the meaning of this message. "The *Kaw'ree*?" she whispered. "*All* of them?"

"Yes, Councilor." Her aide, Matan Tal, struggled for words. "The *sheh'fet* is… It is destroyed. All across the city, the arches are dead. They are… The people are in a panic, rumors are spreading of the Mahr'bal. Of an invasion!"

"Impossible." But it was before her in black and white. And suddenly the truth crystallized, like frost on a winter's morning "So this is their plan. The Tauri have been in league with the Mahr'bal all along. This is why they have attacked our Stargate, why they sent their 'explorers' here in the first place. It is a Mahr'bal plot to destroy us!"

Anger, bright and pure as diamond, ran through her veins. It hardened everything it touched, silenced every remaining voice of reason. "They will not succeed." She skewered Matan Tal with a fierce stare. "Send everything we have to Tsapan. Destroy them – destroy the whole city if necessary, but do not allow a single Mahr'bal or Tauri to escape with their life. Afterward, send our people to the Cordon. The Mahr'bal will pay for this incursion; they will pay with their lives and with the lives of their children." She let the report fall to her desk. "From this moment, we are at war. And it will be the final war. The war that ends all wars."

The attack had started at daybreak, flight after flight of Kinahhi ships, battering the city until it fell to its knees. If it had knees, Jack thought sourly, as he picked his way through the junk heap that had once been an elegant plaza. All around him scattered a ragtag army of Arxanti, disaffected Kinahhi and half-crazed Outcast. Hungry, frightened and losing hope. If they didn't find a way out of here soon…

"Colonel O'Neill?" It was Kenna, coming to trudge at his side. "I believe we have no option but to seize another transport from the military. The one in which we arrived is not armed, and will not hold all our number."

Not if you counted the Outcast. He glanced over at Carter, walking with her familiar long-legged swagger, surrounded by the skeletal creatures. She was almost as pale as them, but looked more herself now that the mark of the *sheh'fet* was fading from her skin. *No one gets left behind.* Not even the dehumanized victims of the *sheh'fet*, according to Carter.

So what about inhuman sons of bitches whose ambition and greed overcame any sense of decency or loyalty to Earth? Did they get left behind, or did honor—

"Colonel?"

"Yeah," Jack pulled his thoughts back on track. "You're right. Any ideas?"

Kenna nodded. "The central landing platform is not far. But it will be well guarded."

"Figures." Jack squinted up into the early morning light. "If we wait for dark we could—"

A deafening explosion, harsh as cracking rock, tore through the city. "Holy *crap*!" Then the shockwave hit, rippling upward, shattering windows and shaking buildings until they sagged on their foundations, cascading rubble like shrapnel. "Find cover!" Jack yelled. "Get out of—"

They were falling. The whole city was falling, like an elevator with its cables cut. Jack hauled himself to his feet, looking for his team. Daniel and Teal'c were to his left, hugging the ground, and Carter was shouting, "Sir, I think they blew the antigrav—"

The elevator hit the ocean. Jack smashed into the floor, landing hard on his shoulder, bounced up again, then slammed down on his knee with a purple burst of pain, cursing. Loudly.

"Jack!" Daniel shouted, staring up in horror. "Oh my G—"

The colossal wave thundered down like vengeance itself. Freezing cold and relentless. Over and over Jack went, tossed like flotsam, dragged through the debris that smashed at his head and body and limbs. He gasped for breath, was thrown sideways, breached the surface again, and saw a claw of brickwork reaching up above the water. He grabbed it, hanging on for dear life while the wave tore at his clothing, trying to drag down into the depths of the violently swaying city as it drained away like water in a tub.

"O'Neill?" Teal'c was standing up shakily, dripping wet. "Daniel Jackson?"

"Over here." Jack climbed down, landing with a painful jolt to his knee. The ground pitched and rolled, making it hard to stay upright. He scanned the ruins, still streaming with water, and saw Daniel struggling to his feet close to the edge of the plaza. He'd lost his glasses and was swiping the water from his face, squinting at the Arxanti, who were scattered like flotsam. Their number was desperately reduced. Nearby, Kenna was helping his boy to his feet, drying the kid's face with a tenderness that tightened Jack's chest painfully. He had to look away.

Carter made her way toward them, stumbling as the ground swayed, surrounded by a handful of Outcast. All that were left? Had everyone else been washed away?

"Sir." Water streamed from her hair, plastering it to her head. "They must have hit the anti-grav generator, we—"

An aftershock rippled through the city. Jack froze, eyes locked with Carter's, holding his breath. And then, with a scream of tortured metal and stone, the entire city listed sharply to one side, sending junk and people alike sliding toward the edge of the plaza.

"Hang on!" Jack lunged for an empty window frame as rocks, debris and water tumbled past, bounced off the walls around the plaza and plummeted into the city below.

"Ah, guys?" Daniel was clinging to the side of parapet, surrounded by the small, frightened crowd of Arxanti. "I think we're in trouble."

Clambering across the suddenly steep slope, Jack, Teal'c and Carter joined their friend and peered over the edge of the low wall.

Holy crap!

"I believe your assessment is correct, Daniel Jackson," Teal'c observed. "We are in trouble."

"I'll say," Carter agreed.

Jack just sighed. "Someone tell me we didn't park down there."

Below them, the ocean gushed into the cockeyed streets and alleyways, churning wildly, battering the city and its once elegant spires.

Tsapan was drowning.

The door to the Kinahhi gate-room was no more than a shattered hole, twice as wide as it once had been, and blackened by the smoke that hung thick in the air.

Hammond counted ten of his men down – at least eight were dead – and the Kinahhi were massing outside for the final push. Only one of the two huge Kinahhi cannons was still in use, manned now by Dave Dixon, whose left arm was tightly bandaged. Hammond himself was crouched behind the DHD with Henry Boyd, the C4 strapped to the device only inches away from his hand. The light on the detonator was flashing, a relentless reminder of his last resort. He was running out of options.

"We can't hold it much longer, sir," Boyd said. He looked exhausted; they all did. "If General Woodburn hasn't sorted things out back home by now…"

If he hadn't, none of them would be going home. "We wait for the signal," Hammond said. "If he's failed, then we have a job to do here."

"Yes, sir." Boyd's eyes moved to the C4. He was thinking of his daughter no doubt. Perhaps regretting his decision to volunteer for this suicide mission.

"It's not over yet, son."

"No, sir."

"*General!*" Dixon yelled from behind the Kinahhi cannon, shifting it to his right as the muzzle of a huge weapon nosed through the shattered doorway. "Incoming!" He opened fire, just as a massive bolt of white heat blasted into the room. The inferno seared the air, sizzling around the Stargate like scalding mist. Even flat against the floor where he'd thrown himself, the air was hot enough to scorch Hammond's lungs. "Boyd," he croaked through an arid throat, "the C4…"

Blisters scarring the side of the young man's face, he levered himself up above the DHD. Dixon was still firing, and someone was screaming in agony. Another blast from the hellish cannon tossed Boyd back to the ground, hair smoking, just as a familiar clunk cut through the heat and noise. Then another. The Stargate was dialing.

"Hold your positions!" shouted Hammond. This could be it – this could be the sign they'd been waiting for. Or it could herald the end. If Woodburn had failed…

Another blast of white heat flamed through the air, licking around the edges of the DHD. But the gate kept spinning. Faster now, chevron after chevron locking, until at last, like a wild cheer, the event horizon erupted into the room. Hammond held his breath, staring at the rippling surface. It shivered, and a MALP crawled out. While the battle raged on, it turned its dead gaze on Hammond. He stared back and prayed to God that he was being watched by a friendly eye.

CHAPTER THIRTY-FIVE

"The lower levels must be filling with water, tipping us like a boat," Daniel shouted over the noise of the waves smashing through the city. "Good job we're not stuck below-deck."

Jack grunted his agreement. "Yeah, I've seen *Titanic*."

"Really? You've seen *Titanic*?"

"Why not?"

"Well, I just—"

"O'Neill," Teal'c cut in. "If we do not reach the landing platform soon, all the Kinahhi ships will have slipped into the ocean."

"Yeah." There was a slight hesitation before Jack answered, so small you might miss it. "Yeah, you're right, Teal'c. We gotta get outta here."

But Daniel had spent his career observing people, and he knew Jack O'Neill inside out. He was hiding something. Turning, Jack braced himself between the stub of a wall and the semi-vertical floor and yelled across the plaza to Kenna. The Kinahhi commander, his son in tow, climbed toward them. He looked shaken, and Daniel wasn't surprised. Within twenty-four hours Kenna had rebelled against his leaders, and now was watching the icon of their security state sink into the ocean. His world was literally falling apart. Under the circumstances, he was doing a good job of holding it together.

Jack had a smile for the kid. "Quite a ride, huh?"

Wide-eyed, the boy just nodded, and Jack reached out to ruffle his hair. But his attention had turned to the father. "How far to the nearest landing platform?"

Kenna blew out a shaky breath. "Not far. Well… It wasn't far. If we can get up the west stairway..." He paused, thinking. "At this angle, it should be possible."

"You'll find it," Jack said. Then he nodded toward Sam, who was perched on the parapet frowning up at the tilting city. Probably calculating how fast it would sink. "Carter's in charge and—"

"Ah, Jack…?"

"Daniel?"

Here it was, whatever the hell Jack had been hiding since he'd leaped out of the *Kaw'ree* chair. "*Sam's* in charge?"

"Sir?" Sam dropped down from the parapet, confused. At her side, Teal'c's disapproval was evident.

"You're in command, Major." Jack didn't look at any of them, shaking water from his Kinahhi weapon. If the thing fired, it would be a miracle. "These are your orders. Take the team to the landing platform, ASAP, and evacuate as many people as possible. Get back to the gate, and get the hell off this world. Understood?"

She frowned, tight-lipped. "Yes, sir. But what about you?"

"Something I gotta do. I'll try to rendezvous later." He looked up then, fixing her with a hard stare that eventually extended to Daniel and Teal'c. "*Don't* wait for me."

"Jack, what are you *doing*? The whole city is sinking!"

"Yeah. Noticed that, Daniel."

"I will accompany you, O'Neill," Teal'c volunteered. "You cannot go alone."

But Jack shook his head. "Nope. One man op, T. This is my—" He snorted derisively. "My debt to pay."

Debt? "Jack… Come on, what's going on?"

But Sam gasped softly. "Crawford."

"He's *here*?"

"He was in the tower," said Sam. "Koash threatened him when I wouldn't cooperate. But after I escaped, I don't know where he—"

"I saw him." Jack raised his sodden rifle and attempted to fire. Nothing happened. He discarded it in disgust. "I saw him in the *sheh'fet*."

So that's what he'd been hiding. Crawford was a prisoner here, just like them.

Sam closed her eyes, saying nothing.

"It is because of Crawford that you were brought here, O'Neill," Teal'c said coldly. "You owe him nothing. He would have seen both you and Major Carter dead. Leave him to the fate he deserves. He would offer you no mercy."

Jack shrugged. "That's not the point. Anyway, you're wrong.

I'm here – we're all here – because I accepted those damn plans from Quadesh and—"

"It was a setup!" Daniel protested. "Come on, Jack, it was a trap."

"And I should have damn well known better than to take the bait!"

Daniel grunted angrily. "So this a pride thing? You made one mistake, Jack. Live with it. It's not worth dying for."

"One mistake? I almost got you all killed, Daniel! I destroyed SG-1, I *lied* to Hammond, cost him his goddamn job. And I —" He sucked in a deep, angry breath. "And I sent Crawford here. I set him up first, remember?"

"Colonel, Crawford tried to have us killed!" Sam argued hotly. "The plans for the anti-grav device were designed to fail. He doesn't deserve anyone's loyalty."

"And he doesn't deserve to drown in that stinking hole, either."

"Better him than you, sir."

Sam's words hung in an uncomfortable silence, and the unhappy glance Jack flung at her held for a moment too long before he turned away. Nothing could bend his resolve, it seemed. "You have your orders, Major."

"Yes, sir."

With a serious parting look he left, adeptly climbing across the scree of rubble on the steep plaza.

"The tower of the *Kaw'ree* is the tallest, O'Neill!" Teal'c called out as Jack reached the top. "It will be the last to sink!"

Jack acknowledged the advice with a wave, then dropped down out of sight.

"I'm telling you," Sam growled, "if he brings Crawford back alive, I'm first in line to kick his ass."

Daniel cast her a wry glance. "Crawford's, or Jack's?"

Her eyes narrowed. "Both."

Moments after the MALP appeared through the Stargate, the Kinahhi gate-room fell silent. Like Hammond, the Kinahhi were waiting to see which shoe was about to drop. Burned air scoured his throat, making him cough as he pushed himself upright. Boyd moved to join him, but he gestured for the man to stay down.

Major General George Hammond would meet his fate on his feet, but there was no need for the rest of his team to risk themselves.

Smoke swirled in the iridescence of the open gate, and even the suffering of the wounded seemed muted beneath the weight of expectation. At last the event horizon shivered. Hammond braced himself, shoulders squared, as Colonel Reynolds of SG-2 stepped out, weapon at the ready. The rest of his team emerged on either side and at an unspoken signal stalked warily down the stairs. Reynolds stopped in front of Hammond, eyeing the smoking ruins of the gate-room. "Sir."

Hammond gave a brief, careful nod. "Colonel."

"General Woodburn sends his regards, sir, and asks if you need a hand."

Yes! Had decorum permitted, he'd have leaped for joy. As it was, Hammond satisfied himself with a jubilant grin. "All the help we can get, Colonel."

On cue, the great muzzle of the Kinahhi weapon shifted.

"Get down!" A blast of fire lashed the room, but Reynolds was on his radio, and moments later men started pouring through the gate. Marines, ducking and rolling as they surged down the steps, their gunfire rattling through the toxic heat of the gate-room. The tide was turning! With a whoop of triumph, Dave Dixon led the charge toward the door.

And behind the Marines arrived the unsung heroes of the SGC – the field medics, Dr. Janet Fraiser in the lead.

By the time they reached the landing platform, the city was tilting so hard that the massive ships were sliding across the pavement, impacting with each other and the buildings that lined the plaza.

Sam squinted up at the towers tilting at crazy angles and groaning under their own weight. How long until one of them snapped, burying them all?

Around her the Outcast cowered, staring up at the distorted, creaking city in fear. She wondered if they understood what was happening, if their minds were still capable of such thought after the abuse they'd suffered. Eytan, never far from her side, grabbed her sleeve and pointed toward the Kinahhi soldiers scrambling around on the skewed landing platform.

"Soon," she told him. "We need a plan first." Glancing over her shoulder, she beckoned Teal'c closer with a nod. "Any ideas?"

He moved to her side, peeking up over the top of the stairway. Or ladder. At this angle, it had been an almost impossible climb. "On the far side," he said immediately. "The largest ship is the only one sufficient to hold all our number."

Sam nodded. "There's a lot of firepower between us and it."

"Indeed." His eyes drifted to the Outcast, and then to the remainder of the Arxanti, gathered around Daniel. "But we are not without force." The city jolted and below them something enormous smashed into the sea, sending up a fountain of water that spattered them all like rain. "We do not have the time to attempt to circumnavigate the platform," Teal'c observed.

"No." The city was sinking faster than she'd imagined, threatening to pitch them all into the ocean as its guts filled with water. She tried not to think about the Colonel trapped down there, and silently cursed his stubborn, implacable drive to do the right thing, whatever the cost. "We're just going to have to rush them," she decided, glancing at Teal'c for confirmation.

He inclined his head in silent approval.

"Stay close to Daniel," she said quietly. "And don't stop for anything."

"Once we are in the air," Teal'c said, "we will be able to search the area for survivors."

He meant the Colonel, and she smiled gratefully at his optimism. "Yeah. Let's get to the ship."

In a few murmured words, Sam gave the orders. Teal'c climbed closer to Daniel, who was in whispered conversation with Alvita Candra and Atella. Quick and agile, the Arxanti had little problem scrambling over the sinking city. And they seemed devoted to Daniel. He looked up and met Sam's gaze with a half smile and a squint. Without his glasses he was at a serious disadvantage in the upcoming battle. He hadn't mentioned the problem, of course, but then Daniel never would.

Teal'c gave a nod. They were ready. Sam turned to Kenna, off to her left, and got the same answer. *Ready*.

The large ship stood on the far side of the platform, crushed against one of the towers. A hundred meters away. The city quaked again, and far above them the leaning tower groaned and shuddered. There was no more time. "On my mark," she said, loud enough for all to hear. "Three, two, one." She glanced at Eytan and nodded. "Mark!"

As one, they poured onto the landing platform and began to run. They'd gotten almost halfway across before the panicking Kinahhi soldiers noticed and opened fire – then people started dying.

Up to his chest in icy water, Jack pushed through the dark corridors. The tang of seawater did little to wash away the stink of the *sheh'fet*, but that was the least of his concerns. With every shudder and jerk of the city, he expected a surge of water to swamp the corridor and trap him forever.

Goddamn idiot, he growled at himself. Teal'c had been right. So had Carter. Crawford didn't deserve his loyalty.

But it wasn't Crawford who filled his mind as he waded through the stinking tunnel. It was Hammond.

"I defended you, Jack. When Ambassador Crawford accused you, I said it was impossible. I told him that we didn't operate that way."

"Sir—"

"I trusted you!"

Truth was, he couldn't go back. One mistake, Daniel had called it, but Jack knew better. It was just the last mistake in a long list. He should never have taken the plans, never have set up Crawford, never have lied to Hammond and never have involved his team in an unsanctioned mission. And all because of what? Because he'd spent a decade hating Frank Cromwell for leaving him behind, and couldn't live with the fact that he'd done the exact same damn thing to Henry Boyd. So he'd ended up lying to his CO and destroying SG-1 just to ease his guilty conscience.

A better man would have made the decision and lived with the consequences. A man like Cromwell. But Jack O'Neill had never been a better man, despite what Daniel might think, and this time he'd proven it. He'd dragged his friends into the stinking quagmire of his self-recrimination and destroyed everything he most cared about.

But if he could save Crawford, if he could use the man to prove exactly what the Kinahhi had been planning, then perhaps he could save his team from Kinsey's clutches. Crawford was the bargaining chip, his knowledge could muzzle the Senator and save SG-1 – even if Jack O'Neill was beyond redemption.

So he pushed on through the darkness, listening and hoping for a miracle.

Daniel dodged the hail of gunfire, squinting myopically into the smoke. Alvita Candra was at his side, Teal'c at his back, but he was hesitant. Racing blindly through the battle, unable to really see his enemy, was terrifying. But it was more terrifying still to know that he was slowing his friends down.

A blast cut too close to his face – he felt its heat strafe the side of his head and dived forward. He hit the ground behind a ship pitched so steeply on the sloping platform he didn't know what held it in place. "Daniel Jackson!" Teal'c dropped at his side as Alvita Candra hunkered down next to him. "You are hit!"

"Just a scratch." Daniel dabbed at the wound with one hand and it came away slick with blood.

Teal'c was glancing backward and forward. "We must not linger."

"I can heal you," the Arxanti woman whispered. "I have the *remem*."

Daniel shook his head. "I'm fine. Teal'c's right, we can't stop." Pushing his feet under him, he ignored the giddy spin to the world and strained to see the ship. A watery blur drifted behind the mist, but it could have been anything. "How far?"

"Far enough."

Daniel glanced at Teal'c's grim face, then out across the chaotic battlefield. "You go ahead," he said softly. "I'll follow."

Teal'c cut him a hard look. "I shall not."

"I'm slowing you down," Daniel insisted, waving at his bare face. "Without my glasses…"

Teal'c answered by looping an arm under Daniel's and pulling him back to his feet. "You would run faster if you talked less, Daniel Jackson."

And so he did, guided by Teal'c out into smoke lanced with angry red laser fire and through the shouts and screams of fighting. Suddenly, something screeched like the spawn of hell above them. Something huge. Something in its death throes. Instinctively, Daniel flung his arms over his head, but when he peered up he could only see a blur of dark shadow against the morning sky. A blur that was somehow getting closer—

"*Run!*" Teal'c yanked him forward, heedlessly bounding into the battle. Alvita Candra shouted out in terror, sprinting ahead and screaming at her people to move. The morning darkened into night as one of the great towers of Tsapan began to collapse on top of them.

The miracle, when it happened, was slow. A gradual increase in the slope he was trudging up, a gradual shallowing of the water, until he needed to grab hold of the rough wall to keep himself from slipping on the slick, steep floor. And ahead of him, in the overwhelming darkness, he saw a faint light. It filtered through the doorway that led to the *sheh'fet*, the door through which he and Carter had been forced.

Gritting his teeth against the stench and the memories, Jack pulled himself up the damp corridor. Water was still streaming past him, confirming his belief that this part of the city had previously been submerged. But as the towers sank, the bottom of the city was rising from the ocean again. For now, at least. But he really had seen *Titanic* and knew exactly what would happen when the water inside reached a critical volume…

But not yet. His fingers were numb with cold, aching as he clutched at the rough sides of the wall and at last heaved himself up into the circular room. He found it easier to stand on the wall than the slanting floor, and through a crack far above him shone a faint shaft of daylight. Its pale gleam caught on the *sheh'fet*, dripping with water. There were bodies inside it still, even though he knew he'd opened the clamps while he'd been sitting in that damn chair. Perhaps some of the poor bastards hadn't been able to get out? Or hadn't wanted to. Or hadn't even realized they could.

But there was only one bastard he was interested in, if he was still here. If he was still alive. "Crawford?"

His voice echoed around the sodden chamber, bouncing off the gray shadows of the murderous machine. There was no answer.

"Crawford!" If he wasn't here, the odds of finding him were impossibly small. But Jack had a hunch; Crawford was a *stay put and wait for the paperwork* kinda guy. "Crawford!"

A noise from far above. A rustle, the clank of metal on metal. Someone was moving. It was coming from the far side of the room, from what was now the top of the *sheh'fet*. Cautiously, Jack edged along the wall. "Crawford?" His fingers itched for a weapon. Who knew who – or what – was hiding in here? One of the Outcast, untamed by Carter?

Another movement, more determined this time. Then a face appeared through the wreckage of the machine, white in the insipid light, eyes wild with shock. Functioning only on the most basic level; surviving but not thinking. He'd been there. Over and over and over…. It stared at him, mouth moving silently, brow creased into a disbelieving frown. Jack stopped, head cocked. Even perched on the edge of reason, the face was unpleasant. Grim triumph made Jack smile.

"You've creased your suit, Crawfish."

CHAPTER THIRTY-SIX

It sounded like the end of the world. Tortured metal screeched and falling masonry thundered as the vast structure snapped at the waist. Everyone fled, the battle forgotten, as the tower smashed down onto the landing platform.

Sam saw Teal'c and Daniel to her right, sprinting and stumbling and running. Side by side, pace for pace. The air scalded her throat as her lungs screamed for air. But it was polluted with dirt and she coughed as she ran, head spinning. And through the noise and the chaos, she felt a scream. Heard it and felt it in her mind simultaneously. Pain and dismay, and huge loss. But no fear, just anger.

She turned as dust clouds billowed around her, and saw a white face staring back at her with desperate eyes – trapped under a chunk of the tower. Eytan. "No!" In horror, she ran back to him. One arm was free and she dropped to her knees and seized his hand. "Eytan, it's okay. We'll get you out."

Lies! It was impossible. Rubble was still raining down around them, the dust so thick she could barely see. She began lifting stones, pushing and shoving with her bare hands, but there was so much and –

"Sam?" Her head shot around as Daniel emerged through the dust like a vision. "I heard you shout."

Thank God! "He's trapped."

Without comment, Daniel began to dig away at the debris. Then Teal'c was there too. He looked at her, at Eytan and at Daniel with a cool eye. "Did you not order us to stop for nothing, Major Carter?"

"He just wants to go home, Teal'c. I can't… I promised him I'd help him go home."

Teal'c touched Eytan's throat. "He will not live."

Damn it. Damn him for saying it! Her gaze rested on Eytan's face and she could see blood now, welling up his torso. But he wasn't dead yet, and with one weak hand he seized hers,

"Ba'bayith?" Going home?

"Soon," she promised. But the lie burned her eyes with tears, the memory of his little girl, his wife, and his desperate desire to see them again raking her soul. "Soon." Gritting her teeth she lifted her eyes to Teal'c. He was watching her with steady compassion. "Go," she said firmly. "Get to the ship. I'll stay with him."

Teal'c shook his head. "You cannot. You must—"

"Wait." It was Daniel, his face smeared with dirt and dust, brow furrowed as he peered at her through the gloom. "Alvita Candra."

"The Arxanti woman?"

He nodded. "She can save him. If we can free him, she can save him."

"He will not survive, Daniel Jackson," Teal'c said sharply. "Even the Arxanti cannot raise the dead."

An odd look crossed Daniel's face, but all he said was, "Trust me."

Always. Sam glanced up at the ragged edge of the shattered tower that hung above them, flitting in and out of the smoke and dust like death waiting to pounce. "We should hurry."

The Kinahhi gate-room had been turned into a makeshift triage station where Dr. Fraiser and her team made emergency assessments of the wounded men. As yet, Hammond hadn't authorized them to dial Earth. The Kinahhi might be waiting for that very opportunity to re-launch their attack, and take the fight right back to the SGC.

As he slowly walked past the bodies of the ten men who'd died under his command, George Hammond forced himself to look at each of their faces, committing them to memory. At the other end of the line, Fraiser was kneeling close to Simon Wells, holding up a drip as she talked to him reassuringly. When she saw Hammond, she passed the drip to one of her staff and stood up. "He's lost a lot of blood," she said as she approached. "I'll need to evacuate him as soon as possible, sir. The others can wait, but Wells—"

"When the rest of SG-13 report back we'll know more, Doctor."

She nodded, and smiled slightly. "If I might say so, sir, it's good to have you back in command."

"We're not back yet, Doctor," he cautioned. "But thank you."

"When I saw what they'd been doing up on Level 17..." Fraiser shivered and her face darkened. "Sir, if Colonel O'Neill and Major Carter were treated in the same way here..." She trailed off bleakly.

"What are you saying, Doctor?"

"Sir, I don't honestly know if the men we found at the SGC will ever recover fully from what was done to their minds. And we can only assume that the device the Kinahhi were using here was bigger, perhaps more sophisticated." She paused. "You should be prepared, sir."

He took a deep breath, mind returning to the day he'd last spoken to Jack O'Neill. He'd lost a friend that day and, in the many days since, had come to realize it was a loss he was unprepared to accept. He owed the man more trust than he'd been willing to give, battered and bruised as Hammond had felt by the plotting of Kinsey. If he never got to regain that friendship, that trust... "I'm not prepared to give up on them just yet, Doctor."

"Me neither, sir."

As Fraiser moved away, back to the patients who needed her, Colonel Dixon appeared in the doorway, climbing over the shattered Kinahhi weapon. Though frowning, he wasn't running like half the Kinahhi army was on his heels. Hammond took that as a good sign. But the Colonel's first words were far from reassuring.

"Something's not right, sir," he reported as he strode across the gate-room. He cast a quick glance at Wells, before turning his attention back to Hammond. "There were about fifty men in the corridor," Dixon continued. "SG-2 and SG-3 are taking care of them, but given the size of this place..."

The Kinahhi should have been throwing their entire military might against the incursion in the gate-room. Hadn't Damaris promised as much? "Something else must be going on," Hammond concluded. "Something bigger."

Dixon snatched off his cap and wiped at his tired face. "SG-

1, sir?"

"Let's hope so, Colonel."

The collapse of the tower, Teal'c observed, had ended the battle. Unlike Jaffa serving a Goa'uld master, the Kinahhi were not
prepared to fight beyond reason. They were abandoning the sinking city like startled birds taking flight, their ships of all sizes and
shapes lifting up and darkening the sky. So much the better.

The body Teal carried slung over one shoulder weighed little,
it was more skin and bone than flesh, but he picked his way across
the slope with care. The angle made it difficult to walk bearing
any burden – however light. Ahead of him Daniel Jackson was
in discussion with Alvita Candra and around them gathered the
remains of the Arxanti warriors. He sensed excitement in the air
and several times saw people look as if in anticipation at him and
the body he carried.

Major Carter was not in sight. She had disappeared into the
Kinahhi ship several minutes ago. As yet, it had not sprung to
life.

"Over here!" Daniel Jackson called.

Teal'c lengthened his stride and lowered the skeletal body to
the ground. "He is beyond aid, Daniel Jackson. He is dead."

His friend just nodded. "Wait," he said, squatting down next to
the body. "Just wait."

Alvita Candra dropped to her haunches at Daniel Jackson's
side. From her pack she pulled the disc Fortus had used back in
Arxantia. As she held it between her hands and closed her eyes
a violet light began to bloom at its heart. The rest of the Arxanti
gathered behind her, Atella among them, animated with expectation.

Around the fringes of this group, hovered the Outcast. They
paced and twitched, and watched. Teal'c wondered if they understood what they saw.

Taking a deep breath, Alvita Candra held the disk over Eytan's
crushed chest. The light of the *remem* spilled out onto the man's
body. Slowly, the wound began to heal – just as Teal'c had seen
his own injury heal. But the Arxanti woman did not stop once
the flesh was reformed, instead she moved the device to Eytan's
head. Her arm began to tremble, as if the disk had become impos-

sibly heavy, but she continued, murmuring in a language Teal'c could not comprehend.

"A prayer," Daniel Jackson whispered, his eyes never leaving Eytan. "A prayer to her ancestors." Suddenly he looked up, head tilted to one side, as if he had heard something. Teal'c followed his gaze, but saw nothing but blowing dust. Daniel Jackson, however, stared hard and then—

"*Bayith*!" The word was spoken strongly, a deep male voice. Teal'c turned back and saw, to his astonishment, that Eytan had been transformed. No longer a creature of nightmare, disfigured by torment beyond endurance, he stared up out of a robust Kinahhi face. And his eyes had lost their animal-like shine; they were haunted, but human. Very human.

With a gasp, Alvita Candra sagged, caught in the arms of Daniel Jackson. "You've—" he breathed in astonishment. "You've... What *have* you done?"

Weakly, Alvita Candra smiled. "As I promised, Daniel Jackson. I have saved him."

"Saved him," his friend echoed. "Yes. Yes you really have..."

Carefully, Teal'c offered Eytan his hand and helped him sit up. But the man's eyes were fixed entirely on Alvita Candra, their expression wide and worshipful. "Arxanti," he said in an awed voice, reaching out and touching her wild hair. "I have seen you in my dreams. You are a child of the Ancient Ones."

A ripple of astonishment ruffled the men gathered behind Alvita Candra, and Eytan lifted his gaze to them. "I know you," he said. "I have seen the truth." And then he turned to Daniel Jackson and his eyes widened further. "You! You are the One."

Daniel Jackson blinked. "I am?"

"You showed us the truth, before the other destroyed the *sheh'fet*. You showed us the truth about Arxantia and the Ancient Ones."

"As the prophesy predicted," Alvita Candra said, rising tiredly to her feet. Atella reached out to steady her. "You showed the *Kaw'ree* the truth about us, Daniel Jackson – you showed it to all within the *sheh'fet* – and now these people, these Outcast, will be the salvation of our people." She reached down and held out her hand to Eytan. He took it reverently and allowed her to raise him to his feet. "Together," she said, "we can change our world."

Teal'c also stood, as did Daniel Jackson, glancing over his shoulder at the hovering Outcast. They were staring hungrily at Eytan.

"Then you can do this for all of them?" Daniel Jackson said. "You can save all of the Outcast?"

Alvita Candra bowed her head. "Not here. The *remem* does not have enough power. But in Arxantia…"

"The healing device!" Daniel Jackson exclaimed. "Of course, you can—"

"Ah, guys?" The interruption came from Major Carter, who stood at the hatch of the Kinahhi transport. "We've got a problem, the—" She stopped dead, staring. "Eytan?"

He turned, a long-forgotten smile tugging his lips. "Samantha Carter! I cannot—"

Suddenly the city lurched, tilting so sharply that Teal'c lost his footing and landed hard on his back, sliding down the landing platform until he collided with the side of the ship below. Several of the Arxanti landed on top of him, and through the tangle of limbs he heard Daniel Jackson shouting, "We have to get outta here!"

After a moment, Major Carter replied. Her voice sounded muffled and came from inside the ship, but her fear was clear as glass. "We can't! At this angle, the anti-grav device won't engage. We can't leave!"

And then the whole city started to move downward, sinking fast beneath the waves.

The Kinahhi had been right to flee. Tsapan, and all left within her, were lost.

Jack shoved Crawford ahead of him as he waded down into the water. The angle was steeper now, the water rising higher. Almost up to Crawford's chest; he'd be swimming soon. But if they could just get out the way Jack had come in, he figured they'd have a chance. Get up to the landing platform, and if Carter had already left – which she damn well should have done – they could snag another ship and get the hell out of the city of the damned.

"I can't…" Crawford's whimper drifted over the slap of water against the walls of the tunnel. "It's too cold, too deep…"

"Shut up, and keep walking."

But the man stopped, pressing his hands over his eyes. "I can't!"

Goddamn it, was he *crying*?

Jack grabbed Crawford's wrist, pulling one hand away from his face. It was too dark to make out his features. "Keep. Moving," he barked. "Or you'll die here."

"Then let me!" Crawford spat. "Isn't that what you want?"

Grabbing the man by the shoulder of his sodden jacket, Jack pushed him back into motion. "If I wanted you dead, I wouldn't have come back."

Crawford stumbled forward. "You don't give a damn about me, O'Neill."

"True." The water was getting deeper now, the gradient of the path steeper. Soon they'd both be swimming.

"Then why—"

"Evidence."

The laugh echoed wetly through the gloom. "You want me to clear your name?"

"Something like that."

"What makes you think I'd—"

Everything lurched, the floor tilted up and out from beneath Jack's feet, and he went under, pushed up from the floor and shot back to the surface, treading water. After a moment, Crawford came up at his side, spluttering.

"What's happening?"

"Shh!" Jack could hear water gushing in, surging closer. His ears blocked suddenly, deaf with the building pressure differential. They were sinking. Fast.

The tower of the Kaw'ree is the tallest, O'Neill! It will be the last to sink!

"We have to go up," he yelled. "There has to be a way up the tower. A staircase, an elevator – anything."

"You stupid bastard," Crawford screamed. "Don't you get it? We're going to die here! There's no point in—"

"Shut up and look." He swam to the wall, peering through the gloom, finger's tracing the rough surface. There had to be a way up, there had to be a stairway or a—

A bone-crushing jolt shook the city, like a car wrecker on overdrive. Metal shrieked all around them, the noise thick enough to cut. Then, suddenly, it stopped and all he could hear was Crawford's shivering breaths. Jack wasn't breathing at all, waiting as the water level rose higher and higher. He raised a hand and the tips of his fingers brushed the ceiling. The water didn't stop rising.

With the city virtually standing on end, Daniel thought it was all over. The Kinahhi ship lay on its side like a beached whale, its bow mere feet from the thrashing ocean. It could only be a matter of moments until the entire city turned upside down, taking them all with it. They hovered on the cusp, a whisper away from death.

Through the window of the Kinahhi transport he saw the blurred shapes of Sam and Teal'c, both struggling to get the ship flying. But at that angle, the anti-gravity device simply couldn't engage. Daniel saw it, clear as day. Clear as the bright day that would be his last.

From the doorway, Alvita Candra was calling to him – and to the remainder of the Outcast he'd come out to retrieve. Too frightened to move, they were clinging to the side of the sinking city like rats with no place to go. He knew how they felt. From up here, even without his glasses, he could see it all spread out before him. He could see the rainbow shimmer of Tsapan swallowed by dark waves, he could see the white froth of the ocean rearing up around them like Poseidon's white horses. And he knew that somewhere beneath them, Jack was trapped. Jack was dying – perhaps he was already dead – and the rest of them wouldn't be long in following. Once the city toppled forward…

Daniel held his breath. Everyone held their breath in that infinite moment of suspense. And then, with a groan and a shudder, the city started to fall. But not forward. Backward. *They had a chance!*

Suddenly Jack was moving forward as the rising river in the corridor became a crashing wave, flipping him over and over along the hall. He hit the floor, tumbled again, then got his feet under him just as Crawford floundered past. Lightning fast, Jack reached out and grabbed the guy by the arm. Crawford's momentum almost knocked them both over again, but the flow was slowing and Jack kept his feet as he hung onto the Ambassador.

Coughing, Crawford swiped Jack's hands away. "What?" he gasped. "What happened...?"

Jack could see it clearly in his mind's eye. "We hit the bottom," he said. "City righted itself." He glanced down at water, rapidly rising again. "And now it's filling up."

Crawford spluttered. "We're under water? The whole city is under water?"

"Yup."

"Oh God, oh God, we're going to die." Crawford began to sob. "We're going to *die*, we're going to——"

"Never say die." Jack yanked him along the corridor. There had to be a way out, a way up.

Crawford's doom-mongering continued, grating like fingernails on a chalkboard. "We're going to die, we're going to die!"

"Seriously," Jack growled, "say that again, and I'll drown you myself."

"Daniel Jackson!" Alvita Candra was screaming his name, the sound lost beneath the vast noise of Tsapan smashing into the sea.

The impact jarred him into motion. "Come on!" he shouted at the terrified Outcast. "Run!"

He snatched an arm and pulled while he slipped and slid toward the open door of the ship. Vast waves were swallowing the city beneath them, seconds away from swamping the landing platform. He staggered, dragging a shivering Outcast behind him, and suddenly heard the sound of engines firing!

When the platform dropped, the angle had to have changed just enough to allow the anti-grav device to activate. A little luck, at last! The ship lifted, hovering a foot in the air. Alvita Candra was still yelling his name and now she was joined by Teal'c ,who stretched out his hand toward him. "Jump!" he urged. "Daniel Jackson!"

But he couldn't. He was still clutching the arm of the terrified Outcast, and five others followed behind. "Take him!" Daniel shouted, pushing the bag of bones toward Teal'c as he turned and grabbed the arm of the next man.

A moment later Teal'c leaped from the ship, hefting the Outcast one-by-one in his powerful arms and throwing them bodily aboard. Daniel spared him a brief look of thanks, when suddenly Teal'c's eyes widened in shock. "Get on board!"

A wall of water was roaring down on them, spilling over the lip of the city like Niagara Falls and surging toward them as the entire structure succumbed to the ocean. They were going under!

With a yell of supreme effort, Daniel flung the last petrified Outcast into the waiting arms of Alvita Candra and threw himself after, up onto the hovering deck of the Kinahhi ship. Teal'c landed beside him with a grunt, as hands grabbed them both and dragged them inside. Sam was yelling, "Seal the doors, seal the doors!"

And then the tidal wave hit.

CHAPTER THIRTY-SEVEN

Cautiously, Daniel opened his eyes. Everything had stopped moving, and he'd finally come to rest in a crumpled heap wedged beneath what had once been an elegant, white Kinahhi seat. It was gray with dirt now, boot prints and sea water all over it. He wiggled, felt a twinge in the shoulder he'd dislocated, but not enough to slow him down as he worked free of the seat.

Next to him, Atella lay flat on his back. A gash to his head bled freely, but when Daniel put two fingers to the man's neck he felt a strong pulse. Getting to his knees, he cast his eyes over the chaotic scene. Without his glasses, everything was blurred. But he could see enough. People were everywhere, tangled together. Some obviously injured, others dazed. There was no sense of jubilation, nothing but confusion. A few had gathered by the far window, staring out at something below. And among them stood Teal'c, his face stony.

Daniel pushed himself to his feet, wincing at a pain that shot down his right thigh and calf. But he flexed the leg and it took his weight – probably only a bruise. Picking his way through the silent, shell-shocked refugees toward Teal'c, he considered himself lucky.

"The city is gone, Daniel Jackson," Teal'c said softly.

Right then he was grateful not to be able to see clearly. But even he could make out the tips of the tallest spires, glittering incongruously in the sunlight while the ocean washed through them with a relentless and destructive violence. Soon, they too would be gone. Occasionally, from far below, a cluster of bubbles breached the surface, an air pocket succumbing to the pressure of the sea flooding the city.

Daniel knew there had to people trapped down there, mostly the Outcast, but probably some Kinahhi too. Fathers, sons, brothers. But it wasn't their fate that clenched a knot in his chest so tight that he could barely breathe.

"The tower of the *Kaw'ree* still stands," Teal'c said in a harsh whisper. It was a desperate hope, but hope nonetheless.

Daniel found he had no voice. *Jack...*

"We'll wait." Sam sounded husky as she came to stand beside them at the window. The hair on the side of her head was matted with blood, her features etched with the grief they all shared. Jack couldn't be gone, not for real. He just couldn't.

They stood in silence, watching the waves break over the towers of Tsapan, until finally people behind them began to move. Daniel was dimly aware of it, of life returning to the traumatized men and women they'd saved. But it seemed far away, he felt no part of it. He felt no relief, no triumph, he felt nothing but loss. He didn't want to move from between his friends, couldn't bear to lose the fragile comfort their presence offered. And so, when he felt a hand on his arm, he shook it off with an angry, "What?"

It was Alvita Candra, wild hair tamed by water into thick black spirals. "We cannot linger," she said softly, her eyes meeting his with a sympathy that threatened to break his heart. "Commander Kenna has detected a flight of Kinahhi fighters heading toward us. They mean to destroy this ship."

"We cannot leave." Teal'c was adamant, not turning from the window. "O'Neill may yet escape."

There was a long silence. Sam sucked in a breath that cracked in her throat, and she coughed. Her face looked as broken as the domes of Tsapan. "Teal'c, the odds—"

"The odds are irrelevant," he replied. "We are discussing O'Neill."

The ghost of a smile touched her face, heavy with misery. "We can't risk these people, Teal'c. The Colonel ordered us not to wait for him."

Teal'c didn't answer, and Sam turned her eyes to Daniel in appeal. He sighed. "Sam's right," he said roughly, though he hated every word. "We can't stay here, we'd be condemning everyone on board."

Silence fell between them. It was as if no one else in the room existed, the quiet babble of voices and movement retreating into the white noise of grief. Daniel reached out and took Sam's hand, placing the other on Teal'c's shoulder. "I can't think of anything to say..." Sam squeezed his fingers, her eyes filling. But Teal'c jerked violently away from his touch. "Teal'c, I—"

"Look." Teal'c moved closer to the window, tense as a hound on the scent. "Look at the dome of the *Kaw'ree*."

Heart thundering, Daniel pressed his face against the glass. But everything was just a blur. Frustrated, he said, "What? What do you see?"

"Something flapping in the wind," said Teal'c. "It appears to be a black cloth."

Sam sucked in a short breath. "One of their robes. It's one of the *Kaw'ree* robes."

Hope and reason were at war in Daniel's heart. "The waves could have washed it out," he said cautiously. *Or maybe it's a signal?* "The waves could have washed it out, and now it's caught on something." *Or maybe it's Jack!*

"The Kinahhi will soon be upon us," Alvita Candra said. "We must leave."

But her voice was distant, it couldn't invade the silent communication taking place between the remaining members of SG-1. Teal'c's eyes fixed on Sam like burning coal. She nodded slightly and glanced at Daniel, seeking his opinion. When he too nodded, she smiled. It was as bright and ferocious as the sun.

"Screw the Kinahhi," she said. "We're checking it out."

Panic fluttered beneath the elegant robes of Councilor Tamar Damaris. Between her elegant fingers she held the latest report, though she hardly knew what it said. She'd gotten as far as, 'Tsapan has been sunk' and stopped reading. The *Kaw'ree* had been murdered, the *sheh'fet* was destroyed, the arches that had guarded their freedom for a generation stood dark and unresponsive, and the enemy was at large.

How was it possible?

Someone behind her cleared his throat. She turned and saw Matan Tal waiting; his fear was as evident as her own, scored into every feature. "Councilor, I have more news."

"Good? Or bad." She could not endure more bad news, she felt as though it might destroy her mind entirely.

But Tal's face was dark. He shook his head, as if the words he spoke could not be believed. "The Tauri in the gate-room have been reinforced from their own world, Councilor. Their hold on the room has strengthened and…"

She let the rest of his words drift past. The Tauri in the gate-room? She'd almost forgotten them amid the other devastating news, but of course this had been their plan. The destruction of Kinahhi had been their plan all along, and she had allowed it to happen. She had feted these people, trusted them. And how had they repaid her? With bloody rebellion.

It took a moment before she realized that her aide had stopped speaking. He probably was awaiting an answer, but she knew not what to say. The presence of the Tauri in the gate-room was nothing compared with the disaster that loomed from the wreckage of Tsapan. If the Mahr'bal landed in the city itself all would be lost. "Have our fighter wings engaged the enemy yet?"

"They have yet to call in," Tal replied.

Damaris turned away, looking out over the false peace of her city. That she should live to see it fall into chaos was unacceptable. "They must not be allowed to land here," she said. "They must be destroyed at any cost."

Everything depended upon it.

The hatch stood wide open as their ship skimmed over the water toward the broken dome of the *Kaw'ree* tower. Sunlight glittered harshly on the waves, the glare making it hard to see, and the roar of the wind and the ocean deafened Sam to everything but the hammering of her heart.

Ahead, the dome grew larger, the waves surging in and out of its shattered elegance. The scrap of black cloth flapped and danced in the wind, offering the only hope they had.

Suddenly Daniel's hand clasped her arm. She turned, and he was squinting up into the sky, the wind whipping his hair in all directions. "Look!" he shouted over the noise, pointing.

She followed his gaze, her sharp eyes fixing on what could only have been a distant blur to her friend. A wedge of dots bearing down on them; fighters in tight formation. Beneath her feet, Sam felt the ship surge. Teal'c must have seen the enemy too and had opened up the throttle.

Closer and closer. The black rag became clearer now, definitely one of the *Kaw'ree* robes. From here she could see that it was high above the water line; there was no way it could have been washed up there. Hope beat painfully in her chest, the wind in her face making her eyes stream. Even if it had been put there deliberately, anyone could have done it. The odds of it being the Colonel...

"What can you see?" Daniel yelled, frustration evident in his clipped tone.

"Nothing," she shouted back. "I just see the cloth, and—" Movement. Something moved in the shadows within the dome.

"*What*?" Daniel sounded desperate, screwing up his face as he peered out. "Sam!"

"I don't know, I saw something move. It's gone, it's— No, there it is! There's someone there!" A shadow, shifting behind the painted glass of the dome, backlit by the sunshine.

Daniel grabbed her wrist, fingers digging deep. "Who?"

"I can't tell, we're too far. I just saw a shadow."

The ship was slowing now, turning sideways as it glided in toward the tower. The booming crash of the waves was louder here, echoing through the remains of the massive dome looming above them. Its rainbow colors were still glinting in the sunlight, a final gasp before the sea consumed the delicate structure.

The shadow moved again, about three meters above the swelling ocean. It looked like it was hiding. "Colonel O'Neill?" Sam called.

"Jack!" Daniel shouted, his strong voice carrying over the waves.

The shadow stopped moving, disappeared, and then after a moment, a couple of feet below, a familiar head peered out from behind a splintered edge of glass. He waved. He waved!

"Colonel!" Sam yelled in triumph. The relief was so intense she almost sagged under its weight. He was alive! Against all the odds, he was alive!

"Yes!" Daniel was punching the air, almost losing his balance and nose diving into the water. "I knew it! I *knew* it!"

Sam ducked her head back inside the ship. "Teal'c!" she shouted toward the cockpit. "He's here! He's okay! Get closer. Get—"

A barrage of scarlet laser fire hammered into the *Kaw'ree* tower, shattering the dome in a splintered line across its apex, sending an avalanche of glass down into the water. Then their ship lurched, shuddering under the impact of multiple strikes.

The Kinahhi had arrived.

Teal'c banked hard as the first wave of the assault began, turning the Kinahhi ship in a tight circle. But it was large, built for transporting troops, he suspected, not engaging in aerial battle. It was, however, armed.

At his side, Commander Kenna manned the weapons console, answering the attack with the ship's powerful cannons. But his face was a knot of anxiety; the boy sheltering in the rear of the ship no doubt preoccupying his thoughts. "We must retreat!" he barked, even as he fired the weapons. "We cannot withstand an assault from two entire wings!"

"We will not abandon O'Neill." The point brooked no further argument.

"Teal'c!" Major Carter appeared in the cramped cockpit, breathing hard. "You have to come around. They're targeting the dome, we have to get him out. Now."

"I am endeavoring to do so."

Commander Kenna fired again, his fist hammering hard on the controls. A Kinahhi ship spun past them, flame blazing from its tail until it drowned in the ocean. "We cannot win this!" The Commander insisted, turning now to Major Carter. "Would you sacrifice us all for the sake of one man?"

From the corner of his eye, Teal'c saw Major Carter shrink from the question. A moment of self-doubt clouded her features, but soon resolve returned. "We don't leave our people behind, Commander." She put a hand on Teal'c's shoulder. "Bring us around for another pass, and we'll grab the Colonel. Then get us out of here."

"On your mark, Major Carter."

As she left, Commander Kenna shot Teal'c a hard look. "The priorities of your people make no sense. The safety of many must come before the life of one man!"

Another hit shook the hull, sounding alarms throughout. The aft stabilizer was damaged. Teal'c said nothing while he fought to keep the ship level, banking and once more closing in upon the dome and O'Neill. But he could not let Kenna's words pass. "Was not that philosophy at the heart of the *sheh'fet*?" The ship was shaking now, the vibrations jarring Teal'c's arms. "The Tauri believe the life of the individual is sacred, whatever the cost of preserving it."

To that, it seemed, Kenna knew no answer.

"What's that?" Daniel asked as Sam dashed back to the open hatch. He was sheltering by the side of the door, peering out toward the shattered dome. "Is it Jack?"

Sam could see the Colonel moving inside, a shadow among shadows, but Daniel was right. Someone else was with him. "Crawford," she said quietly, chilled by the ice in her voice. "I guess he found him."

"Of course he did," Daniel said, on the edge of a laugh.

A new volley strafed toward the tower, and once more the Colonel disappeared from sight. Sam found herself holding her breath, but after a moment he was back. This time, he stood right near the edge, on some kind of platform. Crawford cowered behind him like the gutless creep he'd been from day one. She watched for the Colonel's signal; go left. *Left?* Then he dragged Crawford to his feet. There was some argument, Crawford seemed to disagree with whatever the Colonel was saying. They were too far away for Sam to make out the words, but she knew Colonel O'Neill well – and she knew when his patience, limited as it was, snapped. In one fluid move, he grabbed Crawford by the shoulders and shoved him roughly into the water. The man's arms windmilled, a thin shriek drifting through the noise of the wind until he hit the water and disappeared.

The Colonel looked at them, gestured left again, and dived gracefully into the sea after Crawford. Sam dropped to her belly and edged out until she could see the ocean below. "Teal'c!" she yelled. "Move left, twenty meters. And take us down, right down to the water!"

Overhead, a Kinahhi fighter screeched past, peppering the water with weapons fire. Daniel dropped at her side. "Come on," he murmured, staring down at the choppy sea. "Come on, Jack."

Their ship descended sharply, the ocean shooting up toward them. "There!" Sam yelled. Just ahead, Crawford bobbed to the surface, spluttering. He was screaming obscenities, floundering in panic. "Swim!" Sam shouted. "Over here!"

Crawford's head turned, ducking under the waves, then up

again. He looked exhausted. As the waves swelled and dropped, his head disappeared and reappeared. Another barrage of gunfire raked the water and Crawford shrieked. He wasn't going to make it. He was freaking out, going under, carried by the surge of the waves toward the underside of the dome. Beyond their reach.

"Crawford!" Sam barked, making it an order. "This way. Move it!"

Suddenly, the Colonel breached the surface. He made them immediately and waved, then headed off after Crawford with strong, practiced strokes. He grabbed the flailing man and yelled something, then started hauling him back toward the ship.

"Teal'c, bring her down!"

As the ship edged in, Daniel reached out. The swell was huge this far out, slapping at the underside of the ship. If they got too close, they'd be swamped. "Jack!"

O'Neill pushed Crawford forward, and Daniel was forced to grab the man's scrawny arm. He pulled, the Colonel shoved, and Crawford scrambled up and out of the water. As soon as he was close enough, Sam yanked him into the ship. He dropped to the floor, heaving. She turned away, back to Daniel who now had hold of the Colonel's wrist. But without a little help, physics were against him.

"Sir!" Sam shouted, mirroring Daniel and reaching down with one hand, bracing herself with the other. The Colonel seized her arm too, his hand ice cold against her skin.

"I told you," he grunted as they began to pull, "not to wait!"

"Shut up!" Daniel growled as another fighter barreled overhead. Their ship took the brunt of the attack, shuddering and shaking with each impact. "And climb!"

The Colonel was half out of the water when he abruptly let go of Sam's arm and grabbed onto the edge of the deck. She seized a fistful of his shirt, Daniel doing the same, and together they hauled him up into the ship.

"We've got him!" Sam gasped as the Colonel collapsed onto the deck, blue-lipped with cold and panting for air. "Teal'c, get us back to the gate!

With a stomach-lurching twist, the ship soared up into the air, the enemy fighters right behind.

CHAPTER THIRTY-EIGHT

The Stargate rippled invitingly as General Hammond watched Dr. Fraiser shepherd his injured men back home. With the immediate surroundings secured, he'd judged it safe enough to evacuate the wounded. Whatever was going on beyond the Stargate complex, it seemed to have tied up all the Kinahhi military. That it had something to do with SG-1 was more than likely, in his estimation. But whether they'd come out of it in one piece was another matter entirely.

"General?" Dr. Fraiser stood at the top of the steps leading up to the gate. "Medevac complete, sir."

"Good work, Doctor, we'll—"

A booming crash reverberated through the entire complex, shaking the floor like an earthquake. Fraiser's eyes went wide. "Sir?"

"Go," he ordered. "Get out of here."

She hesitated, eyeing the entrance to the gate-room. "A counter-attack, sir?"

All around, his men had dropped into position, weapons raised. "We'll send word, Doctor," he said. "Get through the gate."

"Yes, sir." With a final backward glance, she stepped into the puddle and disappeared. After a moment, it shut down and the room looked gray and dull again. But the troops never arrived, nor were there any further explosions – if that was what the huge tremor had been.

"Sir?" Henry Boyd appeared in the doorway, part of the advance guard. "Something's going on outside. I can hear fighting."

Fighting? It could mean anything. But it could be his people trying to get home. He couldn't ignore that. "SG-13, SG-2," and with a look at Boyd, "SG-10 – with me."

As one, his men fell in behind as Hammond hefted his P90 and went to find his missing team.

The fighting was intense, the enemy on all sides. Jack was

pinned down behind their crashed ship, Daniel on one side, Teal'c on the other and Carter on their six. Across the courtyard, glaring bright in the sunlight, he could see more Kinahhi emerging from an archway. They fought as though the devil himself were at the door, fear stark in their young faces, mutating into hatred with each shot they fired.

Jack wasn't sure what terrified them most, his team, the Arxanti or the Outcast – an object lesson in the power of fear, hatred and prejudice.

"Sir!" Carter suddenly aimed up at the roof. "Snipers." She took one man out with a single shot, as Jack scanned the rooftops and hit another. Their position had been compromised; they had to move.

"Over there, O'Neill," Teal'c suggested, pointing at the mound of crushed stone knocked out of the building when they'd landed at – or, to be more accurate, crashed into – the Stargate complex. The bulk of the ship would shield them from the snipers, but there was scant cover to the right.

Carter fired again. "Sir, there are more!"

"Move out!" Jack snapped in reply, keeping low as he led Daniel and Teal'c along the side of the ship. Carter followed, still watching the roof. But more Kinahhi were spilling into the courtyard ahead of them, blocking the route to the gate room, the only exit from the claustrophobic plaza. He grunted, hunkering down behind the broken brickwork as the rest of his team crowded in behind. "We need a plan B."

"B?" Daniel muttered, firing over the wall. "I thought we'd gotten to at least E by now!"

"Could we not attempt to enter the building where the ship has damaged it?" Teal'c suggested. "There may be an alternate approach to the gate-room, perhaps one less well guarded."

Maybe. "Beats staying here," Jack admitted. But inside, constricted in the narrow Kinahhi corridors, they'd be—

"Jack?" It was Daniel, head cocked and frowning. "Did you hear that?"

"Hear what?"

The whizz-bang of the Kinahhi weapons continued, but suddenly, like a subtle counterpoint, he heard a different rhythm. A sustained and familiar rattle.

"Sir!" Carter's eyes went wide as saucers. "That's a P90."

Jack scrambled back to his feet, crouching low as he peered over the top of their scant cover. "Question is," he murmured, not daring to voice any hope, "who's firing it?"

A clot of Kinahhi soldiers blocked the doorway that led from the dust-filled corridor out into glaring sunlight. Hammond held up his hand to slow his men; the Kinahhi were too focused on the battle beyond and they weren't watching their backs. So much the better.

With a sharp gesture, he sent Dixon's team ahead. In the close confines of the hallway, SG-13 would have little trouble dispatching the handful of men up front. What they'd find outside, however, Hammond could only guess. And he chose to guess that it was SG-1.

Dixon's team were brutally efficient, taking out the back line of the enemy and causing panic among the remainder. The Kinahhi seemed almost as afraid of retreating into the sunlight as they were of the advancing soldiers, but Hammond had no pity as he stalked along the corridor behind SG-13.

Eventually, the small knot of Kinahhi broke rank and fled, disappearing into the white glare of the plaza. Hammond slowed, regarding the new territory through the sights of his P90 as he cautiously stepped outside.

Chaos was everywhere. Some kind of aircraft had crashed into one of the buildings, and the air was thick with smoke. But through the haze, Hammond saw figures moving. Grotesque figures, bone-white and contorted.

Dixon sucked a breath through his teeth. "What the hell…?"

"Hold your position," Hammond cautioned. "Secure our line of retreat." Whatever the devil this was, there was no sign of SG-1.

Then, suddenly, someone came barreling toward him, screaming like a lunatic. Henry Boyd fired a warning shot and the figure threw itself to the floor, jabbering. It was only then that Hammond recognized the words as English.

"Don't shoot! It's me! It's *me*!"

Crawford?

"Hold your fire!" Keeping his weapon raised, Hammond

stalked forward. The man, his suit in tatters and his face gaunt and red-streaked, cowered in a heap. "Dixon, Boyd, take your teams and form a perimeter."

The men moved past him to surround Hammond, Crawford and the entrance to the corridor in a wide semi-circle. Beyond them the grotesque creatures capered, while the Kinahhi bunched together as if the doors to hell had opened and spewed forth its demons.

Hammond kept his attention fixed on the wreck that had once been Ambassador Crawford; if anyone could give him some answers it was him. "What the hell's going on here?"

Crawford wrapped his arms around his legs, rocking himself manically. "Take me home, take me home."

"All in good time. Tell me what's going on. What are these creatures?"

The Ambassador buried his face against his knees. "They're from the *sheh'fet*," he said, in a shaking voice. "They're monsters. Created by the *sheh'fet*!"

Hammond went cold, his mind returning to what he'd seen up on Level 17. "Created? What do you mean?"

Crawford didn't answer, his shoulders shaking. He was beyond terror; a broken man.

A beat of pity pulsed through the General's chest, but he had more pressing concerns. "Where are Colonel O'Neill and Major Carter? Were they—" His mouth went dry. "Were they in the *sheh'fet*…?"

Crawford nodded, scratching out his answer in a hoarse voice. "I saw them, I saw them in my head…"

Dear God, are they among these monsters? Hammond felt sick to his stomach. "What about Dr. Jackson and Teal'c? Do you—"

"Sir!" The excited cry came from Henry Boyd. "General, look!"

Boyd stood in the tight line of men surrounding the entrance to the corridor, and he didn't lower his weapon as Hammond came to stand at his shoulder. "What is it, Major?"

"There, sir. Look."

It was the only answer necessary. Through the dust and smoke drifting across the courtyard, Hammond saw Jack O'Neill watching them from behind the scant cover of a ruined Kinahhi building. At his side were the rest of SG-1. They looked filthy and exhausted, but they were alive. And they were human. *Thank God!*

Suddenly, none of the rest of it mattered. Not Jack's deception, nor Kinsey's politicking, nor Hammond's own sense of betrayal. It was all washed away in a violent torrent of relief. He'd found his people, and they were alive. SG-1 were alive!

Heart thumping, Hammond pushed past Boyd and out into the courtyard proper. As he did so, Jack visibly started and then, very deliberately, rose to his feet and dropped his weapon. Surrendering? Did expect to be arrested? Hammond felt like laughing! "Colonel O'Neill," he bellowed, grinning widely, "this is going to be one hell of a debrief!"

Major Samantha Carter didn't believe in miracles. She even had a hard time believing in happy endings, but occasionally… Sitting perched atop a broken wall, she watched in astonishment as a miracle played out before her.

Eytan stood at the center of the courtyard, looking around him as if at distant memories. Perhaps he'd known this place before he'd been sent to Tsapan? But as he stood there, his ragged clothing flapping in the slight breeze, Sam noticed one of the Kinahhi soldiers staring at him intently.

A little flare of hope burned in Sam's chest as the Kinahhi woman got to her feet and took a step forward. Boyd was guarding the group and warned her back, but she didn't seem to hear.

"It's okay," Sam called to him. "Let her go."

With a frown, Boyd stood back and let the woman pass. "Major? What's going on?"

Elisha! Oh my baby, my sweet little girl… "I don't know, exactly."

As Sam watched, the woman – maybe twenty-one? – slowly walked toward Eytan. Her face was white, eyes full of doubt as she stopped a few steps away from him. "Papa?" she whispered, almost too quiet to hear.

But Eytan heard. His head snapped around and he froze. After an eternal moment he spoke, his voice cracking with disbelief, "Elisha?"

Her hand flew to her mouth, her whole body trembling. "Papa..."

And then Eytan moved, stumbling forward to clutch the young woman in his arms. *Elisha! Oh my baby, my sweet little girl...*

The memory was raw in Sam's mind, Eytan's desperate longing aching in her chest like the pain was her own. But the little girl was now a young woman and it nearly broke Sam's heart; Eytan must have spent decades trapped inside the *sheh'fet...*

Boyd cleared his throat. "Looks like Colonel O'Neill's ready to move out," he said gruffly.

Boyd was ostensibly watching the Colonel, locked in deep conversation with Kenna, but Sam didn't miss the gleam of moisture in his eyes; Henry Boyd had a daughter of his own who'd grown up without a father. She slid down from the wall and squeezed his arm. "Thanks for coming after us, Major."

He sniffed. "Yeah, no problem."

But his gaze, like Sam's, lingered on Eytan and his daughter. There was so much pain and joy entwined, Sam didn't know if she wanted to laugh for joy or weep with pity as she watched them locked in a fierce and desperate embrace.

"Yo! Carter!" The Colonel beckoned to her from the other side of the courtyard. "Come on!"

Sam swallowed the knot of emotion and took a deep breath. "Gotta go," she told Boyd, with a weary grin. "One last fish to fry..."

Councilor Tamar Damaris fled down the hallway of the Security Council building, Matan Tal at her heels. All around the sound of gunfire filled the air, horrifying and loud and impossible. She couldn't believe it, not here in the heart of Kinahhi.

Her sandaled feet slapped against the polished floor, her robes of state awkward and tangling in her legs as she ran. The rest of the Security Council were already aboard the emergency shuttle, she was the last. The last to leave.

And I will be the first to return, she promised herself angrily. *I will be the first to make them pay for this outrage!*

Ahead of them another corridor crossed her own, the left passage taking her to the safety of the shuttle. Matan Tal, unencumbered by robes and with longer legs, reached it first and disap-

peared around the corner. She cursed him for his cowardice in
abandoning her, mind twisting with rage at a world of injustice as
she hurried after him.

And came face to face with her smiling enemy.

"Going somewhere, Councilor?" It was O'Neill, hair spiking
in all directions, clothes grimy. Matan Tal was trembling at the
point of a weapon wielded by the large alien, Teal'c. And behind
them... Her heart quailed at the sight of the filthy Mahr'bal,
watching her with hatred in their eyes – and the Outcast, animals
that no longer deserved the name human. All here, in Kinahhi!

"What have you done?" she spat, her outrage stronger than her
fear. "Why have you brought these...these...*things*, here?"

O'Neill gave an arrogant shrug. "Cause it's their planet too?"

"Their *planet*? They are killers, monsters and—"

"That's not true, Councilor." Another of the Tauri spoke,
Daniel Jackson. "The Arxanti –" He paused, correcting himself.
"The people you know as the Mahr'bal aren't your enemy." He
glanced warily over his shoulder toward a stick-thin female with
savage hair. She stepped forward, as haughty as any of her kind.
"They are the descendents of a highly advanced civilization that
spanned this whole galaxy," Jackson continued. "We call them
the Ancients and—"

"They are terrorists! They have murdered countless Kinahhi
and—"

"And you have stolen our birthright!" the Mahr'bal woman
shrieked. "Condemned our children to die, stolen our youth
and—"

O'Neill stepped forward, one hand on the creature's arm.
"Okay, okay. This isn't getting us anywhere." He jerked his head.
"Kenna, she's all yours."

Shocked beyond speech, Damaris watched as her once trusted
military Commander stepped out from the rabble blocking her
way. A boy stood at his side, and behind him a dozen of her own
people. But they looked at her with hard expressions, devoid of
all proper deference. "What is this?" she hissed. "What are you
doing?"

Kenna lifted his chin, and his eyes, that had always revealed
too much, showed nothing now but determination. "We're taking
our city back, Councilor," he said. "No more *sheh'fet*, no more

'events' to frighten our people into submission. It's over, Damaris."

She laughed, spat it out in anger and defiance. "You? This rabble, this handful of freaks? All that is over, Commander, is your life. All of you! You will be crushed, and when the *sheh'fet* is restored—"

"Oh, that's gone," O'Neill insisted gleefully. "Down at the bottom of the deep blue sea."

"And we know the truth now," another voice added. She didn't know the man, a Kinahhi dressed in rags and clutching the hand of a young woman. A young woman dressed in Kinahhi uniform! He stared at Jackson, then back at her. "We have seen the truth about the Arxanti and our own people. And we will tell our story, we will shout it from the rooftops!"

Regarding him disdainfully, she said, "And who might you be?"

A bitter smile cut across his face like the slash of a knife. "I am Eytan Lahhat. You condemned me to the *sheh'fet* yourself, Damaris, for raising my voice in protest."

It was possible, she had sent many dissidents to Tsapan. But if he had been absorbed into the *sheh'fet*... Her gaze darted to the demented creatures twitching and capering behind the crazed rabble.

"Yes," the man continued, "I was Outcast, but Alvita Candra of the Arxanti has returned me to myself. As she will all my brethren, when we travel with her people to Arxantia. Then, together, we will return to our homes – to our families – and wash this city of its lies." He bowed gravely toward Daniel Jackson, "For we have seen the truth in ways you could not imagine, Councilor Damaris."

"The truth," she said coldly, "is that your pathetic revolt will be crushed by the might of the Kinahhi military and—"

"Yadda-yadda," O'Neill interrupted. "Kenna? You wanna shut her up?"

With a sharp gesture to two of his men, Kenna stepped forward and took her by the arm. She hissed at his impudence, but he persisted. "Councilor, I am placing you under arrest for engineering the deaths of Kinahhi civilians and—"

"On what authority, Commander? Your own? You have no

right to—"

The man stiffened. "On the authority of the people of Kinahhi.
The free people of Kinahhi." To his men, he said, "Take her to
Plaza 210 and keep her under guard."

"You can't do this!" she screeched, struggling against the iron
fingers of the soldiers who dragged her down the corridor. "I
demand that you release me!"

But Kenna ignored her, talking earnestly to Matan Tal. Her
aide was nodding ferociously, no doubt trading his loyalty for his
life. The only person still watching was O'Neill. He lifted a hand
to his brow in an insolent salute and turned his back on her, saying something to make his people laugh.

Damaris screamed her outrage long and loud. But no one was
listening.

"You've got a tough job," Jack said as they stood in the smoking ruins of the Kinahhi gate-room. Kenna's men were busy
securing the base, fanning out deeper into the complex. And their
ranks seemed to be swelling; it looked good for the future of the
revolution. Or the coup. Or the civil war – whatever the hell it
was they'd started here. Only the Stargate itself seemed undam-
aged in the battle-scarred room, its massive presence dominating
everything.

He was going to miss it.

Kenna's face was severe, his hard voice breaking into Jack's
thoughts. "Damaris was right," he said. "The military will not
simply capitulate. But without the *sheh'fet* to control the people,
and with the Mahr— With the Arxanti openly fighting at our side,
I hope we will succeed."

"I believe you will," said Teal'c. "In my experience, men fighting for their freedom fight longer and with more valor than those
striving to oppress them."

Kenna gave a little bow. "I hope you will return one day."

"Yeah," Jack agreed, clasping the man's arm in farewell. "Me
too." But it was unlikely. After the inevitable court martial, he
doubted he'd be allowed within a ten-mile radius of the SGC ever
again.

The sudden whoosh of the opening Stargate cut through his
brooding, and Jack turned to see Carter and Daniel saying their

own farewells. Daniel was in deep conversation with Alvita Candra, trying, it seemed, to impart everything he knew about the Ancients in one never-ending sentence, while simultaneously edging toward the gate. Carter was hugging Eytan tightly, no doubt making the guy's day on more than one score.

God, he'd miss them. The thought slammed into his gut, physically painful. He'd miss *this*, despite all the hardship and fear and conflict. This was living. This was life!

With a sigh, Jack punched Teal'c on the shoulder. "Time to go."

His friend gave a slight nod of acknowledgment, and together they headed toward the open gate. Crawford was huddled at the bottom of the steps, staring up at the puddle with dead eyes – a broken man. Jack wondered what tormented him more, the horror of the *sheh'fet*, or the fact that Kinsey had abandoned him there? He had no sympathy for the man; if you get into bed with a snake, it's gonna bite you in the ass.

He shifted his attention from Crawford to Hammond. The General stood at the head of his strike team, who were lined up and waiting to move out, his eyes fixed on Jack. They'd had little chance to speak, and Jack was unsure of his footing with the man. A lot had happened since their last conversation in the SGC holding cell, but the fact remained that Jack was still a fugitive.

As he and Teal'c walked past the silent, watchful ranks of SGC personnel, Daniel and Carter fell in at their sides. He tried not to think of it as the final moments of his team – the last hurrah – but it was impossible not to. And from the pensive silence of his friends, he knew they were thinking along the same lines.

At length, they came to stand before Hammond. No one spoke, no one moved. The General was studying them earnestly, his expression difficult to read. Eventually, Jack bit the bullet and stepped forward. "I guess this is where I hand myself in, sir."

Behind him, Daniel muttered under his breath. No one else said a word. The entire room was listening so hard that the silence seemed loud.

Hammond fixed him with a long, steady look. Then a restrained smile touched his lips and he said, "As you were, Colonel."

Jack blinked. "Sir?"

"Take your team home, son."

Your team?

Hammond's eyes glittered as he nodded the affirmative.

"Yes, *sir*!" Jack snapped off a salute and turned back to his team. Daniel was grinning, Carter was trying not to, and even Teal'c looked happy. His own feelings were too ambiguous to allow a smile, but a soul-deep relief washed over him like cool water. SG-1 were going home, together and more or less in one piece. At that moment, nothing else mattered.

"Come on," he said gruffly, "let's go home."

CHAPTER THIRTY-NINE

The sun shone brightly, warming the fall air over Cheyenne Mountain, when Jack stepped past the guard and out onto the steep slope. The trees were turning, dark red against the bright blue sky, and from somewhere far away drifted the tang of wood smoke. It felt like home.

Hammond was already waiting for him, arms folded across his chest as he stood leaning against the hood of a truck and looking down at the small parking lot below. Curious, unsure of the reason for this summons, Jack joined him.

"Nice day for a walk," he said, shoving his hands deep into his pockets.

Hammond smiled. "Too bad I have a 'to do' list as long as my arm, Colonel."

Jack knew the feeling. After an unauthorized absence of over five months his own 'to do' list was— Hell, he'd never in his entire life had a 'to do' list. But there was a hell of a lot of paper spilling out of his in-tray. "So," he said, glancing from Hammond down to the parking lot and the single Humvee parked there, "what are we doing here, sir? Not that it's not a nice view…"

"I wanted to talk to you, Jack," Hammond said, facing him. "Somewhere less official."

Nodding carefully, Jack braced himself. They'd been back two weeks, and the fate of his team was still up in the air. Crawford's testimony had verified everything he and Carter had said about the *sheh'fet*, and Kinsey – like the true rat-bastard he was – had thrown up his arms in horror at the deception of the Kinahhi, and lavished praise on the brave men and women of the USAF. Anything to save his own, stinking hide. Only the fact that the future of SG-1 hung in the balance had kept Jack silent; that and a look from Hammond as sharp as the crack of a whip. But the hearing had been over a week ago… "Have you heard?" he said at last.

"Yes," said Hammond, never one to beat about the bush. "I got a letter from the Pentagon this morning."

Mouth dry, Jack forced himself to ask, "What did it say?"

"You've got a severe reprimand on your file, Jack. But," Hammond smiled, "they agreed with my recommendation – you've still got your job. And you've still got SG-1."

Jack blew out a long breath. "Thank you, sir. I— You don't know how much—"

"I think I do, son," Hammond said kindly, but then his face hardened. "Major Carter will also be reprimanded, but no other action will be taken. Dr. Jackson and Teal'c have been officially reinstated to the SGC."

"Carter doesn't deserve—"

"Doesn't she?" Hammond fixed him with a steady look. "She knew the orders were illegal, Jack, but her personal loyalty to you led her astray. You need to ensure she's not put in that position again. Do you understand me?"

"Yes, sir." On every level. Sometimes life was damn complicated, especially where Carter was concerned. And not just her. He cleared his throat and straightened his shoulders. Apologies weren't exactly his forte, but this one was overdue. "Sir, I just want to say— What I did, taking the plans from the Kinahhi, lying to you about it, going after Boyd without permission… It was a huge, *huge* mistake. And I'm sorry."

Hammond's lips tightened. "I was mad as hell, I won't deny it." The words hit like a slap to the face, making Jack flinch. "I felt as though you'd taken advantage of my faith in you, but when I saw—"

"I was an idiot, sir," Jack blurted. "I hated that we'd left Boyd and his team behind, and I tried to fix it. I didn't realize the price would be too high."

Hammond cocked his head. "Too high?"

"I lost my team, sir. And I lost your trust. That's too high."

"*Almost* lost," Hammond corrected with a half-smile. "You weren't the only one to make mistakes, Jack." Doubting the truth of that, Jack kept quiet and Hammond continued. "When you left to rescue Boyd I knew you weren't going on a standard recon mission, but I let you go. I could have stopped you. Perhaps I should have."

"You let me go because you trusted me, sir. And I blew it."

Hammond shook his head. "There are some people who'd disagree with you on that, son."

"There are *some* people who disagree with me on everything."

Hammond smiled and turned back to the parking lot. "Maybe so," he said. "But I'm not talking about Dr. Jackson."

Jack grunted in amusement, easing the weight of guilt around his shoulders. He took a deep breath and forced his muscles to relax. Below them, a blue sedan was winding its way up the mountain road, the engine noise just audible in the still fall air.

"I was mad as hell, Jack," Hammond repeated after a while. "But then something happened to change my mind."

"Kinsey?" Jack guessed. "The *sheh'fet* set up on Level 17? Kinahhi crawling all over the—"

Hammond held up a finger to silence him. "Wait," he said, watching the Humvee in the parking lot.

Its door was opening, and a guy in uniform climbed out as the blue sedan turned into the otherwise empty parking lot. Even from this distance Jack recognized the airman as Henry Boyd, tense and nervous. The car slowed to a halt and its driver got out, moving to open the rear passenger door. For a long moment nothing happened, and then someone stepped out into the sunshine. Blond hair glinted, and Jack knew her instantly. Heather Boyd. She stood and stared across the parking lot, stock-still, and then a hand shot to her mouth and she started running toward her husband. Boyd met her halfway and swept her into a fierce hug.

His throat suspiciously tight, Jack turned away. The moment was too personal to witness.

After a while, Hammond said, "Look, Jack."

He did, almost reluctantly, and saw the kid, Lucy, holding her mother's hand and walking cautiously across the parking lot. When Boyd reached down to touch her face the kid smiled, stepped closer, and he hugged her tight to his chest, reaching out and pulling his wife into his arms as well.

A broken family restored.

Jack looked away, heart aching for his own loss, one that could never be restored. *Charlie, Sara...*

"You still think the price was too high, Jack?"

He forced a smile past the lump in his throat. "Well, when you put it like that..."

Hammond clasped him on the shoulder. "You brought our people home, son. You did good."

Boyd and his family were slowly walking toward the waiting car, and Jack nodded. Maybe Hammond was right, maybe it was worth the price after all. For this moment, and for the future his team had restored to one family.

Later, in the bustling control room of the SGC, George Hammond looked out into the gate-room with a smile of satisfaction. O'Neill stood talking to Teal'c, prepped and ready to go on the team's first official mission in over five months. Whatever they were discussing, it was animated. At least, O'Neill was animated. Teal'c had an eyebrow lifted in what could have been either amusement, or pain. The General suspected they were discussing hockey.

Major Carter appeared next, bang on time as the gate began to spin and Harriman started the familiar countdown. "Chevron one, engaged." She joined her team with a grin, waving toward the gate and saying something he couldn't hear. O'Neill shook his head, and peered toward the doors. Dr. Jackson was late.

The gate continued to spin, chevron after chevron locking. O'Neill glanced up at the control room with a shrug and tapped his watch. Hammond said nothing. Dr. Jackson would be there, he always was. And sure enough, a moment before it was too late, he came racing into the room, breathless and staring at the gate as if to ensure he hadn't missed anything.

O'Neill made a wry comment, provoking a lengthy explanation cut off by the Colonel's raised hand as the final chevron locked and the wormhole engaged.

For a moment the team in the gate-room stilled, staring up at the familiar magical shimmer of the Stargate. And then O'Neill looked over his shoulder, straight at Hammond, waiting for the order. The General leaned forward and took hold of the mic. "SG-1," he said, with real pleasure, "you have a go."

Colonel O'Neill smiled, flipped a casual salute, and led his team up the ramp. Shoulder-to-shoulder, SG-1 stepped through the Stargate and out into the untamed galaxy beyond.

For once, Hammond thought, all was right with the world. How long that would last was another question entirely…

STARGATE SG-1: RELATIVITY

by James Swallow

Price: $7.95 US | $9.95 Canada | £6.99 UK

ISBN-10: 1-905586-07-8

ISBN-13: 978-1-905586-07-3

When SG-1 encounter the Pack—a nomadic space-faring people who have fled Goa'uld domination for generations—it seems as though a trade of technologies will benefit both sides.

But someone is determined to derail the deal. With the SGC under attack, and Vice President Kinsey breathing down their necks, it's up to Colonel Jack O'Neill and his team to uncover the saboteur and save the fledgling alliance. But unbeknownst to SG-1 there are far greater forces at work—a calculating revenge that spans decades, and a desperate gambit to prevent a cataclysm of epic proportions.

When the identity of the saboteur is revealed, O'Neill is faced with a horrifying truth and is forced into an unlikely alliance in order to fight for Earth's future.

STARGATE ATLANTIS: BLOOD TIES

by Sonny Whitelaw &
Elizabeth Christensen

Price: £6.99 UK | $7.95 US |
$9.95 Canada
ISBN-10: 1-905586-08-6
ISBN-13: 978-1-905586-08-0

When a series of gruesome murders are uncovered around the world, the trail leads back to the SGC — and far beyond...

Recalled to Stargate Command, Dr. Elizabeth Weir, Colonel John Sheppard, and Dr. Rodney McKay are shown shocking video footage — a Wraith attack, taking place on Earth. While McKay, Teyla, and Ronon investigate the disturbing possibility that humans may harbor Wraith DNA, Colonel Sheppard is teamed with SG-1's Dr. Daniel Jackson. Together, they follow the murderers' trail from Colorado Springs to the war-torn streets of Iraq, and there, uncover a terrifying truth...

As an ancient cult prepares to unleash its deadly plot against humankind, Sheppard's survival depends on his questioning of everything believed about the Wraith...

STARGATE SG-1: ROSWELL

**by Sonny Whitelaw &
Jennifer Fallon**

Price: $7.95 US | $9.95 Canada |
£6.99 UK
ISBN-10: 1-905586-04-3
ISBN-13: 978-1-905586-04-2

When a Stargate malfunction throws
Colonel Cameron Mitchell, Dr. Daniel Jackson, and Colonel Sam Carter
back in time, they only have minutes
to live.

But their rescue, by an unlikely
duo — General Jack O'Neill and Vala Mal Doran — is only the
beginning of their problems. Ordered to rescue an Asgard also
marooned in 1947, SG-1 find themselves at the mercy of history. While Jack, Daniel, Sam and Teal'c become embroiled in the
Roswell aliens conspiracy, Cam and Vala are stranded in another
timeline, desperately searching for a way home.

As the effects of their interference ripple through time,
the consequences for the future are catastrophic. Trapped in the
past, SG-1 can only watch as their world is overrun by a terrible
invader...

**Order your copy directly from the publisher today by going
to www.stargatenovels.com or send a check or money order
made payable to "Fandemonium" to:**

<u>USA orders:</u> **$10.82 ($7.95 + $2.87 P&P). Send payment to:
Fandemonium Books, PO Box 2178, Decatur, GA 30031-2178.**

<u>UK orders:</u> **£8.30 (£6.99 + £1.31 P&P).** <u>Rest of the World
orders:</u> **£9.70 (£6.99 + £2.71 P&P). Send payment to:
Fandemonium Books, PO Box 795A, Surbiton KT5 8YB,
United Kingdom.**

Or check your local bookshop — available on special order if they are
out of stock (quote the ISBN number listed above).

STARGATE ATLANTIS: CASUALTIES OF WAR

by Elizabeth Christensen
Price: £6.99 UK | $7.95 US
ISBN-10: 1-905586-06-X
ISBN-13: 978-1-905586-06-6

Series number: SGA-7

It is a dark time for Atlantis. In the wake of the Asuran takeover, Colonel Sheppard is buckling under the strain of command. When his team discover Ancient technology which can defeat the Asuran menace, he is determined that Atlantis must possess it—at all costs.

But the involvement of Atlantis heightens local suspicions and brings two peoples to the point of war. Elizabeth Weir believes only her negotiating skills can hope to prevent the carnage, but when her diplomatic mission is attacked—and two of Sheppard's team are lost—both Weir and Sheppard must question their decisions. And their abilities to command.

As the first shots are fired, the Atlantis team must find a way to end the conflict—or live with the blood of innocents on their hands…

Order your copy directly from the publisher today by going to www.stargatenovels.com or send a check or money order made payable to "Fandemonium" to:

USA orders: $10.82 ($7.95 + $2.87 P&P). Send payment to: Fandemonium Books, PO Box 2178, Decatur, GA 30031-2178.

UK orders: £8.30 (£6.99 + £1.31 P&P). **Rest of the World orders:** £9.70 (£6.99 + £2.71 P&P). Send payment to: Fandemonium Books, PO Box 795A, Surbiton KT5 8YB, United Kingdom.

Or check your local bookshop – available on special order if they are out of stock (quote the ISBN number listed above).

STARGATE SG-1: ALLIANCES

by Karen Miller
Price: $7.95 US | $9.95 Canada | £6.99 UK
ISBN-10: 1-905586-00-0
ISBN-13: 978-1-905586-00-4

All SG-1 wanted was technology to save Earth from the Goa'uld ... but the mission to Euronda was a terrible failure. Now the dogs of Washington are baying for Jack O'Neill's blood — and Senator Robert Kinsey is leading the pack.

When Jacob Carter asks General Hammond for SG-1's participation in mission for the Tok'ra, it seems like the answer to O'Neill's dilemma. The secretive Tok'ra are running out of hosts. Jacob believes he's found the answer — but it means O'Neill and his team must risk their lives infiltrating a Goa'uld slave breeding farm to recruit humans willing to join the Tok'ra.

It's a risky proposition ... especially since the fallout from Euronda has strained the team's bond almost to breaking. If they can't find a way to put their differences behind them, they might not make it home alive ...

STARGATE ATLANTIS: ENTANGLEMENT

by Martha Wells
Price: £6.99 UK | $7.95 US
ISBN-10: 1-905586-03-5
ISBN-13: 978-1-905586-03-5

When Dr. Rodney McKay unlocks an Ancient mystery on a distant moon, he discovers a terrifying threat to the Pegasus galaxy.

Determined to disable the device before it's discovered by the Wraith, Colonel John Sheppard and his team navigate the treacherous ruins of an Ancient outpost. But attempts to destroy the technology are complicated by the arrival of a stranger — a stranger who can't be trusted, a stranger who needs the Ancient device to return home. Cut off from backup, under attack from the Wraith, and with the future of the universe hanging in the balance, Sheppard's team must put aside their doubts and step into the unknown.

However, when your mortal enemy is your only ally, betrayal is just a heartbeat away...

Order your copy directly from the publisher today by going to www.stargatenovels.com or send a check or money order made payable to "Fandemonium" to:

<u>USA orders:</u> $10.82 ($7.95 + $2.87 P&P). Send payment to: Fandemonium Books, PO Box 2178, Decatur, GA 30031-2178.

<u>UK orders:</u> £8.30 (£6.99 + £1.31 P&P). <u>Rest of the World orders:</u> £9.70 (£6.99 + £2.71 P&P). Send payment to: Fandemonium Books, PO Box 795A, Surbiton KT5 8YB, United Kingdom.

Or check your local bookshop – available on special order if they are out of stock (quote the ISBN number listed above).

STARGATE ATLANTIS: EXOGENESIS

**by Sonny Whitelaw &
Elizabeth Christensen**
Price: £6.99 UK | $7.95 US
ISBN-10: 1-905586-02-7
ISBN-13: 978-1-905586-02-8

When Dr. Carson Beckett disturbs
the rest of two long-dead Ancients,
he unleashes devastating consequences of global proportions.

With the very existence of Lan-
tea at risk, Colonel John Sheppard leads his team on a desperate
search for the long lost Ancient device that could save Atlantis.
While Teyla Emmagan and Dr. Elizabeth Weir battle the eco-
logical meltdown consuming their world, Colonel Sheppard, Dr.
Rodney McKay and Dr. Zelenka travel to a world created by the
Ancients themselves. There they discover a human experiment
that could mean their salvation…

But the truth is never as simple as it seems, and the team's
prejudices lead them to make a fatal error — an error that could
slaughter thousands, including their own Dr. McKay.